# The
# Darkest Sin

# The
# Darkest Sin

## CAROLINE RICHARDS

KENSINGTON PUBLISHING CORP.
www.kensingtonbooks.com

BRAVA BOOKS are published by

Kensington Publishing Corp.
119 West 40th Street
New York, NY 10018

ISBN-13: 978-0-7582-4277-8
ISBN-10: 0-7582-4277-8

First Kensington Trade Paperback Printing: June 2011

10 9 8 7 6 5 4 3 2 1

Printed in the United States of America

# *Prologue*

R owena Woolcott was cold, so very cold.
      She dreamed that she was on her horse, flying through
the countryside at Montfort, a heavy rain drenching them
both to the skin, hooves and mud sailing through the sodden
air. Then a sudden stop, Dragon rearing in fright, before a
darkness so complete that Rowena knew she had died.

When she awakened, it was to the sound of an anvil echoing in her head and the feeling of bitter fluid sliding down her
throat. She kept her eyes closed, shutting out the daggered
words in the background.

"Faron will not rest—"

"The Woolcott women—"

"One of his many peculiar fixations . . . they are to suffer . . .
and then they are to die."

"Meredith Woolcott believed she could hide forever."

Phrases, lightly accented in French, drifted in and out of
Rowena's head, at one moment near and the next far away.
Time merged and coalesced, a series of bright lights followed
by darkness, then the sharp retort of a pistol shot. And her
sister's voice, calling out to her.

The cold permeated her limbs, pulling down her heavy
skirts into watery depths. She tried to swim but her arms and
legs would not obey, despite the fact that she had learned as a
child in the frigid lake at Montfort. She did not sink like a
stone, weighted by her corset and shift and riding boots, be-

cause it seemed as though strong hands found her and held her aloft, easing her head above the current trying to force water down her throat and into her lungs.

She dreamed of those hands, sliding her into dry, crisp sheets, enveloping her in a seductive combination of softness and strength. She tossed and turned, a fever chafing her blood, her thoughts a jumble of puzzle pieces vying for attention.

Drifting into the fog, she imagined that she heard steps, the door to a room opening, then the warmth of a body shifting beneath the sheets. She felt the heat, *his heat*, like a cauldron, a furnace toward which she turned her cold flesh. Her womb was heavy and her breasts ached as he slid into her slowly, infinitely slowly, the hugeness of him filling the void that was her center.

Was it one night or a lifetime of nights? Or an exquisite, erotic dream. Spooned with her back against his body, Rowena felt him hard and deep within her. She slid her hip against a muscular thigh, aware of him beginning to move within her once again. She savored the wicked mouth against the skin of her neck, pleasured by the slow slide of his lips. Losing herself in his deliberate caress, she reveled in his hands cupping and stroking, his fingers slipping into the shadows and downward to lightly tease her swollen, sensitized flesh.

"Stay here . . . with me," he whispered, breath hot in her ear.

And she did. For one night or a lifetime of nights, she would never know.

# Chapter 1

"A bloody mess, it was."

"How many days in the water do they estimate?"

"Difficult to tell. Bilious and bloated beyond recognition."

Lord James Lyndon Rushford barely looked up from the table, his gaze intent on the cards in his right hand. "Are we playing vingt-et-un, gentlemen?" he murmured. "I would suggest, judging by your winnings, that you concentrate on the game."

The oil lamps burned low, illuminating the generous proportions of the games room hosting four men, jackets casually draped across chairs, neck stocks undone, who were leisurely and relentlessly bent upon losing money, of which they all had plenty. Crockford's was a private club on St. James, luxurious and discreet, requiring membership that demanded deep coffers and cavalier unconcern. On this Monday evening the crowd was unusually light, consisting solely of players for whom the vice of cards was too hard to resist.

Sir Richard Archer threw down a matched set of queens a moment before Rushford bested him with a sprawl of cards, lazily delivered on the mahogany table.

Archer grinned good-naturedly, blue eyes gleaming beneath a bold nose. "Thought we could put you off your game, Rush, but apparently not."

"Indeed," murmured Lord Ambrose Galveston, leaning forward in his chair, observing Rushford speculatively. "I should have thought that the specter of a soiled dove washed ashore would pique your interest." He was a slight man with a receding hairline that matched his retreating chin.

"Hardly mysterious in this case, I'd warrant," said Sir Harry Devonshire, before throwing down his cards in exasperation. "And I can speak with some confidence. My source of information is not London's chief constable but rather that Irish groom my wife hired last year, a rascal who spends most of his time bedding whatever skirt catches his fancy, whether below stairs or on the riverfront." He drummed his fingers on the table's edge. "Wonder if he knew her," he mused.

"And why should it matter," asked Galveston, "when the body belongs to that of a prostitute?"

"I believe that they determined she was an actress, judging by her finery. Or so reports the Irish groom," corrected Devonshire.

"A very fine distinction," Galveston sniffed. "Actress, whore, it matters little. They do come and go with alarming regularity. What do you make of it, Archer? Clearly, Rushford is not inclined to join us in conversation."

Archer played with the chips at his elbow and shrugged. "This is all prurient speculation. Which means there's not much that need be discussed."

Galveston gave a puff of derision. "I shouldn't wish to offend your sensibilities. Such refinement!"

"I don't quite know what the bother is all about," said Devonshire disingenuously, although all the men gathered around the mahogany table in the library knew precisely why this particular incident—this death—held such resonance. "Besides which and much more importantly," continued Devonshire, deciding to heed the storm brewing on the horizon and decamp while there was still time, "this game has become too rich for me, gentlemen. I shall retire to White's, I believe, for a nightcap before returning home. Anyone care to join me?" Looking about him expectantly, and ignoring the footman who appeared instantly to assist him with his waistcoat and jacket, Devonshire took the last draft from the very fine brandy Crockford's provided to its loyal clientele. "Very well then," he said rising from his chair with a definitive shrug of his shoulders, "I shall make my way to the club and a lonely night of drinking. Good evening, gentlemen." He followed with a curt bow and exited the room.

"I shall follow suit, I think, but prefer to keep my own company this evening," said Galveston, scraping back his chair before jerking his rather meager chin in Rushford's direction. "Although it's difficult to fathom why you shouldn't want to know more about Bow Street's latest gruesome discovery, what with your unorthodox interests, Rushford."

Rushford smiled slowly, the curve to his lips doing nothing to soften his countenance, an assemblage of hard planes and angles that was not particularly welcoming. He slanted back in his chair, ignoring the winnings piled high to the right of his discarded cards. "One needs something to keep boredom at bay, Galveston."

Galveston squared his narrow shoulders. "A highly risible claim. Surely, amateur sleuthing is hardly becoming to a man of your stature. That case you involved yourself in earlier in the year, concerning those prostitutes and their keeper. Truly a noisome situation if there ever was one and with spectacular repercussions, if you'll recall."

Archer cleared his throat in warning, but Galveston continued. "Not much good can come from involving oneself in these matters. And what's the point, after all? The poor and destitute, the morally suspect, shall always be with us, subject to the vagaries of fate."

Archer tensed in his seat as Rushford's smile widened, never a good sign. "So, Galveston, enlighten me, if you will," he said slowly, with a poor approximation of patience. "If this woman recently discovered on the Thames's shore were well born, then you would concede an interest in discovering the crime behind her demise. But given that she may have had to earn her living at a trade of sorts, her life is deemed of no value. Despite the fact that you occasionally avail yourself of services that she and her type might have to offer." The lamps seemed to hiss more loudly.

Galveston pursed his lips, insulted that his extracurricular interests, hardly irregular, would be called into question. He was not quite an habitué of either Cruikshank's nor Madam Recamier's in King's Cross, although he did on occasion sample the wares of either establishment. He smoothed the ivory buttons on his waistcoat with soft hands that had never seen a day's work. "It would appear to me that you're the last one who can afford to cast aspersions, Rushford."

Rushford pushed back his chair, unfolding his impressive physique. Archer followed suit, hoping that Galveston at least had the good judgment not to raise a matter better left cold and dead. Rushford had an unreliable temper, and it was momentarily doubtful that Galveston recollected the fact that Rushford could drill a dime at twenty paces, counted membership in the West London Boxing Club, and was the winner of the Marquis of Queensbury's challenge cup four years running.

"Time to bid adieu, Galveston," Archer said helpfully.

"I shall take my leave."

"Perhaps you would care to finish elaborating your point," Rushford said.

Not a good plan, thought Archer. Galveston opened his mouth to say something, but perhaps it was a primal instinct for survival that he snapped it closed again. Of course, they all knew what he was thinking, what he wanted to say. Instead, with thinning lips, he concluded, "I shall leave you to your dark memories, Rushford. And good evening to you, Archer." Galveston gathered up his jacket and with a backward glance over his shoulder added, "We haven't all forgotten, if that's what you wish to believe, Rushford." He paused meaningfully. "We well realize that your unorthodox diversions are an attempt to make amends, to assuage your guilt—"

Rushford crossed his arms over his chest, the movement straining the superfine fabric of his shirt.

Archer said curtly, "Spare us the preaching, Galveston, and take your leave while you still have time." In response, Galveston made a show of securing the last button on his jacket before turning on his heel, the door snapping shut behind him.

The silence was conspicuous, marred only by the sputtering of one of the lamps as the oil burned down to release a curl of dark smoke. Rushford reached for the whiskey decanter in the center of the table, splashing a healthy amount into his crystal tumbler. He took a mouthful.

Archer raised an eyebrow. "Can't believe I'm saying this, but don't you think you've had quite enough?" Between the two of them over the years, the decanters they'd emptied could rebuild Blackfriar's Bridge.

Rushford glanced at the pyramid of chips next to his chair. "It didn't seem to affect my performance at cards." His eyes were the color of a northern sea and just about as friendly. It was difficult to reconcile the fact that the two men had met two decades earlier at Eton and shared a checkered and overlapping past that included several years adrift not only in the Royal Navy but also in London's backstreets, glittering ballrooms, and Whitehall's clandestine offices. But that was long ago, Rushford reminded himself, before everything had changed.

"We're not talking about your facility at cards. That will never be in question," Archer said dryly.

Rushford raised his glass in his friend's direction. "Thank God. Not that I believe in one. Besides which, your handwringing reminds me of my old nurse."

"You grow more idiosyncratic as you age, Rush."

"I'm not asking you to keep me company."

Archer observed his friend carefully. "You've barely emerged from Belgravia Square since February. And it's now May. Perhaps you should take yourself down to the waterfront and to Mrs. Banks to look at the body."

Rushford placed the now empty crystal tumbler on the table. "Your concern is touching, Archer. You believe embroiling myself in another hopeless state of affairs will ameliorate my ennui. Although I don't think Mrs. Banks would be overly eager to see me." Mrs. Banks was undertaker to the poor, her ramshackle dwelling in the foggiest, nastiest side of Shoreditch, where London's constabulary saw fit to drop off bodies before they found their way to a pauper's grave.

"Your involvement in the Cruikshank murders helped last time, as you very well know. Despite Galveston's palaver about sleuthing, your particular skills and energies are suited to uncovering the truth."

He had scarcely solved the mysteries of the universe, thought Rushford wearily, when he had uncovered what the London constabulary had missed right under their noses. Madam Cruikshank's stable of fillies was being poisoned one by one by her footman, at the behest of a disgruntled client, Sir William Hutcheon. The scandal that had blossomed in the London papers had hardly endeared Rushford to London society, of which Galveston was a particularly vocal example. Not that Rushford cared a whit for society's approbation. "Hutcheon deserved to hang," he said abruptly.

Archer nodded. "This was one crime that could not be kept behind closed doors. Thanks to your efforts."

Rushford reached for his jacket. "Don't patronize me, Archer."

Archer held up a palm in protest. "Furthest thing from my mind, Rush."

"Trust me when I say that I am quite adept at keeping myself occupied."

Archer eyed the whiskey decanter meaningfully before adding, "Does that mean you will pay Mrs. Banks a visit?"

"Christ, you're a nag. Persistently and painfully bothersome." But he shrugged on his jacket, not troubling himself to order his cravat. He would go first thing to Shoreditch in the morning, a reason to rise other than cards and boxing. Archer was bloody right, not that he would say it aloud. They both knew thin ice when they skated on it.

Rushford made for the door, Archer close on his heels. "You ought to forgive yourself," said his longtime friend, to his back. The words burned dully in his brain but didn't penetrate the scar tissue that had closed over his heart.

"Kate would never want you to—" Archer continued carefully.

Without turning around, his palm on the heavy brass knob of the door, Rushford said, "Give it up, Archer. There is nothing left to say." *Or to feel,* he should have added, the shimmer of Kate's beautiful face always in his mind's eye. "I am going home now, with or without your permission, to decant and drain a fine bottle of French brandy." Rushford never got drunk. And never forgot. That was the problem.

Archer shook his head, shrugging on his own coat. "Your work for Whitehall was worthwhile in the end, Rush, despite the fact that you refuse to acknowledge your accomplishments. And if you choose at this time to utilize your talents by immersing yourself in more pedestrian affairs, then so be it."

Rushford turned briefly, his eyes bleak. "Pedestrian? When I think of what was sacrificed for the sake of a few bloody Egyptian tablets that now sit in the British Museum—" He did not finish the sentence but jerked open the door.

Rushford pushed past the footman with barely a backward glance at his friend. The debacle of the Rosetta Stone was one he wished to remove from memory, like a knife from between his ribs. Outcome be damned. Taking two stairs at a time, he did admit to himself that there was something about the body lying at Mrs. Banks's that tugged at his conscience. He wondered briefly why Galveston and Devonshire had been so assiduous in bringing the tragedy to his attention.

Down the stairs and past the discreet entrance off Mayfair,

he pulled up his collar against the nocturnal damp, deciding to walk to his town house rather than signaling for a hansom. Anything to shorten what would be a long, sleepless night. He looked up into the starless sky and then down the length of the slumbering street, sensing that his past was opening like an abyss from which he could no longer look away.

# Chapter 2

Rowena Woolcott assessed the town house off Belgravia Square with a sharp eye. She was reluctant to disturb the servants, aware that at this late hour they would be abed. Having spent the previous ten months as a governess, she knew the habits of those living below stairs all too well.

Skirting the low shrubbery, she moved to the back of the town house where a thick trellis snaked its way to the upper floors. Heavy crenellations underscored a series of windows, architectural stepping stones overlooking a mews studded with shrubbery. Without hoops or crinolines to hamper her, Rowena gathered her narrow skirts in one hand, looping the fabric into her waistband. Although the trellis was slick with dampness, she hoisted herself to the first level, her booted feet finding easy purchase on the lowest stone ledge.

Memories tumbled through her mind. Meredith had never chided her about her hellion ways, she thought, the recollection a poignant collision of pleasure and pain. At Montfort in the Cheviot Hills, she had played outdoors with abandon, riding, swimming, running through the woods during a childhood that was both idyllic and peculiar in its eccentricity. Unlike her sister, Julia, Rowena had led her nurses and tutors on a merry chase, reluctant to bury her head in a book when the sky and the sun beckoned.

A sharp evening breeze fanned Rowena's cheeks, bringing her back to the present and away from her moment's self-indulgence. She could no longer afford to believe in the carelessness of youth, not when that easy, oblivious innocence had been taken from her over a year ago. For the past twelve months, a yearning for retribution had forced her up in the morning and kept her from sleep at night. Anxiety burned in her throat at the thought of her aunt and sister and the danger that pressed close to them from all sides. The high stone walls and thick hedges surrounding Montfort could no longer protect them. She was their only bulwark now against danger.

During those missing weeks after her abduction, she had been suspended between life and death, imprisoned in darkness, but the threat, the voice and words, had survived along with her, haunting every waking hour. She remembered no face or place but merely the voice, speaking sometimes in French, sometimes in English, but always silken with evil intent. The menacing sound insinuated itself into her consciousness, allowing her no freedom from fear.

Fear for Meredith and Julia. *"The Woolcott women. Faron will not rest—until they are made to suffer. Until they are dead."* The voice spooled relentlessly in her mind.

Sinking into helplessness was not in her nature, making her all the more determined to piece together the shards of her broken memories. The dampness of the night curled underneath the collar of her cloak, but she merely stretched her arm higher, grabbing the next rung in the trellis, her feet confidently finding the level of stone upon which to rest. She knew enough not to look down, having climbed trees, and the gazebo in the east garden of Montfort, too many times. From her current vantage point, craning her neck, she saw the still heavy curtains framing the second-floor windows, the rooms beyond obscured by darkness. The third floor, under the eaves, would house some of the servants, which left the second floor, with its empty bedrooms, as the best entry point.

A long narrow window, the casement slightly ajar to reveal the weak glow of a gas-lit wall sconce, beckoned. Rowena took careful steps sideways along the ledge until her hands gripped the casement. All was silent, and if she squinted intently, she could discern the endless black and white tiles of a lengthy corridor typical of Georgian townhomes. Seconds later, she eased open the window and quickly pushed herself through the opening, her feet landing silently on the highly polished floor. Twin sconces burned dully, the hallway flanked by a military row of chairs draped with ghostly drop cloths.

No one was about, as one might have suspected judging the shuttered façade of the town house. Over the past two days, she had studied the exterior from the mews, watching its lone occupant, discovering the solitary rhythms of his life. He was a tall man, his features obscured by the collar of his greatcoat, his strides long and sure. He kept few servants and entertained no visitors. Rowena fingered the information like a blind woman as she glided noiselessly down the hallway, instinct and heedless courage leading the way. It took her but a few moments more to find the double doors of the master bedchamber. The encounter, she told herself, stopping on the threshold, would be awkward, difficult at best, convincing a stranger that she required his clandestine aid. She paused for another moment, her ears straining for footsteps or voices as she quietly eased open the door.

The milky light of dusk filtered through the room, the generous proportions holding a handsome four-poster bed, two matching armoires flanking a window, and a heavy gilded mirror. Rowena shut the door noiselessly behind her, catching a glimpse of her face in the glass. Her eyes were large and shadowed, her hair scraped back into a tight knot at her nape. She was thinner than usual, her collarbones accented by hollows that the simple lace fichu at her neck could not conceal. Reluctant to contemplate the time lost to her, and the alarming gaps in her memory, she stood in the center of the room before surrendering to the need to sit in a high backed chair by the dressing room screen. Now all she had to do was wait and desperately collect the thoughts that seemed scattered to the wind.

Images crowded her vision. Meredith and Julia, their expressions clouded with worry, on one of the last afternoons in the library at Montfort. Julia's voice uncharacteristically sharp, demanding that Meredith allow her to undertake her proposed expedition to photograph Eccles House, Sir Wadsworth's estate. Meredith's anxious reluctance had radiated from the set of her shoulders, the rigidity of her spine. Rowena's hands twisted on her lap, aware now that it was too late, that they had kept too much from her, the younger sister, who was deemed too free spirited, too distracted by life to be freighted down with heavy secrets and dark threats. She had never known anything but life with Lady Meredith Woolcott and Julia, a universe unto itself, protected, guarded, secure. Until that day over a year ago. Behind her closed eyes, Rowena summoned the memory of her last ride at Montfort, followed by the darkness, the heavy current of water carrying her away, the flooding in her lungs. And the dreams. *Dear God, the dreams.*

When she had finally awakened from the darkness and the fog, it was to the fussing concern of the Watsons, an elderly couple who lived in a small thatched cottage in Kent. Like a foundling, she had been deposited on their doorstep a fortnight earlier with a small sack of gold coins and little else. A month had passed quickly under their kind and diligent ministrations, wherein she found herself quickly regaining her strength and gradually the debris of memories, one more jagged and devastating than the next.

*Someone had wished her dead. Worse still, wished her aunt and sister dead.* A permanent heaviness lodged in her chest, pain warring with anger as she dared contemplate the madman, *Faron*, intent on her family's ruin. The name conjured a faceless specter who, she now understood, had presided silently over their lives from a distance before descending upon them with ferocious intent.

*Meredith Woolcott believed she could hide forever.* Meredith's beautiful countenance flickered before Rowena's burning eyelids, her fine features wreathed in concern born of years protecting her wards, secreting them away when they were little more than babes, protecting them from the threat that had overshadowed their lives. It was a shocking realization that the whole of her life, Meredith had been fighting valiantly to keep them safe and in peace. They had all been kept under lock and key, for reasons Meredith had chosen to keep to herself.

Fate had taken a strange course. Rowena would never have known the name Faron if Meredith could have had her way. If he had had *his* way, she would never have risen from her watery grave to unmask the man who would do her family harm.

She took a deep breath, dismayed at what lay behind her and what still lay ahead. She opened her eyes and surveyed her surroundings, impatient to return to the present and intent upon learning something more about the room's occupant. A pyramid of books rested in a corner by the bed, the embossed titles illegible in the dimness, and the faint scent of vetiver, strangely familiar, hung in the air. A decanter of brandy and heavy crystal glasses sat on a small side table over which two landscape paintings, anodyne in their subject matter, presided on a wall lined with hunter green watered silk.

The room gave up few of its secrets, not unlike its occupant. Rowena mouthed the question silently. Who was James Lyndon Rushford? *Lord* James Lyndon Rushford, more precisely, a man who had cared to solve the Cruikshank murders despite the disapproval of his peers, the sensation in the broadsheets, and society's disapprobation at having one of its own sent to the gallows. Rushford was the second son of an illustrious family, she had learned, who had spent many years in the navy and abroad and whose subsequent years might well have been spent gambling away his patrimony, nodding off in the House of Lords, or burying himself in brandy and horses at his family's countryside estate.

No answer to the enigma was forthcoming save for the heavy quiet of the house. To Rowena's jangled nerves, time seemed suspended despite the steady rhythm of the mantel clock. She could no longer stand to wait idly for its main occupant. She took another slow look around the bedchamber, the corners shadowed by the moonlight streaming through the tall windows. The clock chimed close to one in the morning. The chair creaked as she rose to tiptoe over to the oak chest of drawers. Her hands shook as she imagined quietly opening the top drawer to reveal snowy linens redolent of the same vetiver scent that haunted the room. But she would do anything to keep her sister and aunt safe, and surveying a stranger's personal items was the least of it. The more she learned about Rushford, the better she would be able to enlist his assistance. Not knowing exactly what she looked for, her eyes swept across the mahogany finish, expecting to see a brush, a comb, a watch fob, at the very least.

It was bare except for a small, velvet-covered box. With a will of its own, her hand reached out to pick it up. The box seemed to pulse with significance, although she couldn't articulate why. It lay heavily in her hands and she hesitated only for an instant before prying it open. Her breath stopped in her throat as she surveyed the delicate oval of a small portrait nestled against pale rose silk. The subject was a woman of remarkable beauty, with shining dark eyes, a mobile mouth, and a luxuriance of wheat-gold hair. Rowena stared long and hard, unable to look away from the fine portrait, her mind grasping at possibilities.

It was then she heard the footsteps, and in the next instant saw the doorknob turning, giving her a scant moment to shove the oval back in its velvet box before she slid over to stand behind the screen, both courage and plans momentarily scrambled. She concentrated on steadying and silencing her breath, unwilling for the moment to let James Lyndon Rushford know she was in his rooms. Not to ask for help. *But to demand it.*

Rushford moved quietly and fluidly for a man of his size. He was tall, with broad shoulders and a thick head of hair that needed the attention of his valet. He placed a heavy tumbler of brandy on the bedside table and began shrugging off his jacket, discarding it over the end of the bed. Unraveling his cravat with one hand, large but long, elegant fingers extracted a flint from a box on a low table. The candle by the bedside flared to life.

Rowena stilled. Rushford's profile was etched in dark and light, a broad forehead, bold nose, wide mouth, and eyes the color of a dark and turbulent ocean. It was a face that one would not readily forget, arrogant and aggressive in its composition. His expression did not augur well, she thought, counseling herself to bide her time and keep panic at bay until the opportunity presented itself to make her presence known.

Despite her resolve, thoughts skittered through her mind. Would he help her? Could he help her? She had read about Rushford's exploits in the London papers, scavenged from the breakfast table of her employers, the Radcliffes, whose three charges had been hers to educate for almost a year. He had, it was reported, skillfully hunted down the Cruikshank murderer while gathering evidence to ensure that justice would be done. Rowena had been riveted by the account, convinced this was the man who had the expertise to pursue a faceless specter. *Faron*. She could not do it alone.

So much had happened in twelve months, from changing her name and identity, leaving behind the kind shelter of the Watsons, to seeking employment as a governess in a small village in Wales. Without references, she had been forced to take work for modest pay and even longer hours, biding her time until she could scrounge the sovereigns she now intended to offer in return for Rushford's aid.

Not that the man required resources, her instincts told her. Clearly from a wealthy family, judging by the appointments of the town house and the commentaries in the broadsheets, Rushford followed his idiosyncratic pursuits for entirely different and possibly unknowable reasons. A fresh worry, she thought, listening to the steady throb of her heartbeat. Swallowing hard, she watched as Rushford began undoing the ivory buttons of his shirt, then pulling the linen from the waistband of his breeches.

She should have expected something like this. The lateness of the hour. The deserted house. At least he had not retreated behind the screen to disrobe. Heat rose beneath her skin. Rushford's shirt drifted to the floor, revealing a broad back whose intricate musculature reminded her of the sketches she had seen in one of Julia's anatomy books. Hard and sculpted as though from stone, he moved to undo the placket of his breeches, half turning toward her hiding place behind the screen to disclose a beautifully delineated chest, tapered waist, and narrow hips.

Rowena's mouth was dry, her lips tasting of parchment, and she clenched her hands by her sides. It was the strangest feeling, this desire to absorb the heat and smoothness of his skin beneath her palms, to imagine his hardness next to the softness of her body, his nakedness one with hers. She stilled her breath, trying to stop the flow of images, the chafing of her blood. Wherever were those thoughts coming from? Familiar and terrifying at the same time. Her head began to pound, her pulse fluttering in her throat. She had to stop this *now*.

Rushford was facing her. *Facing the screen,* Rowena reminded herself in a panic, watching one large hand grasp his breeches, inching the material down over lean hips. His eyes were hooded, yet Rowena sensed he was staring at her, through the screen, and into her eyes, prepared to call her out.

Her shoulders ached with the strain of standing perfectly motionless. Now was the time to say something, to reveal herself, but it was already too late.

His voice was deep, gravely. "How long do you intend to remain unannounced because, rest assured, I don't disrobe for simply anyone," he said.

Nothing she had read in the broadsheets, or conjured in

her feverish imagination, had prepared her for this encounter. And it was then she realized the full force of what she had set in motion with this strangely powerful man, a portrait of contrasts, a combination of overwhelming physicality and concentrated intellect. All of it, suddenly, focused upon her.

*Meredith and Julia,* Rowena reminded herself. Taking a deep breath, she stepped out from behind the screen.

# Chapter 3

Regret. Like the metallic taste of blood, it left a bitter taste on one's tongue.

*Christ,* Miss Rowena Woolcott was young. Rushford had forgotten, or more precisely had willed himself to forget. Until now, as she stood on the faded aubusson rug of his bedchamber, wide eyed and without a hint of recognition in that expressive, beautiful face. He swore silently, fluently, all the while considering his rapidly narrowing options like the virtuoso card player and pugilist that he was.

"I shan't bother with useless apologies, sir," she began in that low voice that was an unsettling, indelible combination of innocence and sin. Emerging from behind the dressing screen, clasping her hands to her waist, she met his gaze with a boldness bordering on desperation, studiously ignoring the fact that she had not only broken into his home but also interrupted the intimate process of his disrobing. "I had little choice but to meet with you this way," she continued. "Please hear me out before you seek to bundle me onto your doorstep."

Rushford proceeded carefully, taking quick account of her questioning eyes, the downturn of her full mouth, to confirm that she had yet to recognize him. No small wonder, given the circumstances. He kept his mind deliberately blank, disinclined to dissect the exact state of his memories. "I take it that you are not here to make off with the silver," he said, sweeping up the shirt he'd discarded and shrugging it on. Ironic that it was he, a decade her senior, a man who had had countless lovers over several continents, who felt the pull of modesty. "Shall we proceed into the drawing room for this discussion?"

Her eyes widened. They were a dark, impossible blue, he recalled with heavy reluctance.

"Oh, no, I beg of you," she said. "I should prefer to remain discreet. I should rather not have any of your servants alerted to my presence."

Subterfuge was a hallmark of Rushford's existence. It always had been, a mordant reminder of a life spent in shadows rather than light. "Then at least sit down," he said. She startled, stiffening her shoulders, when he moved across the room to drag the chair out from behind the dressing screen. "I won't ask how you managed to enter my town house without arousing suspicion."

"I prefer to stand, sir," she said, ignoring the proffered seat and backing away from him two steps, staring at him as though he were an apparition. "And just so you know, I found easy entrance through the window at the end of the hallway, which was slightly ajar."

He crossed his arms over his chest, aware that his shirt was hanging open. Rowena Woolcott believed she owed him an explanation, a cruel irony of which she was obviously unaware. He smothered another curse when in the next moment, he realized exactly how she had stormed his citadel. "You climbed, didn't you?" For any other woman to do so would have been outrageous. But then again, Miss Woolcott was of another ilk entirely.

Her eyes flickered over to the wide high windows. "If I can do it, I imagine any number of thieves and cutthroats could do the same. I should have that attended to, if I were you."

That scenario was the least of his worries now that this young woman, despite his best efforts over a year ago, had returned to haunt him. She was wearing a simple brown merino day dress, insipid in both color and cut, with a short cloak over her shoulders, none of which gave a hint of the long slender limbs and firm curves beneath. But he knew. He remembered. That was the problem. The warmth of fine French brandy still heated his belly, mingling with a heightened awareness that had everything to do with her presence and his resurrected conscience.

"Thank you for your concern. I shall have a word with my footmen," he said with deliberate calm, leaning a shoulder against the bed's newel post. "But the hour is late, as I'm sure you're aware, so perhaps the time has come for you to tell me what you're about. Before I do decide to call upon the good offices of the constabulary."

In the light of the single lamp, he could see her turn pale beneath the translucence of the finest skin, skin like silk under his hands. He pushed away the recollection, watching as she straightened her spine, her tone hardening. "I'd prefer that you didn't," she said with a shocking arrogance, peculiar for a woman, and for one so young. Unbidden, Rushford heard Kate's voice intruding, bravado lacing her low contralto, that fluent, fluid confidence that came readily to a duchess assured of her beauty and wit.

Rowena's words cut through the inconvenient reverie like a knife through butter, drowning out the cadences of Kate's singular intonations. "I shan't take much of your time," she promised, her spectacular eyes summoning him.

Rushford forced himself back to the present. "So you say," he replied, his voice miraculously even. "And yet you forced your way into my home to do what precisely?"

Rowena took a deep breath, stilling her hands, the slender fingers both elegant and capable, not at all pink, plump, or ladylike. "I come to seek your expertise," she declared, as though it was obvious, and for a wretched moment he thought he had misheard. He was bloody expert at very little these days, as it turned out. "Your expertise as a detective of crime," she elaborated. "I have heard and read of your exploits."

The back of his neck tightened. Of course, the Cruikshank murders. Had he known the uproar the case would engender, he would never have taken it on, goddamn the broadsheets. Galveston's supercilious gaze came all too readily to mind. So that was what Rowena Woolcott was after, *his help*. Now wasn't that rich? Like asking the devil for guidance. "Go on," he said, not liking himself much at the moment.

Gazing upon Rowena Woolcott, he wondered whether she realized how beautiful she was, the effect she could have upon men, if she chose, with the elegance of her profile, those dark blue eyes, slanted at the corners and that mouth, stained like the ripe raspberries of summer. Rushford was the last man on earth who heard poetry in his soul, but experience had taught him a stinging lesson about the siren call of desire. One more complicating factor, he realized, when it came to the fate of Rowena Woolcott.

She was watching him, calibrating his response, as any young woman would, trapped as she was alone in a man's bedchamber late at night. "I read about the Cruikshank murders," she said. "How you spent days and weeks collecting evidence and hunting down the felon," she continued in a low whisper, as though recounting tales of knightly deeds. "Those poor women about whom no one cared, other than you, sir."

Rushford scrubbed a hand down his face, groaning inwardly, the burn of stubble against his palm somehow welcome. "Is that what you believe, Miss? Madam? Forgive me, but I don't even know your name."

She shook her head. "It doesn't matter. For now."

"Ah yes. More mystery." A deadly joke, of which only he was aware.

"But I know you can help me." There was a stubbornness in her tone. "As you helped them."

"Flattery doesn't go nearly as far as one might wish. I am

not the helpful sort, believe me." If the past three years didn't prove that point, nothing would. Ridding himself of Rowena Woolcott would be in her best interests, although she might not appreciate the fact at the moment. It dawned upon him then how simple it could be to be done with her. To frighten her. Drive her off. It was mere coincidence, as opposed to fate or poetic justice, that had delivered her once more into his hands. Thank God. "May I pour you a brandy before I see you on your way?" he asked with no solicitousness in his voice.

Rowena's head jerked up, causing a thick strand of hair, the color of deep burgundy, to fall loose from her chignon over one shoulder. "But I haven't explained. Everything."

Rushford moved over to the bedside table and poured a healthy measure of brandy into a heavy lead crystal glass. "No need." He picked up the drink and strode directly opposite her. A faint scent of soap and something else, achingly familiar, slammed his senses. He shut down the memories, thrusting the glass into her slender hand. Challenging himself to touch her, to see if he dared, he closed her cold fingers around the glass. "I don't need to hear details. Because I am not for hire, madam."

"But I have money," she persisted. "Not much but some." Her fingers tightened momentarily around his, and to his surprise, she raised the glass to her lips and took a sip, closing her eyes as the warmth slipped down her slender throat. *Send her on her way*. The words pulsed in his brain. *As he should have done that first time.*

"I cannot help you," he said simply. Decisively. Any other woman might have implored, begged, or wept, but Rowena Woolcott stared at him with a tensile strength that would have shaken a lesser man.

Her hand on his arm was surprisingly strong, the fingers long and elegant and he'd wager, accustomed to handling a horse's reins with ease. There was a wildness about Rowena Woolcott, he noted not for the first time, a willfulness that refused constraints. She had scaled his town house, broken into his bedchamber, confronted him—he stopped the flow of thoughts, the cool of her hand penetrating the sleeve of his shirt. Most of all, *Rowena Woolcott had survived*—as though he could ever forget.

She removed her hand, taking a few steps away from him, needing the safety of distance to collect her thoughts, to marshal her argument. "At least allow me to tell you of the circumstances—of my circumstances," she amended, getting the facts out brusquely. "This is all about two sisters and their aunt. And a man who wants them to suffer in the worst possible way."

Rushford made his face granite. "Not my problem, alas. I am not a detective, as you seem to believe. The Cruikshank situation was entirely anomalous. I simply had a surfeit of time on my hands. As for your own circumstances, surely a difficult guardian is not unusual."

"He is not a guardian. You don't understand."

"Perhaps I do not wish to."

She took a step closer to him, careless in her courage, the dull dun color of her cloak unable to subdue the subtle radiance of her skin. "But you must," she said, all but stamping her foot. "I was abducted from my home and then left to drown. I don't recall many details, because my memory has somehow been impaired, but I know for certain that someone wishes to do away with me and those I care for the most."

Rushford feigned skepticism. "Murder? I believe we're being a trifle melodramatic here." Of course, her memory would be impaired, given the amount of opiates she had been given. He steeled himself. Rowena Woolcott really left him little choice, but his eyes still searched hers for a glimmer of recognition. He found none. "Still not interested, madam, miss, or whoever you are," he said. "I am not the shining knight in armor or the clever detective whom you seek. You have the wrong man, someone who has entirely no interest in seeking to punish evildoers, in righting old wrongs, or how-ever you choose to frame the situation in your no-doubt overheated imagination. Now I will ask you politely to leave."

"And if I refuse?" she asked with a graceful shrug of her shoulders.

*Christ,* she was young and foolish, he thought for the second time that night. He was tired, unaccountably irritated and determined to rid himself of Rowena Woolcott once and for all. Though overt vulgarity was not in his repertoire, it was the only recourse that readily came to mind. He closed the distance between them and removed the glass of brandy from her hand. "I shall not invite you to leave twice," he said distinctly. "Instead, I may have to act upon my baser instincts, for which few could fault me, given the presence of an uninvited, albeit comely, female in my rooms. Do I make myself understood?"

For once she was speechless, her lips parted in shock. And yet she didn't move, her sensible riding boots riveted to his aged carpet. His fingers reached for the fastenings of his shirt, only to remember that it still gaped open. Shrugging out of the garment, he threw it on the floor before beginning to loosen the waistband of his breeches.

He sat down on the edge of the bed and tugged off first one boot and then the next. Rowena watched in horrified fascination, her breathing having come to a halt sometime between when the first boot and the second hit the ground.

"You have a choice," he said finally, rising from the bed. "Either you depart now, front door or rear window, I couldn't care less, or the breeches come off. And what happens subse-quently"—he paused just long enough to see the darkening of her spectacular eyes—"should not come as a surprise to a woman as intelligent as you appear to be."

She licked her bottom lip, pretending to ignore his outra-geous threat. "So you refuse to help me? Why? When you helped those other women? When you have the expertise to discover who wishes to murder my sister and my aunt." Her response was breathless with shock. "And to kill me."

Rushford shoved his hands into the pockets of his breeches. None of this could come to any good. "You have the wrong man," he repeated. After a lifetime of risk and of loss, Rushford realized that he'd never really experienced this particular sense of dark unease. Not once. Not even for Kate, a small voice echoed. But he felt it now. For Rowena Woolcott. And worse, for himself.

He leaned close, inhaling her scent, watching her tense, the porcelain of her skin pale with alarm and disbelief. He was so ready to touch her, taste her, all in a feeble attempt to lose himself in a physical maelstrom that could never hope to blot out the past. But he balanced this dangerous temptation by giving her one last chance to withdraw from him.

He threw down the challenge like a gauntlet. "You do not wish to become my lover, do you?"

"Your lover?" She mouthed the words, understanding frozen on her face, the pupils of her eyes dilating.

He knew what it would be like. To run his hands from the silk of her cheeks to the slim column of her throat and downward over the planes and curves of her shoulders and waist, across her ribs and then up again to cup her breasts. To test himself, to torture the slight remnants, *nay dregs,* of his remaining conscience, he mentally traced her body through the layers of her clothing, deliberately leaving every button and fastening intact, watching the panic rise in her eyes like an oncoming storm.

It was enough. He didn't have to move or touch her because she had already started to pull away. His gaze still holding hers, he was aware of the tension building inside her, beneath her prim cloak and the plain lace at her slender throat.

He knew the dangerous allure of the game he played. He wondered with a cool dispassion whether he really wanted

Rowena Woolcott to flee, to disappear once more. Then again, the choice was not his to make. She already stood at the door limned in the dim light, a wraith picking up her narrow skirts, slipping away.

Rushford simply watched her go.

The echo of marble and stone was the only sound in the cavernous British Museum. The murmurings of crowds and respectful whispers of groups had long disappeared after the great museum closed its doors for another day, leaving behind hallways and rooms groaning with the treasures of the ancient and modern world.

And as with all treasures, most came with a grievous price. The Rosetta Stone, almost four feet in height and one foot thick, rested in its glass sarcophagus, one thousand and seven hundred pounds of granite, in silent, erudite splendor. The ancient Egyptian artifact carved in the Ptolemaic era had provided three translations of a single passage, two in Egyptian scripts and one in the classical Greek of the country's elite rulers.

Two men stood in the shadows, contemplating the heavy stone with its hieroglyphic inscriptions, their expressions guarded. The taller of the two, barrel chested with hands clasped behind his back, pursed his lips with dissatisfaction.

"It rankles, it surely does." His statement hung in the cool air, as though everything depended on the next few moments.

"What rankles precisely?"

"That this discovery has been here on public display at the British Museum since 1802. For over forty years," the barrel chested man murmured before adding as an afterthought, "Of course, there's another reason our friend insists on the Stone's return to France."

The man by his side raised a dark brow. His was a spare build, compact and athletic, his dark hair brushed back from a high forehead, his linen and demeanor impeccable. "I, for one, am not fooled," he said with a courteous nod toward his

companion. "He wants the Stone in his personal possession."
His English was faultless, save for the faintest trace of French
accent. "Patriotic pride does not come into it. The fact that
Napoleon's scientists and scholars first discovered the Stone
in 1799 makes little difference to him, Lowther."

Giles Lowther smiled thinly. "You, Sebastian, are mistaken. It makes all the difference to him—although not for
the patriotic reasons you may believe." The assertion floated
into the night, illuminated only by two candelabra left behind by a watchman who had been duly rewarded. The two
men took the time to consider their master's motivations
while affecting to read the inscriptions painted in white
below the Stone: "Captured in Egypt by the British Army in
1801" on the left side and "Presented by King George III" on
the right. Despite the curt description, the historical details
were bloody. Both Lowther and Sebastian knew full well that
after Napoleon returned from Egypt to France, his troops
and scientists remained behind with their discovery, holding
off British and Ottoman attacks for a further eighteen months.
The French scholars swore they would prefer to burn their
discoveries rather than turn them over to the hated enemy.

"Our friend," continued Sebastian, gesturing with an elegant motion to the artifact behind glass, "claims that the
Stone was seized by the British from where it had been hidden in the back streets of Alexandria and then found its way
to Britain aboard the captured French frigate HMS *Egypti-
enne.*"

Lowther's eyes narrowed thoughtfully. "All superfluous
detail," he said enigmatically. "What is more important is
that he would like to continue the work Champollion began
over two decades ago." It was acknowledged that the orientalist Jean-Francois Champollion was credited as the princi-
pal translator of the Rosetta Stone.

Sebastian sniffed his derision. "And what did we learn
from the twenty paragraphs? In essence that the Stone speaks
of a tax amnesty given to the temple priests of the day, restor-

ing the tax privileges that they had traditionally enjoyed in more ancient times. Hardly the stuff of legend." His voice trailed away as he glanced sharply at Lowther.

Lowther smiled starkly. "Or so we are led to believe."

"There is more, then?"

"Why else would our friend be so keen to have it in his possession?"

Sebastian tapped a finger impatiently against the glass. His dark eyes were shadowed. "Therein lies the challenge. The situation may prove exceedingly untidy."

"Only because you failed the first time," Lowther said, each word hard as diamonds.

"What is past, is past." He gave a Gallic shrug, "We move on."

"Indeed," said Lowther, a hand at his chin, contemplating what seemed to be an imaginary army arrayed in front of him. "Our next moves must be more strategic. That being said, the actress's demise was a necessity—a tactic—as she knew too much."

Sebastian nodded. "And of course the method of dispatch was meant to be a reminder."

"Our friend delights in symmetry after all." Fire and water, thought Lowther.

"Yet how can we be sure that the drowning will elicit Rushford's interest?"

"It will," reassured Lowther. "Because he was besotted with the Duchess of Taunton. Her death, and his guilt, eat at his soul."

Guilt and passion, thought Sebastian to himself, a powerful, eternally useful combination of emotions. "The Duchess was lamentably unstable. That she flaunted their affair with no thought to propriety or her position—" He paused. "It was not expected."

They both stared at the huge tablet in silence, aware that they had only a few more moments before they must exit the museum. Then Lowther said, "Our friend demands results. A fortnight is all he is willing to give."

"Always impatient." It was a careful observation. Neither man wished to elaborate further because the mention of their mutual friend, the impossibly reclusive and powerful Montagu Faron, always brought with it a measure of fear. And for good reason. Faron was never without his leather mask, shielding the world from the facial tremors that overtook him with unexpected ferocity. And yet, the man was seemingly indestructible, having escaped certain death by fire only one year earlier. And now with scars from the flames all over his body, there were whispers that the great man of science and reason had made a pact with the devil.

"Revenge drives him and his relentless timetable," continued Lowther finally, giving Sebastian the smallest of frowns. "The business with the Woolcotts has never been resolved to his satisfaction, and therein lies the crux of the matter. That tiresome chit, Julia Woolcott, and her new husband, Strathmore, are responsible for more than they know. Good thing that they are far away in Africa, beyond reach for the moment. At least Rowena Woolcott's death slaked some of his thirst for vengeance."

Sebastian's eyes strayed back to the Stone. "I have heard it said that Faron's childhood *amour,* Meredith Woolcott, was behind the tragedy that haunts him to this day. That she was responsible for destroying what many consider one of the world's finest minds." He turned to hold Lowther's gaze, raising one eyebrow. "Although I wonder if that explanation is mere apocryphal legend."

Lowther, who perhaps knew Faron best, both the scientist and the legend, pretended to ignore the question. "We can speculate for hours on end, but for what purpose? I should recommend that we focus upon the matter at hand." He gestured dramatically to the heavy stone behind the glass. "Returning the Rosetta Stone to its proper home."

"France," intoned Sebastian.

Lowther shook his head. "More specifically, Clair de Lune." He referred to Faron's vast estate outside Paris. "Do what you must. And rapidly."

"Don't I always?" asked Sebastian, quick as a snake. He placed a hand on Lowther's shoulder, aware that the familiarity made the other man recoil a little. *Bon,* he thought. No more discussion was required. The two men returned to stare at the silent and ancient Rosetta Stone, its import shimmering in the empty caverns of the British Museum.

# Chapter 4

The past few years had not been kind to East London. The docks had spread east along the Thames, and crowded housing brought epidemics of crime and disease. Mrs. Banks's shanty reeked of decomposing flesh and remnants of fear. Located on the far side of Shoreditch, the abysmal dwelling was the final destination of those who had never been cherished in life and even less so in death. For a fee, she would collect the flotsam and jetsam of fate before the weekly arrangements were made for deposit in a pauper's grave, where twenty-five shillings would buy an open maw to be filled forty feet and thirty corpses deep.

Mrs. Banks had left Rushford alone for the moment, scuttling outside to argue, in a voice rattling with ague, with the char woman. The well-deserved exhortations rained over the woman's cowering head for overcharging on a bundle of wood, dropped hastily at the doorstep earlier that morning.

Inside the narrow building, a dim light barely illuminated dark corners filled with towers of cracked china, glass vases, and the occasional tarnished candlestick or oil lamp. These items were the elastic currency in which Mrs. Banks often chose to trade with those too poor to produce the shillings required to finish off what ill fate had begun. Rushford stood at the foot of a scarred wooden table, looking down at what was barely recognizable as a human form. The rumors had been correct, he thought. *A bloated mess.* He resisted the urge to pull the sheet over the suppurating mass sprawled on the table and topped garishly with a heap of golden curls. The stench was overwhelming, but he forced himself, in a kind of self-enforced punishment, to withstand it.

His eyes lingered on the tangle of hair draped over the bruised throat, his vision blurring as he remembered another body and another time. His Kate. Who, they claimed, had taken her own life by wading into the Thames, her pockets freighted down with stones. Only Rushford knew otherwise.

His mind spun back in time. It had been early spring, sometime before dawn, in the Duchess of Taunton's husband's home, adjacent to Apsley House. Rushford had fought his way into the grand pile, far past caring about the wild rumors, the shocked outrage, and even colder stares of the Earl, who should have been wild with grief. The stench had been just as overpowering then, of white calla lilies, their powdery scent invading every crevice of the mausoleum that the Duchess had never called home.

Kate lay lost on the big bed, staring unseeing into the distance, beyond the high-ceilinged room where they had prepared her for burial for the following morning. Incredulous, he had leaned in close, stroking her cheek, the flesh already cold as stone. Half expecting some response from the still form, he continued caressing her face, feeling the fine bone beneath the blue skin like the map of a familiar territory. Her eyes were open and clouded, the brown indistinct and muddy as the waters in which she had drowned.

He had gripped her hand, the small fingers like stiff twigs. Perhaps he said something, whispered near her cold and parted lips, but she no longer responded to him, her frame still against the pillows, straining against a death that came too soon. For what seemed like hours, although it must have been mere minutes, he continued to sit in the silence she had left behind, waiting for a breath that would never come.

Mrs. Banks's shrill voice, charged with outrage, pierced the fetid air, displacing the scent of lilies with the heavy fugue of decomposition. Rushford placed his left hand to his eyes, but it was as though his right hand still held Kate's. He smiled grimly at his folly, his gaze lifting to the lone begrimed window overlooking a narrow alley. For an instant, he thought that he wasn't quite alone, half expecting a face at the window. In two strides, he was at the dust-streaked casement, peering into the alley. Nothing.

He hesitated for an instant before returning to the bloated form beneath the soiled sheet. He didn't like what he saw. There was a cruel symmetry here. Death by drowning. Another woman whose unexpected and violent demise had been quite deliberately brought to his attention. His eyes moved along the length of the table, and back up to the face that remained unrecognizable. The vivid blue silk and rich lace of the woman's garment poked out from beneath the gray sheet, incongruous details that hinted at a greater story.

Rushford scrubbed a hand down his face. He had all but promised Archer that he would make this pilgrimage to Shoreditch. To accomplish what exactly, he wasn't entirely certain. Perhaps he'd hoped to scare away the demons that regularly bedeviled him.

At the thought of demons, he decided that he didn't want or need to think about Rowena Woolcott for the moment. Their encounter the past night had taken on the shape of a shadowed delusion, yet another ghost come back to haunt him. Fortunately for him, a ghost that was summarily exorcised. He recalled her widening eyes, her shocked expression, moments before she had slipped away from him. This time for good, he hoped, despite his clamoring instincts that told him differently.

He was a man who couldn't afford to believe in happenstance or coincidence. Yet, he convinced himself, there was nothing else behind Rowena Woolcott, in her blindness, finding her way back to him again. The broadsheets had been full of the Cruikshank murders and the name of Lord James Lyndon Rushford, the narrative holding out tenuous hope to a young woman intent on finding answers.

He should feel guilty for turning her away. But he knew

with unshakeable conviction that Rowena was safer without him. He had done as much as he could, as he'd learned in the bitterest way possible. Kate's cold face and unseeing eyes still mocked him.

Behind him, Mrs. Banks's shrill words penetrated the dampness, a wet cold that seemed impervious to the bright sunshine cutting through the small windows of the one room with floors so warped by time and humidity, it was like walking the deck of a rolling ship. She was still arguing with the char woman and had reserves of acrimony to spare, giving Rushford the time he needed to work unobserved.

Mrs. Banks had already stripped the body of anything of worth, including jewels and gold teeth. Even the remaining bits of lace that might have survived their owner's fate would not last long. A woman who believed in neither heaven nor hell, Mrs. Banks had faith only in what she could test with her teeth or barter the next day for a bag of grain or bottle of gin. To confirm his suspicions, Rushford glanced at the corpse's hands; the once plump fingers were empty of rings. The hands rested against the sodden fullness of the silk skirts, the flounces filled out with stones.

"Mrs. Banks. May I speak with you a moment," he said, turning on his heel toward the low entrance of the shanty. He hoped it was not already too late. Unbelievably, the rank air of the narrow alleyway outside Mrs. Banks's establishment was welcome relief. She stood with hands on her bony hips, shaking a fist at the retreating back of the char woman.

"Thievin' doxy." The epithet was more spittle than words. She turned her raisin eyes upon Rushford, shrewdness emanating from every begrimed pore. "Ye've had enough time in there. Now what else is there ye be wantin', guvnor?"

Rushford saw no need for subtlety. "Whatever jewels were on the body. I shall pay handsomely."

Mrs. Banks snorted in feigned disbelief, knowing it was best to play coy for a few minutes at least. "I be beggin' yer pardon, guvnor. I would do no sech thing as takin' jewels from a body barely cold."

Rushford stared down at his boots, the ground dusty beneath his feet, allowing what seemed an interminable amount of time pass by while Mrs. Banks continued with her denials. "How much?" he asked finally, abruptly.

Mrs. Banks grunted something in reply before disappearing for a few moments into the narrow building. Returning promptly, she held out a dirty handkerchief to Rushford in one gnarled hand.

Without undoing the knot to take note of the contents, he repeated, "How much?"

"Ten guineas."

"Done." Rushford pulled out the coins from his jacket pocket. Glancing down the narrow street and then up into a sliver of blue sky revealed by the narrow buildings, he added, "Is there anything else you'd like to tell me?"

"For a price, guvnor."

Rushford returned his gaze to Mrs. Banks. "I shouldn't have it any other way."

Mrs. Banks grunted. "There was a gentleman here last evenin'."

"Go on."

"A Frenchie by the looks and sounds of 'im. Medium height, scrawny I'd say; 'air black as a raven's wing."

Rushford's gut tightened. *Coincidence* was a word used when one couldn't see the levers and the pulleys. "And what was he about?"

Mrs. Banks shrugged. "He didn' say, not that I was expectin' 'im to. Jest wantin' to let you know you didn' get 'ere first, guvnor." She clucked her tongue against a series of missing teeth. "Not the type to disturb the body. Too squeamish like."

"And had you already stripped the body by that point?" Rushford asked bluntly.

Mrs. Banks nodded. "He left after five minutes. No more."

Probably could not endure the stench, thought Rushford. He pulled out another two guineas. "Thank you, Mrs. Banks. Most helpful as always."

Pocketing the handkerchiefed bundle, he walked toward
Molton Street, not bothering to glance over his shoulder,
aware that he was, once again, being followed. He kept a deliberate pace, wending his way outside the warren of streets
before ducking into the last tavern on Blackall Street. All but
deserted midmorning, Rushford found a table in the back of
the low-ceilinged room. In a few moments, he had untied the
bundle given to him by Mrs. Banks, holding the remnants of
a life in his hand. Three gold teeth, a filigreed silver bracelet,
and a man's signet ring, the gold winking dully in the dimness. The crest was familiar. A capital G, festooned with laurel leaves.

Suspicion flared as suddenly as his thirst for a brandy.
Rushford signaled the sleepy publican from his slumbers behind the length of a sticky counter. His mind was already
planning an evening of gambling at Crockford's, where the
company of Lord Ambrose Galveston beckoned. In the interim, he thought, eyeing the low doorway of the tavern, he
would await Rowena Woolcott's arrival.

The heavy pall of ale in the air and sawdust underfoot did
little to dispel Rowena's growing unease. Pulling her cloak
more tightly around her shoulders despite the warmth of the
tavern, she ignored the stares of the publican who was in the
process of filling a tumbler with spirits and glowering at her
with unconcealed dislike. Unaccompanied women had no
place in a drinking establishment. Convention, Rowena reflected desperately, had less place in her life than ever before.

After a short and sleepless night at her lodgings on Holburn Street, she had risen early to return to the town house
on Belgravia Square, observing Rushford from what was
now a familiar place in the mews. He had uncharacteristically chosen to hail a hansom cab rather than walk to his regular boxing club rendezvous, which he kept as regularly as a
cleric did his Sunday sermons. Rowena quickly followed suit,
quelling the reservations uppermost in her mind. *You do not
wish to become my lover.* Rushford's intimidation, meant to

strike fear into her heart, drummed stubbornly in the background of her thoughts, the implications scalding. Yet, she conceded with suppressed panic, the prospect made a kind of wild sense.

She had alighted from the hansom at the far end of the narrow streets that leaned in upon themselves like collapsing bookshelves. Watching from a distance, she had seen Rushford duck into a low entranceway from where a stick figure of an older woman had emerged, shaking her fist threateningly. The street had been all but deserted as Rowena followed a serpentine of alleys that wound their way to the back of the narrow building and a window dark with soot.

Her eyes had taken a few moments to penetrate the grime and adjust to the room's dimness. She could still hear the rush of blood in her head when she first saw the corpse, a hellish blue-green of mottled skin and rotted silk, and Rushford standing beside it, lost in thought, his eyes flat and expressionless. Her skin crawled. Absorbing the scene a moment longer than was wise, she had been left with the implausible impression that, for at least one instant when Rushford had looked up at the window, almost meeting her gaze, his expression had changed from one of cold objectivity to intense longing. Impossible, she thought, as her mind attempted to make sense of what she saw.

Pulling back from the window, she waited outside, around the corner of a tavern, losing herself in the neighborhood of pickpockets, thieves, and prostitutes slowly awakening to the demands of the day. Behind the torn awning of the tavern, she observed another abbreviated conversation between Rushford and the old woman, watching as he took a dirty bundle from her hands. Rowena waited until he nodded curtly and began walking away, following behind him a discreet distance. In short order, his broad back was absorbed by the thickening crowd until at the last moment, he ducked into an entranceway.

Rowena quickly retraced her steps toward the old woman, whom she discovered still standing, one hand on her bony hips, the other counting the coins Rushford had given her. Without looking up, she said, "What you be wantin' with Miz. Banks, eh?" The old woman spat on the ground, before surveying Rowena with immediate suspicion. "We don't be needin' any good works here. Too late for all that. Me customers are all dead." Men of the cloth, dour-faced women intent on good deeds—she had no use for either. Last time a rector had tried to close her down, he'd been arguing for proper burial for paupers. Wasn't that precisely what she provided?

Rowena had secured her reticule beneath her cloak but extracted several coins from her pocket. "I'm not here to do good works, madam."

The woman's eyes glinted. "What you be wantin' to know, then?" Her shrewd glance reassessed Rowena's muted dress and anxious demeanor. "Lookin' for a missin' relative? Well, don't know what ye will find 'ere." Mrs. Banks deftly pocketed the coins Rowena pressed into her bony hand. "Lots of people certainly are lookin', let me tell ye. She must be somethin' important. Or at least, important to somebody."

Glancing up and down the narrow street to discern whether they were calling attention to themselves, Rowena sized up Mrs. Banks for the businesswoman she was and seized the advantage. "Mrs. Banks—who has been here inquiring about the poor woman who lies dead inside?" she asked coolly. "Aside from the gentleman who just left?"

"Ye know 'im, do ye?"

Rowena thought it useless to lie. "Yes, I do. Lord Rushford."

A tabby cat slunk along the stoop, wisely avoiding Mrs. Banks's skirts. "A strange one, 'e is." The old woman curled her upper lip, communicating her unease. "Don't happen very often to have all these guvnors sniffin' around. Before Rushford came another," she said, deliberately vague, her foot shooting out to chase the cat away.

Rowena was loathe to let her eagerness show. "Another man? How do you mean, Mrs. Banks?" she asked, sensing that she was getting somewhere. "Do you have a name or a description?"

A wet series of coughs was the answer. Thumping her chest, Mrs. Banks made a great show of clearing her throat. Rowena dug into her pocket to extract another coin. With a surprising swiftness, it was snatched from her outstretched palm.

Hauling in a deep breath, Mrs. Banks seemed to recover, wiping her eyes with the back of the hand clutching the coins. "Another 'igh born one, 'e was. All dressed for the opera or some such." Rowena's frustration grew, listening to the old woman describing half of London. "And 'e had black hair, slicked back like from a 'igh forehead, with pomade."

Of course, he had not introduced himself, as such courtesies were neither necessary nor wise when going about business in Shoreditch. Disheartened, Rowena asked with a painful smile, "I'm certain your powers of observation are acute, Mrs. Banks, so I'm to wonder whether the gentleman in question displayed any other distinguishing features."

Mrs. Banks followed the cat's progress with her eyes, as though rummaging through her store of memories. "'E was alone," she concluded, watching the cat's tail curl around the broken leg of a stool. "An' yes, I be forgettin'. 'E 'ad an accent, Frenchie, I would say."

Rowena's heart ballooned in her chest. The voices never far from her hearing reverberated through her mind. A Frenchman. She dropped through the floor and back into the nightmare she was struggling to escape. Her throat closed shut, and she nearly tripped over the cat in her haste to back away from Mrs. Banks's stoop, murmuring an abrupt goodbye. She suddenly wanted to scream, but she could hardly breathe, instead stumbling in the direction that Rushford had taken minutes earlier, the morning sun hot on her face. Securing her cloak around her shoulders, she kept her head low. She almost missed the low doorway into which Rushford had disappeared.

The aroma of ale and sawdust assaulted her nose. She bent

down to enter the tavern, opening the heavy door, her eyes adjusting to the dimness of the interior. Wavering on the threshold would do little good. She swept up her skirts from the sticky floor and walked toward the lone man who sat in casual disarray, booted legs stretched out beneath a bench, in the far corner of the hostelry.

Rushford did not feign surprise at her sudden appearance, but nonetheless his gaze was fixed on her with an intensity that made the tavern with its miasma of stale ale and sawdust fade away. She blinked rapidly, her eyes curiously raw. He had been expecting her.

"Difficult to believe that I could be in such demand. Twice in twenty-four hours," he said, rising to pull out a chair for her, dressed in his usual somber black suiting and white broadcloth shirt, which did nothing to mute the impact of his presence. "Although if you persist in following me, I promise to offer you advice as to how you might better remain invisible. I noticed you two blocks away from Mrs. Banks's establishment."

Rowena bit back a sharp reply, hoping to muster a civil tone. She needed this man—to help her find the Frenchman. She pretended to fuss with her skirts as she sat down, the echo of her conversation with Mrs. Banks making it difficult to collect herself. She had been catapulted back into the netherworld of her abduction, reluctant though she was to cross the threshold again. When she looked up again she cleared her throat, but the words were tentative nonetheless. "I don't expect you to understand, my lord," she said, "to what lengths I have been driven. Please believe me when I say that I am hardly practiced in this type of endeavor." A Frenchman. It could have been Meredith or Julia lying on Mrs. Banks's table. She swallowed her panic, finding strength in her burgeoning anger to continue. "You might have saved us both time and effort had you listened to my appeal yesterday evening."

Rushford threw an arm across the back of his chair, inclining his head, as though preparing for an attenuated conversation. "I'm beginning to think that you enjoy spending an inordinate amount of time skulking about in dangerous places," he said. "Clambering about my roofline is one thing, but that alleyway behind Mrs. Banks's is far from safe."

Safety had nothing to do with anything, Rowena thought, the sharpness of a hundred emotions warring with good sense. Her instincts had been right. Faron would not give up, for whatever his twisted reasons, in tormenting her family. She had returned from the dead and she would climb mountains, swim rivers, challenge armies—rooftops and alleyways were minor encumbrances. "I was indulged as a child and young girl," she said curtly, not trusting herself to say more. "My aunt encouraged all our interests—including physical pursuits." Closer to the truth was that they had been raised in a man's world, with Meredith's example anything but that of a conventional female. They had learned nothing of flirting, of empty conversation, of hiding behind a mask of frivolity and silliness. Their existence had been comprised of books and science, of foreign languages, of riding and marksmanship.

"I'm not surprised," he said. "You demonstrate unusual courage." It was unclear whether the observation was intended as a compliment.

Rowena regarded Rushford warily, folding her hands neatly on the table dividing them. Keenly aware of his height and the length of his legs, she tucked her ankles beneath her chair. "Were you acquainted with her?" she asked in an abrupt change of subject. They both knew to whom she referred.

Rushford's eyebrows went up at her question, but he shook his head, and she chose to believe him, although why she couldn't say. "I do not know the dead woman in question," he said, removing his arm from the back of his chair to face her directly, his expression unchanging. Heavy footsteps sounded from behind as the publican came over to their table, apron straining over his girth, and placed two tumblers of brandy, both chipped, in front of them. Rowena was about to refuse the drink and then thought better of it. It was barely noon, but she needed the fortification, and she took a sip of the strong drink, aware that Rushford was watching her carefully. "I don't usually indulge in spirits," she said for no reason, her tone hopelessly prim in contrast to the welcome warmth in her chest.

It was obvious that he did. Rushford shrugged, taking a healthy mouthful. "Immaterial to me," he said. "And by the way, the answer is still no."

Rowena almost jerked from her chair but then sat down again, hiding her disappointment beneath a brittle bravado that barely held her nerves in check. "I haven't even had the opportunity to pose the question," she said. She wanted nothing more than to leap out of the tavern and return home to Montfort, to reassure herself that all was well with those she loved most. But it was impossible. In the past, hers had been a direct, forthright nature, but now she realized that circuitousness had its place. Setting her glass down carefully, amazed that her hands did not tremble, she tried another tack. "Why were you at that dreadful place this morning? I can only assume that you were investigating the possible causes behind another suspicious death."

Rushford's glance flicked away from her to the bar, where the publican was arranging a row of glasses on the dusty rack in preparation for the regulars to take their place under his rheumy gaze. "That dreadful place," he said, returning his attention to her, "belongs to Mrs. Banks, East London's undertaker. There are hundreds if not thousands of suspicious deaths in the city each year, although few receive undue attention, but that is another matter for discussion at another time." Rowena wondered whether he was thinking of the Cruikshank murders, of the prostitutes about whom no one cared. "And to answer your next question," he interrupted her thoughts, "which I'm certain is forthcoming, the cause of death in this instance was by way of drowning."

*Drowning.* Rowena's mouth was suddenly dry, her hands in their leather gloves cold. It was not his words so much as the incisive tone that pushed her close to the edge. "Was he or she . . . could she have been . . ." Rowena struggled to finish the sentence.

"She," Rushford supplied.

The implications crowded her thoughts. "Is that why you were called to Shoreditch? There is something of a sinister nature behind her death," she said, answering her own question.

Rushford smiled grimly. "In all probability there is something untoward going on. Most actresses are not partial to midnight swims fully clothed in the Thames. Besides which, bruises on her throat lead one to believe she had been strangled—asphyxiated." Rushford stared at Rowena over the table. "And her body was weighted down."

Rowena paled. "Weighted down? To do that to someone—" She straightened in shock, struggling to keep her own nightmares from piercing the light of day. Her throat closed on memory of the water flooding her lungs, her heavy skirts pulling her inexorably lower. The cold, stiff body on Mrs. Banks's table could have been Meredith's or Julia's. The horror repeated like an incantation in her mind. Her eyes tracked the scratches on the wooden trestle table. She chose her next words with the exactness of a surgeon, as though they could form a bridge away from madness toward reason. "I know you may choose not to believe me," she said, her voice sounding hoarse to her own ears, "but there is every possibility that there is a connection here . . . between me and the woman lying at Mrs. Banks. Which would make your involving yourself in my situation—"

"Advisable?" He completed her sentence and followed with a short laugh, his strong white teeth flashing in the dimness. "I don't quite follow you. Why would there be a connection between you and an actress lying dead at Mrs. Banks's?"

"I do not know how to explain it." She did not understand it all herself. She swallowed hard. "You see, it began over a year ago, at my home in Cumbria." She attempted to keep her description spare and unemotional, aware that he could just as easily bolt from his chair and leave the tavern. *A calm, rational explication.* "I last recall riding my horse on the estate," she continued, "when he stumbled, which is absolutely uncharacteristic of Dragon." Her beautiful Arabian, headstrong and willful, but as reliable as a rocking chair. "I came off, and then I remember nothing more but awakening to darkness and remaining in this impenetrable fog for what seemed like days or perhaps even weeks." She stopped abruptly, wondering whether it wise to continue, to tell him about the voices and the dreams, all the while fighting the urge to confide in this man who, she reminded herself with effort, was a stranger. "I remember very little except that I was found all but dead on the banks of the Birdoswald River." She paused. "I had been left to drown." For one fleeting second, she thought she caught a hint of what—knowledge, awareness in his eyes? But it was gone before she could name it, and he did nothing more than tilt his head to one side, as though contemplating a great mystery. "Continue with your story," he said.

"It is not a story," she insisted, her voice strained to the breaking point. "It's the truth. Why else would I be entreating you to help me?" Dear God, she sounded like a bedlamite. "I do not know what more I can say to make you believe me." She paused to clear her throat, which was thick with emotion. "I sense," she resumed more slowly, enunciating each word and recapitulating her argument, "that there is a connection between the dead woman and my dilemma."

Rushford absently fingered his glass. He had beautifully formed hands, Rowena observed, the thought only adding to the rush of confusion muddling her thoughts.

"That's a rather wild connection to make," he corrected her flatly.

She took a deep breath, ignoring the knots tightening in her stomach. "Please hear me out," she said, wondering desperately if he admired her at least for standing her ground.

Rushford managed a smile. "If it prevents you from scaling the edifice next door, I will, but let's begin with something simpler, such as your name," he demanded.

She hesitated for the barest second. "Miss Rowena Woolcott." A strange feeling of relief flooded over her, like the beneficence of a confession. The knot in her stomach loosened, and for some unknown reason she believed that she could entrust her identity to this man. "I would ask you to keep this in strictest confidence," she said, "as knowledge of my existence could endanger those closest to me."

"You have my word," he said simply. "By this point in our short if unorthodox acquaintance, I understand that it is your wish to remain dead to the world."

Rowena bit the inside of her lip to keep her expression calm. "I realize this sounds mysterious but only because you don't yet know all the elements at play here, not that I know myself, which is why I've come to you . . ." To stop herself from rambling, she clasped the tumbler on the table before asking finally, "Then you will help me?"

His smile widened at the entreaty in her voice, the hard lines of his face transformed into an expression she wished desperately to interpret as warmth. Rowena blinked and then just as suddenly the smile faded. "Miss Woolcott," he said, her name on his tongue unreasonably pleasing to her ears, "much as I would like to help you, I must reiterate what I said to you yesterday evening. I am not the man you think I am. Trust me when I say that your consorting with me can only bring you more harm. The best I can do is offer you funds so you may return to your home safely. Otherwise, you will simply be compounding an already difficult situation."

"Difficult for whom?" Her hands curled into fists. "I get the distinct impression that there is something you are unwilling to reveal here, sir. Why is it that you are keen to unravel the mystery behind a stranger's death, but you will not help me?" The words left her mouth before she knew it. She was, after all, as much a stranger to him as the actress lying cold and dead on Mrs. Banks's table in Shoreditch.

He raised a brow. "Simply because I found myself embroiled

in the Cruikshank murders does not mean that I am prepared to involve myself in every lamentable situation that comes my way."

Rowena flinched at the dismissal in his tone, narrowly reining in the urge to tell him the whole truth, or at least what she knew of it.

Rushford continued, "In short, Miss Woolcott, I suggest that you flee the scene as quickly as you are able."

"Then you admit that I am in danger. How could you possibly know that, sir?"

"You've told me on several occasions, if you'll recall."

"And now you believe me suddenly. So what has changed?"

"You would have made an excellent barrister, Miss Woolcott," he said drily, a glimmer of admiration in his eyes.

She unclenched the fingers on her lap. "Then I'm not finished questioning you, my lord. Why is it that you find yourself embroiled in these nasty situations, the Cruikshank murders and now this poor actress? There is something at work, I'm convinced, that compels you to come to the aid of those who have nowhere else to turn. It is the reason behind my appearance at your town house last evening and the reason why I am sitting across from you here today, my lord."

He considered her over steepled hands. "You are tenacious, Miss Woolcott."

"Merely desperate," she corrected him. "There is no one else to whom I can turn for the appropriate expertise. You are a man who could spend his time gambling or boxing or riding in Hyde Park, and yet you choose to devote your time to matters far outside your station. Why?"

Rushford placed a hand over his heart in mock surprise. "I protest, Miss Woolcott. It is you who are the sleuth, shadowing my every move and gathering the most intimate of information about my personal habits. Given your propensities, you most likely know how much I wagered last night at Crockford's and the condition of my linen."

Despite her desperation, Rowena felt her cheeks warm, the image of Rushford's impressive musculature, and the memory of his attempt at intimidation, difficult to banish. He was teasing her, she knew, as only a man of his experience could do. Well, she was no schoolroom miss, ready to run with her hair aflame at the thought of being alone with a man. Still, the thought caught her unawares, like the tendrils of a dream at dawn. "I had no choice but to meet with you as I did," she said in an attempt to justify her actions. "Of course, I had to learn everything I possibly could, and it seemed to make perfect sense at the time . . ." Inexplicably and illogically, all of this felt somehow right, like the tumblers of a complex lock falling into place.

Lord Rushford was a stranger, she reminded herself again, which did nothing to account for the compelling force that drew her toward this man. Perhaps, if she was totally honest with herself, she was simply confused, the strain of her recent experiences tingeing her actions with a hint of madness. The troubling, outrageous dreams, so flagrantly erotic, were somehow responsible for this uncommon, unaccountable response. It was time for reason to resurrect itself. Lord Rushford was but a means to an end, she told herself, looking directly into the dark gray eyes across the table.

He took a last draught of his drink. "If you dare not return home, do you require funds, Miss Woolcott, to settle elsewhere?" He had clearly made his decision.

Her chin jerked up. "How did you know that I cannot return home? Do you believe me now?"

He shrugged at the accusation in her tone. "You mentioned something about a difficult guardian."

"Your words, your assumption, not mine," she said tersely. "And I do not require funds. I require your *assistance*."

"I believe we have a stalemate, Miss Woolcott. Particularly if you persist in shadowing my every move. What will it be next—Crockford's and the West London Boxing Club?"

In response, she gulped the last of her brandy, the heat searing her throat. She bit back a cough, placed the glass on the table, and adjusted the collar of her cloak. "I shan't give in," she said, amazed at the conviction in her voice, "until you help me. You, Lord Rushford, are the only one who can."

For the first time, she detected a hint of weakness in his armor when he said, softly, "Why me?"

"I just know," she said, although she really didn't. "And I have a plan."

"Why does that not surprise me?"

"You yourself suggested it."

He appeared to stifle a smile. "I can hardly contain my impatience. I'm certain you're eager to regale me with the details."

The sound of deep-throated laughter cut off her rejoinder. Three men entered the ale house, their boisterous shouts attracting the publican's attention. She and Rushford were no longer alone, and she welcomed the diversion, a dilution of the tension, an illusion of safety. Leaning forward, she placed her hands on the table, summoning the courage to make her declaration. "You suggested," she said softly so only he could hear, "that I become your mistress, that we become lovers." The words, outrageous and desperate, pulsed between them.

Rushford did the unexpected. He, too, leaned forward, his voice dropping to an intimate growl, to grab her hand, his grip warm and inescapable. "You don't know what you're asking, Miss Woolcott," he said just above a whisper. His voice was deeper than usual, sending a shiver down her spine. "You're asking for the impossible."

Rowena nearly jumped from her place as his hand warmed the inside curve of her wrist. Layers of fabric did little to lessen the imprint of the heat of his fingers on her skin. Worst of all, she couldn't bring herself to take her hand back. She struggled to maintain her train of thought. "I don't mean in reality, of course, Lord Rushford," she hastily amended, "merely as a ruse so we may spend time together without arousing suspicion. It would be dangerous for me, Miss Rowena Woolcott, to appear to employ your services, you understand."

"My services?" he prompted.

Rowena jerked her hand out of his after what seemed an eternity. "You deliberately misunderstand me, sir. Together we could move at will amongst the demimondaine, the world of the poor creature lying dead at Mrs. Banks's," she said, gathering the collar of her cloak more closely around her. She could not repeat the shocking words and suddenly wasn't sure of what to say at all. She was drowning again, but this time in an entirely different way.

Rushford's glance was hard. "I warned you last night, Miss Woolcott, and here you are today taking me up on my offer."

"Don't be ludicrous," she huffed. "You deliberately misunderstand."

"Then what did I just hear?"

She scraped back her chair to rise, and he immediately followed suit, towering over her and in that one movement asserting his dominance. The three men who had entered the tavern earlier looked up from their tankards of foaming beer, eager to take in some light entertainment. Rowena fastened the toggles of her cloak. "I believe we are finished here," she said tightly.

"I sincerely hope so, Miss Woolcott." Rowena's view was filled with the wall of his chest, mere inches from her nose, the faint scent of vetiver tantalizing. "As I mentioned several times, I'm not the man you're looking for."

"I shouldn't be too sure." The words sounded feeble, all the more so when she flinched away from him. Raw, potent desire was making her begin to tighten and ache in a way that was both familiar and disturbing.

"What will it take to finally frighten you off, Miss Woolcott? Don't you already have enough with which to concern yourself?" He leaned down, his breath fanning the smidgen of skin left bare at her throat. She forced herself to look into the flat gray of his eyes. "Mistress? I don't think so," he said.

Despite their audience, Rushford pulled her close against

him, the pressure of his hands on her arms enough to slip her easily into his embrace. Then he lowered his head slowly and kissed her.

A rush of confusion. Fear and danger blended with an intoxicating gust of desire. Rowena's body began to fight against the logic of self-control at the first touch of his lips. She had never been kissed before, yet the contact with this stranger felt overwhelmingly familiar, her lips blooming and responding to his as though she'd been born to it. The incursion of his mouth began slowly and leisurely, as if they had all the time in the world, an easy exploration of every soft corner of her mouth, subtle and dangerous. The fire he stoked flicked through her veins, like a hot bath after a cold day outdoors, until she thought she'd die from the pleasure it invoked. His hands tangled in the knot of hair at her nape, his palms cradling her against him, sampling and seducing, until she no longer knew where his mouth left off and hers began.

His tongue was rough velvet, tasting and teasing. What began as one slow kiss multiplied, the dance of his tongue conjuring erotic images, mirroring the tasting and touching, the thrust and parry, as shocking images flashed through her mind. Her legs wrapped around his waist. Her breasts brushing his chest, the tips swollen. The fullness between her thighs, inexorable and undeniable.

She was brought back to earth when he pulled away from her mouth, only to begin trailing his lips down her cheek, to her chin and to the pulse that beat at her throat. He dragged his tongue along the small strip of skin made available by the collar of her cloak. His hot breath scorched, and she arched her back as he pressed her body more closely against him. Her thigh slid instinctively and familiarly between his legs, and even with the barrier of her skirts and his trousers, it felt strangely like coming home. Shocked, her mind suddenly clear, she pushed him away. Rushford released her instantly.

Her breath was coming quickly. "I know what you're

doing," she said, a sob nearly escaping her throat. "And it won't work." She stepped away from him, sawdust sliding beneath her boots, until she was halted by the table at her backside. Stingingly aware they were not alone, she retreated into herself with mortification. The three men at the adjacent table were sniggering into their tankards, while Rushford seemed entirely nonplused at the scene they had recently provided.

"I was merely demonstrating," he said distinctly and as though their shocking embrace had never occurred, as though he had no trouble shaking off the effects of passion to instantly recall the issue at hand, "the inadvisability of following through on your plan." He lowered his voice. "I urge you to be cautious, Miss Woolcott. Your first instinct to remain in the shadows is in all probability your best choice. And now if you will excuse me, I must return home and prepare for what you probably already know is an evening of gambling pleasure far away from Mrs. Banks's charnel house and your unwise demands. In short, stay away from me."

Rowena stepped back, her balance suddenly unsteady, struggling against the flush of desire and the specter of defeat. Her heart ached as she thought of Montfort, her sister and aunt, imagining them standing by her side. She fought the longing for their arms around her, to make her feel shielded, safe, and as though nothing had changed. Losing them would be the cruelest blow of all and made this moment in a Shoreditch tavern with Rushford seem worth the humiliation. Impetuous, impulsive, and relentless she might be, but those qualities formed the steel in her spine that would finally convince Rushford he had no choice but to do her bidding. The threat of the Frenchman stiffened her resolve, fueling a dangerous logic that refused to give way.

Rushford took her arm, the matter closed—but only for the moment. "Allow me to escort you to the street and secure you a hansom cab," he said, moving them toward the tavern door and into the light of the alleyway. Moments later, alone in the swaying carriage, Rowena considered her prospects as the image of Rushford, lifting his hand in salute, faded away. The conveyance surged forward, the aroma of leather, vetiver, and worse still, the indelible imprint of their embrace lingering in the close air. There was no room for hesitation, she thought, blood pounding in her ears. Meredith and Julia would not pay the price for her cowardice.

# Chapter 5

A scant three hours later, Rowena looked at the reflection in the cracked glass that leaned against the pockmarked wall of a shop below her lodgings on Holburn Street. The warm afternoon sun streaked through the dirty windows, its bins filled high with a kalaidescope of velvets, silks, and lace. If one failed to examine too closely, it was simple to overlook the smudges of grease and dust that turned gold into dross, evidence of past lives lived in corsets and gowns now for sale to desultory bidders.

"You are a delight, my dear, let me assure you," announced Mrs. Heppelwhite, the owner of the dusty establishment and Rowena's erstwhile landlady, whose attempts at genteel tones could not entirely obscure her Cheapside roots. Widowed in her prime, she had boldly continued in her husband's footsteps as landlord, with the addition of opening a small shop on Holburn's street level. All too often, unable to afford their rent, lodgers paid with a collar of Valenciennes lace, an evening gown which they would never have a chance to wear again, or a rabbit muff they could no longer afford to warm their hands with on damp winter days. A keen judge of character, Mrs. Heppelwhite had sensed immediately that this one, with her fine skin and lithe elegance, was of a different cast altogether. Clearly a lady of quality, judging by her educated, dulcet tones, Miss Frances Warren, as she called herself, had fallen on hard times but was destined for better things, and perhaps an illustrious protector, thought Mrs. Heppelwhite in a flight of romantic fancy. Not that she encouraged such goings-on in the five rooms above the store on Holburn, she reminded herself with a dose of righteousness. She only let rooms to women of reputable character.

"The red velvet is perfect," she fussed, nudging the gown with its portrait collar lower on Rowena's shoulders. "Do not hide your assets, my dear," she advised, shrewdly assessing her customer's superior qualities. Long legs, a waist designed to fit a man's hands, wonderful shoulders, firm but, alas, small breasts. "You are a trifle slender, perhaps, with regards to fashion's dictates, but that can be easily remedied." Producing two small sachets from a drawer with a flourish, she proceeded to tuck first one and then the other into Rowena's bodice. "There, you see?" she asked triumphantly.

Rowena bit back a grimace, acknowledging that she would accept any assistance Mrs. Heppelwhite had to offer, from her reasonably priced lodgings to the contents of the shop below. Her transformation would have to be both convincing and complete, and accomplished with the smallest portion of her meager reserves. Her head still spun at the outlandish plan, so brazen that it took her breath away.

She glared at the image in the mirror. "This is considered stylish, then, Mrs. Heppelwhite, and perhaps a trifle provocative?" she asked, soldiering on yet having no idea as to the vagaries of fashion and even less knowledge of how a mistress might comport herself. At Julia's behest, she had read the various epistolary novels coming out of France, offering a cynical worldview of romance and flagrant immorality. Mistresses were practical, clear-eyed creatures unprincipled in their cravings for wealth and pleasure, their behavior and appearance designed to entice and beguile. Rowena's life at Montfort had prepared her for neither, most of her time spent in the countryside. There had been ventures into London to visit a modiste once every year, during which Rowena had never paid the slightest attention to her wardrobe. Both she and her sister had other interests with which to occupy themselves, Julia her studies and daguerreotypy and she riding, the outdoors, and her poetry. Even so, she preferred Wordsworth and his paens to nature over the rogue Byron whose overblown treacly romanticism made her teeth ache.

Although their pursuits would have been considered unorthodox for gently bred ladies, Rowena breathed a silent prayer of thanks for Meredith's insistence that her charges become learned individuals not tied to the dictates of proper feminine behavior. It was almost as though their guardian had suspected her neices would one day need great reserves of strength and fortitude. Alone and unmoored, beset with recurrent dreams that pushed at the edges of her sleep and sanity, Rowena had little choice but to persevere.

*Think before you act. You are far too impulsive, Rowena.* Julia's voice called out to her. And it was true. She rode Dragon far too wildly. She shocked the vicar with her outrageous pronouncements. And she had thought nothing of besting their groundskeeper, McLean, with her marksmanship. Unlike Julia, who could not hit the broad side of the gazebo on Montfort's east lawn, Rowena could peel the bark from a tree at fifteen paces, nine times out of ten.

Now that combination of impulsiveness and perseverance was responsible for this mad scheme. Leaving the tavern earlier in the day, Rowena had made the decision with lightning speed. Rushford was a gambler, and he would discover she was prepared to raise the ante and match intimidation with intimidation. His words were prophetic, she thought with strange satisfaction that intensified the knots in her stomach. She refused to think about the pressure of his lips on hers, the hard body pressed close, his breath hot on her skin. She had no intention of becoming the man's lover, absolutely not.

She would have to think about how to convince him to participate in the masquerade. He was as interested as she in getting to the bottom of the actresses's murder, and once his hand was forced, he would see the judiciousness in collaboration. Lord Rushford and his mistress and the demimondaine, she thought.

"What else do I require to complete my ensemble, Mrs. Heppelwhite?" she asked, not sparing a second glance in the mirror for fear of what she would see.

The landlady placed a finger on her chin, contemplating her creation, before producing from a drawer beneath the counter a sparkling necklace of paste, the gems the size of robins' eggs. "I do believe we need something to call attention to your outstanding shoulders," she said. The necklace against Rowena's pale skin glowed, but the older woman quickly shook her head. "No, I was quite mistaken, my dear. No use gilding the lily and covering up that flawless skin," Mrs. Heppelwhite murmured, more to herself than anyone else. "What of your coif, then?" she asked. "Perhaps you could dress your hair with these?" They both knew there was no maid to help with the task, but the older woman held up the necklace in any case, the paste glittering in her hands in the harsh afternoon light.

Her hair was a dark auburn, and her most distinctive feature. Suddenly, Rowena felt heavy with exhaustion, the burden of the past year almost too much to bear. She could not waste another moment in the purgatory where she'd been cast, neither dead nor alive, destined to remain ineffective and in the shadows. She plaited the worn velvet of her skirts in her right hand, the movement an attempt to soothe her agitated thoughts.

"Are you quite all right, my dear?" the landlady asked. If truth be told, she had rarely enjoyed herself as much, dressing this young woman in the once sumptuous evening gown, which, though she had not given it much thought, would net her a pretty penny. Her lodger was obviously primping for a suitor, whose intentions might not be quite honorable. But then such was life. "Is your gentleman," she probed carefully, "difficult?"

*Difficult,* echoed Rowena under her breath. She should have expected that Rushford would be an unusual sort, eccentric perhaps given his unusual interests, but nothing had prepared her for the intensity of his presence, simultaneously alarming and compelling. She could not begin to account for her physical reaction to the man, the flush of desire rather than embarrassment that had overtaken her at the tavern, the sensations at once foreign and familiar. She thought again of her nocturnal fitfulness, and most disturbing of all, the dreams.

Impatient with herself, she said, "The difficulty, Mrs. Heppelwhite, is that my gentleman prefers women with fair coloring. Is there a solution that you may have at the ready?"

Bloody ridiculous, men, thought Mrs. Heppelwhite, her own late husband included in the mix, who had seen fit to die inconveniently and with a mountain of debt that she had somehow managed to shoulder. Nonetheless she clucked consolingly for Miss Warren's benefit. "Aren't these gentlemen silly with their preferences? But pay no mind, my dear." She eyed the thick head of hair. "Bleaching is clearly out of the question, but I do have several wigs at hand." Never mind that they had come from old Mrs. Grenville, whose vanity had far outstripped her ability to pay her rent. "Oftentimes the ladies prefer to change their look at the whim of their gentlemen," she rambled on, all the while congratulating herself on scraping together a small living rather than subjecting herself to the whims of so-called gentlemen.

Leaving the young woman in front of the mirror, Mrs. Heppelwhite bustled to the mustiness of her storeroom, returning shortly brandishing Mrs. Grenville's yellow curls in her hand like a spring bouquet. "And real human hair," she exclaimed, promptly slipping the confection over Rowena's head, scraping loose tendrils beneath the tight fit. In a matter of moments, Rowena's features were transformed, her eyes a darker blue and catlike in tilt, her lips darker and fuller against the light canvas. No one would connect this arresting creature with the nondescript governess from Wales, and better still, no one would ever recognize her as Rowena Woolcott who had died over a year ago.

"I believe this shall do, Mrs. Heppelwhite," Rowena said. The landlady beamed her approval.

* * *

Felicity Clarence had been a fine morsel. Galveston settled into his box at Covent Garden, the shrieking of the well-padded soprano onstage undermining the comforting satiety of knowing that all was right with his world. Beside him, his wife Lucinda sat in rapt attention, not at all focused upon the swelling music emanating from the orchestra pit but rather upon the fashionable company that attended such events. Her ridiculous sausage ringlets quivered in anticipation of meeting Lady Sophie Crittendon's new son-in-law, a freshly minted duke from Italy. Her hopes momentarily dashed, she raised her lorgnette from her ample bosom in anticipation of catching the Duchess of Osborne in her box. Securing an invitation to her weekly salon was her fondest desire.

Galveston rested his head on the velvet cushion of the settee, shutting out his wife who, with a dowry and allowance as generous as her form, had allowed him to pursue his leisurely pursuits as should have been his birthright. The fact that generations of his family, on both maternal and paternal sides, had squandered their patrimony on horses and brandy was of no account. Lucinda's merchant-class bona fides were unfortunate, save for the munificent sums that flowed consistently from her family's coffers.

The soprano's voice soared in supplication, an annoying counterpoint to Galveston's more pleasurable ruminations. *Felicity had been a tasty morsel indeed.* The images repeated themselves in his mind. He missed her rather salacious enthusiasm most of all. When he had first been introduced to her at Garrick's in the West End by the Baron Francois Sebastian, an aristocratic gentleman who traveled in the same discreet circle as most of Madame Recamier's guests, he had been delighted. The actress had been as voracious in her appetites as in her penchant for trinkets. But it was Felicity's irritating ambition to rise above her station that had halted the enjoyable proceedings, most inappropriately. Not the thing at all, to ask him to be introduced to the more august personages in his sphere, the diplomats and the earls who littered his realm. He recalled the glitter of determination in Felicity's eyes.

It had all ended rather in a muddle—were it not for Sebastian, who had been most helpful with his suggestions for a tidy cleanup, a way of sending Felicity her *congé*. The Baron had unwittingly encouraged Galveston in his own dark directions, with an enthusiastic Felicity happy to comply. A familiar tightening in his groin joined with images of the actress, her head flung back, her mouth in a rictus of pain. *Until that last evening, when matters took a rather drastic turn.* It was difficult to remember exactly who had suggested the little game. Was it the Baron or the slyly lovely Miss Barry? Galveston did not care to recall.

It was unlikely that the body recently disgorged by the Thames belonged to the actress. Even if that did prove to be the case, there was no way to connect her disappearance to Lord Ambrose Galveston, or so Sebastian had assured him. As long as Rushford did not insert himself into the mix, thought Galveston darkly. Baiting him last evening at the club had been about as wise as baiting a lion in its den, but necessary all the while. Galveston had wanted to remind Rushford of the dangers of revisiting his past.

Galveston, annoyed at the tapping of her lorgnette on his shoulder, turned to his wife. She pointed somewhere into the sea of theater patrons, but he could not hear her words over the soaring voice of the soprano. No matter. He nodded in any case, following her gloved hand as she discreetly pointed in the direction of the Duke and Duchess of Osborne. But it was not the Duchess's bejeweled diadem that caught his attention.

The Baron Sebastian, sleek as an otter in his evening clothes, sat in the adjacent loggia, his dark eyes finding him like a bullet homing in on its mark. Galveston ran a finger around the stiff collar beneath his cravat. The crush of people, the cacophony of voices onstage, and the Baron's gaze closed in upon him to a distressing degree. Excusing himself abruptly to a startled Lucinda, Galveston exited their box, his mind already on a night at the gaming tables, always soothing to unexpectedly frayed nerves. The last images of Felicity Clarence flashed through his mind. Uncharacteristically disturbed, he shook off the vision with impatience, standing on the steps of the theater, summoning his carriage with a flick of his gold-handled cane.

# Chapter 6

It had been surprisingly straightforward to storm the citadel that was Crockford's Club. Rowena had simply swept the major domo who attended the door up and down with an imperious stare and demanded that he make way for Lord Rushford's mistress, Miss Frances Warren. Accustomed to the irregular behaviors of a demanding clientele, the major domo had summoned Hastings, the establishment's manager, who came onto the scene with great alacrity and a barely raised brow before sweeping the winsome and confident Miss Warren inside the notorious town house.

The club was, as Rowena had expected, extravagantly decorated, the heavy greens and golds meant to suggest the vastness of distant ducal palaces despite the reality of the narrow confines of a warren of salons, which encouraged intimate tête-à-têtes and hushed conversation. An abandoned gallery ran high along one side of the tight hall, its gilt arches pointing toward a rollicking gallery of cavorting mythological figures. Rowena wandered for a few minutes, trying to take the measure of the place while avoiding any specific invitations to join a circle.

She had met with cursory interest in her entrance, but in red velvet and fair curls, she passed scrutiny in what was regarded as a thoroughly dissolute circle that devoted itself to gambling and other barely reputable pastimes. Allowing a half smile to appear on her lips, she assessed the small crowd, mostly men and a few women, in the atrium and the adjoining salons. The laughter trilled a little too loudly and the colors of the silks and satin shone too brightly for decorum, but the club was known for its eclectic mix of high brow and low. Rowena stood on the threshold of one of the salons, a glass of champagne spirited into her hand by a passing servant, her attention captured by a man with heavy white mutton chops leaning over the décolletage of a red-haired woman.

"I shouldn't be surprised if a few fortunes are overturned this evening," he said, the turquoise satin of his waistcoat catching the gaslight.

The redhead, the jeweled combs in her hair flashing, placed a plump hand to her bosom. "Do you believe so?" she asked in a breathless voice schooled to flirtatious perfection. "Lord Rushford is a difficult man to intimidate across a card table."

Rowena took a sip of her champagne, fixing her eyes on a painting of a clutch of cherubs above the mantel, pretending to study the brush strokes closely as she eavesdropped from a modest distance.

The man's brow lifted in amusement. "I shouldn't try, my dear Constance, as I don't have a fortune to lose. My dear and careless father made certain of that some time ago, alas."

The red-haired woman made a moue of disappointment. "Do not tell me that I am wasting my time, Cecil, darling. I simply could not bear it. The House of Braemore in straitened circumstances! Only imagine . . ." She ended the sentence with a girlish giggle.

It was Cecil's turn to laugh. "You always were refreshingly direct, my dear," he said, reaching out playfully to stroke her hand in its silk glove, "but If you are looking for an engagement, perhaps you should try Lord Rushford. The man clearly has deep pockets and remains stubbornly solitary."

"Deep pockets perhaps," Constance mused, a curve to her rouged lips, playfulness still in her tone despite her companion's disappointing confession. "Much as I find the concept appealing, you and I both know that Rushford is reluctant to, shall we say, *engage*. Since the scandal." She paused significantly, looking at Lord Braemore as though she had secreted a priceless gem away in the bodice of her gown. "Not that I don't relish a challenge," she continued, lowering her voice further, "although I sensed there was something different about him this evening. I did snag him by the lapel of his jacket for the briefest moment earlier," she added. "I couldn't say precisely what struck me as unusual." She narrowed her feline eyes contemplatively.

"He seemed as indifferent to the world about him as ever when I last espied him in the library." Cecil sniffed. "Cold water for blood, that one."

Constance shivered dramatically, the silk tassels on her bodice keeping time. "I shouldn't be too sure of that. I hear he does have a fearsome temper. Albeit rarely on display."

Cecil's brow inched higher. "Now do not tell me that you have frequented the boxing club, eh?"

"I'll never tell," Constance said archly. "Except to say Rushford is quite the specimen of a man, particularly in full bout. Little wonder the late Duchess lost her head over him. Sacrificed everything." She shook her head. "Rumor has it that it required five men to hold him back from killing the Earl. Of course, he was distraught." She wagged a finger at Lord Braemore. "And you believe he has ice water running through his veins. I should love to prove otherwise."

Rowena was overcome by a sensation so physical that it threatened to bend her body in two. How strange, she forced herself to observe, that she should be so affected by the thought of Rushford with a woman.

She startled at a hand on her elbow. Turning away from the couple whose heads were bent closer in conversation, she prepared a bright smile for the gentleman who sought her attention. Fixed squarely in a shaft of light slanting from a tableside candelabra, he looked as though he had simply materialized there, a tall man of middling age with an imposing physique.

"I trust I am not interrupting," he said. The light cast his features in sharp relief, revealing eyes both inquiring and intelligent. Rather too inquiring and intelligent, thought Rowena, extending a gloved hand.

"Not at all," she said, lying, attempting to school her mind and emotions into a semblance of order. "I was merely admiring the delightful painting," she said, gesturing to the canvas over the mantel.

"Rather unfortunate, isn't it?" the gentleman asked rhetorically, a grin lighting his stern features, his eyes glinting over the prow of a bold nose. "I don't think I've ever seen a cherub quite that shade of pink."

Rowena shook her head, unable to stop a widening smile. "Indeed. Although I shouldn't think that the club is much concerned about the selection of paintings for these walls."

The gentleman relinquished her hand with an abbreviated bow, admiration in his gaze. "You are honest in your estimations, madam. And now that we have established the fact that we share impeccable taste in art, if I might be permitted to introduce myself? Lord Richard Archer."

His humor gave Rowena a false sense of courage. "Miss Warren," she said briefly. "Pleased to make your acquaintance." That she was an unaccompanied female did not seem to matter to Lord Archer, who merely crossed his arms, a ghost of a smile tugging at one side of his mouth as he regarded her with frank interest.

"Pleasure," he said. "I noticed your entrance earlier in the evening, when you caused a ripple among the men, like a new species swimming into the pool. And yet, you seem to have spent most of the evening attempting to hide in full sight, Miss Warren."

Rowena took another sip of her champagne. "I wasn't hiding," she countered.

"Merely eavesdropping?" Lord Archer rewarded her with a speculative glance, nodding discreetly toward the couple still posed under the painting. "Rushford finds himself at the center of conversation more often than not. Particularly recently."

An inner voice warned her to retreat, but she ignored it. She straightened her shoulders, unaccustomed to the low drape of her bodice and a stranger's scrutiny. "From what I could glean, he's quite the unusual man," she said neutrally.

"And a close friend," Archer said with an appealing frankness. "So you will hear no gossip from me, Miss Warren."

"I am relieved," she replied, reining in her strong curiosity. Somehow she had not considered Lord Rushford as having friends. He seemed a man disposed instead to isolation, shuttered away in his town house save for the few excursions and unorthodox pursuits he permitted himself. Lord Archer was observing her like a scientist intent upon discovery and made no effort to disguise the fact of his interest. She lifted her chin defiantly, aware that there was no use in holding off the inevitable. "Lord Rushford is a friend of mine as well."

Archer's dark brows snapped together. "My, my," he said. "Rush has been keeping secrets. But then he is a man who plays his cards close to his chest. How do you know him—or is it prudent to ask, Miss Warren?"

The lie was outrageous, she knew, but entirely necessary. The pause lengthened as he waited for her to offer elaboration. A small twinge of conscience was defiantly repressed. "I am," she said slowly, suddenly all too aware of her borrowed costume and hastily conferred identity, "Lord Rushford's mistress."

Archer's brows shot up, his keen gaze quickly taking in her ensemble, from the improbable tint of her hair to the crushed velvet of her red dress, missing no details Rowena feared. A burst of laughter, followed by a volley of raised voices, prevented whatever he was going to say next. The knot of people in the salon craned their heads in the direction of the hallway to see what the commotion was about.

"You will excuse me, Lord Archer," Rowena murmured, turning toward the threshold, "I believe I should hasten to Lord Rushford's side. In the library," she added with a tilt of her head in farewell before she began threading her way through the melee heading toward what she hoped was the library.

"This could get very exciting." The woman named Constance was behind Rowena, the scent of gardenias wafting along with her wide skirts. "From my vast experience in these matters, Cecil, it appears as though someone is on the precipice of winning a great sum."

"It's been some time since a great fortune was lost," Lord Braemore murmured in return. "Crockford's is losing its edge, I fear."

Rowena walked on, relieved to have left Lord Archer behind in the melee, quickly relinquishing her glass of champagne on a sideboard. She stood on her toes to peer into what was clearly the gambling room, painted a more somber green and gold but with none of the bookshelves one would expect in a library. Instead, two tables dominated the space, with only one currently occupied. All the other players had presumably abandoned their games to stand on the sidelines and watch the contest of vingt-et-un that was unfolding.

The cards were being shuffled, signaling the beginning of the end for one of the two men. Lord Rushford, in contrast to the prevailing mood, sat at the table with unconscionable disinterest, dressed simply in a black evening coat, his cravat a subdued cream silk, directing his gaze to the skillful hands of the dealer rather than on his opponent, whose complexion had taken on the grayish cast of a November sky. Rowena watched Rushford closely, noting there was nothing aggressive about his posture or movements, nothing to indicate that he cared a whit about the game's outcome. Yet, with his height and distinctly unfashionable athletic build, he dominated the room and his opponent, an aggrieved looking gentleman with a retreating hairline, matching chin, and ashen cast.

Behind Rowena, Constance whispered to her companion. "Dear Lord. The amount on the table is frightening. Too much money for Galveston to lose." The pile of chits, and tension as tight as piano wire, proved the truth of the declaration.

"Galveston's wife's family will absorb the losses," came Cecil's reply. "Although Ambrose appears to be having second thoughts. I suppose it's a big enough sum to toss."

The club's dealer, as gaunt and serious as an undertaker, oversaw the proceedings. A king for the man named Galveston, who called for another card with a sharp rap of his knuckles on the table.

Rushford drew a queen, followed by a six of hearts, with the nonchalance of a leisurely Sunday ride in Hyde Park. The hush in the library deepened.

Rowena knew little of gambling, save for whist and chess, which she and Julia had played as children. However, the tension in the library, already as tight as a bow string, was difficult to ignore. Even Rowena sensed that the pile of chits on the table was fearsome. Perspiration gathered under the wig and velvet dress.

Galveston nodded abruptly for his last card.

An eight of clubs snapped onto the table, and Galveston's face hardened into a mask of disappointment. The onlookers released their collective sigh in one breath, punctuated by polite applause, and a few outstretched necks waited for Rushford to collect his winnings. Rushford did not relax farther into his chair, however, nor did he reach for the chits at the center of the table. Instead, with the steadiest of hands, he signaled for the dealer to draw another card.

Over a collective hiss of surprise, Rushford said, "We can do better than this, can't we, Galveston?"

"I play by gentlemen's rules, Rushford," Galveston replied with a distinct whiff of desperation. "Although I shouldn't expect you to understand."

A soft murmur went through the crowd. The dealer's hand hovered over the deck. Behind Rowena, Cecil whispered, "Whatever is going on between those two?"

"From what I understand," Constance said, her voice thick with secrets, "Ambrose cannot forgive Rushford for his involvement in the Cruikshank murders. A betrayal of his class and whatnot."

"As though Rushford gives a damn," Cecil responded. "There is more than that behind it, I'd wager."

Impossibly, the tension heightened when Rushford nodded almost imperceptibly at Crockford's dealer. In a moment, the card was placed face up on the table. A five of hearts. *Vingt-et-un.*

The library erupted in applause and hoots of approval from the coterie of regulars who called Crockford's, after White's and Boodle's, their second home. Rushford appeared not to notice, his expression neutral, but the crowd quieted instantly when he shoved his cards aside. "I advise you to be careful as to the rules of the game, gentlemen's or otherwise," he said softly to Galveston, a hard and undeniable undercurrent to the casually delivered statement.

Galveston's smile tightened as he produced a handkerchief to mop the sheen from his brow. But he made no move to rise and quit the library. "You do tempt fate, Rushford," he said, his hand trembling. "One would have thought that you had learned your lesson."

"I've been told that I'm a quick study."

"Not quick enough," Galveston said. "At least by my reckoning," he continued, "not at all." The needling voice carried on. "As a result, I wish to challenge you to another game. This time double the winnings on the table—or nothing."

The temperature in the library notched up. A monumental amount was on the table. And something else. Rowena was sure of it. It was as though they were speaking of something other than the game of vingt-et-un. There was a shared history, and spilled blood, behind the fortune that rested on the table between the two players.

Rushford smiled slowly with a look of utter boredom, like a wolf circling his prey with elegance and ease. "If you prefer, Galveston," he said softly. "Although it must be said that you sorely try your wife's resources. My conscience feels twinges of remorse."

THE DARKEST SIN    71

Galveston's eyes narrowed and his mouth tightened as though prepared to spit rather than speak a reply. Instead, he signaled the dealer, who began the somber ritual of shuffling the cards. All eyes were riveted on the tableau around the polished mahogany table in London's most venerable gambling club. Years later there would be talk of this night.

There would never be a better time, Rowena told herself, her mind summersaulting. For some reason, she suddenly remembered what it was like when she'd dared herself to jump into the cold, spring-fed lake at Montfort—in February—goaded by the groundskeeper's son. Her hands formed fists in her evening gloves, and her voice seemed to come from far away. But she spoke firmly, without hesitation, her low voice carrying throughout the library and into the hushed stillness. "Lord Rushford," she said, drawing out each syllable.

Rushford's eyes snapped up from the cards in the dealer's hands. Rowena once again felt a gust of emotion, an agonizing awareness that tightened her throat. She drew upon the curious sensation to inhabit her role as Miss Frances Warren and moved slowly from where she stood in the doorway to the center of the room, deliberately positioning herself by Rushford's chair. Attentive to the open-mouthed stares of the assembled onlookers who had parted to allow her to pass, she lay a gloved hand on Rushford's shoulder.

"My darling," she said, dragging her fingers across his back, "It's close to midnight. How long do you intend to keep me waiting?" Her tone was dark, sultry. Or at least, she hoped so.

There were any number of rejoinders Rushford could have chosen. As decorum dictated in the presence of a lady, he rose from his chair and fixed her with a surprisingly warm smile. "You always seem to surprise me, my pet. One of your many charms," he said. "And of course you know that few others could lure me away from the gaming table." As he leaned his hip against his chair and turned his back to Galveston, his tone expressed pure pleasure at her presence. For a moment, his approbation, although patently false, tasted like honey in

Rowena's mouth. Rowena was not sure what she'd been expecting, but this was not it. Beyond them the small assembly gaped at this unexpected turn of events, the prospect of financial ruin suddenly transformed into amorous intrigue.

Her limbs as stiff as a marionette's, and acutely aware of their audience, Rowena nonetheless moved in closer toward Rushford until the velvet of her skirts almost kissed his knees. "I've been bored all evening, Rushford," she said in what she hoped was a continuation of her sultry whisper but one that she knew could be heard at the back of the library. "Whilst you have been occupied with this dreary card play. So do let us have some amusement at long last."

"As though I could ever keep you waiting," Rushford returned with a small smile exclusively for her, although his eyes remained inscrutable.

Rowena lowered her lashes. "Confess, my lord. You have been keeping me waiting for an unconscionably long time." She tapped his chest in mock outrage.

Galveston did not bother to clear his throat but scraped back his chair. "This is ridiculous, Rushford," he declared, flicking a dismissive gaze at Rowena and the riveting tableau they presented. "I do not relish this interruption by your doxy. I trust I will not be required to have the house intervene. We have more than enough witnesses to attest to my upping the stakes and your acceptance of the ante."

Rowena looked down and across the table, fixing Galveston in her sights. "If I were you, I should welcome the interruption, sir," she said softly, a hint of warning in her eyes, "judging by your performance this evening. Lord Rushford's decision to spend the rest of the night with his *doxy* is entirely in your favor, I should think."

A murmur went through the assembly at the affront, and from one so young and obviously unknown. Who was this woman who, in truth, was little more than a girl? Galveston purpled, and the crowd around the room bent collectively closer, a frisson rippling through the library. "This appears to be a new low even for you." He directed his remark to Rushford. "To allow yourself to be dragged from the gaming tables—and by such a woman."

"I believe she has a point," Rushford said slowly, an arm encircling Rowena's waist as though it was the most natural gesture in the world. "You would be wise to return home to Lady Galveston with at least a few coins in your purse."

Rowena stiffened and then forced herself to relax against Rushford, seeing her advantage. "Lord Galveston," she said smoothly, "I feel as though I must rectify matters. It is only right, given your assumptions." Her eyes widened in feigned dismay. "It turns out that I am, after all, not simply a doxy but rather," she said distinctly, aware that Galveston refused to acknowledge her presence in any way, "Lord Rushford's mistress."

Another ripple of shock coursed through the room, the mountain of chits, the indeterminate acrimony, suddenly yesterday's scandal. The hum of talk among the audience was suddenly deafening, and Rowena was aware of Galveston's staring up at her with mute fury. The words had had the desired effect. She could not take them back.

The world now knew that Lord Rushford had taken a new mistress at last.

# Chapter 7

The resolute dark blue of Rowena Woolcott's unmistakable gaze under a fringe of blond hair reminded Rushford of another place and another time—a pugilistic ambush that had been swift, strategic, and merciless. He had barely survived the attack in the ring and now seriously considered whether he would survive whatever silken assault Rowena Woolcott held in store. But if he had learned anything in his considerable experience in the Royal Navy, the boxing arena, and in the backrooms at Whitehall, a defensive strategy was never a good idea.

He had unwisely allowed Miss Woolcott to lead the charge far too long, keeping his own powder dry. It was time to load the cannons.

He managed to continue smiling at her despite his aching jaw, his acting skills honed through years of subterfuge. "You are quite correct. I have been remiss and, as always, I detest seeing you deprived of anything at all, darling," he said, aware of another charge running through the audience, reflecting an unsavory but entirely expected delight in witnessing his private life exposed. He had always been discreet in his affairs, never so much as in his involvement with the Duchess of Taunton. In contrast, her intemperance had known no bounds, her emotions as transparent as glass. Most of London still whispered about the night she had publicly threatened to leave the Earl for Lord Rushford, creating a scene of epic proportion after a reception at Hawkesbury House. Liaisons were tolerated, but indiscretion was not. Worse still, full blown love affairs were regarded with all the approbation of a potentially rampant contagion, dangerous to the extreme. Many would concede, with lowered voices and thinned lips, that the Duchess's untimely and scandalous death was not entirely unexpected—or unwelcome. Rushford's arm instinctively tightened around Rowena's narrow waist.

He said, "However, I know that you will oblige me in indulging Galveston's whims, just for one moment longer." He insinuated subtly that it shouldn't take more than a final hand to put the man in his rightful place. "After which you will have me entirely at your disposal." Galveston was not far off from losing his composure. A moment longer, several thousand pounds lighter in his purse and heavy with humiliation, he would be ready to lash out. He would be easy to break, a soft man who had never been tested by life. Something that Rushford counted upon.

Rowena smiled up at him from under her dark eyelashes and ridiculous wig. Rushford reminded himself to burn the horror first chance he could. "If you promise me that the next hand will be your last," she said.

Galveston shot daggers at them from across the mahogany table, a faint tremor appearing at the downward pull of his lower lip. "With your permission," Rushford said to Rowena, relinquishing her waist and taking his seat. Galveston remained standing, wearing an ugly expression, his eyes darting around the room as though looking for a solution to his predicament. Then he found it, a satisfied smile slowly appearing on his face. "One moment, Rushford, if you will," he said with a sudden and exaggerated politeness.

Surrender was not forthcoming. "I should like to add to the winnings on the table. To make our gambit all the more interesting," he said.

"Don't be tedious, Galveston," Rushford said genially, cursing under his breath at what was coming next, aware of the importance of keeping Galveston in play. "Out with it."

"Your mistress." The two words were stark, the implication unmistakable, as Galveston waved a palm in Rowena's direction. Rowena's hand on Rushford's shoulder stiffened while he quickly ran through his options and the odds, neither particularly good at the moment.

"What of her?" Rushford asked although he knew exactly where next Galveston was headed. His gaze, if not exactly lascivious, had a proprietary gleam. Not the worst turn of events after all, thought Rushford coldly. It had happened before in places like Crockford's, wherein chattel had been won and lost with the toss of a dice or a flip of a card. Miss Woolcott would do well to pay attention to what she had unleashed when she'd decided, unilaterally, that she would play the role of mistress.

"This is highly irregular," Rowena snapped as though reading his mind, the hand on his shoulder tightening.

Galveston merely shrugged. "That would be for Lord Rushford to decide, no?" He shot a glance at his opponent, who was calmly contemplating the fresh deck of cards in the center of the table before turning to look over his shoulder at his mistress.

"No need to concern yourself," he said to Rowena, watching the cascade of emotions on her expressive face. He saw that her youth and willfulness were proving impossible to contain. She appeared as though she was about to say something, but for her own good, Rushford imperceptibly shook his head before returning his gaze to Galveston. "Very well, Ambrose. What do you say that we toss in a night with my mistress against something that I find myself coveting."

A pistol might as well have gone off in the room. Witnesses to the delicious outrage would be dining out on the incident for weeks. *The beautiful young mistress and Rushford in a scandalous altercation with Lord Galveston.*

Galveston fingered the handkerchief still in his hand. "You're a greedy man, Rushford. I should think that the winnings on the table would be enough for you."

"Just as you wished to make the play more interesting by including my companion in the mix, I, too, should like to add a certain edge to the game," Rushford said, glancing at his opponent's hands twisting the handkerchief. "It's only fair. And when you hear my request, you should be quite relieved. After all, it's only your family's signet ring that I covet."

Galveston turned from gray to ashen, disbelief skittering across his face. Reflexively, he placed his bare fingers beneath the table. "How dare you, Rushford. Beneath contempt . . ." he sputtered.

"Ah, I see," continued Rushford disingenuously, "you are not wearing the ring. Now why might that be?"

"This is preposterous," stuttered Galveston, eyes flicking around the room, aware of the astonished audience who was clearly wondering why he was totally apoplectic at the prospect of wagering a gold bauble. "And totally insupportable," he sputtered. "An insult to my family name."

"Absolutely no insult intended," Rushford said benignly. "I merely covet something that I cannot have, all the more so because there is no evidence of the ring on your person. I wonder why that might be."

Galveston took a moment for consideration, squirming in his seat. He mopped his brow. "Very well," he said, his voice hoarse. "Your doxy is off the table."

Rushford inclined his head, as though in thanks. "A wise decision, sir. With your permission, then."

The room exhaled in a hiss, watching as the impassive dealer extracted a fresh pack of cards, cutting it cleanly before dealing the initial cards face down. The young and certainly unknown mistress remained standing behind Rushford, relief evident in the set of her shoulders, her heavy lashes obscuring her expression.

Galveston signaled for his next card, a slow confidence

blossoming in the narrowing of his eyes as he tipped the corner of his initial card. A four of spades. Rushford nodded imperceptibly, and the dealer rewarded him with a ten of hearts. Neither man flinched.

Again the dealer offered and Galveston gestured impatiently and was rewarded by a six of clubs. This time the library was preternaturally still, arching closer toward the mahogany table like a well-choreographed ballet. Rushford's nod brought him a six of spades. With a smug smile, Galveston flipped his first card, an ace of diamonds. One digit short of the prize.

The dealer, his long face schooled to passivity after years of watching men win and lose fortunes with the turn of a wrist, waited for instruction. Rushford quickly considered the odds, decidedly not in his favor, and tapped a finger on the table. For the barest of seconds, perceptible only to the hardened habitués of Crockford's, the dealer hesitated before deftly placing, face side up, a three of hearts. With a fluid motion, Rushford tipped the corner of his initial card, with the three of hearts.

A two of spades. Vingt-et-un.

A polite spattering of applause, a collective exhalation of breath, but there hovered in the library a sense of anticlimax, a premonition that the two men at the table had yet another score to settle between them. Galveston jerked to his feet, almost overturning his chair, muttering under his breath. The knot of onlookers parted as he stormed from the library.

Despite having won a small fortune along with Lord Galveston's pride, Rushford was not finished with his opponent just yet. "Wait for me here," he growled at Rowena, his mask slipping for an instant, the insouciant charm and easy manner wiped clean. Her eyes widened in concern. "My Lord, I shall go with you," she said, disobeying him completely and following him from the library, her wide skirts making it difficult to keep up with his strides as they made their way through the club, past curious onlookers, and down the narrow hallway to a closed door at the back of the residence.

Rushford ignored the rush of skirts at his side, intent on finishing this game with Galveston. He jerked open the door to what he knew was a private study for the use of Crockford's patrons, beyond caring that Rowena had slipped in behind him.

Galveston's respite, in the form of a generous tumbler of Crockford's best brandy and solitude, was not long-lived. Rushford slammed the door behind him, stalking toward the man whose hand trembled as he set the glass down. "You cannot do this, Rushford," he gasped, assessing the situation instantly. "I shall call for the major domo at once. I shall have Hastings ban you from the club in perpetuity."

"You won't have time," Rushford muttered, "before I've dealt with you." Rowena had planted herself by the door in stunned silence.

"Now see here," said Galveston, dragging his hands through his thinning hair. "You are taking this too far. It was merely a game, if you'll recall, that you won fairly, I'll concede." He slumped against the sofa, his necktie undone. "No offense taken."

"I'll decide that," Rushford said, wishing to have the man in the ring with him, yet knowing that the competition would be wholly unfair. But then again, he could easily reach across the study and pummel him into oblivion. He wondered briefly at the source of his anger.

"First things first," he said succinctly before reason escaped him. There were people beyond the door, waiting like vultures to fall upon any morsel of scandal and gossip that came their way. "If you ever again even refer to my mistress, as a doxy or otherwise, I shall rip out your throat. Understood?"

Galveston retreated farther into the sofa, swallowing hard, his breath louder than the ticking of the ormolu clock on the gilded mantel. Dread filled the study like a noisome odor.

"I did not quite hear your answer, Galveston," Rushford snarled.

"Understood," Galveston finally said, praying he would not be dragged from his feet. His tremulous hopes were quickly dashed. Jamming up the sleeves of his evening jacket, Rushford stalked across the parquet floor until he had seized Galveston by his shirt front, pulling him into a standing position where he wavered like a flag in a breeze.

"Rushford. Please," Galveston whispered. "What the hell is wrong with you? This is not the Duchess we're talking about here, for God's sake." Panicked, shaking as though with ague, he realized instantly that he'd reached for the wrong antidote. Rushford drew back one arm, prepared to shatter his jaw. Then before Galveston could cringe away, the taller man's rage seemed to coalesce and harden, staying his arm in midflight. Raw emotion flickered across his face, and he dropped Galveston onto the sofa in a heap. He turned back to the door, unseeing and unaware of Rowena, who stood frozen, wide eyed with a hand to her mouth.

Rushford released his breath in a stream. Then he turned back to face Galveston, who looked as though prepared to face the wrath of God. "My sincerest apologies. I was not thinking properly."

Galveston shuddered. "Absolutely, no offense intended," he muttered uselessly, holding both hands, palms up, in supplication. "Take your winnings, fairly won."

Rushford stared down at him as though from a great height. "I overestimated your intelligence, Galveston, among other things. This has little to do with vingt-et-un or my mistress." His voice was harsh. "I don't give a damn about the fortune you lost and which I won. But I do care about your signet ring. Where is it? And don't try lying. Because it will hurt if you do."

Galveston's shoulders fell farther into the sofa's plush cushions. "Good Lord, Rushford. Ring? Why do you care about a bloody ring?" His look was incredulous.

"You are most unwise if you expect me to remind you." Rushford's voice was lethal. He pushed his sleeves back down and shot the cuffs of his shirt to keep his hands from curling into fists.

Galveston's eyes darted around the room as though looking for answers. Then like bolts sliding into place, his expression changed from fear to comprehension. "The bloody whore," he whispered, turning his head toward a cushion to shield himself from dawning awareness. "Dear God, the bloody vixen!"

Rushford's eyes were hard and his voice cold. "The bloody whore, as you call her, is dead, and happened to have your signet ring on her person. Why should that be, I wonder?"

Galveston set his fingers to his temple. He knew enough not to deny the charge. "How am I ever to explain this all?" he muttered, a cushion absorbing his moans.

"Let me help," Rushford snapped. On the periphery of his vision, Rowena had backed up against the study wall as far as she could without actually leaving the room.

Galveston rose slightly from the cushions. "Felicity Clarence meant nothing, a mere entertainment," he declared. "Things got into a bit of a muddle. You of all people must understand how such things occur, Rushford." Galveston's mouth twisted at the memory, his face ashen.

Rushford took another step toward him, his evening jacket pushed back by the hands on his hips. "Who helped you dispose of the body?" Patience was wearing thin, and he spared Galveston a more detailed confession. "You could hardly accomplish such a feat alone." Galveston had never been asked to move so much as a feather tick. "And don't ask me to repeat myself," he ordered. "I expect the truth."

Galveston appeared as though he wanted nothing more than to cover his face with his trembling hands. "Surely you understand. If it hadn't been for the Frenchman, the situation would never have gotten out of hand. He encouraged it, as a matter of fact." Galveston's confession proceeded in no particular order, one non sequitur after the next, panic overtaking logic. He seized on the excuse of the Frenchman like a dying man. "And then he was there," he continued, "when I summoned him. When I realized that she was dead."

Rowena's gasp was quickly stifled. She clutched a handful of her skirt to keep herself upright. Rushford rapidly considered the wisdom of letting her hear the rest of Galveston's story. "You may spare us the sordid details until later," he said. But there were other specifics for which he was unprepared to wait.

In the next instant, the smaller man was jerked to his feet again. "What is the Frenchman's name and what does he want?" Rushford asked slowly, tightening his fist in Galveston's collar.

The smaller man's eyes bulged. "What do you mean? I don't understand." The collar tautened persuasively around his neck, which did everything to encourage the flow of Galveston's next words. "The Baron Francois Sebastian introduced me to her last autumn at the Garrick Theater, on Charing Cross Road. She had a reputation, even among the other actresses . . . It all went swimmingly for a time—" He choked out the words, beads of sweat reappearing on his forehead. "Felicity adored certain . . . diversions . . . and perhaps we went too far. She wanted the usual in return, the baubles and trinkets, and then began asking me to introduce her here and there." His voice coarsened. "But when she asked me to introduce her . . . she reached too far above her station. And that final night . . . it was she who suggested that we . . . I never expected that it would lead to her asphyxiation . . ."

Disgusted, Rushford released him. He strode to a desk in the corner and snatched a piece of vellum from the blotter. "Your signature and confession. And a promise of your further cooperation, which if you're exceedingly fortunate, may mitigate the court's judgment of your actions," he demanded. "Or I shall inform the magistrates in the morning of your involvement in Felicity Clarence's murder."

Galveston sucked in a breath and took the pen that Rushford offered like a piece of hot coal. Turning to the side table, he scribbled down several lines. Relief smoothed the lines of his face when he quickly finished. "You are very generous, my lord, to allow me this reprieve . . ." he opened his mouth to begin, but the rest of the words faded on his lips.

"This isn't a reprieve, Galveston," Rushford corrected him coldly.

Galveston tried to repair his rumpled clothes, shrugging his coat over his shoulders, attempting to knot his cravat. "See here, Rushford, the Cruikshank situation and of course the Duchess—" he began awkwardly but was silenced instantly by Rushford's glacial stare, suddenly more frightening than the physical threat of violence.

"We've concluded here this evening, Galveston," said Rushford, watching the smaller man exhale slowly, a trace of color coming back into his face. "I shall let you know when I've finished with the Baron and, rest assured, we shall resume our discussion. I don't foresee you fleeing to the continent; you wouldn't have a farthing without your wife's largesse. If you cooperate, we may be able to mitigate the charges brought against you."

"How is that possible?" he asked in a choked voice. "How could you possibly circumvent an investigation once it is opened?"

Rushford declined to answer, glancing instead at Rowena, who gazed at him questioningly. She moved away from the wall and the door, sensing that Galveston was close to making his exit.

"I sense you are eager to depart," Rushford said, standing aside. Galveston hurriedly smoothed back his hair, straightened his jacket, and then scuttled from the room like an insect. The door closed behind him and Rushford turned to Rowena Woolcott.

# Chapter 8

Rowena's limbs were stiff from holding herself rigid, her mind flying off in several directions, trying to make whole cloth of what she had just witnessed. She refused to back away from Rushford, who held her in the crosshairs of his dark gray gaze.

"Where is your cloak?"

"I don't have one. I came without."

He nodded brusquely. "Very well. There is an exit at the back of the house, by the mews."

"You are clearly familiar with the escape route," she remarked.

"And a good thing," he said, grabbing her arm. His eyes flashed his irritation. "We shall return to my town house unimpeded, if all goes well."

Rowena drew herself up a notch. "Your town house? I don't think so. I shall return to my lodgings."

Rushford jerked open the door, flicking her a dismissive glance. "You are my mistress now, are you not, self-declared?"

With his dark suiting marred only by the pristine cream of his cravat, he looked the devil incarnate, thought Rowena, and just about as powerful. At least, she thought with fatal optimism, she had finally captured and now held Rushford's interest. "I did what I deemed necessary," she said. "And don't be preposterous, Rushford. We need only inhabit the roles for the sake of our audience. As tonight demonstrated.

You were prepared to wage a night with your mistress, as I recall."

She tried to pull away from the hand on her arm, but he had already propelled them into the hallway, taking long strides toward the back of the establishment. A few voices could still be heard in the distance, the sound of crystal mingling with general laughter. "I trust I did not pique your vanity," he countered tightly.

She ignored the taunt, endeavoring to keep up with his strides. "At least you now agree on the wisdom of assisting me, given the interesting parallels that have risen to the surface this night." The Frenchman and the drowning were uppermost in her mind.

"You were the one who forced my hand," he gritted.

"As though anyone could," she muttered, adjusting her wig, which had angled to the side in their rush to leave the club. "Do not play coy with me. Your appearance at Mrs. Banks's this morning had to do with your suspicions, some of which possibly involve my circumstances, as I tried to explain to you at the tavern."

"This is not the place to discuss whatever parallels your imagination conjures, Rowena."

"Why do you persist in pushing me away? When we clearly have interests in common? Do you believe it is coincidence that you were alerted to the drowning of that poor actress? And what of the late Duchess—your duchess—whom everyone is so keen on mentioning, sotto voce, of course."

"You know nothing of my life, Rowena," he said, warning in his voice. Copper pans hung overhead as they made their way through the kitchen, deserted now.

"Was she your mistress?" Rowena asked. "The Duchess? It could explain your hesitation—"

Rushford stopped, slamming her up against a counter, the pots clattering, his eyes bleak, his jaw hard. "Rowena." His voice was quiet. "I do not wish to speak of it."

Rowena was shocked at the heat of his body inches from hers. "Very well," she said carefully, wondering at the iron in his voice, and at the boundary she was not to cross. "However, I shall not return to Belgravia Square with you," she said, sagging against him.

"I don't care what you wish," Rushford snapped. "You set the wheels in motion this evening, Rowena, not I. And you will live with the consequences."

She stiffened against him, raising a fist to push him away. His broad shoulders were hard as a slab of stone beneath his coat. "This is not what I intended, as you realize full well." He caught her wrist and jerked her even closer against him. "What are you doing?" she asked, confused. For a long moment, their eyes locked, their breaths mingled, suppressed rage and frustration bubbling between them. And then, as though there was no recourse, Rowena felt the urge to draw nearer to this man, dragged by the heat pooling in her stomach, familiar and yet exotic sensations that she chose not to consider too closely, not to consider at all. As though in a dream, she removed her fist from his broad hand and brought it around his neck, pulling his face down to hers.

Before this day, she had never been kissed. And had certainly never initiated a kiss, a second kiss, as a matter of record, and certainly not experienced the dizzying power of raw masculinity. It was heady, this combination of anger and lust, coaxing at the tendrils of a dream yawning deep within her. His mouth was an inch from hers, she noted in the suddenly hazy recesses of her mind, and beautiful. In an instant, he'd closed the distance. A hungry urgency took over, their bodies molded together as though nature had intended the union, at once unmistakably familiar and unbearably exotic.

The dance of his lips against hers was intoxicating, the silk of his heavy hair rich under her fingers. His tongue stroked and coaxed and she knew that this was not right, and yet every sweep of his tongue and thrust into her mouth was stealthily stealing her will. Rushford groaned into her lips, his tongue entwining with hers, capturing it, playing with it, his hand sliding around her waist, pushing closer to her, the hardness of the counter on her backside fading away.

Unwilling to think, Rowena slid a hand around his chest beneath his coat, liberating the scent that she had come so quickly to associate exclusively with him. The faintest aroma of vetiver claimed a primal sensual ground, settling around her in opulent warmth. She would not lie to herself. She wanted him when she didn't even know why or what precisely her feelings meant. His mouth moved over hers, his tongue languorously teasing as his free hands wandered over the boning of her corset.

It was utter madness. It was anger, which she had witnessed in the study with Galveston, mixed with lust. Her frustration and her inexplicable attraction to this man. Nothing more. But it didn't matter, any more than his hard thigh sinking between her own, his chest against her breasts, his lips sliding along her jaw. She could lie to herself, pretend it was another of her dreams, the heaviness between her legs becoming an intense ache.

She closed her eyes, willing the dream, *her dream,* to wash over her. Her womb was heavy and her breasts hurt, as she savored the wicked mouth against the skin of her neck, pleasured by the slow slide of his lips. She reveled in his hands, cupping and stroking, his fingers slipping into the shadows—

A door slammed somewhere nearby, and Rowena's eyes flew open at the sound, alarm drying her dream to a fine dust. Rushford did not wait but hauled her into his arms. Her head began to swim again pressed close against his chest, the profile of his hard jaw cut by the sensual mouth hovering over hers. Rushford jerked open the kitchen door and the night air swept over them both.

The streets had been empty given the late hour, rendering their journey to the town house on Belgravia Square short. Dismissing the curious looks of his driver and butler with a curt good night, Rushford had bundled Rowena up the back kitchen stairs toward one of the five guest rooms in the back of the residence. He'd managed only two steps away from the bed, upon which he had deposited a mutinous and dangerously silent Rowena, to mentally brace himself against the oncoming onslaught, his pulse pounding and his breath coming as though he'd been running for days. The hardness in his groin mocked him without mercy.

The memories came rushing back, making it no easier for him to forget what had transpired in the club's kitchen or resist tearing off Rowena's gown, the red velvet pooling around her in a crimson heap. The offensive wig was partially askew, the gold lush against her white skin. As though reading his mind, she pulled the curls from her head, revealing a sleek topknot and the elegant bone structure of her face. It was the last thing he needed. She pushed herself up against the pillows, ready to swing her legs out of the bed. "I cannot stay, Rushford. You cannot hold me here against my will."

For a brief moment, snared by the brilliance of her beautiful, intelligent eyes, he wondered who was the captive. Would she ever remember, he wondered, feeling a tightening around his conscience as well as his pounding erection. Philosophical flexibility should have been his for the taking, buttressed by a jaundiced worldview and a personal cynicism that had been forged by years of professional betrayal and cemented by the murder of his Kate. *Christ,* he was feeling guilty for the uncontrollable desire he felt for this girl sitting awkwardly on the wide bed. Desperate, he struggled to resist what was but a paler version of a passion he'd believed would never be his again. His enforced celibacy had been a form of self-torment, punishment for allowing the monstrous to have happened.

He ran a hand through his hair and said without looking at her directly, "You need not flee, Rowena, I shan't touch you again. You have my word."

She did not move from the edge of the bed, her slender neck bent as she seemed to contemplate the complex pattern of the parquet floor. "I apologize," she said, glancing up at him after a moment. "I take full responsibility. The fault was mine. For whatever reason . . . I cannot hope to say why . . . I cannot account for . . . but I was the one who initiated the embrace this evening. I am simply embarrassed." She bit her lip. "Perhaps it was the strain of the evening. However, it will not happen again, I assure you, my lord."

It was excruciating, the pain he felt at the innocence in her voice. When it was he who had taken advantage, and not for the first time. His mind spun back, hopelessly in thrall to the memories that her presence so easily conjured. Before the images could coalesce, he shut them down with brutal swiftness. He was wasting time—and endangering Rowena further. It was the bitterest irony that she had come to him for assistance when he would simply lead her back into the vortex of Montagu Faron's making, so chillingly outlined by the foolish, unwitting Galveston earlier in the evening.

"I take full responsibility," he said abruptly. "Enough said about the matter."

Rowena sighed her relief. "Enough said," she echoed. "Then I can return to my lodgings and we can meet tomorrow to discuss how you intend to resolve the murder of Miss Clarence, now that you have Galveston's confession."

Relieved at this turn in conversation, Rushford shook his head. "Galveston is more valuable to us at large just now. His day of reckoning will come, never fear."

"I sensed that there was more." Rowena swung to her feet. She moved elegantly, thought Rushford, in total control of her body without any of the simpering daintiness typical of her sex. "This Frenchman, for instance—" The sentence remained unfinished. Her eyes shone clear, without guile.

And nearly killed him. "We can finish our discussion tomorrow morning," he said tersely.

"Very well, then, I can see myself out, my lord. Please, if you would be so kind as to arrange for a carriage, so as not to alert your servants to my presence."

"It's a trifle late for that. And you're not going anywhere. You are safer here," he said, hoping to enlist her compliance for once. He walked over to the window, bracing his palms on the sill, turning away from her. The darkness of London stared back at him. "Let me know the location of your lodgings, and I shall have your belongings sent for."

"I thought we'd resolved this matter."

Rushford rubbed his chin, already rough with morning stubble. "You have declared to the world that you are my mistress. So tomorrow I shall have my solicitor see that you are established in appropriate apartments." He turned back and glanced at her critically, taking in the rumpled, red velvet dress. "And we shall have a new wardrobe, the proper jewelry."

"Is all this window dressing necessary?" Rowena asked with the arch of a brow, her arms crossed.

"Absolutely," he said briskly. "Lord Rushford's paramour should look the part, particularly if we are not to raise suspicion."

She cocked her head to one side. "I have but one question."

The corner of his mouth lifted slightly. "Just one?"

"Why the sudden volte-face, my lord?"

Now was not the time for the truth. Rushford gazed up at the ceiling, ornately plastered with gilded laurel leaves, searching for an explanation that would satisfy. When he found none, he said, "You would not believe me if I said that you'd won—nay—worn me down. So let me just say that you have resurrected my chivalrous nature."

She nodded her head slowly, as though deciding whether to believe him. "I trust there's more to your chivalrous instincts than you let on."

"You yourself have told me that you and your family are in grave danger, now more so given that you have exposed yourself to the world. The unfortunate wig, notwithstanding," he added dryly. They both glanced at the curls lying discarded on the bed.

Rowena fingered the knot of hair at her nape, long, lustrous and heavy in a man's hands, Rushford thought suddenly. "It served its purpose, did it not?" she said. "Although we must find a replacement since you find it so odious and obviously not suitable for Lord Rushford's mistress."

"All in good time," he muttered.

She picked up the discarded wig, contemplated it for a moment, and then tossed it back down on the bed. "You are using me, Lord Rushford," she said sweetly.

He was a man who generally had the power and the cunning to get what he wanted, and it amazed him that this young woman saw through him like a pane of glass. "As you intend to use me," he said, keeping his voice even.

She lifted her nose. "I can afford to pay you for your time and expertise."

"That's ridiculous, as well you realize. I've never taken money from a woman, and I don't propose to start now."

"However, you have no qualms about using a woman, do you?"

As he had in the past. Again he wondered how much Rowena remembered in the shadowy recesses of her consciousness. His own memories, far too close to the surface, pierced him to the core. "It doesn't signify if we both get what we want," he said bluntly, deciding on a partial lie. "I will concede that there might be some connection between the murder of Felicity Clarence and your situation."

"But that's not why you've finally decided to assist me," Rowena said with a surprising insight into his character, or lack thereof. "At this point, having a mistress on your arm could help you achieve your own ends, making it easier for you to move in Miss Clarence's and this Frenchman's circles," she analyzed with an astuteness that was shocking in its cynicism. "It's clear to both of us that Galveston, horrible man though he is, doesn't understand the half of it."

Rushford had underestimated Rowena Woolcott, but there was little use in holding back credit where it was due. "Well played," he said, sensing that she wasn't quite finished. And he was right.

"I suspect," she continued fearlessly, "that there is something more you seek, besides apprehending Galveston for the crime of murder. Something to do with this Frenchman. *Se-*

*bastian.*" She pronounced the name with the proper French inflection. And, although she didn't say it, something to do with his duchess. With Kate.

"We will discuss the situation further tomorrow morning, when you are rested," he repeated, wondering if he sounded even remotely convincing. Rowena Woolcott managed to open doors that should remain firmly closed. "If you require anything"—he gestured to the bellpull by the bedside—"the servants will be pleased to assist you. Your possessions will be delivered to your new apartments post haste." There was a studied formality to his tone, a suit of armor hastily donned.

And then he left her, just in time.

For the first time in weeks, Rowena slept deeply, undisturbed by dreams or nightmares, awakened late by a morning sun saturating the heavy curtains shuttering the bedchamber. Before she could rationalize her decision to remain at the Belgravia town house, a discreet knock at the door opened to reveal a middle-aged woman in a mob cap, hesitation marking her face.

Rowena came instantly awake, murmuring her thanks and motioning the woman to place a tray holding a steaming pot of tea on the table at the foot of the bed. She pulled the sheets to her bare shoulders, aware that she was clothed only in her shift. Accustomed to informality with the servants at Montfort, she smiled brightly at the maid, who was busy opening the drapes and smoothing the counterpane.

The bedchamber was of grand proportions, its wide four-poster enveloped in a gold embroidered canopy, the furnishings glossed to a high sheen. As with the rest of the town house, the atmosphere was cold, as though the walls and rooms had never heard laughter, the footfall of children, or the barking of dogs. It was not a home, merely a residence where Rushford chose to abide when he was in London. As she made to leave, the maid bobbed a curtsy and pointed to the smooth, ivory vellum on a silver salver by the breakfast tray. "For you, my lady," she said before gathering up the tray and disappearing through the door.

Rowena threw back the covers and sat cross-legged, reaching for the note and quickly scanning the contents. A carriage would take her in an hour's time to her new apartments in Knightsbridge. Rushford, it came as no surprise, had had his solicitors working quickly to ensconce his latest mistress in her new home.

*Mistress.* Wide and largely unsupervised reading had taught Rowena the meaning of the term—the female lover of a man who is not married to her. A mistress was a kept woman, a courtesan, showered with extravagant clothes and jewels in exchange for sexual pleasures. A mistress existed in the shadows of the demimonde, expected to be educated and adventurous, a companion for theater, certain ballrooms, and, of course, the boudoir.

A strange concept to learn, however secondhand, in a household of spinsters, Rowena considered. She moved over to the washstand by the dressing room screen. In the eyes of the villagers living in the Cheviot Hills, Montfort was a grand fortress that kept safe three women, living without men, who managed well for themselves. No husbands, no brothers, no uncles, no amorous protectors. Rowena splashed cold water on her face from the washbasin, feeling heat and color spring into her cheeks. Too young and too wrapped up in herself, she had never looked beyond the surface of the pastoral existence that Meredith had created for them. Their aunt had never spoken of her past, their parentage, or the quiet life she had deliberately chosen for them to lead. They could well have traveled the continent, been launched into society, resided part of the year in London. Rowena now realized that those possibilities would only have invited the attention of Montagu Faron.

Her hands shaking, she dried her face with a fine linen towel, then quickly donned her corset, neatly laid out over the dressing screen, followed by crinolines and the velvet dress with its difficult hooks. Mrs. Heppelwhite had served as her dressing maid, but she would now fend for herself. Mercifully, as she was not going to be going about in public, the yellow wig could wait.

An hour later, she stood in the graciously appointed apartments Rushford had arranged for her. She might have expected a garish heap suitable for a fallen woman, but the series of rooms on the second floor of a Palladian mansion was exquisite. With a private entrance to the side, away from the prying eyes of Brandsome Street, marble steps led up to a wide, flat terrace, surrounded by a pale stone balustrade. Inside, the main salon was large with a high ceiling of cream medallions on a lemon background, and walls that were hung with shimmering peach-colored silk. The room held several wide divans, low tables and was fitted with cherrywood paneling. The overall feel was of decadent opulence, entirely appropriate for its purpose, Rowena decided.

"All is well?" Mr. Smythson, Rushford's solicitor, asked attentively.

"Yes, thank you," she said, trying not to be intimidated by the man with his high starched collar and dignified air. They had made small talk about the weather and the environs, just south of Knightsbridge. It was not too rarified and yet not too louche, the buildings well tended, the gardens neat and tidy with their rows of hedges interspersed by rose bushes.

Rowena glided across the marble floors to inspect two bedrooms, one the master chamber with an oversized bed that required a footstool to scale its high mattress and with walls obscured by ornately framed mirrors on every side. And in one corner, next to the dressing room door, stood her small trunk, delivered as promised.

The bathroom was charming, with a copper tub and porcelain washstand, and again, a repetition of the same ornate mirrors, reflecting every possible angle—. Rowena's face flushed, overcome with a sudden exquisite mortification. She scarcely recognized herself any longer. Rushford had inveigled himself into her thoughts and emotions in a way she could scarcely explain. She had behaved outrageously, even for her, allowing herself to give in to desire for a stranger, a man whose life and experiences were far beyond her ken.

The chamber was suddenly stifling, and she turned decisively back to the main salon where Smythson waited patiently for her. "If all is in order, then, Miss Warren," he said, using the alias given him, "I shall take my leave presently. I should like to inform you that a cook and a maid have been retained as well. If they do not meet your approval, simply let me know and I shall make other arrangements. Permit me to add," he said, turning his hat in his hands, "that Lord Rushford has asked me to engage a modiste on your behalf who should be arriving"—he glanced at the ornate ormolu clock on the fireplace mantel—"one hour hence."

Rowena nodded her thanks, although not in the least grateful. She wished never to be beholden to Rushford in any way, and the thought of the expenses he was incurring made her distinctly uncomfortable. "Lord Rushford is too generous. He does nothing by half measures, it would seem," she said.

"Indeed," said Smythson, often referred to as the "vault" by those who knew how much he prided himself on his discretion and faultless service to two generations of Rushfords. Impeccably dressed in gray trousers and severely cut jacket and waistcoat, he had produced a rabbit out of a hat for Lord Rushford on a minute's notice. There was no hint of censure in his deferential gaze, which emboldened Rowena to ask, "Lord Rushford's parents—do they reside here in London or in the country?"

Smythson pursed his lips, spinning the edge of his hat in his hands. "I'm afraid, Miss Warren," he said reluctantly, "they passed away many years ago, along with the elder son, when Lord Rushford was at Eton. A fever took them," he added with appropriate solemnity.

Rowena felt a stab of sympathy and then quickly considered posing another question to the solicitor, driven by a hunger to learn more about Lord Rushford. "And no other siblings?"

Smythson shook his head. "Regretfully, no."

They were both orphans of a sort, thought Rowena, finding the correspondence intriguing. Neither she nor Rushford had grown to adulthood having known their parents. The ghost of an idea coalesced, and she stopped on the threshold, the impulse to ask more questions strong. Smythson cleared his throat once more, however, recovering his full legal hauteur and clearly reluctant to disclose any more than necessary pertaining to his employer. "If you are finished with your inspection, Miss Warren, I have further instructions," he said with a hint of awkwardness in his tone. "If I might suggest that I accompany you to the library."

"As you wish." She followed his tall narrow back to a rose and ivory jewelbox of a room with its shelves only half filled with books. A feminine escritoire sat in the corner upon which rested three heavy boxes, embossed with what she took, upon closer inspection, to be the Rushford crest.

"Oh, no, this is not necessary, Mr. Smythson," she said, understanding dawning. "Totally unnecessary, truly," she tried again, her protests trailing away.

"I have my instructions," he continued, his hands making surprisingly quick work of the intricate locks on the first box. A choker of pearls, like rich cream, nestled in the silk lining. Smythson efficiently peeled back the silk to reveal another tray upon which lay a bracelet of rubies and emeralds. Then a diamond-studded pendant. A king's ransom, thought Rowena, blanching.

"Yours to use for the time being," Smythson explained. "Upon Lord Rushford insistence, Miss Warren." He added with an approximation of kindness, "No worries, of course. Important family jewels are not amongst the sampling here." Naturally, Rowena thought, Rushford's mistress could not be seen wearing paste and borrowed gowns. *We must not arouse suspicion.*

Soon thereafter Smythson departed, having locked the boxes away in a recessed drawer behind the porcelain fireplace of the library, leaving Rowena little time to agonize over her next challenge: the modiste. Madame Curzon and her coterie of seamstresses invaded the apartments like a tempest. Instantly, Rowena longed for the warmth of Mrs. Heppelwhite, who had not regarded her with thinly arched brows and clenched teeth after ordering her to disrobe and stand in front of the bedchamber's many gilded mirrors. "I don't require too much, Madame Curzon, a few gowns, perhaps a day dress," Rowena began before she was asked to stand on a hastily procured footstool to be surrounded by mirrors reflecting her from every possible angle.

Madame studiously ignored her words, ordering her acolytes to produce bolts of fabrics ranging from the softest silks to gossamer satins, which she then began draping around Rowena's shoulders. "I do not like overly fussy styles of dress," Rowena said as her words were muffled by a swath of lace descending over her head and neck, "and I do not wish to incur too great an expense, preferring a style that is somewhat understated."

Madame knit her brow, her fingers covering her mouth at the abomination. "Impossible. No great expense? Lord Rushford would have my head," she said, her French accent faltering. Her eyes narrowed, making a quick reassessment of her newest client. "You are young, *alors*. Part of your charm, this hesitation." She took a step back, a birdlike figure in black bombazine. "However, we do not wish you to be lost in a cloud of innocence, not for a man with the sophisticated tastes of Lord Rushford."

Rowena stiffened at the implication, wondering not for the first time about Lord Rushford's late duchess. A beautiful woman, without doubt, one who could hold the attention of a complex and overwhelmingly masculine man. She saw again Rushford's bedchamber, and the small painting of the woman with the dark eyes and tumble of hair, which she had held in her hand.

"Was she very beautiful?" she asked, surprised that she had spoken aloud.

Madame quickly replaced her frown with a convincing smile, unwilling to risk alienating a nervous young woman who was not long out of the schoolroom, clearly, and yet one with such promise. "No need to concern yourself with what is past, mademoiselle," she said with the pragmatism that came naturally to a businesswoman who had fled East London decades earlier, never to return. Rushford was known for his discretion and it was not for Madame to tell tales out of school. Better to calm the waters. "What is beauty when one has youth and spirit on her side?" she asked with forced bonhomie.

Unbidden, the image of the delicate oval danced in Rowena's vision. A woman of remarkable beauty with shining dark eyes, a mobile mouth, a luxuriance of wheat gold hair. Rushford's duchess.

"The past is the past," Madame Curzon said, steepling her fingers together as she contemplated Rowena from another vantage point. She took a step back, determined to change the subject to her benefit. "I envision several day dresses, perhaps in oyster and gray satin, trimmed with pearls. Perhaps a champagne tulle for evening. So wonderful with any coloring, whether you decide to go au naturel or blond," she enthused, instructing one of her acolytes to produce a bolt of peau de soie, which she then began to pin around Rowena's waist. Her hands fluttered around her shoulders, gesturing her eagerness. "Such a lovely, lithe figure, such a tiny waist and youthful bosom. We will ensure all the bodices are cut accordingly, eh? We would like to keep the illusion of the maiden but with some mystery and temptation also."

Rowena acquiesced, at this point almost convincing herself that Rushford was correct. She would need the appropriate armor to do battle if she wished to carry off her deception successfully. Despite her determination, she could not escape the sense of doom slowly settling around her, as heavy as the emerald brocade Madame Curzon was wrapping around her shoulders and neck. Suddenly, she wanted nothing more than to finish with the fitting, to flee the elaborate apartments and the charade of Miss Frances Warren, Lord Rushford's young mistress.

She heard herself saying, "I believe five or so garments will be sufficient, Madame, three day dresses and two evening gowns." The room seemed to spin around her, a kaleidoscope of colors and textures.

Madame clucked disapprovingly, waggling her ringed fingers in protest. "You are young and naïve, my dear. Lord Rushford is a wealthy man and requires that his mistress be appropriately gowned, if she is to appear on his arm." She added with a shrewd look, "And if one is to seek a man's approval and keep his attentions, perhaps there are a few lessons that a young woman would seek to learn." Bustling with renewed efficiency, she produced two bolts of the finest lace. "Valenciennes, bien sur. You and Lord Rushford will adore the chemises and corsets we will assemble for you."

Entirely unnecessary, Rowena wanted to say while holding still for the couturier and her assistants, who spun the wisps of fabric and measuring tape around her bosom and waist. She closed her eyes, feeling like the fragile, porcelain dolls she had never played with as a child.

"I could not agree with you more, Madame Curzon," a deep voice said. Rowena opened her eyes, a soft chill sweeping across her now exposed skin. She stared at Rushford with mute shock, watching as he sank into a peach-colored divan at the foot of the bed, casually loosening the snowy cravat at his neck. "My darling," he added with a raised brow, "I would heed Madame's advice at all costs."

Madame puffed up her chest like a guinea hen, swelling with pride, directing her seamstresses to produce more of their lacy offerings. Murmuring enthusiastic statements about mademoiselle's beauty and youth, she and her acolytes danced around Rowena, who was clad in only her chemise, corset, and white stockings.

Choking out a perfunctory greeting, Rowena wished she

could close her eyes and disappear from sight, vanish in a puff of smoke, spirit herself away to Montfort in a return to her careless, oblivious youth. Was it really so long ago that she had spent mornings riding Dragon until they were both breathless? Or played chess with Meredith and then spent the afternoon with Julia, reading her latest poems while her sister busied herself with her daguerreotypes?

She wished desperately she could leave now, trying in vain to ignore Rushford's presence several feet away from her and the dangerous emotions he aroused. Aware of Rushford's eyes following her every move, she longed for her velvet skirts and stiff bodice, discarded over the foot of the bed.

Sensitive to the growing tension in the room, Madame Curzon, no stranger to the desires of men and their new mistresses, suddenly began murmuring apologies, declaring that they had finished for the day and would deliver the first of the garments in two days' time. "For you, my lord, especially," she crooned to Rushford before clapping her hands to her seamstresses and turning on her heel.

The double doors closed decisively, taking the tempest with them, but Rowena did not know whether to welcome the reprieve or hurl insults at Rushford. "What are you doing here?" She had all but forgotten that she was almost naked, one stocking-clad leg on the footstool and the other hovering over the floor.

He shrugged nonchalantly. "I do believe I have every right to visit my mistress, at any time of day or night."

Rowena looked frantically for her clothes, conscious of her plain cotton undergarments; the bright lights of the room were unforgivably revealing. Unapologetically, Rushford took in the whiteness of her skin, the flash of her backbone and hips, as she turned around to face away from him. "Don't be ridiculous. Once and for all, this is a ruse," she hissed, refusing to turn around and face him. "I am no more your mistress than the man in the moon."

"It's a trifle late for modesty, Rowena," he said casually. "Or would you prefer that I continue addressing your backside, perfect though it may be."

"This is too much," she said over her shoulder. "And entirely unnecessary. You knew very well that Madame Curzon had arrived to prepare my wardrobe." Stretching out his long legs and crossing them at the ankles, he looked thoroughly relaxed, and it occurred to her that the situation was outrageously familiar to him. The Duchess, no doubt, and a phalanx of women before her had probably spent thousands of Rushford's pounds on gowns and jewels, and in apartments much like this one.

"If we are to continue with this ruse, as you call it," he continued, his eyes on her form reflected from every direction by the mirrors in the room, "we shall no doubt find ourselves in similarly intimate circumstances. So I should advise you not to reach for the smelling salts just yet."

She raised her chin at him. "I have never had to avail myself of smelling salts in my life, Lord Rushford," she snapped, making no effort to face him directly. "And I don't intend to begin now." To prove her assertion, she finally turned around to face him, slipping her arms into each sleeve of her chemise in an attempt to coax the fabric up to her neck.

She realized that Rushford was enjoying himself. He rose from the divan with an exaggerated sigh. She refused to take a step back, her hands gripping the fabric at her neck. "You are made of sterner stuff, I suppose," he murmured, moving toward her until his knees touched the cushion of the footstool and the two were face to face. It was happening again, the awareness, the thickening tension in the air whenever they found themselves together. With excruciating slowness and an outrageous familiarity, Rushford slid the fabric of the chemise down, exposing her collarbone. Rowena did not protest, could not protest, when he bared her shoulders, helping the garment along until it slowed on the swell of her breasts.

"What are you doing?" she asked, when she should have asked, *what are we doing*?

"We are going to have to behave as though ours is an intimate relationship."

She stiffened beneath his hands. "I am a good enough actress that I don't need the practice, my lord."

"That may well be," he said, continuing his work unabated, unlacing her corset before tossing it aside. Underneath the sheer cotton of her chemise, her flat stomach was smooth and unmarred. He spanned his hands around her waist, her skin cool marble beneath the fabric.

"We decided," she said shakily, "that this would never happen again."

"Yes, we did," he answered calmly.

Rowena knew that she had every chance to back away from him, to bolt, that he would make no move to stop her. Yet she was honest enough to admit that she desired him. Seeing him so close, the austerity of his face, the wide mouth, the dark eyes, reminded her of what more she wanted him to do—to her. Her pulse leaped in rapid staccato, fueling the mad idea that he was a substitution for the man in her dreams. Aware that her breathing was coming fast and erratic, she focused her gaze past his shoulders, on the cream-colored plaster medallion overhead.

They stood for an eternity, a frozen tableau. "This is but a dress rehearsal, Rowena," he said softly, and then nodded as though coming to a decision. He strolled across the room, away from her.

When she found her voice, she said, "What do you mean?"

"Do you believe that whoever is after you and your family," he said, standing by the fireplace mantel, this time not bothering to hide the mockery in his voice, "will be easily misled? This is a dangerous game you and I are about to play. Deception is never as easy as it looks."

His accusation stung. "You believe that I will not be able to carry off this plan, to play the role of your mistress."

He took a few steps back to lean a shoulder against the

mantel. "Well, isn't it true? You came to me with the preposterous proposition, going so far as to force my hand yesterday evening at Crockford's, and now you cringe like a
convent-bred schoolgirl at the very prospect of my proximity.
Yet we shall be called upon to play the besotted couple, over
and over again. And yes, in public." He straightened away
from the fireplace, his fluid movement startling her. He
moved so differently from other men she'd encountered.

Rowena shook her head, unclenching the fabric in her
hands. "I will do anything to enlist your assistance in uncovering the threat to me and my family. And I can assure you,
my lord," she insisted, stepping off the footstool in only her
chemise and stockings, "that modesty, false or otherwise, will
never stand in the way of our achieving *our ends*. What is fair
is fair," she emphasized. "I will do whatever is necessary to
ensure that you uncover what it is you are after." She wished
desperately to ask what, precisely, that might be.

Instead, she hastily began gathering up her clothes, as un-
selfconsciously as possible, stepping into her velvet skirts and
then fastening her corset, before finishing with the damnably
long row of small hooks on the bodice. Her fingers fumbled
under Rushford's cool gaze, but she was relieved when he finally moved from the fireplace to wander over to the cur-
tained windows, giving her time to collect herself. When she
was finished, she turned toward him, took a breath, and gestured to the divan. Her need to explain was acute. "It's impossible to continue like this," she said, "unless we have
candor and truthfulness between us."

He remained standing by the window, and Rowena
thought she saw compassion in his gaze despite the neutrality
of his voice. "What is it you wish to tell me?" he asked, reading the anxiousness in her eyes.

Rowena sat down on the divan. "There is only one place
to begin this discussion, and that is with the man who wishes
my family ill—Montagu Faron," she said abruptly. "I do not
know why, but I do know that he is the reason behind my abduction and a continued threat to my aunt and sister." She

paused, trying to interpret his expression. "Does the name mean anything to you?"

"It may well," he said ambiguously. "How do you know this Faron is the man who represents the danger to your family?"

She acknowledged silently that her assertions sounded far-fetched, and even now she had difficulty separating the strands of reality from her recurrent dreams and fractured memories. She shook her head in confusion. "During my abduction, I remember little else but hearing his name, over and over, and his threat to make the Woolcott women suffer," she continued, her voice low with distress. "I awoke in a haze of dull pain, several times, and I remember a voice urging me to drink something vile. I kept my eyes closed, waiting for the pain and nausea and confusion to subside. And always the voices . . ."

"Whom else have you told about this? Have you confided in anyone?"

Rowena thought of the few acquaintances in their small circle at Montfort, none of whom she would wish to entangle in her plight. "I've told no one and have not contacted Meredith for fear that I would make things worse if our enemies discover that I am still among the living and that their plan had failed. The last thing I wish to do is to add flames to the fire."

Rushford sat down beside her. "Do you have any idea as to why Faron would wish the Woolcotts harm?"

If only she did. "I don't know," she said with desperation, burrowing back into the cushions of the divan and into her years at Montfort. "It all seemed to begin after my sister Julia published a monograph featuring her botanical daguerreo-types. It was against my aunt's wishes, as she was acutely afraid of any kind of notoriety, any activity that might prompt outside attention. In the village, Meredith was always considered somewhat peculiar because of her independence and need for privacy. She was always hesitant about letting us go out in the world, and in retrospect, I now see

that she was mightily afraid of something—of someone—
finding us."

Rushford listened patiently.

"I don't remember much after my abduction, about which
I have already told you," she paused, the moment heavy with
guilt, fear, and desire. She placed her hands on her flushed
face. "And the rest I can't recall other than this anxiety that I
must somehow find Faron before he can get to Meredith and
Julia. And yet, I wish desperately to tell them that I am still
alive. Their anguish must be—" Rowena could not finish, de-
spising her weakness when Rushford reached for her and removed her hands from her cheeks. His face was blurred by
her tears, and she blinked to hide the evidence of her torment.

She swallowed the lump in her throat. "I realized that once
I recovered, I had no choice but to go to work as a governess.
There was little else I could do to support myself and earn the
means to find Faron." She did not try to hide the hope in her
voice. "And then I read about your exploits in the broadsheets."

His hand tightened on hers, adept at sensing her responses,
knowing her better, somehow, than she knew herself. She realized that she should be worried, but pushed the doubts
away. Instead, she looked at the man so close to her, wondering if she would ever see behind the gray eyes that watched
her as though he knew her most inner workings. There was a
connection between them both, if she could only grasp it, but
it melted like fairy dust between her fingers.

Her head hurt and her eyes burned with unshed tears. "I
wonder if I know anything anymore, if I can possibly recall
something, something that's missing." She sounded incoher-
ent now, even to her own ears. Struggling to maintain her
hold on reason, she said, "I can't say why but I sense the situation with Galveston and Miss Clarence is somehow associated with Faron."

Rushford was silent, and his weight shifted away from her.
As always his proximity was disturbing, making it hard for

her to think clearly, trust giving way to misgivings. She smoothed her cheeks, warm under her palms. "I have told you all I know, Rushford," she said simply. "But there is more, I suspect, that you have been reluctant to reveal to me."

He sat back on the divan, watching her carefully. "Perhaps not everything is as complicated as you suppose, Rowena," he said. "After spending several years abroad, I found myself at a loss upon my return to London. You yourself have pointed out that I have little enough to fill my days, save gambling and boxing. "

"But what of the Cruikshank murders?"

"Mrs. Cruikshank was an acquaintance of mine. She confided in me one day the distressing fact that three of her courtesans had suddenly passed away." He shrugged. "Out of courtesy and yes some curiosity, I began to investigate the peculiar circumstances. And you already know the outcome."

Mrs. Cruikshank a friend? Highly doubtful, thought Rowena, that Rushford would count a madam as merely an acquaintance. Annoyance now mingling with her anxiety, she struggled to keep her counsel and pursued doggedly onward. "What about Miss Clarence?" she persisted.

Rushford stretched an arm across the back of the divan. "My reputation precedes me, as you have noted several times. The situation was brought to my attention," he said. "You are not the only one who read about the resolution of the Cruikshank murders."

An amateur sleuth. Why did the mantle sit so awkwardly on his broad shoulders? "I still believe that you're concealing something from me," she said, aware that she was treading on dangerous ground. The late Duchess. She had no right to ask, but nonetheless she resented his reserve about the life he had led in the years and months before their meeting. Looking around the overtly feminine bedchamber with its lemon-colored walls and peach curtains only managed to heighten her unease.

"Galveston and the Frenchman—Sebastian—is that what you're referring to?" he asked. Rowena read the challenge in his eyes and met it by forcing herself to relax, smoothing the folds of her skirts with damp palms.

"To begin with—yes." Even though there was so much more she wished to know.

"Because the two are French?" he asked doubtfully.

"There is that commonality, tenuous, I'll concede. But then the modus operandi is curious. Murder by drowning. A mere coincidence?" She paused awkwardly. "More importantly, of all the murders in London, why did you choose to investigate the Clarence drowning?" *How did your duchess die?* she really wanted to ask. The question intruded like an ugly stain upon a pristine swatch of silk. She broke off, unable to continue, momentarily staggered by the words that hovered on her lips.

His eyes darkened, and she wondered whether she'd gone too far, if he could indeed read her mind. "You're wondering if I'm hiding some dastardly secret? Some unfathomable sin?" he asked, injecting a humorous tone in his voice, a deliberate attempt to diffuse some of the tension between them.

Her face warmed. "You needn't condescend, Rushford. You misunderstand. I am merely inquiring about your motivations. You yourself said to me earlier that Galveston is merely a means to an end. Why is it so unusual that I wish to learn more, or that I suspect there is something more . . ." she rambled, embarrassed. She trailed off hopelessly to examine the intricate embroidery of the brocade divan.

The silence weighed heavily. Then Rushford touched her arm. "My apologies. I did not intend to be condescending," he said, rising and forcing her to look up at him. "You are absolutely correct in your assumption that there is more to this recent drowning than meets the eye, particularly if Galveston is in any way involved. The man has a penchant for getting into trouble in areas far outside his comprehension. Which, to answer your question, leads me to suspect that we must discover more about Felicity Clarence's last days and the whereabouts of the Frenchman, Sebastian. And perhaps that will lead us to your Faron."

His answer both raised her hopes and doused them. On the one hand, she had succeeded in gaining his assistance. However, she also sensed a guardedness that was years in the making. She was reminded of a cunning animal in the wild, protecting its territory from dangerous incursions. Rowena clenched her fingers together in her lap to keep from reaching out to him, to touch her fingers to his forehead, the slant of his nose, the hard lines of his jaw, as though reading a topographical map.

"And there you have it," he said, interrupting the disturbing drift of her thoughts and closing down the discussion neatly. "Tomorrow evening we shall have our first excursion—we shall go to the Garrick and visit with Miss Clarence's coterie of friends and colleagues. And in the interim, I shall endeavor to discover what I can about Sebastian and Montagu Faron. I promise you."

Rowena nodded halfheartedly, realizing that she should be grateful. She now had a powerful ally in her quest to find Faron. She studied the profile of the man about whom she knew almost nothing but who now held her fate—and those she loved most—in his hands. "I should like to thank you, my lord," she said.

He was already at the door and turned briefly, his eyes unreadable. "Thank me? That's the last thing I want," he said. "I cautioned you, Rowena, about going ahead with your mad scheme. So just remember, you started this." And then he was gone.

# Chapter 9

Rushford left the Knightsbridge apartments as though the hounds of hell were at his heels. The cool afternoon air hit his face as images unspooled in his mind with fierce intensity.

Rowena on the stool, her profile turned toward him. Several strands of her hair arced toward her mouth, her full lips pressed tight.

Rowena's beautifully naked back, the delicate indentations of her spine a magnet for his lips and tongue. It had taken every ounce of self-control not to trace a kiss down the expanse of skin, his palm pressed into buttocks barely covered by her pantalets.

He growled to his driver to return to Belgravia Square, slamming the carriage door shut. He leaned back against the squabs, attempting to ignore the heaviness in his groin. The mirrors in the apartments had given him Rowena Woolcott from every outrageously erotic angle. He'd forgotten that mouth, sensual without any need of rouge, the startled blue of her eyes with their flared brows. Her hands had gone up to clench the sheer fabric around her neck, the motion curving her young, lithe body away from him.

*This had to stop.* Once and for all. Not for the first time since Kate had been murdered, Rushford sensed the earth suddenly sliding from beneath his feet, felt a downward pull toward the deep hole of guilt he'd been attempting to crawl out of ever since. Kate had been made for him. They had been made for each other, he believed. He'd been a reformed cynic who had spent years casually sampling the world's female bounty before being stopped dead in his tracks by the Duchess of Taunton. He'd first clapped eyes on her across the crowded lecture hall at the Royal Geographic Society. He had forgotten what the lecture was all about and could only recall the challenge in the Duchess's dark eyes as she lured him into a spirited conversation about the latest contretemps over the Elgin Marbles. It did not take long to discover that the Duchess's marriage was a typical arrangement predicated on bloodlines rather than passion. And certainly, Kate was not the first married woman with whom Rushford had involved himself—but he knew from the start that she would be his last.

He would be forever hurt, betrayed and furious at her death, and he mourned her acutely, missed the swift cut of her mind, her physical beauty, her courage. She was the strongest woman he'd ever known, and the most vulnerable. Vulnerable to the passion they had created between them.

The carriage swung around a corner, the cobblestones grinding beneath the turning wheels. He had thought that the pain of losing Kate would lessen but it hadn't, and now he was searching for excuses for his indefensible behavior. There was no justification for the lust he felt for Rowena Woolcott, born of a moment of susceptibility and need over a year ago, heightened by drastic circumstances that had tumbled out of control. That she did not remember was his good fortune, but for how long? She sensed, rather than knew, there was a connection between them, as evidenced by her blind insistence that he was the only man on earth who could help her.

And it was bloody well true. But in helping he could also do her grave harm—the late Duchess of Taunton was proof. He clenched his fists in frustration, swallowing the urge to have his driver take him to the London Boxing Club on Maiden Lane, in the Strand. He wanted nothing more than to sweat away his frustration in the ring.

The carriage pulled to a stop on Belgravia Square. Rushford leaped from the conveyance and up the stairs, brushing past his butler and into his study. Dust motes spun in the afternoon air, the clock on the fireplace mantel ticking entirely too loudly for his liking. The drinks table beckoned, but he turned away from the brandy decanter, sitting down and throwing his legs up on his desk. He needed to think—and to plan.

Rowena's faith in him was entirely misplaced. Of course he knew of Montagu Faron's whereabouts and had for a long while. Claire de Lune was outside Paris in the Loire Valley, and about as penetrable as Faron's medieval fortress of a soul. Despite rumors to the contrary, that Faron had actually set foot in England over a year ago, no one had seen the devil, hidden behind his omnipresent leather mask, for decades. His acolytes killed and lied on his behalf, single-mindedly intent upon the collection of ancient relics and scientific spoils.

When Rowena Woolcott had reentered his life, Rushford had merely been suspicious, but the demise of Felicity Clarence had intensified his unease that he was being strung along. It all had the markings of a well-laid trap, especially Galveston's readiness to give up the name of Baron Sebastian, one of Faron's lesser known disciples. Rushford gritted his teeth. And all for a few ancient tablets.

"You seem more miserable than usual, Rush."

Rushford uncoiled from his chair at the familiar voice coming from the doorway. Archer was an imposing figure as he stood smiling just inside the study, his broad frame filling the doorway. He moved damned quietly for a man his size.

"And you more cheerful than usual. Gives me a bloody headache, Archer."

Archer's smile broadened. "Happy to be of use. I didn't think you would mind my intrusion, and I didn't want to ring the bell and disturb your skeleton staff. This place looks like a mausoleum, by the way."

"Your opinion means the world to me, as you know."

Rushford sat back down and stretched his legs on the desk again, strangely grateful for his friend's intrusion. He knew better than to ask how Archer had gained entrance to his town house, aware that the man could make himself a ghost, if needed, remembering another time and another place. The port of Alexandria in Egypt, when Archer had saved the day by materializing with preternatural timing to head off an ambush set up by the Emir Damietta. Rushford allowed himself a ghost of a smile. "Have a seat," he said, "and pour yourself a drink. I think the butler's disappeared."

"You've retained one? I'm utterly amazed. Now if you could only do something about all of these drop sheets. Good Lord, it's as though nobody lives here."

"I hadn't fully realized your penchant for the domestic."

Archer crossed his arms over his chest. "And what would you know of it?"

"Last time I checked, you'd been living at White's. You're never around long enough to visit that pile of stone in Essex, which is probably ghost-ridden by now. And my solicitor mentioned recently that you have leased out your family's London town house for the fifth time in ten years."

"You know how restless I get," Archer responded. "Don't like to plant my feet anywhere for more than a few weeks. I've got enough to keep me busy in London for the next while, however."

"Do tell."

"I fully intend to."

"Although it will be for naught, I promise you, Archer. I do not wish to involve myself in anything that concerns Whitehall. And by the way, you haven't poured yourself, or me for that matter, a drink. The least you can do is stop hovering on the threshold and sit down."

Archer acknowledged the invitation by moving farther into the room. "Never mind Whitehall," he said casually. "What's going on with you? It's not like you to be so bloody mysterious. I'm your friend, remember? And you could have introduced me, by the way," he continued. The two men had dispensed with social politesse years ago. Archer walked by the drinks table to stand beside the unlit fireplace, glancing at the ash-strewn interior with a small frown.

"To whom?" asked Rushford.

"To the winsome Miss Frances Warren, of course," Archer replied, turning back from the fireplace but ignoring the proffered seat. "She seems a little young. Not your usual type."

Rushford considered his options, lying for one, but Archer's knowing glance wouldn't let him. The two of them had been through enough weather together to make obfuscation pointless. "She's not my mistress," he said bluntly, examining the tip of his boots across the desk.

"Then what are you doing?" Archer's look was skeptical. "I thought you were going to rip Galveston's throat out. Haven't seen you quite that riled in a long time." Not since Kate, was what they both knew he really wanted to say. "What's going on exactly? It's not like you at all to enact this sort of drama. For a man who doesn't seek attention, the business with the Duchess and then the Cruikshank murders should have been more than enough."

Rushford leaned back against the arch of his chair. "It is a drama of Miss Warren's own devising."

"She appears far too young and innocent to devise much of anything. And she doesn't seem the avaricious · sort," Archer said, going down the list. "What is she after—I might wonder."

"She's not after anything. It's the safety of her family that drives Miss Warren's life at the moment. And while you're so intent upon these intrusive questions, would you like to know what happened at Mrs. Banks's?" Rushford asked peremptorily.

In reply Archer took his seat, settling across from his friend, his eyes watchful. "Desperately eager, particularly since you don't seem disposed to answer further questions regarding Miss Warren. So—what do you make of the drowning?"

"Besides the fact that the actress's death was deliberately

brought to my attention, as you'll recall?" Rushford looked thoughtful. "I subsequently discovered that Galveston is our murderer, no real surprise there. Mrs. Cruikshank had mentioned to me once that he had been barred from her establishment, given his unpredictable tastes."

Archer frowned his distaste.

"The victim's skirts had been weighted down with stones so the body would sink. But she didn't drown. There were bruises around her throat. The whole business seems rather clumsy in comparison with the Cruikshank situation. Poisoning is much more subtle than strangulation."

"You made the connection to Galveston how?"

"His signet ring was on the body—or at least until Mrs. Banks got to it."

Understanding dawned. "I was wondering why you were so keen to have the ring included in your wager the other night. Thought there must be a very good reason."

"Now you have it," Rushford said. "Further still, Felicity Clarence was an actress who, I've since discovered, wished to enter influential circles."

"Entrapment you think?"

Rushford shrugged. "Very possibly. She entertained Galveston's perversions to gain entry or at the very least introductions to eminent personages. At least according to Ambrose. The name Sebastian came up as well."

Archer straightened. "Are you certain?"

"Galveston seemed almost eager to name him." He would discover more once he and Rowena began making the rounds of the demimondaine. The prospect was hardly appealing. She was much too young and innocent for this business. "But you and I both know that Sebastian is a runner for Montagu Faron." Rushford felt the anger in him leaking from an old wound. "The drowning has Faron's handiwork all over it— the man does love to send a message."

"You could just let this go, Rush," Archer said softly.

Rushford's jaw tightened. "I lost Kate because of him and

because of my own hubris, and I insist on finishing this the way it was meant to finish. It's no longer a game."

"I'm not sure you're in the proper frame of mind—" Archer stopped himself, then continued in more measured tones. "What do you hope to gain from this? Other than helping Miss Warren with her immediate concerns? Perhaps you'd be wiser to allow someone else to play the role of knight rescuing the fair maiden."

"Don't think I haven't thought of alternatives. I endangered Kate's life because of our liaison, and now I could well do the same with Miss Warren."

"Miss Warren. Isn't that a trifle formal?"

"I already told you she's not really my mistress."

"Then why did you decide to become involved with her?"

"She forced my hand."

"Oh, you don't say?" Archer crossed his arms over his chest, watching his friend closely. "I've known you for twenty-five years, and I can't recall your doing anything you don't want to do."

Rushford jerked out of his chair and walked around to the front of his desk. "Your insights are astounding, Archer. Truly," he said with a measure of sarcasm. "But there's more to this than meets the eye, as I'm sure you've gleaned, being the perceptive bastard that you are."

Archer rubbed the bridge of his nose, hiding a smile. "She's very beautiful. And intelligent."

"Don't be preposterous."

"The attraction between you is rather obvious, Rush, and obvious to the roomful of onlookers at Crockford's the other night. Even without the Galveston drama, the two of you could have set the library ablaze."

Rushford sat back down, denial tensing his muscles. "Sod it, Archer. Leave it be. We are talking murder here—and worse possibly, as you well know. That's why you're here, isn't it?" he asked darkly.

Archer grunted and then reached into his coat, retrieving a

packet of papers and then throwing them on the desk in front of Rushford. "See for yourself what Faron has planned," he said. "I just came from Whitehall."

Rushford reached for the dossier, his eyes skimming. "Bloody fucking hell" he said softly after a moment. "The damn Rosetta Stone. *Again*. Why am I not in the least surprised." He shoved the papers back across the desk to Archer. "I never did believe the rumor that he had died in the fire at Eccles House. And this proves it," he continued. "The man's made a very pact with the devil, I swear."

"It's the only intelligence we have for the time being." Archer leaned forward in his chair. "But I need to ask—are you ready for this reprise?"

Rushford left his seat, unable to remain still, pacing around his desk. "Don't even ask, Archer. I cannot let it stand, not this time."

"You did what your conscience ordered you to do. You safeguarded the Stone."

"For fuck's sake," Rushford fumed, his voice a low growl in contrast with Archer's calm tones. He took a step back and let out a short breath to slake the fury that made his hands shake. "I won the battle but lost everything in the bargain. And for that alone, if I have the chance, Faron will pay."

Archer stood, meeting his friend's eyes. "Whitehall wants you back."

"I'm not doing this for goddamned Whitehall," he ground out. "And if that makes me a lesser man, so be it. I'd rather spend my time at the gaming tables, in the ring, or helping the Madam Cruikshanks of the world."

Archer held his ground. "And what about the girl? Miss Warren. How is she involved in all of this?"

Rushford's gray eyes darkened. "Despite my lamentable record, I shall protect her." *And use her*, his conscience taunted him. "Most of all from Faron. I've learned from my mistakes."

Archer assessed his friend. "The mistakes weren't yours to

make, Rush. It was Kate's decision to become involved with the Stone. Remember, she'd been married to a diplomat and was far too accustomed to putting her nose where it did not belong." Bored senseless by the never-ending cavalcade of social events that marked the life of an ambassador's consort, Kate had unwisely turned to other interests. Rushford included, thought Archer sadly. He realized that his friend believed grieving was not enough, that it was his obligation to set things right. "Everything else is superfluous. The Rosetta remains in British hands due to your efforts," Archer concluded with finality.

"For how much longer?" Rushford asked, his eyes glittering. "The contest begins again, but this time I've learned that a defensive strategy is not the answer. Last time, Faron went after us. This time, I propose that we change the nature of the game." He gestured to the dossier lying on his desk. "And you've just confirmed my reasoning."

"You're hardly a novice," Archer said, acknowledging Rushford's vast experience in a world few knew anything about. "But this young woman . . . to drag her into a maelstrom of events that she is totally unprepared for is hardly fair."

Rushford acknowledged the warning, and what was left unsaid, with a look. "I won't allow another cock-up. Trust me on this one, Archer. Miss Warren and her family will remain unharmed."

"I don't have to tell you that Faron has an unerring instinct for weakness."

And for innocence, Rushford thought, but hesitated only a moment. This time, instead of sending Miss Woolcott to safety as he'd done over a year ago, he would take her into the heart of darkness itself. But unlike Kate, he vowed, Rowena would emerge alive.

The rolling thunder of applause shook the seats of the Garrick Theater in London's West End. The melodramatic tale of Buckston's *The Dream at Sea* had titillated its audience with its double entendres and bawdy repartee. Rowena sat stiffly with Lord Rushford in a private box, wearing the pale gray satin gown with its daringly low-cut portrait collar encrusted with mother-of-pearl delivered that afternoon by Madame Curzon's. The lavish creation was as distinctly foreign to her experience as the drama unfolding before her eyes.

She and Julia had read the entire works of Shakespeare, Molière, and Johnson, but nothing had prepared her for the sights and smells of a crowded theater, and an energetic plot bristling with scheming villains, lurid details, and bosomy heiresses, many of whom she guessed had been compatriots of Felicity Clarence. The box gave them a strategic view not only of the stage but also of the audience, of the women turning to survey each other's plumage, lorgnettes and opera glasses raised with serious intent. In the dimness, Rowena scanned the neighboring boxes, looking for an as yet unidentifiable threat.

As the lights rose after the final act, she leaned against the plush velvet seat, going through the motions of clapping, her hands cold in her gray lace evening gloves. She observed Rushford's profile discreetly, the boldness of his nose and chin. Slowly, his steady gaze turned to meet hers.

"Try not to look as though I'm about to devour you, Miss Warren," he said once the applause had subsided and the audience began to move to the atrium for champagne and ices and morsels of gossip. "We've a whole evening ahead of us."

She responded with a brilliant smile, more for the benefit of onlookers than for Rushford. "You're too arrogant by half, Rushford. It is not you whom I fear," she lied, snapping her ivory fan for emphasis. She had not been able to keep her attention on the farce, her own personal drama intruding. For the moment at least, she wished she could ignore that sharply planed face, strong and austere, and that tall, tightly coiled body whose imprint still burned against her skin. She unclenched her jaw. It did neither of them any good to remember those moments, at the tavern and at Crockford's or for that matter in the bedchamber at what she privately referred to as *Miss Warren's apartments*. Although Rowena's hands were cold, the air around them seemed far too warm.

Suddenly eager to leave the privacy of the box, she made to rise. "I can't say that this play was quite what I was expecting. Although Miss Barry's performance was impressive," she added, making mention of the evening's leading lady. "Despite the material with which she had to work."

"My thoughts exactly," said Rushford, already standing next to her. "It was hardly *Hamlet*." He crooked a smile. "Yet we were so obviously impressed by Miss Barry's prodigious talent that we wish to engage her attention in the salon downstairs."

Any excuse would do. "I'm certain a woman as beautiful as Miss Barry is accustomed to adulation," Rowena said. "Although she might be surprised to learn that her prodigious talents are not what we're interested in but rather anything she might reveal about the company the late Miss Clarence chose to keep—and why," she finished as they moved to the back of the box. It required all her concentration to focus on Rushford's words. His physical presence was even more potent in the confines of the private box than when he'd first arrived at her apartments to convey her to the theater. His impeccably cut evening jacket, made less severe only by the dove gray of his waistcoat, emphasized the breadth of his shoulders and the length of his legs.

Rushford would handily attract the interest of the exotic actress, thought Rowena, unwilling to examine her flash of irritation at the prospect. "Perhaps Miss Barry may snatch you away from your current mistress," she said aloud, surprising herself.

"Impossible," he replied with a smile.

"No need for flattery, Rushford," Rowena said crisply. "I shall play my role with appropriate insouciance and worldliness that should allow Miss Barry plenty of room to practice her wiles. And for us to glean what we require. I am certain that Miss Barry is aware of our presence, given the entrance we made earlier this evening." She recalled the carriage with its simultaneously discreet and distinctive crest, sweeping them to the entrance of the theater, whereupon they had made their leisurely entry. To her great relief, there was not one familiar face in the melee, making it easier for Rowena to move confidently through the crowd in her role as Miss Warren. Uneasy, she touched a hand to the fair curls of a newly procured wig, courtesy of Madame Curzon, before her hand drifted to the heavy ruby necklace encircling her throat.

She thought back to the moment at the apartments when Rushford had reached into his pocket and withdrawn something in his fist. "As I recall, a gentleman always brings a lady some token of his affection," he had said. "Please turn around, Rowena."

She had presented her back to him, and he'd placed something around her neck. His fingers worked the back clasp, brushing her skin, sending flickers of heat coursing through her. When he'd finished, she went to one of the many mirrors in the room and gasped. About her neck was a magnificent necklace of rubies inlaid in intricate gold work. She had touched the stunning piece tentatively before letting her hand drop to her side.

Now in the dimness of the theater, Rushford's gaze swept over her with uncharacteristic intensity. "No flattery, only the truth. You look beautiful, Rowena. Never fear. You will have everyone convinced that you have snared my undying interest." The last words held a tinge of mockery. Rowena reluctantly looked up from the necklace to meet Rushford's focused gaze, his eyes a smoky gray. She had to say something, to respond. "Thank you. For the loan of the necklace, that is. It's lovely," she said, licking her dry lips, acutely aware that a more sophisticated, experienced woman would respond differently, with rapier sharp wit or a double entendre. Her mind had seemingly stopped working whenever he was near.

She moved ahead of him toward the door of the box. Gathering her wide skirts with a hand that also gripped the fan at her waist, she did not need to glance over her shoulder to confirm Rushford's proximity. His gaze scorched her naked shoulders. It seemed an eternity until they reached their destination in the theater foyer. It was filled with a stream of players, most still in their costumes, a dazzling parade of furbelows and greasepaint. Several of the actresses flitted their fans to smile coquettishly at their male admirers, as aware as their audience that many liaisons were forged in such salubrious circumstances. Behind Rowena, several men craned their necks, looking about the salon for the latest seductress whose favors were in high demand.

The murmurs in the crowd increased. Miss Barry had decided to make an entrance of her own, smiling for the small cluster of men who gathered around her, their hands clapping in enthusiasm. She had changed from the wedding dress required for her role as Anne Travinion into a sumptuous gown of bronzed brocade, with a daring bodice overlayed in black lace and paste diamonds.

"Enchanting."

"Incandescent performance."

"A veritable siren!"

The chorus paid homage to the woman in their midst, her black hair piled high on her head, emeralds from her last admirer, a count, glittering at her swanlike throat. She was smaller than she looked onstage, with fine, doll-like features highlighted by the contrast of white skin and dark hair.

Rushford offered Rowena his arm, and they glided toward the lovely actress, whose eyes narrowed appreciatively, her gaze devouring Rushford. Nodding generously to her admirers, she then held out a slender hand to Rushford with a tilt of her head.

"What an honor, Miss Barry," Rushford said, bending over the diminutive figure, aware of the crush of devotees watching enviously from the sidelines. "Lord Rushford and Miss Warren," he said smoothly by way of introduction.

The actress looked up at the man who stood nearly a foot taller than she, purring her response. "The pleasure is surely mine, my lord." Her heavily kohled eyes lowered assessingly.

"And your Miss Warren is certainly lovely"—she parted her red lips in a smile—"and so very young."

Well done, thought Rowena, opening and shutting her fan with a decisive click. Miss Barry had effectively advertised her highly vaunted experience and expertise in the amorous arts in one simple phrase that put the young mistress precisely where she belonged—in the schoolroom.

Rushford bent toward her, his warm breath brushing her ear. "No need to blush, my darling," he said, his words bringing her instantly back to the conversation and pointedly reminding her of her role. "I was just about to inquire of Miss Barry whether we might take some refreshment, perhaps somewhere quieter, more private." This was a different side to Rushford, who was suddenly, irritatingly charming. His gaze swung back to Miss Barry.

The actress rewarded him with a devastating smile that could not obscure the faint lines around her eyes under the heavily applied makeup. "Delighted! What a capital idea, my lord. As a matter of fact, I should be more than pleased to give you a tour of the very private and fascinating areas behind the stage, where I happen to have champagne cooling at the very moment," she said, waving her hand with the flourish of an accomplished performer. "Do follow me, Lord Rushford, Miss Warren."

Making her second dramatic exit of the evening, Miss Barry clung to Rushford's arm, her skirts in full sail, supremely confident of ensnaring every pair of eyes in the salon. As the disappointed groans and murmurs of the audience faded, the opulence of the salon abruptly gave way to a narrow hallway and then a labyrinth of narrower passageways that comprised the theater's spine and skeleton. Old scenery canvases lay against the walls, interspersed with portable spiral staircases and rolls of canvas. "Fascinating," Rowena said for the actress's benefit, turning around in a show of appreciation before following Rushford and Miss Barry through another door into what appeared to be a dressing room. A large mirror was propped up against the wall, reflecting a dressing screen draped with corsets and lacy undergarments, to the left of which sat a bottle of champagne, chilling as promised. A lavish canvas was propped against the opposite wall, depicting a Venetian canal complete with gondola and gondolier. Miss Barry collapsed in an extravagant heap on a narrow brocade chaise, taking Rushford with her.

"My kingdom," she said with a sweep of her hand. She leaned forward deliberately, her jutting breasts barely concealed by the immodest bodice encrusted with black lace and rhinestones. "Alone at last," she said dramatically. "Now we may talk privately." Her eyes narrowed on Rowena. "Now wherever did you meet this sweet young thing, Lord Rushford?" she asked, raising her fine eyebrows mockingly.

"Miss Warren and I have acquaintances in common," Rushford answered, incongruously seated amidst plush cushions and a waterfall of dainty undergarments. He did not, Rowena observed, look in the least uncomfortable.

Miss Barry nodded understandingly, pulling up a rounded leg, a generous calf peeking out from beneath the froth of her skirts. "It does not really signify how you met, does it? As long as you find one another entertaining. As I'm sure Miss Warren continues to be," she said with halfhearted conviction, as though the premise itself was indeed doubtful. She had the look of a cat that had consumed a surfeit of cream, eyeing Rowena once more before turning back to Rushford with barely disguised cunning shining from eyes that had bewitched thousands of theater patrons. "I don't mean to be forward, my lord, but clearly there is something that you seek, that I could perhaps provide," she said in her lilting voice, accustomed to coaxing intimacies from both the reticent and the eager.

"You are indeed a woman of the world, Miss Barry," Rushford said.

"Life is brief, my lord. I did not become a great actress of the stage by pursuing a false modesty. And having reached the pinnacle of my career, I do not easily bestow my talents nor my favors."

"I shouldn't doubt otherwise."

"Then there is no reason for hesitation, my lord," she continued, patting his thigh with easy familiarity. "I am without a protector at the moment, of my own choosing, of course, not for the lack of suitors. Although in truth, at the moment I am a trifle confused," she continued with a brief look at Rowena, "given that you are already *engagé* with Miss Warren. Or have I missed something?"

"Perceptive, as well as talented and beautiful," Rushford said easily.

Miss Barry paused. "Perhaps your young Miss Warren," she continued delicately, "requires further introduction to the wider world. Some tutelage, as it were."

Rowena stared uncomprehendingly while Miss Barry's mouth made a small moue of concern. "I'm certain you are a marvelous lover, Lord Rushford, if you will excuse my candor. Although you are unusually discreet, I have heard tell that the amorous company you keep is accordingly sophisticated. Married women and widows are your preference," she said matter of factly.

"You are exceedingly well informed, Miss Barry."

The actress bowed her head briefly at what she perceived as a compliment. "*Scientia est potentia* said our Francis Bacon, if I recall," she quoted, "and I must say experience has proven him correct. Knowledge is indeed power. As is candor, I suspect, particularly when it is called for, as in this situation. It does give one cause to ponder whether someone as young and, frankly"—she gestured elegantly in Rowena's direction—"as untested as Miss Warren is enough to sate your appetites."

Rowena was deadly silent, aware that Rushford appeared thoroughly at ease with the unfolding conversation. He nodded as though he had just received a kernel of wisdom from an important sage, she thought with simmering anger. "How insightful of you, Miss Barry," he murmured politely. "I am, of course, never averse to entertaining suggestions."

The actress bowed her head in acknowledgment. "I thought not. You will forgive my frankness."

"Of course. Nothing to forgive. However, I must confess that you have more than piqued my curiosity, Miss Barry." His gaze met Rowena's over the actress's upswept hair, bidding her to remain silent. "Lord Galveston," he continued after an imperceptible beat, "whom we may count as a friend in common, recommended your company highly. He confessed that you and a coterie of friends spent many pleasurable hours together at country house weekends and the like."

The actress laughed, the sound lush with promise. "Galveston—my, my. His proclivities, from what I hear, require a certain amount of stamina." She patted Rushford's arm as though they shared a private joke.

"According to Felicity Clarence at least," he supplied, his expression supremely unconcerned.

"We all make our choices," she said cryptically, a strange smile touching her lips and eyes. She heaved a dramatic sigh, her glance landing upon Rowena once again. Her gaze swept over the younger woman's figure, outlined in the gray satin, lingering on the ostentatious ruby choker, before making another moue of distaste.

"And while we are on the topic of certain proclivities, if I might say, Miss Warren is darling in a diverting, simple way, I suppose, but one would have thought something a little more voluptuous, and seasoned, would be to your taste."

"I should not entirely agree with you, Miss Barry, as innocence does have its allure. That's not to say that an introduction to the wider world of experience would not have its place, as you helpfully suggested," Rushford said, deliberately looking away from Rowena, as though she were no longer in the dressing room. Rowena forced herself to smile to mask her growing anger. If this was a test, to determine whether she was prepared to take on her role as Rushford's mistress, she was determined not to fail. Sauntering over to the chaise, she returned Miss Barry's look with a conspiratorial quirk of her lips. "I bow to your superior experience in such things, madam. I shall do whatever is required to remain in Lord Rushford's good graces," she said with a lingering hand on his arm. "Don't I always, darling?" she asked with mock concern.

His eyes bored into hers. "All part of your many charms," he said, pulling her toward him, until her hips were nestled at his side.

"Your wish is my command," she murmured.

"What an intriguing concept," he said a half smile on his lips before he turned to the actress. "Miss Warren is a quick and willing study, and inordinately amenable. Are you not, darling?"

Miss Barry did not wait for Miss Warren's answer. To her mind, the matter was entirely resolved. She arose from the chaise in a tidal wave of bronze, her arms extended in invitation. "Then it is settled," she said, her hands fluttering extravagantly rather than finishing the enigmatic statement, "and we must, absolutely must, have our champagne." She hovered indecisively for a moment. "However, my darling Rushford, I have entirely forgotten about the time. One of my many admirers, the Baron Sebastian," she continued with no false modesty, "has insisted that I join him and a small set of friends after the theater. I cannot possibly disappoint. However, I should be absolutely downcast should you refuse to accompany me." She looked at the two of them expectantly, hands at her breast, deliberately framing herself to best advantage against the canvas depicting the Venetian canal.

"You are too kind, Miss Barry," Rowena responded instantly upon hearing the Frenchman's name. "We should positively love to attend. I have never met a baron before." She beamed at Rushford. "Darling, I am so excited! Have your carriage brought round instantly. Miss Barry, I'm sure you would like a few moments of privacy. May we meet with you at the backstage entrance?"

Rowena deliberately looked away from Rushford—who was already propelling her toward the dressing room door. "Indeed, thank you for your generous invitation, Miss Barry," he said over his shoulder. "We shall see you shortly."

The dressing room door closed behind them, leaving them in the narrow corridor leading in one direction to the stage and the other to the street. The odor of greasepaint hung in the air. "What are you doing?" he asked.

"Playing the role of your mistress."

"I should like to congratulate you on your performance," he said tersely, his arm around her shoulders. "Well done."

She tightened against him. "I have some small talent, it appears." The tension was suddenly thick between them.

"I believe we've made some progress. You may return to the apartments whilst I accompany Miss Barry."

Rowena shook her head and took one step back, throwing up her hands to hold him off. "I don't believe I understand. We have come this far together this evening, and now you wish me to return home?"

"Whatever happened to the amenable, biddable Miss Warren?" Rushford leaned back against the stained planking of a makeshift boat, eyes hooded. "I don't have to explain, Rowena. If I discover anything about Faron and your family, you will hear about it immediately."

Rowena stared at him in infuriated bewilderment. "I am fully capable of going through this charade, Rushford."

Rushford remained unmoved. "Don't be naïve, Rowena. Faron and his people are dangerous. You yourself claim to know that, and yet you would place yourself directly in his path. A wig and evening clothes will not protect you if you insist on going into the lion's den."

She waved him aside, continuing toward the door leading onto the street. "I do not have to follow your orders. Did you not hear—Baron Sebastian? Galveston's man." The moment the words left her lips, she realized the truth. "Of course, you knew all along, didn't you? The reason you chose this theater and this play, with Miss Barry in the lead role."

"I had some time on my hands to investigate the matter," he said shortly.

"This gambit of ours is not going to work if you continue withholding information, Rushford," she said. "How am I to play my role convincingly if I don't know what's transpired? Ignorance is what's dangerous. All the more reason that I need to attend this evening at the Baron's—accompanied by you."

He had obviously not heard a word she was saying. "You will plead a headache. You declined the invitation in order to take to your bed," he informed her coolly. "We have no time for argument at the moment. You asked for my assistance— demanded it, as you'll recall—but there are conditions. That you obey me implicitly. For your own safety."

The authoritarian tone grated. Rowena turned around to face him directly. "I don't recall discussing any such conditions," she declared, jabbing at his chest with a forefinger. "You are not my—"

"You are my mistress," he said, catching her fingers. "Or have you forgotten already?"

Rowena drew a breath deep into her lungs. He was still holding her hand, and there was a sudden intensity in the eyes resting on her face. Rowena pulled her hand from his grip. "It will look suspicious if I do not accompany you," she repeated, turning to pull on the tarnished knob to pry the door open. If she took a step back, her body would collide with his chest. "You cannot stop me."

"Your intemperance is going to get you into trouble," he growled, "and not for the first time, I'd wager." He tugged her backward, tightening his hold and pressing his mouth to her temple. "I will not have you hurt, Rowena, not under my watch."

"We don't wish to keep Miss Barry waiting. She will be here at the stage door any moment."

His hand wrapped more tightly around her waist, and she was relieved that she did not have to look into his face when he said, "This is hardly wise. Do you realize what might transpire this evening?"

"And do you not yet realize that I will do anything to keep Meredith and Julia from Faron's grasp?"

"At your peril," he whispered. Rowena jerked from his grasp and pulled the door open wide. Gaslight flooded the dingy hallway, and she took a cleansing breath, exhaling the sting of anxiety and greasepaint. Her every instinct warned her to run away from this man and from this evening, but she knew she never would.

"I shall have the carriage take you to Knightsbridge," Rushford said.

Too late. He lifted her easily, and her hands grabbed reflexively at his shoulders, their bodies entirely too close. She was enveloped by the feel of him, the scent of him, the heat of his hands burning through the fine silk of her gown. She could not pull away if she wanted to. And she didn't want to.

It was then she heard the lilting tones of Miss Barry. "My, my," she trilled, sweeping toward them, a velvet shawl with swinging gold tassels wrapped dramatically around her tiny frame. "I do so hope that I am not *de trop?*"

# Chapter 10

"**Y**ou brought guests?" Baron Francois Sebastian uncharacteristically revealed his surprise as he watched a footman pour champagne into two crystal goblets in the salon of his town house off fashionable Cavendish Square.

"I didn't think you would mind." Miss Barry eyed Lord Rushford, his head bent to catch something Miss Warren was saying, a proprietary arm around her waist. They seemed to be insensible of the throb of guests around them; the heat between the pair was palpable. He was devastatingly handsome, in an overtly masculine manner that very definitely caught Miss Barry's interest. As for the young mistress, she was quite the mystery. Her vanity pricked, Miss Barry peered at her reflection in the glass over the mantelpiece and tucked a straying wisp of hair back into place. She smiled approvingly at her reflection before catching the Baron's eyes in the mirror. "I thought perhaps that you would like to meet Lord Rushford, given his acquaintance with Lord Galveston, and the fact that he very deliberately sought out my company after this evening's performance."

Sebastian pressed a goblet into her hand, well aware that Rushford was not the type to cool his heels at theater doors. He did not elaborate, extracting a slender cigar from the case in his pocket.

"I would introduce you, of course, but it appears that you already know the man."

THE DARKEST SIN   131

"I know of him," he said, rolling the unlit cigar between his elegant fingers, regarding the couple through assessing eyes. "Although I doubt that he is made of the same malleable material as our friend Galveston." His mouth moved in the semblance of a smile. "Would you not agree, madam?" he asked in his near flawless English.

"He seeks a liaison to add some spice," she said blandly. "Nothing unusual there. The girl is much too young and inexperienced to hold his interest for long. Innocence, however despoiled, loses its charms very quickly."

"That remains to be seen," Sebastian suggested. He stuck the cigar in his mouth and felt in his pocket for his sulphur matches. For some reason, he then changed his mind, putting the cigar back in the silver case and sliding it into his waistcoat pocket. He reached instead for his champagne, his eyes drifting across the room. "It's clear that she is quite beautiful, indisputably what first attracted Lord Rushford's interest."

The actress frowned, her hand automatically going up to smooth her brow.

Sebastian smiled at her vanity. "Nevertheless, aesthetics and youth aside, indulging in the whims of important men is what you do best, madam."

Her smile was brittle. "And Felicity . . . What was her special talent, Sebastian?" Sometimes the price seemed too high, she thought acidly. Although she and Felicity had been more rivals than friends, Ellen Barry, known in her previous life as Gwen Shandpepper, was smart enough not to delve too deeply into her adversary's demise. Galveston had been a beast, a self-indulgent coward who loved to inflict pain in order to shore up his fragile sense of masculinity. They had seen his ilk too many times before.

"Do I detect a hint of empathy," Sebastian asked with barely contained sarcasm. "This is most unlike you."

The actress wisely did not rise to the bait. "Felicity made several errors in judgment."

"Fatal ones, as a matter of fact."

They both let the subject drop, drinking their champagne

and watching the couple across the room. "She is quite beautiful, the more I look at her," Sebastian murmured after several moments. "But there is something familiar about her, the way she moves and a certain watchfulness. I cannot help wondering if she will last as Lord Rushford's paramour. As you know far better than I, madam, not all women are as, how might I put it"—he paused—"ah, yes, morally flexible as you."

"Shall I introduce you after all?" she asked smoothly.

"Of course," Sebastian murmured with a calm smile. "I should be remiss as a host otherwise."

From the corner of her eye, Rowena watched the approach of Miss Barry and the impeccably groomed man at her side. He was of medium height and a spare build, the blinding whiteness of his cravat an impeccable contrast against the midnight blue of his evening coat. When she and Rushford had first arrived, the heat of their argument still simmering under a cool façade, she had been struck by the ornate luxury of the town house in one of London's most fashionable streets. She had yet to swallow her shock at the sight of the grand salon on the second floor. Scantily clad women sauntered around the room, draped in wisps of corsets and petticoats with black stockings rolled to just below the knees. Their lips were moist and red, their faces painted and powdered to give the look of patent invitation. Worst of all, no one but Rowena seemed to notice. The two dozen or so men and women seated on plush chairs were clearly habituated to the scene around them. Rushford's nonchalance, she noted, seemed entirely natural. To suppress her sparking anger, she gazed at the crystal and gold beads of the chandelier overhead, all the while wondering why she could not rein in her overblown response to Rushford.

Rowena smiled mindlessly for what seemed to be the hundredth time, her cheekbones aching, when Ellen Barry's fan tapped her arm. "Darlings," the actress said, looking out from under her luxuriant lashes for Rushford's express benefit. "May I make the introductions . . . Lord Rushford. And, of course, Miss Warren. May I present Baron Francois Sebastian."

The Frenchman executed a small bow, bending over Rowena's hand. "Lovely to meet you."

Rowena's anxiety froze to shock. The voice. Her heart pounded so strongly that she feared everyone in the room would hear.

"Are you feeling quite well, Miss Warren?" the actress asked. "You appear to have blanched suddenly. You are paler than usual."

Rushford stepped so close to Rowena that she could see the stubble on his jaw. He swept a finger down her scalding cheek, watching her closely. "Miss Warren is merely a trifle fatigued," he said, his voice deliberately unconcerned. "Perhaps another restorative sip of your champagne?" he asked, bringing the flute to her lips like the concerned lover that he was. They were all talking, making the requisite noises, when all Rowena could do was clench the fragile stem of the crystal, hoping it wouldn't shatter. Despite the champagne, her lips were dry and she had difficulty forming words, her mind grasping to follow the conversation.

Sebastian smiled, revealing small white teeth. "The pleasure is without doubt mine, Miss Warren. You are indeed as lovely as Miss Barry promised," he said with only a trace of a French accent. "Isn't it wonderful that the love of the theater brings us all together." It was difficult to tell whether the irony was deliberate. "Both of you, Lord Rushford and the lovely Miss Warren, enjoy such excursions, I presume."

"We certainly do," Rushford said.

Miss Barry leaned in confidingly. "Of course, the theater is but a reflection of life. When we allow the imagination to soar, there are many adventures to be had. Am I correct, Lord Rushford?"

"But of course," Sebastian interrupted silkily. "Why should one seek to curtail one's experiences?" He looked expressly at Rowena.

"Not unlike our dear friend, Lord Galveston," Miss Barry finished.

Sebastian continued where she let off. "Another theater lover, Lord Galveston. He is an acquaintance we have in common," he said, turning to the actress, "or so the lovely Miss Barry informs me."

"We've crossed paths on a number of occasions." Rushford's tone was ambiguous.

Undaunted by Rowena's stillness, Sebastian continued. "Quite the adventurer, our Ambrose, as it turns out." Rowena's breathing was shallow, and it seemed that the chatter around them dimmed, the dozen or so guests in the room fading into the background.

Rushford smiled, his expression at odds with his next words. "Indeed, Galveston and I had a chance to review his recent conquests just the other evening." The last phrase hung in the air, heavy with implication.

"Is that so? The world is smaller than one might expect," Sebastian said with veiled derision, the source Rowena could not quite identify. "Of course I have heard of your recent exploits, Lord Rushford, concerning the Cruikshank murders. You are quite the sleuth and champion of the everywoman, as it turns out."

It would not do to remain silent much longer, Rowena told herself, aware that she was required to deliver a performance. That the Baron was the voice she'd heard in her nightmares, and very possibly part of the reality of her abduction, would not stop her in her tracks. She thought briefly of Meredith and Julia, her nerves making her bold. "It is unfortunate that we were never able to make the acquaintance of Felicity Clarence," she said finally, her voice sounding surprisingly normal despite her panic. "Lord Galveston never could stop talking about her appearances in the West End." She forced herself to meet the Frenchman's gaze unflinchingly.

The diminutive actress giggled. "To which performances was Galveston referring, those onstage or off?"

Rowena managed to smile serenely, aware of Rushford's hard arm around her waist.

The actress tapped a finger to her lips. "Not that Felicity pretended to have a tendresse for the man," she continued, and then took a dainty sip of her champagne. "I do believe theirs was a liaison predicated on far more practical concerns." She fluttered a hand in Rowena's direction. "Do not look so shocked, my dear. If you were to survey this salon more closely, you would discover that its female occupants are mostly kept women, mistresses of wealthy men, such as yourself, my dear. And then we actresses, of course, bathing in the adoration of our audiences, onstage and otherwise."

"And a good thing," Sebastian murmured. "Women crave nothing if not our adoration."

"I'd never heard it put quite that way before," Rushford said, his voice having taken on an edge. "It makes one wonder whether the late Miss Clarence would agree with you, monsieur."

Sebastian made the appropriate noises, deliberately misunderstanding. "Yes, such a tragic end. One almost believes that a love affair might be to blame. To cast oneself into the river . . ." His remark seemed to target Lord Rushford specifically, Rowena thought.

Miss Barry arched her thin brows. "Don't be ludicrous, my pet. After that debacle at Eccles House, Felicity swore off such romantic nonsense. She was a practical girl at heart."

"A tragic accident, then," Sebastian concluded.

Rushford focused on the Frenchman lounging casually before them. "Of course, Eccles House," he drawled, as though something had suddenly stirred his memory. "Sir Wadsworth's country estate."

For a moment, Rowena felt light-headed. Beside her, one of the scantily clad women trilled with laughter. Rowena swayed on her feet, yielding to the support of Rushford's hard body. "I'm so sorry. Did I hear you mention Sir Wadsworth?" *The man who had invited Julia to his estate.* Rushford discreetly tightened his arm around her waist. "Are you feeling quite yourself, my pet, or should I call for the carriage to be brought round?"

*No.* She would not, could not leave even if they carried her out of the town house. They were talking about her sister. "Absolutely not," she said, forcing a smile to her face. "I feel perfectly splendid," she added brightly. "Now that you have me intrigued about the goings on at Eccles House."

Sebastian gave a half smile, removing a slender silver box from his waistcoat and turning it idly in his elegant hand. "You like gossip, then, do you, Miss Warren?"

"Of course, what woman doesn't?" she replied. Feeling as though she might shatter, she gave a small laugh bordering on hysteria. She focused on the silver box in Sebastian's hand.

The Frenchman turned to the actress at his side. "Then I shall give you full permission to regale us with the tawdry bits, my dear." He glanced at Rushford consideringly. "We men shall try not to be bored."

Miss Barry put a hand to her bosom. "Oh, really, gentlemen. If you are looking for something shocking, you may wish to look elsewhere. This is quite the boring little tale. As it turns out, our dear, departed Felicity let it be known that she had set her cap for Lord Strathmore at Eccles House, only to be rejected by the man."

"A first for her, I'm assuming?" Rowena asked, continuing to lean into Rushford, placing a hand on his chest to keep it from trembling.

The actress shrugged. "Who knows? I believe it was her pride that was hurt more than anything else. Strathmore actually chose a nondescript country bumpkin, a veritable blue stocking with the most bizarre interests, over the enchanting and alluring Felicity Clarence. *Only imagine,*" she added sarcastically.

Rowena's heart stood still. Julia. Her Julia with her outsized interests in botany and daguerreotypy. Sebastian observed her closely. "You seem quite intrigued, Miss Warren."

"Only mildly," she said, suddenly desperate to bring the conversation to an end, afraid that it might lead in a direction where she would lose all control. She straightened away from Rushford, who nonetheless kept a hand around her waist. "Although I do hope that a thwarted love affair was not the reason for Miss Clarence's decision to end her life."

Sebastian asked cynically, "Who can afford love, after all, Miss Warren? When there are reasonable facsimiles to be had. Am I correct, Lord Rushford?" Once again, subtext shimmered beneath the question.

"As experience would attest," Rushford said, his grip around Rowena's waist tightening infinitesimally.

"All the more reason I should like to invite both of you to Alcestor Court, my estate in Dorset, this coming weekend," the Baron pronounced smoothly, "so we may pursue our common interests." He turned to Miss Barry, smiling broadly. "And we are most grateful to Miss Barry here," he remarked, "who had the keen foresight to forge ahead with these introductions."

"Too kind," Rowena said grimly, watching in silence as the actress placed a dainty hand on Sebastian's proffered arm. "We look forward to our visit, do we not, my lord?" Rowena turned to Rushford with an attempt at a flirtatious smile. All she could think of was Julia, questions frozen on her lips. Questions for Rushford, once she had him alone.

Lowther waited for Sebastian in the study on the second floor of the house. The sounds of revelry were muted by the richly paneled walls, but he immediately recognized Sebastian's silhouette in the doorway. They were in no way alike, thought Lowther with typical objectivity. The Frenchman was an elegant aristocrat in his bearing, and Lowther knew he bore the blunt features of his English dockyard parents. However disparate their physical bearing, they were both equally although differently in debt to the man they now served.

The door clicked shut, and Lowther gestured to Sebastian to take the seat across from him. A fire burned brightly in the hearth despite the warmth of the spring evening.

"Rushford succumbed to the temptation," Sebastian said, sliding elegantly into the chair. "Galveston, Felicty Clarence, and, of course, the beauteous and beguiling Ellen Barry performed brilliantly. He and his lovely young mistress will be joining us at Alcestor Court this coming weekend."

Lowther nodded approvingly. "Well done. At least thus far, although I'm not entirely surprised by the turn of events. Did I not predict Rushford's response? The guilt is eating him alive."

"Yes, you did indeed, Lowther."

Lowther ignored the comment, tinged with resentment, tapping his thick fingers against the polished wooden arm of his chair. "He believes he can assuage his conscience, bring the Duchess back to life by involving himself in these sordid events, bringing resolution elsewhere because he can find none in his own life. I should have expected more of him, given his rather jaundiced view of the world, but then again there is no accounting for emotions when they get in the way of reality."

"Works in our favor," Sebastian said with the practicality of a Frenchman.

"Only if we proceed carefully. Remember, Rushford has in the past offered his services to Whitehall, until the proverbial scales fell from his eyes upon the death of the Duchess. But let us not forget that he single-handedly prevented a virtual praetorian guard from stealing the Rosetta Stone on Faron's behalf."

"Is that how you choose to describe our efforts, a praetorian guard?" Sebastian mused. "It is amazing that a man as clever as Rushford still has no idea . . ."

Lowther smiled. "Love is blind."

The trite statement drew a chuckle from Sebastian. "Hard to believe." He shook his head in wonder. "And yet that love was not enough to remove Rushford from the mission. I despair, truly," he sighed.

Lowther peered moodily into the fire. "We believed the Duchess would be Rushford's weakness, and the Earl's, but we were wrong. Let's not err twice. Faron would not be pleased if we were to fail again."

"No possibility of that," Sebastian corrected calmly, crossing one leg over the other, examining the high gleam of his evening shoes. "Particularly since we intend that Rushford shall steal the Stone on our behalf. What could be simpler?"

The bald statement drew Lowther's gaze from the fire. "Let's hope not too simple, particularly after having our first attempt thwarted. Although I suppose Rushford paid the higher price. Sacrificing the Duchess cost him dearly, I'm sure." He paused. "Although I hear that he's taken a mistress. You don't find that peculiar?"

It was a ridiculous question to ask a Frenchman. Sebastian smoothly retrieved the silver case from his waistcoat pocket, extracting a slender cigar. "In what way is it unusual for a man of Lord Rushford's station to take a mistress? A man has needs, after all, and what better way to assuage those needs than by engaging the affections of a young and beautiful woman. I don't begin to understand your question, Lowther."

"Who is she—and don't tell me that you haven't the slightest idea."

For a moment, Sebastian thought to lie but then thought better of it. "Miss Frances Warren is who she is, young, beautiful, and entirely too intelligent for her own good. You know how I detest intellect in a woman. It takes from their natural femininity," he elaborated. "There's an intensity about her that I find disturbing."

"How so?"

"Difficult to explain."

"She is quite different from the Duchess, I take it."

"The Duchess was complexity and subterfuge, sophistication and elegance. A fine wine, in other words. In contrast, Miss Warren is as transparent and refreshing as a glass of water."

"You do not seem overly impressed. Although based on your analysis of her character, I have the notion you have met her before. Not entirely surprising given the circles in which you roam," Lowther said with a hint of sarcasm. "What—is she an actress, or did Rushford find her amongst Mrs. Cruikshank's fillies? Does it matter, in the end? Perhaps Miss Warren is entirely beside the point."

"I wish that were so," Sebastian said cryptically, leaning toward the fire to light his cigar. It flared to life in a small burst of orange. "Of course, I recognized her immediately, despite the frightful wig."

"So she is not really Miss Warren," Lowther said impatiently. "Her name is Sally Grimshaw or some such, and she hails from the dockyards or worse parts of London. It would not be the first time a young girl has taken another name so as to burnish her appeal. What of it, Sebastian?"

Sebastian drew on his cigar unhurriedly, exhaling a slow plume of smoke. "The situation does rather complicate matters and adds a wrinkle to our plans. Faron will not be pleased to hear of it." He rather liked stringing Lowther along. He knew the man preferred to be in control and to believe that Faron's wishes were his alone to execute. It was tiresome, really, for a guttersnipe like Lowther to have risen so far in the ranks of Faron's legion, Sebastian thought. But then again, a man of foresight, Faron collected acolytes from far and wide, looking only for extraordinary intelligence and loyalty, in equal measure, among his recruits. There was a story told that when he was a brilliant student at the Sorbonne, Faron had saved Lowther from the gallows. Whether the tale was true or not, Sebastian hadn't a clue. Sebastian now contemplated that same man twenty years later, impatience in every line of his bulky body, as he sat across from him.

"Out with it," Lowther growled, half rising from his chair. "Who is she and why ever would it matter to Faron?"

Sebastian tapped the tip of his cigar against the fireplace grill, the ashes falling onto the grate. "I am as perturbed as you will be, Lowther," he said, slowly releasing rings of smoke into the air. "Do sit back down."

"You are trying my patience."

Sebastian continued, "No need to concern yourself. I have it all well in hand." Was it his imagination or did he hear Lowther grinding his teeth? "You will be pleased, relieved, and grateful to learn that I have a contingency plan in place."

"Enough with the enigmatic ramblings," Lowther said, returning to his seat reluctantly. "I suggest strongly that you don't wait to enlighten me."

"Very well. Our lovely Miss Warren, mistress to Lord Rushford"—Sebastian blew another plume of smoke, locking eyes with Lowther—"is no other than Rowena Woolcott, come back to life. You look positively apoplectic. Are you surprised? I certainly was."

# Chapter 11

Rowena did not trust herself to speak in the carriage ride back to the Knightsbridge apartments. The silence was suffocating; overwhelming shock and fatigue blurred her thoughts. She wanted to go home, to run to Montfort, to discover for herself that Julia and Meredith waited for her there. She knew it was out of the question though. One look at Rushford, at that cool enigmatic face across from her in the carriage, and she realized the dangerousness of her yearnings. How much did he know that he wasn't telling her?

With typical efficiency, he had them both in the apartments moments later, the discreet housekeeper who had been recently engaged opening the door and disappearing just as quickly. Rowena strode into the center of the salon, pulling the wig from her head and running a shaky hand through her hair. She turned on her heel to face him.

"What in bloody hell have you been keeping from me, Rushford?" she demanded.

"Would you please sit?"

"No. I have questions that I should like answered."

"I can see that." He blocked the door.

"What do you know of Eccles House, Wadsworth, and my sister?"

He appeared entirely and infuriatingly unconcerned, his hard jaw shadowed with stubble against the crisp white of his shirt. "I made inquiries the past few days." He stepped into the room, forcing her to move closer to the divan.

"And did not share them with me?" she asked, her voice low with anger, battling a dangerous rush of memories, of Montfort and her sister.

"There was nothing to share."

"So you say. All of this is entirely too fortuitous, Rushford. Your knowing Galveston, Sebastian, Faron, the situation at Eccles House. What is going on?" She put a hand to her forehead as if to contain her swirling thoughts. "If you don't tell me immediately, I swear I shall make my way back to Sebastian and confront him directly." She drew off her gloves and threw them on the floor.

"You are acting like a child, Rowena, when you do not fully comprehend what you're dealing with."

"Then tell me," she challenged outright with a lamentable lack of finesse.

"You know nothing of it. Trust me, it is better that way. Recall that you were the one who pushed your way into my life, and now you assume you have the right to tell me how to go about my business."

"That is hardly fair," Rowena interrupted, outraged. "As though anyone could push their way into your life if you did not want them to."

"You offered me little choice," he interrupted in turn, with a bleakness in his voice she had never heard before. He paused for a heartbeat before continuing. "And if I am to resolve this matter successfully, you would be wise to trust me and do as I say."

For a brief moment, she considered what lay behind the starkness of his words. Then impatience won out. "Oh, please stop." She threw the words at him with ringing scorn. "You are entirely too condescending. And dismissive." There was a heaviness in the room and a barely contained fury beneath the attempts at civility. "I have much more at stake in this than you. The fate of my family is involved. Whilst you are going about this business with Felicity and Faron as though on a lark. Are you merely whiling away the hours in your day, Rushford?"

Rushford's direct gaze was unambiguous. "Believe what you will. And then let's leave it at that," he said. "There is little else I can do or say to convince you otherwise."

Rowena shut her eyes briefly against the intensity of her feelings. Sebastian's voice rang incessantly in her head. She drew in a shallow breath. "I don't believe you." The words echoed hollowly between them.

"Then believe this." His voice was gruff, heated, an undertone of resentment rising to the surface. He closed the distance between them in an instant, suddenly gripping her shoulders, his fingers biting into her flesh. "I sent word yesterday to Montfort to inquire as to the well-being of your aunt and sister."

She wrenched herself from his grip, protectiveness for her family making her strong, her head suddenly clear. "You had better know what you are about, Rushford," she said. "If Faron's people discover that someone is inquiring about the Woolcotts . . . I have died a thousand times, wishing that I could send word to them." The words faltered on her lips. She walked away from the divan to cross the room and sit down in a small occasional chair, fear for Julia uppermost in her mind. She steadied her voice. "Please tell me what you know of Julia and Eccles House." He could do that for her at the very least.

Rushford exhaled swiftly. "She is safe. Married. And in North Africa."

"Good God. North Africa? Married?" Relief and anxiety swept through her simultaneously. "That's not possible," she began, and then the pieces of the evening's conversation came back to her. Strathmore and his bluestocking—her sister Julia. "Who is this Strathmore?" she asked.

"Lord Strathmore is a renowned explorer who, I discovered after reading the banns published last year, married your

THE DARKEST SIN  145

sister and took her to North Africa with him. Do you know what that means, Rowena?"

Rowena hid her face in her hands, not answering the question. Julia was safe. Far away. Under Lord Strathmore's protection, as his wife. Relief was so sweet that she could have wept with gratitude. When she looked up again after several moments, she said, "I can't begin to tell you how grateful I am to hear those words." She drew herself up straight. "Now I have only Meredith to worry about, at least for the time being." Thoughts whirled through her mind, driven in equal measure by nerves and dread. "Once we arrive at Alcestor Court, we can formulate a plan to discover Sebastian's connection to Faron. And Faron's whereabouts," she said, her thoughts running away with her.

How she would proceed once she confronted Faron, she had no idea. She was so deeply immersed in her ruminations and planning that she nearly jumped when Rushford's hand fell on her shoulder. He crouched down in front of her. "You've had a shock. A number of shocks tonight, Rowena. And now we are getting ahead of ourselves," he said quietly.

Rowena looked up at him. "I must do this. I can't stop thinking about it." His hand slipped to clasp the nape of her neck, warm, comforting. Suddenly, the anger and anxiety of the previous moments dissipated, subtly altering to something else. For the second time that night, Rowena found herself leaning into the firm pressure Rushford's body so easily and readily provided. Her muscles and limbs relaxed. "I am so tired," she confessed, feeling shrunken inside her whalebone stays, corset, and voluminous gray silk.

"Of course you are," he agreed. "I propose that we continue this discussion tomorrow morning." He glanced at the clock on the mantel. "It is close to three." But his fingers tightened around the slim column of her neck as if he could not bear to let her go. Or so Rowena suddenly imagined.

"I agree," she said. They remained silent for a few moments, Rowena acutely conscious of Rushford's even breathing, the warmth of his body. She realized unexpectedly that she'd become accustomed to such moments, to touching a stranger, enveloped in his warmth and his strength. And she didn't want him to leave. At that instant, as though in response to her thoughts, he let his hands fall from her, rising to his full height. "Off to bed with you. Shall I ring for the maid?"

"No need. I can manage," she murmured as he held out a hand to help pull her to her feet. Only inches separated them.

"I'll bid you good night then."

The words burst out of her. "Don't go." Rowena breathed in his scent, stealing the warmth from his body, potent memories, hazy and indistinct, driving her on. "I don't wish to be alone with my dreams—and my nightmares." She reached out and touched his arm, trying to remember all the reasons that he should leave. "Please don't go." Her arms slid around his waist.

"This isn't right, Rowena," he said, his voice low.

"I'm not asking for anything," she said, lying to both of them. She didn't know what she wanted herself, other than to feel his strength next to her. And to banish her nightmares.

"None of this will help. I will only hurt you if I give in to what you believe you want." Gently he unclasped her arms and stepped back.

"I'm sorry," she whispered.

"Don't be. You are simply enervated and acting out of shock," he said. "You are exhausted and will fall asleep quickly."

"I understand," she said. "I simply don't wish to be alone."

His jaw clenched. "You would regret it later." He drew a shallow breath.

"I'm not sure of anything right now," she conceded. "With the exception of the nightmares and the dreams. I don't wish to face them. Not tonight."

"What are your dreams and your nightmares? Perhaps it would help to talk about them."

She could only shake her head mutely. Words would only serve to bring them to life.

"I can hold you for only a moment." His voice was heated, but he made no move to touch her. "We shouldn't be doing this. We promised—I promised, more importantly—that this would not happen again."

"It's my decision."

"You don't know what you're asking, Rowena." His gaze was fierce. "Surely you can't be that naïve."

"I am not naïve," she said with conviction, aware suddenly of the decade and breadth of experience that separated them. But she somehow knew what she wanted—desired. Yet how could that be? She slid her hands up over the satin lapels of his jacket while he stood rigid under her ministrations. Raising herself on her toes, she slipped her hands around his neck. "Please," she whispered. "Stay with me only an hour." Her voice was liquid longing as she tugged his head down toward her.

When their lips were a whisper apart, he said, "I can't do this, Rowena." He pulled her arms from around his neck and stepped back only to come up against the barricade of the wall. "Go to bed. You will thank me tomorrow."

And leaning forward, he lightly kissed her mouth, and then, straightening, immediately stepped away.

# Chapter 12

It was only when he heard her footsteps recede and a door close in the distance that Rushford exhaled. He swore fluently under his breath, cursing the fact that his feelings refused to cooperate no matter how much he reasoned with himself. It had been so long since he'd acknowledged any feelings other than pleasure that he wasn't certain he could recognize real emotion anymore.

He'd made the mistake once in a bid to comfort Rowena Woolcott, and he would not make it again. He needed a drink to distract himself, although he questioned the logic of further numbing his already shaky self-control. Striding over to the drinks table, he poured himself a brandy. He should leave, he told himself, instead of lingering a few feet away from the object of his desire like some love-struck schoolboy. But he didn't. Draining his glass, he reached for the decanter placed conveniently on the floor beside his chair and poured himself another drink, at a loss to explain his motives or Rowena Woolcott's irresistible allure. She was young. She was beautiful. But she was definitely not Kate.

No answers came to mind, no easy resolutions except for the guilt that rose like bile whenever he forced himself to think back over a year ago. Bloody hell, she had been so young and had needed him so much. And what had his defense been? He had needed her, he decided with brutal honesty. *No excuse.*

The irrepressible sun heralded the breaking of dawn, turning the curtains into incandescent flame. Life went on, wasn't that the lesson of the greatest tragedies? He was no further along in solving his dilemma. Worse still, his decision to allow Rowena even the smallest role in his unfinished business with Faron was suspect. If she pressed him further on the morrow, he would give her the truth, or at least a half-truth, about the Rosetta Stone and his original role in ensuring its safety. That is, if she didn't awaken to her own memories, courtesy of her dreams and nightmares, before he could do anything about it. He swore softly. He should leave now. It was simple as that. He inhaled deeply, swallowing the last of the brandy. If only he could.

A low sobbing jerked him out of his stupor and into full awareness before he realized what it was. In what seemed like two strides he was jerking open the door of Rowena's bedchamber, finding the room suffused with early-morning light.

She was sitting up in bed, tears sliding from her closed lids, rocking her body from side to side as though seeking comfort behind a mountain of blankets.

"Rowena," he whispered, shocked to his soul, guilt swallowing him whole. She did not respond, and he touched the bare skin of her back where the ribbon of her night rail had come undone. He repeated her name again, just as softly, his palm cupping the damp curve of her shoulder. Her eyes remained shut, and the sobs continued. Deeply asleep, she sat with her knees drawn up, reliving an anguish whose contours he knew too well. She had warned him. The nightmares. The dreams. And he realized exactly what they were about.

"Rowena—wake up." He spoke quietly but with force, kneeling on the bed to grasp her shoulders and prod her awake. "You're fine, Rowena. You're with me. Wake up."

Her eyes slowly fluttered open, the torment in them staggering. Her hair clustered around her face, clinging to cheeks damp with tears and sweat as she stared at him, uncomprehending. Then it was as though time unspooled in her mind, and her eyes lit up with the same joy and relief he remembered from over a year ago. It robbed him of breath.

His eyes raked her face, finding her expression calm, the dark blue of her eyes returning his scrutiny openly.

"How do you feel—are you all right, Rowena?" When she didn't answer, he swept a lock of hair back from her cheek, the skin scalding beneath his hand. "Please answer me. Say something."

"I remember," she said simply.

Rushford's world shattered at the innocent longing in her eyes, the lush feel of her body against his, weakening his already equivocal resolve, his body automatically responding to her nearness.

"I remember," she repeated. "You were the one who saved me," she breathed. "I wanted you then and I want you now." She moved her hips against his growing erection. Her eyes were dark blue, untouched by doubt, her mouth inches away from his. He dropped his head slowly, while his hands drifted lower, sliding down her back, cupping her bottom and pulling her hard against his body. Then he kissed her as she sighed into his mouth, confident and greedy in her desire, reveling in his acquiescence. Melting against him, she tasted him deeply.

He dragged his lips from hers to whisper, "You remember. Tell me. I need to hear it." He gently pushed her away. "It can't simply be gratitude."

She frowned, a hand on her forehead. "Gratitude? How can you think that when it was so much more?" she asked, all innocence and youth. "I was so cold, so very cold," she said. "And I heard my sister's voice, calling out to me."

Rushford sat very still on the side of the bed, watching Rowena limned in the light of the rising sun, the mahogany of her hair catching fire. "Time started and stopped, and then I remember water pulling down my skirts. I tried to swim but I couldn't. Even though I'd learned as a little girl in the frigid lake at Montfort," she said with a ghost of a smile. "But I didn't sink like a stone. Strong hands found me in the current and held me aloft. And those same hands—" She broke off.

The silence lengthened before she continued, knowing what he needed to hear. "I dreamed of those hands," she said with a shaking voice, "saving me, enveloping me in a combination of softness and strength. I heard steps, the door to my room opening, then the warmth of a body shifting beneath the sheets. I felt the heat, like a cauldron, a furnace into which I turned my cold body." It was as though she was reciting a poem, an incantation. Her voice, low and soft, drifted around him. He fought against his desires, knowing it could lead to nothing but hurt, knowing that he shouldn't give her what she wanted.

When he finally trusted himself to speak, he said, "I was the more experienced. I should not have given in to my desire." There was an undertone of regret in his words.

She shook her head. "Our desires. Not simply yours."

"At the very least, I should explain," he muttered brusquely, struggling against his base impulses. And that's all they were, he convinced himself.

"Later," she murmured, moving toward the edge of the bed and melting against him, her needs and her terrors driving her, as though nothing mattered but feeling him inside her.

The warmth of her body, the soft pressure of her breasts, her hips, her thighs burned through the fabric of his evening clothes, stripping him of his defenses and bringing back the memories with blinding force. It did not bear thinking of. How could this slight young woman so arouse him, when he knew that the only woman he'd ever loved was dead?

Agony tore through him. Then, before he realized what was happening, all he could smell was her warm skin tinged with the freshness of youth. His mouth found hers, tasting sweetness as pliant lips opened beneath his, allowing his tongue to run lightly over her mouth. Her body was pressed to his, her heart beating against his chest. His arms went around her, his hands spread over her back under the thin lawn of her nightdress, feeling her supple slenderness. For a moment, their tongues played, slowly and sensually, until he moved his hands to grasp her head, holding her strongly as he drove deep within her mouth with a fervor that in some faraway part of his brain seemed long past due. He was not prepared for what was happening. He responded from some deep, passionate part of himself that was not simply mired in lust. He wanted Rowena, to feel her and taste her, as vitally as he had ever wanted any other woman in his life. Including Kate.

He pulled away, regarding her with unsmiling eyes. "Yes," she said, softly, simply nodding in response to his silent question. His hands went to the ribbons of her nightdress. Forcing himself to slow down, he pulled the silken bows, one by one, until they came undone. Rowena sat motionless under his hands. He then lifted and turned her wrists, unfastening the tiny pearl buttons before pulling the nightgown's sleeves from her arms. The fabric pooled around her waist, and he looked at her, bare in the early-morning light. She remained still for the long, deliberate scrutiny, her nipples lifting and hardening in the cool air.

He held the swell of her breasts in the palms of his hands, his thumbs flicking the nipples, his eyes holding hers before he lowered his head and drew his tongue in a slow, easy stroke, first over the right breast and then over the left. Rowena caught her breath, stilling her voice, as though they were both afraid of breaking the silence that held them in its thrall.

Rushford caught her waist and lifted her effortlessly from the mattress, sliding the nightgown off her legs. Slowly, he unfastened the tapes of her pantalets, pushing them along her hips. Then he rose and looked down at her as she lay on the bed, vulnerable in her nakedness. He had never seen her in daylight, he realized; his hands had been those of a blind man. Now he saw her long limbs and the gentle curve of her hips, the surprising fullness of her breasts, high and firm.

He swiftly took off his coat and neckcloth and pulled his shirt over his head, memories, honor, and scruples a spot on the far horizon. He reached for the buttons on his breeches, greedily drinking in the young woman before him, hair tumbling on her shoulders, trembling in her eagerness. He slid the buttons free and slipped his trousers over his legs, stepping out of them. Then sitting down beside her, he lowered his head to lightly kiss her lips, pushing her hands away, easing her thighs open. Trustingly, she closed her eyes and eased herself into the cushions while he slipped a finger between the sleek moistness between her thighs, gently stroking her pulsing flesh.

She arched her hips against the sensation and sighed against his lips. He eased his fingers in another small distance, watching the play of emotion over her face. She moaned softly, and he massaged her with practiced skill, slowly sliding deeper, touching and stroking. She kept her eyes shut, lost in sensation, floating in a blissful sea of concentration centered between her legs. The tempo of her breathing increased, and she moved her hips in a slow undulation, reaching for a pleasure point, lifting into his hands for his heated touch.

Rushford had done this hundreds of times with all too many women, but never before had he watched so closely the flush of arousal color a woman's skin or observed so scrupulously the panting gasps as he slowly penetrated and withdrew, taking careful note of the increasingly frantic arching of her slender hips. He kissed her again, inhaling her whimpers while stroking her fevered flesh, wanting her with a fierce violence that was foreign to him. His self-control had been tested over the years but never like this. Schooling his impatience, he murmured against her mouth. "No more bad dreams, Rowena, only this. You'll feel me deep inside, sliding infinitely slowly, filling you." His hands continued cupping and stroking and as he spoke, the heat inside her burned higher with each hot word. "But this time you will remember every instant, with every nerve in your body."

She arched a final time into his hands, her climax tensing every muscle, a low moan escaping her mouth, the breath hot on his lips. They lay that way for what seemed an infinity until finally the cadence of her breathing slowed and she lay replete, eyes shut, a small smile on her lips. "I knew there was something about you, something familiar . . ."

"I suppose my vanity should be pricked that you'd forgotten." His voice was teasing, his arms still around her.

Her eyes slowly opened and her smile widened. "Don't make fun, Rushford," she said, reaching up to touch his hard chest. "I remembered in some part of me, how your body felt so right next to mine, your scent, the way you made me feel safe."

"What else do you remember?" he asked carefully.

She turned her head away, stretching with unalloyed pleasure against the sheets. She was finely boned and taut, the years of riding and outdoor pursuits honing her body to perfection, he thought, with none of the easy plumpness of women of leisure and rank. "I do not wish to speak of it right now," she said, "particularly when I sense we're far from finished here."

"As long as you're sure this is what you want."

"I knew the first time," she murmured without hesitation. "I would have died without you in my arms. Don't ever forget that." Once again, he was struck by her startling honesty, totally without pretence.

"Why didn't you tell me?" she asked, breaking her own promise not to delve further. "When I first came to you that night in Belgravia Square?"

The bare bones of the story were all he was prepared to reveal. He stroked the silk of her cheek. "In some ways your fractured memories were a gift—which I did not want to destroy."

"And why you continued to push me away?" She frowned. "Even as I thought you a complete stranger, I sensed that you were not telling me everything." Pausing, she plucked the linen sheet. "We have much to discuss."

"Later."

Her eyes shone, her mood quickly transformed. "At last we agree on something wholeheartedly." She wriggled beneath him enticingly.

He smiled faintly. "I sense that you're not satisfied yet?"

She waved an arm in his direction languidly. "You are insufferably arrogant. Of course, I'm satisfied and you well know it." She leaned up on her elbows, arching her back, giving him a view that lengthened his erection by several inches. "But there's always more." She had the eager look of a young girl surveying a box of bonbons.

Her frankness surprised and delighted him. The women in his past were much more coy about their demands. "I have my share of masculine pride," he said with a glimmer of self-mockery touching his eyes.

Rowena's fingertips brushed over his chest. "I'd never have believed it," she murmured.

In response, he simply smiled his promise, lying down next to her, moving a leg over her thighs, drawing her close against the warmth of his body. It was his turn to close his eyes, the scent of her skin filling the air around him. He inhaled greedily, his hands running over her back, learning again the curve of her hips and buttocks, the smoothness of her skin, the delicate flare of her spine. He felt the press of her breasts against his chest, the tautness of her nipples as he tasted of her mouth with a searching tongue. His need was urgent, eclipsing everything but the immediacy of his delayed desire. With a soft moan, Rowena moved against his hard flesh, her thighs tightening as she held him in the warmth of her body, sliding her hip against a muscular thigh. Her words whispered against his mouth.

"Don't think. Not now, Rushford," she said with ferocity, as his palms flattened against the silk of her thighs, opening her. He touched her slick core, and she moaned her need. He lifted his head, gazing down at her as she sprawled beneath him in abandon, her hips lifting unconsciously, her thighs parted, moisture on the satin of her skin glistening in the glow of the morning light. Her tongue touched his lips and she said, "Now, please . . ."

A wildness surged through him, and somewhere inside he knew he was irretrievably lost. He feasted his eyes on her body, taking in the skin that stretched taut over her rib cage, curving into the hollow of her stomach. He lowered his head to lavish his tongue into the shell of her navel. He moved over her, and his hands lifted her hips to meet his hardness, sliding an inch into her. A slow smile spread over her face, and her eyes widened as he moved in farther, the incursions short and then longer. All the while his hands continued to roam, finding the places that made her wild with desire, stroking and then backing away.

He kissed her again, more forcefully this time, the blood simmering in his veins when he finally entered her with a swift thrust that forced a cry from her throat. He renewed the rhythm, slowly and then faster; Rowena's breath came in gusts from her throat. She sought his mouth with her own and clawed at his back, arching up to meet his thrusts, driving him deeper and deeper still, assuaging a shared hunger.

Lust clawed at his senses, and he brought her legs to rest on his shoulders, filling her to the hilt, balancing them both on the edge of pleasure and pain, punishing her and most of all himself with the most exquisite torment he'd ever known. This wasn't right. And yet it was right, so right, he thought, biting back a groan. Rowena reached with her hands, pulling him down toward her so he would fill her more deeply still, not wanting gentleness, preferring the savage thrusts that were driven by a need that more than matched her own. She kissed him hungrily, moaning her rapture into his mouth as their breaths merged into one.

When the climax came, it jarred him to his bones, the shocks reverberating through their joined bodies. It all but killed him, but he pulled out in time, her legs still spanning his shoulders, her heart pounding against his. They lay locked in each other's arms, shattered by what had passed, not for the first time, between them. They were drained beyond reason, their bodies hot and damp. Rushford rolled off Rowena, but they continued to touch, shoulders, breasts, legs, despite the emotions he tried to shutter behind the mask of his closed eyes. He settled down beside her, throwing one arm across her shoulders.

"Stay here . . . with me," he whispered, the echo hot in her ear. And she did.

Rowena awakened several times, the warmth of the morning sun turning into the heat of daylight.

Now when she rolled on her side and looked at Rushford, everything was familiar to her, from the breadth of his shoulders against the linen sheets to the clean lines of his jaw, the strong nose, the deep-set eyes. How could she ever have forgotten him? *Forgotten this?* She didn't want to think and she didn't want to remember but only to feel. Moving by instinct, she slid her body over his, watching him close his eyes and absorbing his tremor of pleasure. He caressed her bottom and then dropped his hands on the bed. Sitting up, she straddled him, gazing into his face, the silence heavy around them. Taking a deep breath, she reached out to brush back the hair that had fallen onto his forehead, studying his every feature, understanding fully that while they shared a passion, they knew little of one another.

As though she had done it all her life, she mounted him, impaling herself slowly upon his pulsing erection, holding hands, fingers interlocked as she rode him up and down, moving around in little circles. Her breath caught in her throat, her pulse exploding, the pleasure acute. To be in control of his every movement, to have him where she wanted him, while he caressed her core with those clever hands and fingers, she could feel him growing harder and bigger, on the edge of lust. They were both holding back, desperate for another taste of sexual oblivion.

He squeezed her hand tightly, and never taking his gaze

from her eyes, he pressed his lips to hers and then trailed small kisses to her breasts. His kisses turned to sucking and then biting, encouraging her to ride him, harder, faster. She came first, long and strong and overwhelming, lost in a vast void of bliss, scarcely aware of his pulling away to spill his seed on the smoothness of her abdomen.

If they wanted to say things to one another, the opportunity never came. It was only there in their eyes, the passion and urgency and lust. They spoke with their bodies. Later, as the sun rose still higher in the sky behind the curtains, they rose from the bed. Moments later, overcome with renewed passion, Rushford held her up against the peach silk-covered wall and she wrapped her legs around his waist. He started again with her mouth, with deep kisses while his hands caressed her breasts. He played with them, burying his face between them as his erection throbbed inside her. He was lost, she somehow understood, placing her hands firmly on his shoulders and leaning back and away from him against the wall so he might continue his kissing. Her legs were still wrapped around him, and she used her grip to ease herself on and off his penis. He moved in time with her, controlling the tempo with exquisite, drawn-out ease.

They came. And then they slept, waking again when the sun began its afternoon decline. He took her on her knees, with him behind her. He had a way of tormenting her with desire, teasing her and holding back until she begged for more. She loved the warmth of his lips on hers, the demand of his tongue in her mouth. His kisses could take her over, and she felt herself giving in to him as the day turned once more into night.

When they finally emerged from the bed, it was well past dusk. "You can come out now," Rushford said, glancing at her shape under the covers. "You must be starving. No worries. I asked the servants to leave trays outside the door."

She sat up slowly from beneath a mound of sheets, watching with appreciation as he walked resplendently nude to the

door, returning with a tray balanced on each hand, then placing them on the bed.

"You make a superb manservant, Rushford," Rowena
said, reaching for the hand he held out to her, easing into a
seated position.

His smile was infectious as he watched her lift the silver
covers from the plates before her and take in the rich venison
stew, small dauphinoise potatoes, and green beans. "Will you
not join me, my lord?" she asked. "Your recent endeavors
have surely sharpened your appetite."

He looked at her propped up against the pillows, di-
sheveled from their lovemaking, her nakedness only half covered by the disarray of linens. "My appetite is only for you,"
he said.

"That sounds decidedly romantic. I almost feel as though I
should believe you."

"Perhaps you should."

A small silence fell while Rowena told herself she didn't
dare think any further into the future. She glanced away, uncomfortable with her thoughts. She knew this man was not
for her to have by her side where she suddenly, desperately
wanted him. The realization stunned her, and she tried to
concentrate on the simple task of moving the fork to her
mouth. They had been thrown together by a twist of fate,
nothing more. But she didn't want to think about that now.
His cool murmur forced her gaze back to his. "We have to
talk, Rowena," he said.

She patted the napkin to her lips. "You're angry. Regret-
ful."

"No. Absolutely not." They had both agreed to the step
they'd taken.

"There is nothing to regret," she said forcefully. "You
found me in the river and saved my life. I'll never forget that.
And then when I needed something more . . ."

"Sex is not comfort, Rowena." His voice was different
now, cooler, more remote.

"I am no child, Rushford, despite what you believe. Do you think that what we did over a year ago and these past hours was in any way based on an emotion as pallid as comfort? If you do, then you are sadly mistaken." Inadequacy burned in her chest. "I know I am not as experienced as Miss Barry or any other of your mistresses might have been," she began.

He interrupted her, catching a gesturing hand in midair. "Don't slight yourself, Rowena. You are simply superb. Perfect. No argument." His voice was low, scarcely audible.

He kissed her palm before releasing it. She said wisely, "Then let's enjoy this veritable feast for the moment. We can speak of these things later."

The concession was his to make. Rushford reached for a linen napkin and sat opposite her while Rowena lounged on the bed. They ate in companionable silence broken only by murmurs of appreciation and sips of wine that Rushford had decanted.

"That was wonderful," Rowena said finally sinking into the pillows at her back. "But you didn't eat much. And you're very quiet."

He glanced up.

"You're looking at me as though you've despoiled a maiden."

"You're not exactly what I'm accustomed to." He lifted his wineglass to his lips.

A flare of anger lit in her chest. "I think we've already established that fact. You mean that you are unaccustomed to virgins. I'm your first—is that right?" she asked with her usual candor. "Or more correctly, perhaps, I was your first virgin when we met over a year ago." She folded up the napkin on her lap. "I'm becoming increasingly irritated by your condescension, Rushford. I am not some silly doll-like creature who doesn't know her own mind. You should know that by now."

"There's no possible way I could overlook that fact," he said dryly. The sound of a door closing, followed by footsteps and the splash of water, interrupted their conversation. "I ordered us a bath," he said, and she noted that he appeared to welcome the disruption, nodding toward the small door in the corner of the bedchamber, which led to the water closet.

"Us?" She smiled flirtatiously, her ill humor suddenly fleeing as she acknowledged that she was the one who had Rushford for the moment. She also recognized full well that she could never compete with the pantheon of women who had come before her. But she wouldn't think of them now. Throwing the coverlet aside, she slid her legs over the bed. "I'm more than capable of making my own decisions," she continued. "Which is precisely the reason I came to you in the first place."

"You mean the second time."

Her brows rose. "You found me the first time, the details of which I'm anxious to hear. And yes, I made my way back to you, unwittingly, although something drew me toward you. Obviously the memories, the dreams, and the nightmares I had suppressed." She gathered the linen around her body, though unaccountably unembarrassed by her nakedness. "How did you find me?" she asked bluntly.

"How about your bath first?"

Moments later, he sat a distance away from her while she sank into the copper tub's steaming water. She watched him from beneath her eyelashes, wondering what it would take to tempt him to leave his chair. The knowledge of her power, newly discovered, was alluring. She took a sip of the wine balanced on the stool beside the tub.

Picking up the fragrant bar of soap, she bathed with a deliberately unflustered disregard for his presence, as though she had done so countless times before with a man present. Then she sank back into the water.

"Now you're the one who is quiet," he said, watching her

trace her palm over the surface of the water, causing light ripples to wash over her submerged breasts.

"I'm waiting for you."

"To answer your questions." He leaned forward in the chair but stared off into the middle distance as though something required his entire concentration.

"Yes," she said with conviction.

"Very well, then." He nodded, returning his gaze to hers. "The basic facts are these. I found you floating face down in the Irthing River, near to Birdoswald. It was close to one in the morning, and I thought you were dead," he said brusquely, clearly unwilling to add any more detail to the narration. "I couldn't be sure whether you still lived, so I threw off my jacket, jumped in after you, and pulled you to shore."

Rowena fought against the remembered sensations, the heavy drift of her skirts pulling her down. Her lungs close to exploding. Rushford watched her expression carefully before continuing. "You had obviously been fed opiates because it required two days for you to awaken fully. I had taken you to a small inn nearby, and I was reluctant to leave you as you were racked with fever."

When she could finally speak, she said, "I remember being cold and then warm . . . and the nightmares . . . being held captive in the dark."

"Do you wish me to continue?" he asked.

"I don't have any other choice," she said, sinking farther into the copper tub until the water covered her shoulders. "I must know."

"There were no indications of harm, Rowena, no marks." His face was granite, but she sensed that he was alert to her every reaction. "On the third day you awakened, your fever having broken. Do you remember?"

She thought for a moment, the images unfurling in her mind's eye. Rushford at the side of her bed in a cramped, slope-ceilinged chamber with room for little else save a bed, an armoire, and a small side table. She had been distraught, woken from a nightmare when he had taken her in his arms. He had begun to rub her back with strong fingers, finding a slow, lulling rhythm. As his fingers worked, she had felt her muscles and her anxiety let loose their punishing hold. Slowly and in an unhurried silence, he massaged the small of her back, circled his thumbs upward toward her shoulders, and worked the length of her arms. It had been the beginning.

She looked up from her position in the tub. "I regret nothing," she said simply, seeing reflected in his eyes the moments they had stolen together over a year ago.

"You are wise for a young woman," he replied after a moment. "Regrets are useless."

"You are referring to something more, I sense."

"It's of no account," he said, his voice neutral. "You refused to tell me your name or where you lived," he continued, "and I believed once you were physically recovered it would be best to leave you in the care of an elderly couple I knew of in Kendal, far enough away from Birdoswald." He caught the flash of worry in her eyes. "We were together a total of three days and nights."

And Rowena could suddenly account for every last moment of every hour with him, like the individually precious pearls on a string. "What were you doing there? So far from London?" she asked awkwardly, grasping for an explanation that could set her world to rights.

"Going after someone. Something."

Rowena regarded him for an instant through narrowed, disbelieving eyes. "As usual, that tells me very little." She'd shared enough with Rushford to recognize that whatever was troubling him ran deep.

"Have you heard of the Rosetta Stone?" he asked with what she discerned as instinctive reluctance. It was time to return to the real world, he had somehow decided. Or that he owed her that at least.

She nodded, easing her head back until it rested on the lip of the copper tub. "It is an ancient Egyptian artifact. Meredith took us a few years ago to the British Museum, where we saw it in a collection of Egyptian monuments captured from the French over thirty years ago."

"Montagu Faron wants it. Badly."

Rowena's head snapped up, water sloshing onto the floor with her abrupt movement. "And that's why you were close to Birdoswald that night?" The pieces were beginning to fall into place.

"We had heard that he had landed in Calais the night before and was making his way to Eccles House, where we were endeavoring to intercept him."

Rushford, she realized, was far from the amateur sleuth who had involved himself in the Cruikshank murders. "Who is *we*? Or will you even entertain that question?"

Rushford stood abruptly, utterly careless of his nudity. "The Rosetta Stone is still in British possession. So you may surmise the rest," he said briefly.

A shiver ran through her as the water cooled on her skin. *Who are you really, Rushford?* she wanted desperately to ask. Instead, she attempted to moderate her desperation. "At the very least you must tell me who this man Faron is and what he wants with the Stone."

"Montagu Faron is a difficult man to explain, other than to say that he has the power and the resources to get whatever he desires—including some of the world's most valuable, ancient artifacts."

She frowned. "For his own gain?"

He crossed his arms over his chest. "From what we know, Faron is many things, chief among them an amateur scientist and explorer whose hubris leads him to make unwise decisions."

"Such as trying to steal the Rosetta Stone?" she prompted.

He agreed with a somber nod of his head, before gazing at her directly. "What that has to do with the Woolcotts I'm not certain, if anything."

For a moment she fell silent, then said, "You are telling me the truth finally. I sense it, Rushford. You know nothing of the reasons behind Faron's obsession with my family."

"But we shall learn more when we visit with Sebastian and the lovely Miss Barry this coming weekend. That I promise you." His gaze raked her face, but her expression remained calm, her blue eyes returning his scrutiny with resolve. "I know that's what you wish," he said, continuing to regard her for a moment, then nodded as if satisfied.

"The Rosetta Stone is still in the British Museum, you say?" she asked, unsmiling now. "I suppose I will not learn much more from you," she amended, answering her own question, Rushford filling the frame of her gaze. He was tall, broad-shouldered, honed to physical fitness, a man who, she sensed, would not accept failure. Ever. She had sensed that from the first. A rush of desire flared, burning a path through her senses. Amazing, how accustomed she had become to the combustible effect of his nearness.

"What of your bath, my lord?" she asked, having had enough of reality for the moment. A heartbeat later, he stood at the foot of the tub, exhibiting a splendid erection. Rowena forced herself not to stare.

"I thought you would never ask," he said, stepping into the water before she had a chance to react. He sank to his knees between her legs. His hands slid under her bottom.

"How often can we do this?" she asked, naturally curious, balancing a calf on the edge of the tub to accommodate him.

He grinned. "As often as you like." As they had already proven in the past twenty-four hours.

She sighed her contentment as he lifted her gently until her pulsing core met his hard length. Water rippled around them as he forced his rigid erection downward, easing into her sleekness, moving forward by slow degrees. Rowena gasped as he filled her, lifting her mouth to his, murmuring with inchoate longing. "Don't ever stop," she breathed, his penetration all encompassing, chasing away all thoughts of danger or the future.

"I'm here," he whispered, and glided a fraction deeper, reckless as he had never been before in his life. His thumbs moved to trace the shape of her neck, his palms flattening against the curve of her cheeks. How could he do this to her, Rowena thought helplessly, reduce her to whimpers with the slightest touch?

One of his hands moved between them as he held himself motionless against the mouth of her womb. Rowena arched her back, the world dissolving, a heated ecstasy overwhelming her mind and body, every nerve drawn to a feverish pitch. Water sloshed over the edge of the tub as he began to withdraw. She clutched at his back, trying to keep him inside her.

"Don't worry. I'm here," he said, his voice low. And then he reached the limits of his withdrawal, plunging in once again as she tightened around him and he buried himself in to the hilt. Sensation shook their bodies; they moved in the heated water in a concerted flow, sending waves onto the tile floor. They partook wildly, greedy, impatient and consumed by a hunger that scorched away anything else but their shattering climax, leaving them both bereft of breath, conscious only of the all-consuming present.

"I thought I'd died," she said, her head thrown back, her arms still around him.

"I think we both just did," he growled, his forehead resting on the edge of the copper tub.

"Just remember, this does not make me your mistress in actual fact." The words left her in a rush, a statement she was convinced both of them needed to hear.

He turned his head and met her dark blue gaze. "Lover then," he said softly. "Undeniably."

"As long as we're both clear." What she really wanted suddenly alarmed her, and she needed to put some distance between them.

"Whatever you wish."

For now, she thought, finishing his sentence, knowing full well that theirs would be a continuing contest of wills. She moved her hips in the smallest of undulations, aware of the one area upon which they unequivocally agreed. Impossibly, he had grown rigid again, the sensation bringing a smile to her lips. This, at the very least, she could control.

"Whatever I wish?" she asked with a cheekily raised brow. His response was to lower his head to hers.

# Chapter 13

"Where is she?" Faron demanded, pacing in the hall of mirrors on his estate, Claire de Lune, outside Paris. His voice behind his leather mask was raw. "Why is Rowena Woolcott alive when we believed otherwise?"

Lowther, accustomed at managing the violent and unpredictable demands of Montagu Faron, stood patiently with his hands behind his back. "Montagu," he soothed. "I was as surprised as you to learn of this turn of events, but Sebastian assures me that he will remedy the situation post haste."

"I do not reward you to be surprised, Lowther," Faron said, gesturing for emphasis. Lowther tried not to be repelled at the line of raised scars on the back of the Frenchman's hands, a souvenir from the night at Eccles House not so long ago. "It enrages me to think that Julia Woolcott is not only alive but safe with Strathmore in North Africa after deliberately causing the fire that almost killed me. And now to learn that her sister has not been dispatched as I asked?"

Lowther cleared his throat, focusing on the line of oak trees framed in the French doors. "I do understand your concern about the Woolcotts," he began carefully, "but we have rather more important matters to discuss at the moment."

A momentary pause. "I decide what's important," Faron snapped, beginning to pace again along the hall, his tall, lithe form reflected in the multitude of mirrors. "I'm assuming you are about to apprise me of the whereabouts of the Rosetta Stone. The Woolcott matter having thoroughly escaped you."

Lowther bowed his head, waiting for the storm to pass.

"I demand that all of my requests be executed. Neither is more important than the other."

"I understand completely," Lowther said. "So you will be pleased to learn that we intend to have the Stone in our possession and dispense with Rowena Woolcott at the same time."

Faron's barking of laughter echoed in the cavernous hallway. "Intend? Your intentions do little to inspire my confidence. So do try to bolster my enthusiasm and enlighten me," he said caustically.

Lowther had planned to explain the plan earlier, but Faron had shut himself in one of his elaborate laboratories for several days, playing with his beakers and specimens, declining to meet with anyone. At least one of his uncontrollable rages had not overtaken him, Lowther thought with relief. He recalled how several weeks earlier the Frenchman had completely destroyed one of his laboratories, leaving behind a small mountain of broken glass. He was far from the gentleman scientist, retiring genteelly to his laboratory, to be served tea by the housekeeper and to jot notes of profound significance in his journal. Lowther took a deep breath, wishing he could delay the inevitable. "Rowena Woolcott is with Lord Rushford," he said finally.

The Frenchman halted his pacing, turning around slowly to face Lowther. The features behind the smooth leather of the mask, Lowther had heard, were handsome and unblemished but oftentimes beset with wild tremors beyond the Frenchman's control. And now only a pair of dark eyes stared back at him with focused venom. "Impossible," he hissed through the leather slit of his mask. "I won't have it."

Experienced with the wild swings in mood, Lowther continued undaunted. "You'll recall, Rushford interfered with our plans for the Rosetta Stone last year, despite his involvement with the Duchess of Taunton."

"I recall—and with some displeasure." Faron's voice had become so quiet that Lowther had to move closer to hear the words. The low timbre was not a good sign.

"We were in Cumbria," Lowther continued, marching into the breach, "dealing with Rowena Woolcott. Rushford was in the environs as well, having learned of your intended visit to Eccles House. He'd been following our trail but happened instead upon the Woolcott chit floating half-dead in the Irthing. He never did get to Eccles House."

"Details. Always details. They don't interest me in the least if the objective is not reached." The dark eyes bored unwaveringly into Lowther's. "At least Meredith and the wretched sister still believe her to be dead. A small consolation."

Lowther bowed his head. "Rushford saved her life, ensured that she recovered with a family in a neighboring village, and in turn, Rowena Woolcott is now intent upon working with him to ensure your downfall."

A man who was wealthy beyond belief, damned by a family fortune that gave him unrivaled power and had led him down the darkest of paths, Faron demonstrated his displeasure with a string of curses. "The Woolcott women are all cut from the same cloth," he said softly, the words laced with poison. "Meredith has ensured that they are endowed with the same irredeemable qualities that she herself possesses—a feral recklessness that has done nothing but bring sorrow into her life. I have made sure of that."

Lowther knew enough not to ask why. There had been rumors for years that Montagu and Meredith Woolcott had spent their childhoods together and that she was somehow responsible for his mental imbalance.

"You should be concerned that Rushford is at Woolcott's side," Faron added scathingly. "The man is a formidable opponent, and if you need more proof, recall how he willingly forfeited the Duchess's life in order to fulfill his duty to his country. Totally unexpected. I trust you have a worthy plan in place."

"We do. Both for the Woolcott woman and for the Stone."

Faron glanced at him briefly, a jerk of his chin the only reply. Then he turned away, looking out to the parterre beyond the windows, gazing down a long tunnel of memory. "I don't like this, Lowther. I don't like this at all."

"What might we do to win your confidence?" Lowther asked dutifully.

Faron turned from the window, his hands clasped behind his back. "Just what I should like to hear at long last. Surely it's time that you do something to earn my confidence. Although you truly do not understand the power of motivation, do you, Lowther?"

When Lowther did not reply, Faron gave a small shake of his head. "Use Meredith Woolcott, you fool," he said in little more than a whisper. "The Woolcott women will do anything to protect one another, don't you see?"

"Use her?"

"Use them both. When Meredith learns that Rowena still lives but is once more within our grasp, she will wish her ward had perished a year ago," Faron said harshly. "And as for Rowena, dispose of her in any case. As a matter of pride, for God's sake, if nothing else."

With Julia's departure and Rowena's death, Montfort, though little changed, felt deserted. For the past year, Meredith Woolcott had watched the seasons change from the windows of the drawing room in the medieval fortification where she and her charges had lived safely for close to twenty years.

Dusk hung about the salon like a heavy mantle, despite her best efforts to shake it loose. She had tried to alleviate her malaise by taking a ride earlier in the day, finally ending her exertions at the stables where Rowena's horse, Dragon, still waited patiently for his mistress's return. There the ghosts of Rowena and Julia's childhood lingered, their laughter mingling with dust motes in the air. It seemed both an eternity and only yesterday that the two girls had played and planned their time together. Julia with her wide-eyed but cautious curiosity, and Rowena the hoyden with her boundless energy. What innocent times those were, times when the consequences of their aunt Meredith's actions had never entered the minds of her young charges.

Leaving the stables, Meredith's eyes had automatically scanned the expansive green of the estate, expecting to see Rowena on her horse, harboring a deep-set hope that her younger ward was still alive, although she knew it to be an illusion. Shaking her head at her folly, she had wandered restlessly toward the house, which posed majestically against the gently rolling green hills now enshrouded with fog.

At least Julia was safe with Strathmore, far away in North Africa. Their wedding in the small chapel at Montfort, their passion and love for one another, had been a comfort. Julia had found the protection with Lord Strathmore that she herself had been unable to provide.

Meredith was neither a weak nor emotional woman, and had done her best for her wards for many years. In a strange twist of fate, she had inherited wealth that had allowed her to shelter her young charges from the evil that she had had a hand in creating. But she would always carry the burden of knowledge that she had not done enough.

Rowena lay dead, somewhere at the bottom of the Irthing River, the loss forever mired in Meredith's heart. She could not bear to spend one moment thinking of the man who was responsible for the heinous crime, her hands shaking as she tried to contain her anger. When she had learned that Faron still lived, she thought she would go mad with impotent rage. Yet she could do nothing for fear that Julia would be harmed. About herself, she no longer cared.

Meredith stepped back from the window and surveyed the room. There were small reminders of her girls scattered about the place, Julia's favorite books, Rowena's riding jacket that Meredith could not bear to put away, and Rowena's favorite pen in its ebony box on the escritoire. She wandered over to the desk and picked up Rowena's favorite copy of Wordsworth's poems. It made her feel close to Rowena, to hold the source of her joy.

She stood there for a time, hoping for a miraculous gift, looking out the wide windows of Montfort where the horizon was a gunmetal gray. She could see nothing, but it didn't matter. She can't be dead, her conscious mind cried, even though logic told her that she must give up the illusion and give in to her grief. A full year later, she could not believe that Rowena would not come home.

Her stomach clenched, and she forced herself again not to think of Montagu Faron, not to remember that last afternoon so many years ago when they had ridden through the Loire Valley, the lush green of the countryside bounteous in the late summertime. As the sun set, it had cast a delightful glow upon the land, creating a feeling of magic. They had ridden to Blois just as the sun was slipping behind the low hills of the small city. Together they meandered through the narrow, empty streets and along a narrow road beyond prying eyes. Finally they dismounted and walked the rest of the way, the horses' reins dangling loosely in their hands.

Behind them stretched the valley of kings, extending along the river in a deep serenity and an aura of splendor and history. Presently, they had stopped at a small cottage with an arched door and a tangle of rosebushes. The sight of the charming domicile brought a smile to Faron's young face.

"Entirely unexpected, no?" he asked in English. "You are surprised, Meredith?"

Meredith had caught the intimacy in his voice. She had looked at him then with young love in her eyes, at the tall and handsome youth in the evening light. He had raked a hand through his coal-black hair, his cloak slung over his arm and a loose white shirt open at the throat. "Shall we go in?" he asked, producing keys from his cloak. Outlined against the golden light of early evening, he looked like the image she'd first had of him, the image from her dreams. He was dark and brooding like the heroes in the novels she loved to read. He was her soul mate, sharing his interests in science and the wide world. They had spent hours together in his father's laboratories, scoured ancient texts in the chateau's library, and exchanged heated words in heated debates about everything from galvanization to nitrous oxide.

Meredith remembered the vivid red of the roses as though it were yesterday, recalling how she and Faron had lingered on the cottage threshold. She had always known they would be together one day, and had felt an inexplicable premonition of a shared fate. And so she had put her hand in his, watching as he studied her face seriously for a moment and then pulled her to him with a searing kiss. Then he tore his eyes away and unlocked and opened the door. Lifting her in his arms, he had carried her inside.

Meredith raised her head from her reveries, the pain in her chest unbearable. Looking into the darkening sky surrounding Montfort, she wondered how her life had taken such a perverse turn and why the only man she had ever loved was now the man she would hate to her grave.

# Chapter 14

The first night at Alcestor Court, Rowena slept fitfully, desperately missing the warmth and security of Rushford beside her. They had arrived late Friday evening, and their host, Baron Sebastian, had not made an appearance to welcome them to his country residence but rather preferred that his butler show his guests to their appointed bedchambers. Rowena and Rushford had been placed at opposite ends of a long hallway, in the tradition of country house weekends, where couples were encouraged to play elaborate games of sexual *rondeau*.

The Baron had clearly attended to the disposition of the bedrooms, having each guest's name written neatly on a card and slipped into a tiny brass frame on the bedroom door so male guests would not blunder into the wrong rooms. Or so Rowena had guessed, insisting to Rushford that they sleep alone in their appointed bedchambers, so as to fit seamlessly into the weekend's baroque choreography.

"Lock your door. And keep the key in the lock," Rushford had growled, reluctant to let her out of his sight. But Rowena had pushed him away, needing some time to regain her equilibrium after having spent three scorching days in Rushford's bed. She wished to clear her head and her heart, to focus on the matter that was her only concern. Faron.

She awoke before the maid brought the tea tray. Springing from the bed, she flung open the curtains and looked out on

a perfect early-spring morning with a pale sun already
sparkling on the green expanse of lawn beneath her window.
She turned away from the window as the maid knocked and
entered with her tea. She shivered in her thin nightgown, gossamer threads held together with satin ribbons and delicate
lace.

"Shall I lay out your riding habit, madam?" The maid
straightened from arranging the tray, and Rowena recalled
the butler's announcement the previous evening that the day
would begin with a hunt.

"Please do." Rowena poured her tea in a rich aromatic
stream from a silver pot, her pulse jumping at the thought of
riding again. She blocked out images of Montfort and
Dragon and instead observed the maid holding her new riding boots of cordovan leather up to the light, examining
them for marks. The maid proceeded to bustle around with
jugs of hot water, then laced Rowena into her new riding
habit. Leaving her fair wig in the bottom of the armoire, she
fitted a snug hat over her hair, a clutch of trembling feathers
its sole decoration.

An hour later, with the maid leading the way, Rowena proceeded along a deserted hallway and entrance hall to the
breakfast room, where a footman jumped to open the door.
Momentarily startled, she found herself alone with Rushford.

"Good morning," she greeted him with a casual smile and
as if they had not recently spent days indulging in the heights
of passion. There was a studied coolness in her tone, an af-
fectation she had thought best to rehearse and adopt, at least
in public, in an attempt to mimic Miss Barry's easy sophistication and *sang froid*.

"I've been up since the early hours of the morning," he
said shortly, barely looking up from his place setting.

"Quite unlike you from what I've seen these past three
days," she said cheekily, lifting the lids of the chafing dishes
on the sideboard. They were entirely alone aside from two
footmen who studiously avoided looking at them. The guests

were obviously still abed, and Rowena wondered how many would actually make it to the hunt.

Rushford's response was a grunt.

"You did not sleep well, I surmise, judging by your tone and lack of conversation."

He looked up at her from his empty plate. "I think this is a mistake," he said abruptly. Rowena knew exactly to what he referred—her presence at Alcestor Court.

"We agreed," she said briefly, helping herself to a dish of eggs and a slice of toast. "There is nothing to discuss. We're here now. Together." She sat down at the far end of the table, as far away from Rushford as possible.

"You can return to London. It's not too late."

"I'm sorry, Lord Rushford." She looked up in innocent inquiry. "I didn't quite catch that."

"Your hearing is quite selective."

"Enjoy your breakfast as I'm certain the hunt will be demanding. I quite look forward to it. It has been sometime since I've ridden," she said with a serene smile. "And while you're about it, my lord, could you please pass the teapot?"

Rushford pushed back his chair with a deliberate scrape against the polished floor, picked up the heavy pot, and marched the length of the table, depositing it beside her tea cup. "At the very least, follow my lead," he said, staring down at her. "And we are sleeping together in the same bedchamber this evening, twisted conventions be damned."

Rowena tried to contain her physical response to his nearness—and his proclamation. He was already in his riding attire, his stock snowy white against the hard planes of his face. He'd taken her breath away when she'd first seen him in the breakfast room, although she trusted she hadn't given him the satisfaction of seeing it. He was older. He was experienced—the hours spent in his bed were a testament to his finesse as a lover. And he had saved her life. All the more reason she needed to ensure she didn't lose her head over a man who held the fate of those she loved in his hands.

"I suppose," she murmured, taking a bite of her toast, "that we should not appear too possessive. It's clearly not the thing. Particularly if we are meant to engage with the Baron."

"Stay away from him." The words were stark.

"Isn't that precisely the point? To spend time with the man?" She would not let Rushford know how the Frenchman's voice alone sent shudders down her spine.

"Only if you are at my side," he amended unhelpfully, his eyes darkening.

"And leave everything to you, of course," she said. She rose from the table so they were almost at eye level and she could lower her voice. "You have yet to share with me your strategy for finding your way to Faron, never mind your intentions regarding the Rosetta Stone. And I have a feeling that you intend it to stay that way."

He placed his hands palms down on the table, his face bending toward hers. For a moment, she imagined that he would lower his lips to hers, but his expression was unforgiving. She blocked out a sudden urge to throw her arms around his neck and to kiss him deeply, to move her hands up through the thickness of his hair, to devour him and transport them back to Miss Warren's bedchamber in Knightsbridge. His next words stopped the madness and brought her back to reality with a decisive jolt.

"I promised to apprise you of whatever I discover about your family, Rowena. That is all. Anything more is entirely too dangerous."

She let out an exasperated breath. "Just because we have shared a bed, Rushford, does not mean that anything at all has changed. I am not a child but a capable woman. You are not responsible for my well-being."

"Then why did you approach me in the first place?"

"For your expertise at solving crimes. Nothing more." She paused to straighten the dark emerald pin securing the white muslin cravat at her throat. Loathe to admit to him or to herself that there was more binding them together, she sat back down at the table. "You saved my life, and I'm grateful. Forever," she said quietly. "But that does not in any way make you responsible for my safety in perpetuity."

"Let me decide that," he muttered darkly, turning on his heel and leaving the breakfast room.

Rowena Woolcott was correct in her assumptions, Rushford thought later, when the blasting horn of the hunt interrupted his dark ruminations. He saw her immediately when he stepped through the front door of the grand eighteenth-century Palladian country house, and stood looking down at the half dozen riders and dogs congregating on the circular gravel in front of the house. Rowena wore her hat with its feathers caressing her shoulders, auburn hair tucked away. She sat on a roan hunter, her skirts swept to the side. As if aware of his observation, she turned slightly and looked directly at him. He was too far away to see her expression clearly, but he could imagine the questions in her dark blue eyes, her lush mouth turned down in concern. For an instant, he thought that she was holding him with her gaze, robbing him of his will, this young woman who had so suddenly become a seductress. Then she broke the spell, curving from her waist to adjust a foot expertly in the stirrup. Each of her movements expressed the sinuous vitality of a woman in control of and at ease with her body. She looked at one with her horse; her face, as Rushford approached, glowed with suppressed excitement.

A groom brought Rushford a gray hunter, and he mounted swiftly, easing his horse to Rowena's side. Guiding her mount to the edge of the circular drive, she deliberately looked away and cast her neighbor a quick glance. A man with heavy muttonchops was laughing with the Baron at something he had said. Introductions had obviously been made.

"So you are an experienced rider, Miss Warren," Sebastian chuckled, resplendent in a dark brown riding jacket with bronzed braiding.

"Guilty," she said, her gloved hands resting comfortably on her mount's neck. "I've ridden all my life."

"You were raised in the countryside, if I might inquire? Your accent seems to hold a shadow of the north country."

"Well done, Baron," Rowena responded calmly and as though she had nothing to hide. "And if you would permit me, I should say that your accent, slight though it may be, is distinctly Parisian."

Sebastian bowed his head in assent. "It is indeed, Miss Warren. Although I am an anglophile and have spent many years in England and outside France. As well, my late great-uncle was an Englishman, and it is to him that I owe a debt of gratitude as he bequeathed me Alcestor Court upon his death." The house loomed in the background, rising up from the parkland below. Classical in style, with a large portico and strong vertical lines on the exterior, it was built of pink sandstone and gray granite.

"Will Miss Barry be joining us?" Rushford heard Rowena ask.

Sebastian and the other guest, familiar to Rushford as Lord Braemore, laughed heartily. "Miss Barry won't see noon, I shouldn't think," he said. "Besides which, she is not an equestrienne."

"Hers is a sport of a different kind," Sebastian added drily, gathering up his reins in his gloved hands. "This evening's diversions are more to her liking." He turned to Rushford. "Good morning, my lord."

Rushford nodded briefly, irritated by the Frenchman and his proximity to Rowena and even more so by the emotions she engendered. Lust and passion and protectiveness—that was all, he had convinced himself. The last thing he wanted to do was understand her or know anything more about the workings of her soul, of her favorite pastimes, her politics, if she had any, her love of riding, or her fondness for poetry. He had thought, mistakenly, that taking her to his bed once more would banish such inclinations and reveal the origins of his responses for what they were, pure physical desire for a beautiful young woman who had appeared in his path at a difficult juncture in his life. Nothing more.

The huntsman blew for the start, and the dogs set off in a howling exuberant mass, the grooms encouraging them. The group of riders moved down the long drive. Rowena expertly positioned herself in the front, directly behind the hounds, as Rushford watched expectantly, not in the least surprised to discover that Rowena Woolcott was an aggressive and accomplished rider who was perfectly familiar with the sport. He drew alongside her mount, offering a brief nod of greeting.

"I realize I've already broken the first rule in daring to converse with the Baron without you," she said without preamble but with a sideways glance and a hint of challenge. Clearly, the prospect of physical exertion agreed with her. The statement was delivered in dulcet tones above the baying of the hounds.

"And you will break many more before the weekend is done," he said, and found himself smiling.

"I never promised to be biddable, except of course, for the benefit of Miss Barry," she admitted with a smile of her own. "And for now, I'd like to forget about all this skullduggery and focus on the hunt, on the thrill of moving and galloping through the forest on this fine specimen." She leaned forward to give her horse a firm pat.

"We can't let down our guard."

"The first rule of skullduggery, I suppose," she said, urging her horse into a trot and forcing Rushford to keep up.

"Remember, someone wants you dead." His exclamation was low but nonetheless forceful. He did not want to add that she had been abducted when riding on the grounds of Montfort.

"But not right now," she continued as if she hadn't heard him. "They know me as Miss Frances Warren. I think it's best not to have these conversations in public. Besides, I wish to have a little sport and some amusement for a change."

As though he needed reminding how young she was. And how vulnerable.

"You know I'm correct, at least for the moment," she said.

"Nothing can happen when we're in this melee," she added, gesturing with a gloved hand to the riders and hounds around them.

"Miss Warren, I wish I could share your optimism," he said, falling back as they reached a gate leading to a covert. The dogs surged forward, and the riders followed more slowly. Rushford hung behind, allowing Rowena to move ahead, his objective to keep an eye on her at every moment. He watched her perfect posture, her easy seat, as her head snapped up at the huntsman's horn, searching the pack. The horn blew again, and the dogs tore across the meadow toward the fox, which had broken away.

The entire group surged forward, breaking out of the trees, hooves pounding the soft ground. A long slope of meadow lay ahead, and Rowena abruptly pulled her mount aside as the riders pushed past. She was sensible enough to wait for him, he noted with some small satisfaction. She was unaware that he was as intrepid an equestrien as she was. He arrowed toward her, but she had already charged ahead of him toward a thicket hedge at least six feet in height. Before he could register Rowena's intention, he watched her gather her horse together for a jump.

Rushford realized she was physically daring, maddeningly courageous, but he hadn't expected this. The jump was impossible, a reckless and wild gambit. He had no time to respond except to collect his own mount, adjust his stride, and then sail through the air after Rowena Woolcott. He had barely landed on the other side of the hedge, his horse narrowly avoiding a wide trench, when he was forced to urge the animal forward. Because Rowena was racing ahead of him again, across a rolling pasture, the thrill of the hunt clearly heating her blood.

Rushford gave full rein to his mount, arcing over another hedge until he was alongside Rowena, who was totally oblivious to his presence, aware only of the sounds of the huntsman's horns and the pounding hooves filling her ears. Bending low over the neck of her mount, she was focused on the fox, a reddish-brown streak that had gone to ground. Together they pounded behind the hounds and into the bracken, the rest of the riders left behind.

Rowena collected the reins and slowed to a canter, watching the hounds lose the scent and scatter in all directions. She was panting slightly, but her tone was jubilant. "That was incredible. A wonderful run. I've never enjoyed anything more," she confessed. The feathers in her hat were slightly wilted, and her face had taken on a pink cast. "I'm almost happy we lost the fox." She wrinkled her nose. "I'd prefer not to run him down."

Rushford didn't know whether to haul her from her mount and take her back to Alcestor Court or revel in her unwise exuberance. "You could have broken your neck," he declared instead.

The sounds of their breathing sawed the air, the only other sound the hum of crickets. "I am an accomplished rider, Rushford," she said, tilting her chin. "I've ridden every day since I was five years of age. And that hedge we just jumped is nothing compared to what . . ."

"Hardly an excuse." He interrupted her. "We are here to keep you safe until we can find Faron and eliminate the threat to your family. Or have you forgotten?"

Stung, she stared at him uncomprehendingly. "What are you saying? That I would jeopardize Meredith and Julia for a moment of recklessness?"

"Yes," he said flatly.

"Then you know me less well than you think. Perhaps you were the one who found the jump daunting." It was a ridiculous assertion as she well realized. His mount was bigger and more powerful than hers.

They slowed to a trot. "You never contemplate the consequences of your actions, do you?" He wondered at the source of his anger, gathering the reins of his mount into his right hand.

"I won't disappoint you, Rushford. I shan't do anything reckless," she said, glaring at him and at the frustrated pack of hounds behind them. "And in the interim, I assume you will continue to see specters behind every bush." Then before he could respond, she turned her horse skillfully to the left and cantered off across the field, away from him. But she could not ignore the hooves following her, as he leaned low over his horse's neck, keeping pace until they both emerged onto a stretch of flat land. Rushford nudged his mount's flanks and the animal broke into an easy gallop.

They raced across a common, up a hill and down the other side. Perhaps because of his greater height, he saw the farmer and his shotgun in a copse of trees first. The man raised the muzzle of his rifle. Then a volley of shots ricocheted into the sky and Rowena's mount reared on its hind legs, the golden light of the sun silhouetting them. She struggled with the reins regaining her seat, experienced enough to know that the slightest mistake would be enough to throw her off balance and have her hurtling to the ground.

Although Rushford kept his eyes open, all he saw was Kate, her face on the pillow, whiter than was possible for living flesh, her eyes open, accusing him of not keeping her safe. In front of him, as though time had slowed to an agonizing crawl, Rowena fought to control her horse, and when he pulled himself out of the jaws of memory, he glimpsed something else by the copse of the trees. Rowena's mount was frantically dancing toward it.

Rushford's eyes had been trained to see what others missed. He knew it was useless to shout out, his roar would only panic the horse further. Then for a dizzying moment, Rowena was in the air, her mount collapsing to its knees in a heap, panting, reins hanging loosely from its neck. On the ground beside the roan, in a shallow ditch covered lightly with branches, Rowena landed in a sprawl, her hat flung several feet from her body, her rich auburn hair spread over the hard earth.

Rushford reined in his horse and threw himself from the saddle, dropping to his knees beside her. His hands loosened the emerald pin at her cravat to feel for her pulse. It was faint but steady beneath his fingertips. Beside them her mount struggled to rise to its feet, whinnying softly in distress.

At the sound, Rowena's eyes flew open, her lips slightly parted as she attempted to sit up. "Is he all right?" she croaked, her unfocused eyes looking up into the flawless sky.

"Don't move," Rushford said. Casting a quick assessing glance over her body, Rushford rose from his knees to go to the horse, running his hands down the length of its strong legs, testing for lameness. "All is well, it seems," he said after a time. His fingers traced the girth straps, grimacing at what he found.

"Thank God," she murmured as Rushford returned to her side. "I would never forgive myself otherwise."

He watched her carefully, silently, looking for injury and finding none. She struggled to sit up, her hand at the small of her back. "I don't know how I bloody well let that happen," he said with quiet ferocity. Rowena regarded him with a puzzled frown. "Do you understand now what I've been warning you about? Why I did not like the idea of your coming with me to Alcestor Court?" he asked tersely, gesturing to the ditch.

"I am posing as your mistress so that we might gain entrance to the Baron's circle. And that requires my being here by your side. Besides which," she continued, "this incident was an accident." She endeavored to rise to her feet, pushing his hands away. "Where is my hat? I must have it." She straightened her skirts and walked several unsteady feet before grabbing at the scrap of fabric and, with shaking fingers, pushing it back on her head.

"No accident," he said abruptly, rising. "I suspect that they know your true identity," he said, watching as she shoved the last tendrils of her hair under the hat, its plumage irredeemably crushed. "Someone just tried to kill you. Not Miss Frances Warren but Rowena Woolcott." He brushed at the grass on his knees.

She shook her head, wincing. "I've had worse falls. And I'm quite all right," she said. "The farmer simply could have been watching for poachers." She leaned against her horse to regain her equilibrium, stroking its quivering flanks, murmuring softly into its muzzle.

"You think so?" he asked, walking to her side to draw the horse's girth straps to her attention. "Deliberately cut," he said curtly. "You would have come off sooner or later, but the gunshot and trench were extra assurance."

Rowena's eyes widened in disbelief.

Rushford walked over to the shallow pit, no longer covered with bracken. "And if you're seeking further evidence, it's impossible to explain this away," he said brusquely, shoving the twigs and branches aside with a booted foot to expose a three-foot hollow into which Rowena's horse had stumbled. Rowena refused to look where he stood, her lips tightening, but she took a moment to run her hands along the girth straps, examining them closely while speaking soothingly to the horse. She pulled the saddle to the ground. Still ignoring Rushford, she looped an arm around the horse's neck and pulled herself on its bare back without assistance. "If you're at all concerned, I have ridden bareback many times. And as they say, if you come off, for whatever reason, get right back on," she said coolly, unwilling to allow shock to rob her of reason.

She had not broken her neck, but Rushford was ready to do it for her. He was equally angry at himself for acknowledging the strength emanating from this young woman sitting proudly astride the roan, her eyes already on the horizon. And there was something else. He felt himself responding to her wildness, and to the passion and fearlessness that drove her.

Unbidden, he remembered holding her in his arms over a year ago, stroking the damp hair from her forehead as she wept after one of her nightmares, her body rigid against the pain. She had clung to him, shivering in her fever-soaked nightgown, and he hadn't known how to comfort her except to hold her and infuse her with the warmth of his own body. When her weeping ceased and her eyes opened, he had gently rocked her, then kissed her eyes, her nose, her cheeks, and her mouth. She had slowly warmed beneath his touch and welcomed the heat of his body lying along hers, drawing strength from the passion and possession they shared.

Her reality, past and present, was grim. Standing in the fields of Alcestor Court, he pushed aside the memory, and in the next instant knew he would send Rowena back to London. He would contact Archer to ensure she would be protected. He pulled himself onto his mount, aware that Rowena had read his mind because there was no mistaking the stubborn glitter in her eyes. She would not leave Alcestor Court without a fight.

Their course took them across four fields, and Rowena was close at his heels throughout the ride. They took the longer route, through fields and over ponds and streams, the warm air streaming past them. Hooves crashed over the furrows of plowed fields, and they plunged through a copse, Rowena leaning low to her horse's neck to avoid branches whipping by them, her expression set and determined.

When they arrived back at the circular gravel drive of Alcestor Court, their mutually enforced silence continued. Rushford expected Rowena to exhibit fatigue or at least the aftereffects of shock. But she did neither. Instead, she swung down from her mount without assistance. Rushford's sharp eyes noticed that she wavered for a second before her feet touched solid ground and that she held her shoulders straight with effort. He dismounted and watched as the groom led both their mounts away, then put a hand lightly under Rowena's elbow as they climbed the steps to the open front door. The atrium was deserted, the riders still at the hunt and the rest of the guests still abed.

Rowena had no chance to turn him away at her rooms. He opened the door and thrust her inside, regarding her unsmilingly. His hands immediately went to the row of buttons on the bodice of her riding habit. In leisurely but determined fashion, he undid them one by one. Rowena stood motionless under his purposeful hands, and he could feel his blood pounding in time with his rising anger. He didn't know if it was rage, lust, or just plain relief at having her safe and alone in his arms.

Lifting her wrists, he unfastened the tiny ivory buttons before parting and pulling the bodice from her arms. He tossed the garment aside and stood looking at her, bared to the waist in the morning light, her corset and chemise a pale foil against the satin of her skin. She said nothing but endured his intense scrutiny, her response only to begin loosening the fastenings of her corset, parting the stiff fabric to let it slide to the floor.

Rushford needed no other inducements to take the swells of her breasts, covered in the finest lawn, in the palms of his hands, his thumb flicking the nipples, his eyes holding her before he lowered his head to tongue first one breast and then the other. Rowena caught her breath, folding her hands in the thickness of his hair, unwilling to break the spell of silence.

Rushford seized her waist and lifted her onto the bed before pulling off her riding boots and stockings in turn. He wondered if she realized that he was doing this for the last time, that he would send for Archer to meet his carriage with Rowena Woolcott as its lone passenger. *It was the last time.* And yet, he forced himself to go slow. As though they had every moment of the morning left to them, he deliberately unfastened the waistband of her skirt, lifting her off the bed again to push the garment from her hips. Finally, she lifted her arms like a child as he pulled the chemise from her torso.

Rushford felt her shiver, and he lowered her to the bed. She smiled into his eyes and said, "You seem to like carrying me around, Rushford." Her voice sounded strange after the intensity of their silence. Rushford looked down at her as she lay on the bed, open in her nakedness. He smiled in return. "Perhaps it's the only way I can ensure that you remain safe—in my arms." Or at least the illusion of safety, he wanted to add, but didn't.

"There is nowhere I would rather be," she said, and he wondered whether she realized the impact of the staggering honesty of her words.

He shrugged off his riding jacket and shirt and came down on the bed beside her. For the next few hours, they made love furiously, stingy with their words and generous with their passion, in a feeble attempt to hold the menace outside the bedchamber door at bay.

"I can't bear it. This is almost too much," Rowena managed to gasp at one point, her head falling back, the column of her throat arched. His fingers bit into her flesh as she convulsed around him. She fell forward with a moan, her forehead resting on his right shoulder, and he held her as his own orgasm slowly subsided.

She raised her head, still astride him, her lids heavy with spent passion. "Is it always like this?" she asked. It was precisely the question he didn't want to answer. "I have no way of knowing," she said with her usual brutal honesty.

Rushford did. The other women he'd known, and one in particular, did not readily jump to mind. How the bloody hell had that happened, he asked himself silently, running a finger over Rowena's lips. He hoped his expression was not as bewildered and open as hers.

"No," he said finally, unable to lie to her or to himself. "This is different."

Her dark red hair tumbled over her shoulders, and her long legs stretched astride him. "In what way?"

"Some things are difficult to describe." He lifted her off his lap, aware that his answer satisfied neither him nor her. "And we don't have the time at present to discuss why we happen to enjoy sexual congress as we do," he continued, no longer able to delay what was inevitable. She could not stay at Alcestor Court. "Even the Baron's guests might be shocked if they guessed how we've been spending the afternoon." He shook his head, taking in the sprawl of Rowena's naked limbs beside him, the unruly tangle of hair, her eyes soft with satisfaction. He watched as she gathered up her chemise and pantalets. "Particularly if the Baron believes that you have met with an accident."

"I refuse to run and hide," she said, her head emerging from a froth of silk.

"I'm sure running and hiding undermine your very principles," he said, leaning forward to begin closing the small buttons on the chemise. "However, that doesn't help us with the unpleasant reality facing both of us. And do not deny the facts. You saw the girth straps and trench as well as I did."

"All the more reason to stay. We are obviously getting closer to Faron, if your hypothesis is true."

"Consider this, then, Rowena," he said. "If my hypothesis is true and they wish you ill, they have probably discovered that you are not Miss Frances Warren."

Her expression remained surprisingly calm. She took the drawers from the bed and stood to slip them over her feet, raising her hips to pull them up. "I believe it is Sebastian who recognized me," she said tonelessly.

His chest tightened, and he didn't recognize the sensation until a moment later. Fear—for Rowena. "What makes you say that *now*?" he asked carefully. He tried to ignore how she lifted her right leg and slipped a lace-trimmed garter up to her thigh and then completed the same action with her left leg.

"His voice sounds familiar," she said.

"Familiar?"

"Similar to what I remember." A slant of her hair obscured her profile and expression. "What I recall from my nightmares about the abduction."

"Why did you not tell me earlier?" he asked, knowing her answer before she could respond. "Because you knew that your recognizing Sebastian would have been one more reason to rule against your coming to Alcestor Court." He paused deliberately. "That places Sebastian at the scene of your abduction."

Concentrating on lacing up her corset, she did not meet his eyes. "I can't be sure."

She crossed her arms over her chest, turning around to face him. "I don't relish your choice of words, Rushford. I was raised by my aunt to be an independent woman who definitely does not wish to be *ruled against*."

Rushford rose from the bed. "Even if your life is at stake? And the lives of your family?"

Rowena immediately stopped getting dressed, awash in a sudden rage. "How dare you imply once again that I don't put my family first, sir? When you, I warrant, are more concerned about your bloody stone tablet than anything else. You would prefer me to disappear from view for fear that I might put at risk whatever plan you have in place regarding the Rosetta Stone—"

"Hold off!" he ordered, his voice dangerously soft. "The Rosetta Stone is no business of yours, as I've told you a dozen times. You will only endanger yourself and your family further if you become embroiled in this situation."

"As though you know anything at all about loyalty, or love for that matter, Lord Rushford."

"I would be careful what you say, Rowena."

"I will say whatever I wish, sir," she interrupted, her complexion paling, her eyes dark blue pools. "You have absolutely no power over me. I shall do precisely as I wish."

Rushford seized her upper arms, and in reaction Rowena attempted to swing her palm against his cheek. Her hand hung an instant in the air before she spun away from him in horror. There was a lengthening silence as he looked away from her to gaze out the window. "This is all a mistake . . ." The rawness of the encounter left him drained. "I shall send for the carriage."

"I'm sorry," she said, her voice shaking. "I don't know how we arrived at this juncture." The words between them were ridiculously formal.

"I wish you to return to London."

"I refuse." The silence elongated, grew heavy; then Rushford turned, shrugging on his riding breeches and shirt, and left the bedchamber, closing the door decisively behind him.

It was late and the dinner party in full play when Rowena finally presented herself, without Rushford on her arm, in the dining room. She did not know precisely what awaited her, and she dreaded it, along with the blaze of lights and music. Immediately, the dozen guests turned their heads to mark her entrance. Baron Sebastian's friends were perfumed and dressed in finery that glittered like jewels, all of them seemingly talking at once.

"You look divine, Miss Warren." Lord Braemore was the first to speak, escorting her to the table and to her seat. From the periphery of her vision, she noticed Sebastian assessing her presence without surprise. She had waited for Rushford to return to her rooms to collect her for dinner, rehearsing how she'd intended to approach him and sweep all his objections aside. She would not return to London, she decided, dressing carefully for the evening. She was armored in a delicate dress of pale crepe de chine, matched by long silk gloves, and her blond wig piled high and fixed in place with a diamond pin from one of the Rushford family store of jewels. Drained and shaken by their last encounter, she had proceeded through the movements of getting dressed with curious detachment and careful deliberation, waiting in her rooms for Rushford until the sun was setting and the maid had arrived to light the lamps. Deciding to linger no longer, she'd descended the grand staircase alone.

"You were positively magnificent today at the hunt," exclaimed Lord Cecil Braemore, taking the chair next to hers.

Miss Barry, resplendent in a glittering gown of gold brocade, concurred from across the table. "Positively Amazonian, from what I've heard," she said, her smile brittle. "Of course, I was still abed. I do so loathe the outdoors, I must confess," she added with a delicate shrug of her bared shoulders. "Thank goodness we have Miss Warren here to join the gentlemen in their exploits."

Rowena smiled and answered with a playfulness she didn't remotely feel. "I certainly enjoyed the fresh air and the opportunity to ride. You keep a wonderful stable, Baron," she said, bypassing the actress and directly addressing Sebastian down the length of the table.

As always, his attire was impeccable, the superfine fabric and exquisite tailoring of his waistcoat and dinner jacket the height of sophistication. His black hair was slicked back from his forehead, his eyes concerned. "How ever did we lose you and Lord Rushford during the run?" he asked. "As your host, I was quiet anxious, truth be told, my dear Miss Warren. I should not wish anything untoward to transpire over the course of these few days."

Cecil nodded energetically in agreement. "Lord no! We shouldn't want anything to befall you, my dear."

"Lord Rushford and I had quite an adventure," she said. The Baron's brows shot up. "Indeed?"

"A little mishap with the girth straps of my saddle. Nothing more," she demurred.

The Baron's frown deepened. "I shall have my groom look into the matter at once. This is inexcusable, and I offer you my heartfelt apologies, Miss Warren."

Lord Braemore patted her hand with relief. "Your experience as an equestrienne no doubt held you in good stead, Miss Warren. And at least you're back safely now in the bosom of Alcestor Court. Although such a shame that you missed the conclusion of the hunt. It was quite spirited."

A footman placed a heavy linen napkin on Rowena's lap. "To be entirely candid, Lord Braemore, I don't actually like to hunt."

The Baron's brows rose once again. "How can that be when you ride so superbly, my dear Miss Warren?"

"I have no desire to witness a bloody slaughter."

"That's simply nature you are recoiling from," the Baron

answered smoothly. "I shouldn't have thought you to be so timid."

"Hardly timid, sir, merely empathetic to an animal's plight."

"A tender heart, then," the Baron concluded.

"If you will."

"Speaking of which," Miss Barry interrupted with a flutter of a small hand, "where is that charming escort of yours, Miss Warren? Perhaps he has lost his appetite?" she inquired slyly.

Rowena did not reply, concentrating instead on the dish of quail placed before her. Conversation murmured around her, and she answered the occasional question directed to her mechanically and with as much false charm as she could muster. She looked about at all the rapacious faces around the table, her unease sharpening. Where was Rushford, she wondered, alarm blossoming like a bloodstain.

The Baron was explaining how he had come into possession of his country house in Dorset, his homes in France and Italy, and his peripatetic inclinations when it involved roaming the world. Soon after there were various remarks about retiring early, accompanied by sidelong glances and languidly exchanged looks. Her anxiety growing, she contemplated the last course of ices and petit fours placed in front of her. She was half listening to something that Lord Braemore was saying, her mind weighing the wisdom of forging ahead with Baron Sebastian—with or without Rushford. Planning ahead, unlike her prudent sister Julia, was clearly not her forte.

Rowena felt a hand on her shoulder. Turning, she saw Cecil's eyes burning into hers, fueled in good part by too much claret at dinner. All around them, chairs were being pulled back, and couples drifting from the hall to the salon beyond. Miss Barry had already exited, she noticed, as Braemore leaned in closer, the overwhelming scent of heavy cream sauce on his breath. "I was hoping perhaps," he began, bringing his face closer and lowering his voice for her ears alone, "that you might be in some ways tenderly disposed toward me, Miss Warren. Might a gentleman hope for the favor of an evening stroll through the grounds?"

Rowena knew well enough that it wasn't a stroll he had in mind. Night had already fallen, and she realized any stroll would take place upstairs in Cecil's bedchamber rather than on the dimly lit grounds. Yet this was the expected behavior of a mistress at a country house weekend, she thought, watching as Cecil put a finger to her chin and leaned forward to kiss her. Her stillness was all the encouragement he needed. He leaped upon her like a man at a feast, taking her face in his hands and kissing her crudely, allowing his fingers to wander the cleavage that had tantalized him from the moment she had entered the room. Stiffening in shock, with one part of her mind telling her this interlude was a necessity of the role she had taken on, she pushed him away. Her distaste trumped her good sense. She shot to her feet, the fine crepe de chine of her gown straining against Braemore's grip. "My apologies," she murmured, ready to tear from the room.

Before she could take a step, the Baron appeared at her side. "I believe Miss Warren requires a few moments to herself, Cecil," he said carefully as Braemore slowly released a handful of crumpled silk. "Shall we retire to the conservatory, my dear?" he asked, proffering his arm, and ignoring the other man's frustrated expression. Rowena had no desire to be alone with either man, but the look in the Baron's eyes, shocking as a flood of ice water, made her nod her head in assent.

When Rushford thought back on it, he should have been better prepared upon returning to his rooms. He had felt rather than seen the three men behind the door, and then very definitely registered their hands, firm and insistent, gripping his arms. Briefly, he thought of Rowena, waiting for him in the dining hall, but then he refused to think of her again.

"Do you know why you were invited to Alcestor Court?" one of the men asked. He was short but aggressive in his posture. Still, if his hands were not tied to a chair, Rushford could have taken him in the ring in under a minute. Pity he would never have the opportunity.

"Why don't you ask the Baron?" Rushford replied. One of the other men, weighing at least two hundred and fifty pounds, drew back his arm and smashed his fist into Rushford's sternum. Pain seared through his chest, and he felt the warm wetness of blood fill his mouth.

The shorter man smiled his approval and clapped a hand on Rushford's shoulder sympathetically.

"We have all night for this discussion, if you choose to be difficult, my lord. You will just simply miss the festivities below."

The next few minutes passed in a blur. The big man had once studied boxing, Rushford decided; he knew the location of the body's internal organs and how to target them with lethal force. The man who addressed Rushford introduced himself between the blows as Crompton. Crompton watched as the pugilist named Johnston performed his duties with detached interest, interspersing the volley of punches with the occasional question for Rushford.

"Are you here because of the Rosetta Stone?"

Rushford told him that he had no idea what they were talking about, that he had been invited to a country house for the weekend by the Baron for no other reason than to disport himself among his guests.

"With your mistress?" Crompton asked.

"With whomever the Baron decided to invite."

"Your mistress is not Miss Warren but rather Miss Woolcott, is she not?" The room spinning, Rushford replied that he had no idea what they were talking about. This time, Crompton held him while the other man punched him repeatedly in the stomach. The huge four-poster bed with its crimson canopy swam before Rushford's eyes. He was close to vomiting and on the verge of blacking out.

"It would be a shame to have Miss Woolcott share the same fate as the late Duchess of Taunton, would you not agree?" The voice was Crompton's, although it came from a great distance away as it filtered through the haze of Rushford's brain. He allowed the image of Rowena's face to dance momentarily in front of his mind's eye, his senses consumed by pain. A fist to his right ear rang in his head, accomplishing what he could not have done alone. It banished thoughts of Rowena.

"We are clearly losing our patience, my lord, with your disinclination to oblige us."

"Then perhaps try asking me questions that I can answer," he said, his voice still surprisingly strong. The pugilist raised his fist again, but Crompton held him back.

"What would you like to tell us about the Rosetta Stone?"

"It is where it always is—the British Museum."

"Then why are you here at Alcestor Court?"

Rushford closed his eyes, a tide of weakness tugging him into the shallows. "I already told you."

Crompton pursed his lips, a cupid's bow, incongruous with his stocky frame. "Very well then. How much do you care about Miss Woolcott? It perhaps doesn't truly signify, since you already have the blood of one innocent on your hands?"

Dimly, Rushford considered telling them what they wanted to hear. That he would allow them to steal the Stone but only if Rowena Woolcott and her family were left in peace. The insight gave him a strange confidence. The Baron would find an appealing symmetry to the idea, of having both the Woolcott dilemma and possession of the Rosetta Stone resolved with one elegant solution.

Crompton's voice droned on. "Despite your amazing resilience," he continued serenely, "our aim is not to dispatch you, my lord, although we easily could. Another body found floating in the Thames— You are known as a man who loves his drink and who is still lamenting the death of his former mistress, the Duchess of Taunton. No one would be overly surprised, I shouldn't think."

They would not kill him yet, Rushford knew. They would

leave him to his own devices for the time being, he predicted, to allow the chill of threat to permeate his already aching bones.

Crompton said, "I believe that Johnston here deserves a reprieve, Lord Rushford. Take some time to ponder your opportunities. And let's not forget how Miss Woolcott is spending her time at the moment—with the Baron. How fortunate for them both."

# Chapter 15

Rowena felt a curious mixture of despair and relief. Relief that she had the monster Faron in her sights and despair at the impossibility of escape. Despite his small, lean frame, Sebastian seemed to fill the conservatory. "You are looking disarmingly beautiful, Miss Warren, I must say."

His air was one of formality, and she followed his lead with a slight bow of her head. "Thank you," she murmured.

Sebastian looked about the gracious room, running his hands over the rich sheen of his waistcoat, as if wondering what to do with them. She noticed that he did not have his cigar case on his person.

"You are welcome to take your brandy and cigars, if you choose," she said. "It does not disturb me in the least."

"Most thoughtful of you. Shall we stroll, Miss Warren?" he asked, the timbre of his voice all too familiar. Rowena concentrated on steadying her breath.

"There are some wondrous species of orchid and lily that my gardener has taken great pains to cultivate," he continued. "And then we may converse at our leisure." When she didn't immediately respond, Sebastian asked, "Come now. Surely a sedate stroll is preferable to what is going on in some of the bedchambers at the moment, Miss Warren? Your virtue is safe with me, if that's your concern."

"Where is Lord Rushford?" she asked abruptly.

"I haven't the slightest idea. Perhaps he has taken up with Miss Barry, who, we all noticed, seemed particularly enamored of him. Don't look so downcast, my dear. You will hardly survive life as a courtesan if you do not inure yourself to such things. Is that not precisely why you've accompanied Lord Rushford this weekend? To round out your education, as it were?"

Rowena's throat felt blocked, but she squared her shoulders and said as carelessly as she could, "I am certain Lord Rushford will disport himself as he wishes while I welcome the opportunity of getting to know you better, Baron."

"How brave you are, my dear," he said. "Perhaps the prospect has you nervous."

"I have absolutely nothing to be nervous about, now have I? Lord Rushford looks after his own interests, as do I," she claimed, responding to the Baron's gestured invitation that they commence their walk around the periphery of the glass enclosure. The Baron began pointing out a species of lily discovered in South America, his meandering disquisition more nerve-racking than if he had pulled Faron like a rabbit out of a hat.

"You are so wise for one so very young," Sebastian said with mock admiration, pointing out the furrowed leaves of a vibrant yellow orchid. "Life is so much more pleasant when one is accepting of one's fate."

Rowena stared at the orchid, its color rich against the dark green foliage. "Such as the accident arranged for me earlier today?" she asked. Her anger must have shown as she lifted her eyes, for his own flashed unexpected fire.

"Whatever do you mean, Miss Warren? I trust you are not referring to the unfortunate incident that befell you earlier today. And I do so hope that you are not accusing your host . . ." he began with a halfhearted indignation that did not match the expression in his eyes.

"Clearly, I don't accept my fate," she interrupted. "And not for the first time, Baron Sebastian. Otherwise I might be found on the bottom of the Irthing River."

The Baron registered her words with an unblinking stare. "Never truer words spoken, *Miss Woolcott,*" he concurred, resting his hands in the pockets of his evening jacket. There was a moment's silence, and it seemed to Rowena that even the stars shining overhead through the glass conservatory dimmed. The sweet and heavy scent of the blossoms seemed suddenly overpowering.

"You abducted me from my home," she said finally, pausing significantly as if to let the words take on their full weight. "And left me for dead. You were there, were you not?"

The Baron's dark brows rose in surprise. "I didn't expect you to be quite so blunt, Miss Woolcott."

"I have nothing to lose."

"Except your aunt and sister," he finished deftly. "Faron is most displeased to discover that you are among the living. So it would stand to reason that he may set his sights on your aunt."

Rowena clenched her fists in her evening gloves. "Which I intend to forestall," she said heatedly.

"That remains to be seen."

She thought of her pistol, at home in Montfort, and imagined drilling a tidy hole in the Baron's forehead. But it was not to be. There was another moment's silence as she lowered her eyes so that he wouldn't see her thinking, or detect her anger. "Sebastian," she said softly, breaking the air of formality between them, "there must be some way we can reach an accommodation." When she dared to look up, she found his eyes, dark obsidian, upon her.

"What makes you say that?" he asked in a calculating tone, his head bent toward a giant calla lily, openly admiring its dusky color. "You have little with which to bargain." He turned to look at her, and she recognized then from the expression in his eyes what the price of accommodation would be. It sickened her, but in some way, it also hardened her resolve. Suddenly, only Meredith and Julia mattered, and she knew what she had to do, and realized that she had the strength to do it.

"Faron tried to kill me. As you did today. At his behest, I surmise."

"What do you remember of what transpired a year ago?"

"You were there. I remember your voice," she said. "Distinctly."

"That may well be," he mused. "I can't entirely account for my presence during that period."

Rowena flinched, suddenly cold in the thin silk of her gown. "You find the prospect of murder amusing?"

"Murder? You are standing before me today, my dear Miss Warren. Due entirely to Lord Rushford's timely intervention, upon both occasions," the Baron reminded, deliberately testing her. "I wonder how difficult it would be," he continued crisply, "to work against the man who has saved your life not once but twice."

"Are you inquiring about my loyalties, sir?"

"Of course, my dear," the Baron answered, suave as ever. "How else can I determine whether you would truly see fit to betray Rushford's confidence?"

"You are mad."

"Hardly, my dear Miss Warren. I am entirely rational in believing that you would give your loyalty to your aunt and sister before you would give it to the man who has taken you as his mistress."

Rowena quickly thought beyond the present, envisaging a future where life at Montfort would be as vibrant and full of promise as in the past. "I shall be honest," she said. "If I could, I would kill you here and now for what you and Faron have done and still intend to do."

The Baron smiled with satisfaction. "I shouldn't doubt it. You are an unusual young woman, and I value your truthfulness." He picked a wilted leaf, rolled it between his fingertips, and discarded it with the flick of a wrist. Patting his pockets, he produced his silver cigar case. "If you would permit me?" he asked again, the courteous host, extracting a thin cigar.

Rowena's mind worked quickly. If he wanted something in exchange, she would give it to him. "Let's dispense with civilities, Baron. I refuse to speak to you any further about my loyalties, divided or otherwise. I will resolve the situation regarding my family with Faron directly," she said stonily. "From you, I wish only to know of Faron's whereabouts."

He looked vaguely amused. "What you ask is difficult." He produced a match and lit his cigar. "You understand that Faron wishes you dead. I should not like to disappoint him—again."

"However, I may be worth more to you both alive. For the time being at least." Despite the humid warmth of the conservatory, she felt chilled in the thin crepe de chine gown.

His sleek brows rose. "My dear girl, what is it that you are offering? It must be of great value, please understand."

Rowena met his eyes evenly. "Anything I might have to pay."

The Baron smiled at her through a haze of smoke. "I have never needed to coerce a woman for her favors." A look passed between them that Rowena couldn't fully understand, but it had in it the raw light of truth. If he guessed her real intentions or feelings in that moment, he would let her know. He merely took another puff of his cigar and allowed his gaze to wander. "Women's bodies are abundantly available, a fact which at your tender age, you have yet to learn. However, you are beautiful and young and belong to Lord Rushford, for the moment at least. You need not tell me whether your arrangement is predicated on need or gratitude, my dear. Neither matters in the least. Regardless, despite my baser inclinations, I would say that your offer is not nearly enough to entice me to come to an agreement." He punctuated his statement with a keen look through a plume of smoke.

"I was not offering my person," she said, although she would have, she admitted to herself honestly. "What else do you wish from me?"

He stopped their perambulations abruptly, took one more

draw from his cigar, his eyes suddenly darker and alien. "You have become close to Rushford. I'm sure he could be persuaded to confide in you. If he has not done so already."

"About what precisely, Baron?" she asked, her voice surprisingly hard.

"Has he spoken at all of the Rosetta Stone?"

Rowena stared blankly. "Yes, the Rosetta Stone," continued the Baron, leaning against the wrought-iron table in the conservatory. "Surely, Lord Rushford has confided somewhat in you?"

Rowena thought quickly, aware that she should feign knowledge of Rushford's intentions regarding the Stone despite the fact that he had been reluctant from the first to reveal anything of substance to her. It was a form of leverage, of power that she had over Sebastian and Faron. Her story would be pure fabrication, if need be, and cause no harm to Rushford's plans, whatever they might entail. If it brought her closer to Faron, all the better. "Of course," she said with feigned confidence. "He explained how he foiled your plans to steal the Stone some time ago."

"Anything more?"

"Certainly," she said. "He mentioned that there were plans afoot to steal the relic once again and secret it out of England."

"My dear, you are playing coy, which will get you no closer to what you want."

Her mind grappled with plausible developments. "There are details, of course, to which I am not wholly privy," she continued, measuring out what she knew. "But I shall endeavor to bring more information to you as I uncover it."

"And I have your word?"

"Yes."

"Well your word means little to me," the Baron said abruptly. "I shall be honest with you. Should you refuse to be scrupulously honest with me, there is still your aunt, at Montfort—"

Rowena placed a gloved hand at her throat. "That is not

necessary. Entirely unnecessary," she said softly. "You have my word. But if any harm at all should befall her—"

The Baron chuckled. "And what could you possibly do?"

"Ensure that you never get your hands on the Stone," she said, her words as hard and clear as glass.

The Baron examined the tip of his cigar. "And what do you wish in return for your assistance, in addition to securing your aunt's safety?"

"To meet with Faron," she said clearly.

"He will no longer travel to England."

"I will go to him in France."

"An interesting proposition," Sebastian said, tilting his head to one side before releasing a stream of smoke. "Perhaps arrangements can be made."

"At the very least, tell me where he resides," she said, trying to keep desperation from her voice.

"I don't suppose it could do any harm. Claire de Lune outside Blois is heavily protected. You would not gain entry without Faron's assent. And who knows, he may at this point derive some kind of twisted pleasure out of meeting you in the flesh. Although, he would still see you dead."

*Claire de Lune, outside Blois.* Rowena held on to the nugget as though it were gold. She struggled to concoct something regarding the Rosetta Stone that would hold Sebastian's interest. He observed her carefully, leaning gracefully against the glass and wrought-iron skeleton of the conservatory. "I don't suppose he's told you," the Baron mused.

There was a change in tone and Rowena shivered, wishing she had brought her shawl from the dining room.

"I suppose he has never mentioned the Duchess at all."

The image of the beautiful portrait danced before Rowena's eyes. Now would be the worst time to examine her feelings too closely. "You are referring to Lord Rushford's former mistress."

"Indeed. I don't suppose he divulged how she died. Perhaps you should be apprised of the details as it may make a difference in how you perceive your divided loyalties—to him and to me."

"What do you mean?" she asked, endeavoring to keep the tremor from her voice.

"It may make the situation a trifle easier for you, my dear." Sebastian stared moodily at the stars overhead. "You see, theirs was a torrid affair, a *coup de foudre*, as we say in French. She was willing to sacrifice everything to be with Rushford, including her marriage to the Earl and her position in society, from which she would be forever outcast should a divorce have ever taken place." He paused as though shaking his head at the folly. "And yet, I am loathe to reveal, Rushford was more than willing to sacrifice his duchess in order to achieve his own ends."

Rowena listened wide eyed, her mouth dry.

"The Duchess of Taunton became involved in the Rosetta affair, to her peril when Rushford was given the choice to give up the Stone or forfeit the Duchess's life." The Baron shook his head with affected remorse. "Alas. He did not choose well." He held Rowena's gaze for a long moment. "Hardly the hero of the story, I am most sorry to say."

They had left Rushford manacled to a chair, which in turn was chained to the armoire by the window. Of course, it was all child's play, Rushford reflected in the moments after they had left him alone. There was little he had not experienced and survived. He was a man who had been beaten in the past, not only by those with everything to lose but also in the ring by men twice his size. And in the navy, captured by a Spanish galleon with a particularly sadistic captain, he had once been kept in a cell slightly bigger than a coffin for a fortnight on the island of Majorca. And there had been the days after Kate's passing when he'd wished he was dead, and he'd been left to explore his own vulnerabilities and guilt so intimately that he knew precisely what he could tolerate and when he would break. As Crompton had discovered, he had a high threshold for pain and feared physical torment far less than what they could do to his mind.

Rowena, he thought. *They will try to use Rowena against me.* The only time he'd been vulnerable in his life was with Kate, and now they knew he would do anything in his power to prevent the senseless death of another innocent. He gritted his teeth and strained once more at the chain connecting the cuffs securing his hands, although the effort was useless. Iron, he thought mordantly, attached to a heavy chair. He heard the door to the bedchamber open and saw the Baron, still in his evening clothes, step forward into the lamplight.

"Good evening, Lord Rushford." His voice was low and rich. "So disappointed that you failed to attend our lovely dinner this evening." He sauntered farther into the room.

"You were missed, of course, particularly by Miss Warren, whom you will be relieved to know, I took under my wing for a stroll throughout the conservatory. It is particularly lovely this time of year, what with all the lilies and orchids in blossom." The Baron paused deliberately. "I should really not wish for Crompton and Johnston to have to return," he said conversationally. "As you know, Johnston can be quite persuasive, and Crompton believes that questioning you into the night should help you reconsider your opportunities, or so he tells me."

"He's wrong." Rushford forced himself to speak.

The Baron nodded contemplatively. "I thought you might say that, alas."

Rushford's mouth was dry. "What's in this for you, Sebastian? Did Faron promise you another chateau or English castle or perhaps a packet of sovereigns?"

A flicker in Sebastian's eyes. Rushford had learned some time ago that turning the tables was part of the mastery of fighting back.

"We do not speak of Faron," the Baron said with regal hauteur. "And to answer your question, we simply require your cooperation, and I'm here to ask for it. I hope not to resort to threats."

"Although beatings are permissible."

Sebastian shrugged. "Your choice. If you indicate that you are ready to be more amenable, Lord Rushford, I'd like you to pick up the pace. In the interests of civility, let us not delay. What do you intend to do about the Rosetta Stone?"

Rushford half rose from his seat, the violent movement instinctive. The two men stared at each other, and neither budged save for the faint tremor of Sebastian's hands.

Rushford sat back down. "I intend to do nothing."

"Nonsense," the Baron tossed off, his eye on the chains around Rushford's wrists and the heavy chair upon which he was seated. "Pure, unadulterated nonsense," he added succinctly.

Rushford's eyes flicked toward his. "I suggest that you will discover your efforts are futile."

Sebastian shook his head. "All for nothing? Hardly. That would be most unfortunate as I should be forced to bring Miss Warren into the mix. Or should I refer to her as Miss Woolcott? Once again, your decision."

Rushford stared at him, anger rising in his throat. "Do not fuck with me, Sebastian," he warned.

"I have little choice," he returned genially. "And I'm afraid the fate of Miss Woolcott just may hang in the balance should you refuse to offer your assistance in the matter of the Rosetta Stone. Such a shame, given the situation with the late Duchess . . ."

Rushford tensed his shoulders against the chair. "When I am free," he said, "I will kill you, Sebastian. With my bare hands. Nobody uses Rowena Woolcott to get to me."

"But Lord Rushford," the Baron reminded him gently, "we already have. From the very beginning." There was a pregnant silence as Rushford strained against his manacles, all the hatred and guilt of the past two years blazing in his eyes. "I have just finished speaking with Miss Woolcott, who is ready to betray you for whatever it is that she wants. Her family's safety—I believe it is. The Duchess of Taunton, Felicity Clarence, Galveston, and now the Woolcott girl. It really is mysterious, how a man of your experience could be deluded not just once but several times."

A thick miasma filled the room.

"You appear somewhat discomfited, Lord Rushford. I have heard it said that you have a fierce temper."

With sudden violence, Rushford thrust himself out of his chair, the chain attached to the armoire breaking loose with a bone-crunching sound. "Deluded," he spat out, his manacled hands clanking against the chair. Sebastian retreated a step but not soon enough. With his fingertips, Rushford lifted the edge of his seat and hurled the back of the chair, legs first, at the Baron. It struck once, and though Sebastian stepped instinctively backward, one of the legs caught his cheek, the cut instantly welling with blood.

"Johnston," the Baron called calmly, pulling a handkerchief from his vest pocket, "it would seem that Lord Rushford requires extra inducements to convince him to oblige us." The large man appeared almost immediately, his heft invading the room. He attempted to push Rushford back in his seat. Instead he found himself kneed in the groin, pushed to the ground with one of the chair's legs and his pistol taken from his waistband.

Rushford's breaths came evenly. "Now let's review our options again," he said calmly as he aimed the pistol with both hands steadily at Sebastian, its blunt nose pointing through the legs of the chair. "Beginning with these manacles, shall we?"

Still holding the handkerchief to his cheek, Sebastian smiled nastily. "How prescient of you, my lord. We no longer need the manacles, nor as you shall soon see, do you need use of the pistol. You will quickly understand the wisdom of assisting us in our endeavors. As a matter of fact, the decision will be all yours—when it comes to Rowena Woolcott and her dear aunt. You could have left her to die in the Irthing and gone after Faron. But you didn't. And now you're together again after all these months. Whether or not you believe it to be true, you care for the girl, Lord Rushford." He dabbed the handkerchief against his cheek before calling for Crompton. "The keys, if you will. Lord Rushford is prepared to be obliging. I shall predict that he has had a change of heart."

Rowena awoke to a dimly lit room. Her sleep had been so heavy that for minutes she couldn't move her limbs although something told her she was not alone. Finally she was able to turn her head and open her eyes.

Rushford was sitting at the end of the bed, a glass of brandy in his hand, watching her with a granite expression. Everything rushed back to her in a dizzying flood of panic. She sat up in bed. It was then she noticed the shadows beneath his eyes, the bruise on his jaw, and the blood on his torn cravat.

"What happened? You're hurt," she began. She had never seen him this way. He appeared more of a stranger than the first night she had met him in his bedchamber on Belgravia Square, and as unreachable as the farthest shore.

Rushford interrupted with a wave of his hand. "That's the last of our worries, Rowena." His next words were soft, freighted with lethal menace. "What did you agree to tonight? And by God, don't lie."

There was a beat of silence. Where had he been? With the Baron as well? "You don't understand," she began, her thoughts disorganized. "Let me explain."

"No explanations. I asked what you agreed to tonight. With Sebastian." The tone of his voice was ugly.

She became immediately defensive. "I divulged nothing to Sebastian. I have nothing to divulge because you have told me nothing," she said, panic making her ramble.

"And that was a damned good decision on my part. Because you wanted to." He stood up in one swift, angry movement, the glass falling from his hands and breaking on the floor.

Feeling vulnerable, Rowena slid to the edge of the bed, looking for her wrap, watching as he advanced upon her. With one desperate and silent plea, she swung her legs to the floor, avoiding the shards of glass, and stood up. The room was dark save for a slit of light emanating from behind the closed door to the hallway. With shaking hands, she lit the lamp by the bed.

"Let me explain," she began again, turning her profile away from the light. "I only promised to tell him what I learned in exchange for access to Faron. And protection for Meredith."

"About the Rosetta Stone."

"About which I know nothing," she said, exasperation in her voice and posture. She rubbed her hands against her bare arms. "In exchange, Sebastian revealed where Faron resides, knowledge which surely is of help to you."

Rushford laughed, the sound bleak. "I already know where to find Faron, you little fool," he said.

"And yet you didn't tell me?" she demanded. "Now who is betraying whom?"

"So you could go rushing off to France with some wild notion and be killed?"

"Why did you not tell me?" she continued, ice in her veins. "I believed we were working together, if for different purposes, against Faron."

He stood over her, his face a mask of fury, his eyes deadly. The bruise on the side of his jaw was purpling, and in the candlelight, she could now see a rip in his shirt, the collar smudged with smears of blood.

"What happened to you?" she asked again, her head spinning, and she was suddenly more frightened than she had ever been in her life. Even more, if possible, than during the lost days of her abduction. "You do not look well. You don't look like the man I know."

"I'm far from well, Rowena," he said with the same soft savagery. "And you don't know me. What did you promise to do? Seduce me—in exchange for information about the Stone?"

Rowena stood up slowly as the words tumbled in desperate explanation from her lips. "Of course I would not tell the Baron anything of value. I would merely mislead him but allow him to think that he . . . And in exchange he would guarantee Meredith's safety."

Rushford's face was gray in the dim lamplight, his eyes dark in his face. "You once told me you would do anything to protect your family, and I clearly didn't listen," he said in a voice devoid of emotion. "And yet you dared wonder why I was reluctant to reveal matters relating to the Stone."

"No!" Rowena shook her head vigorously. "Never! How can you believe I would ally myself with a man like Faron?" His eyes blazed with a ruthless rage, and she suddenly knew why. She felt as though her heart was breaking. "Why do you not believe me, after everything that has happened between us?" She regretted the words the instant they left her mouth.

Rushford stepped back from her, a bitter hostility in his eyes, but he was once again in control of himself. He said nothing. Rowena swallowed. "You cannot tell me that what we have shared means nothing to you. Or that it means nothing to me."

"You used me," he said finally. "Or you were prepared to, if you only knew how. And if you could."

Rowena gazed down at the floor, at the broken glass, looking for words of defense. He spoke only the truth. "Yes," she said in a low voice. "You're entitled to that interpretation, I will concede, but I never led you to believe otherwise. I have always said openly that I would do anything to protect those I love."

"Including betraying me."

She looked up, meeting his eyes, seeing the bitterness there. "No, not betrayal," she said desperately. "I would never betray you after all you have done for me. And yet, I don't understand what happened tonight and what's changed." She searched his face, seeking answers. "You spoke with the Baron."

"I did. And we came to an agreement."

"About which you will refuse to tell me."

"Correct," he said darkly. "I thought I was protecting you by keeping you from learning things that might prove a danger to you. Instead, I discovered tonight that by doing so I ended up protecting myself."

Rowena struggled with the grim picture he was presenting. "You have your loyalties, as do I. Yours are to your country—" She paused with difficulty. "And to the Duchess. And yet what happened with her, between the two of you," she said softly, carefully. "A woman whom everyone says you loved to distraction—" she could not continue, reluctant to put into words what she had learned from the Baron. Suddenly she understood that she had been fooling herself not only for the past three days but also for the past year, lulled into believing that the man who had fished her from the river cared for her. His feelings for her were but a pale imitation of his love for the Duchess. The memories flooded back, and she turned her head aside, reaching for her robe, not wishing him to see her pain.

Rushford said flatly, "She was murdered. By Faron's men. Drowned."

Rowena took a deep breath, forcing herself to look at him and confront her own truth. Yet another drowning, and this one Rushford could have prevented. So much made sense now. She laid a hand on his arm, immediately feeling the muscles strain beneath her fingers. "You loved her very much," she stated quietly, her own instincts urging her on. "And yet not enough."

"I don't want to talk about it. Not to you. Not to anyone."

Yet he had betrayed the woman who had seemingly meant everything to him, given up the woman he loved most in the world. For what? There was something in the darkness that he would not permit her to see. "You are allowing the past to color your future, Rushford," she said. "You refuse to believe me when I say that I would not betray you—a man who saved my life. But you can't make proper sense of this situation because you are still in mourning. I can sense it," she persisted. And something else. Something worse. She took a step closer and placed her arms around his shoulders. Brushing the bruise on his chin softly, she watched as he closed his eyes as if to hide the truth in them. She wanted to gather him into her arms, hold him against her body, allow him to weep for his duchess and the love they'd had. The love that he had betrayed.

He did not push her away, and they stood like that for what seemed a moment and an eternity. "What do we do now?" she asked finally, feeling as though she had aged a decade in the short time they had known one another.

He opened his eyes and deliberately removed her arms from his shoulders. "We go on. You get what you want and I get what I want." He did not have to say that there was no use in hiding behind subterfuge, because it would be of little use. He would be cutting her from his life like a cancer from his flesh. "You will remain safely at the Knightsbridge apartments," he said, "until I decide otherwise. And when I tell you what you need to say to Sebastian, you will do it. Understood?"

"I will not betray Meredith or Julia." Somehow she had to bring Rushford back. "You would not force me?" Rowena looked into his eyes and saw her own reflection in the flat gray. There was something in the depths that she didn't want to read, something that sent renewed chills over her skin.

"Don't even ask what I am prepared to do," he said.

# Chapter 16

Lord Rushford stood in his shirtsleeves by the windows of his study on Belgravia Square, looking out into a late spring night made miserable by the rain that lashed at the glass. London rain was as predictable as the world spinning on its axis, but this storm seemed to be gaining strength, the pellets of water beating against the drains and bouncing off the walkways in the street below.

The stormy weather matched his mood. Still staring out the window, he pulled the stopper from a decanter of brandy by his side and turned to pour a glass. The spirits, he knew, would do nothing to wash away his anger and guilt. At least the path he had to take was now clear. He tossed back half the brandy, savoring the slow burn down his throat.

He had not seen Rowena in the five days since they'd returned in stony silence from Alcestor Court. What he'd learned from Sebastian had shaken him to his core, even though, tonight, he simply ached for her. She was young and she was inexperienced in the games that men like Faron and Sebastian played—yet that would not have stopped her from betraying him if she could have worked the treachery in her favor. The knowledge hurt far more than it should. At least he knew. Bloody hell, he'd seen that expression before. But he had never expected it from Rowena Woolcott.

He thought back to the night at the edge of the river over a year ago now. How he had hit the water like a knife, swimming toward the small form, a silvery shimmer in the current of the river. Impenetrable blackness, a dark, great void, and long timeless moments passed as he propelled his arms and legs in the water, coming up for air and then going deeper. He kicked out hard with his legs, going as long and hard as his breath wood allow, the current threatening to suck him under. His lungs were about to burst, his muscles screaming against the heaviness of the current, when he surfaced again, breathed and looked up for the fourth time. Then he saw her, a faraway stain of silver floating on the surface, almost indistinguishable in the river's undulations. With strong, certain strokes, his objective in his sights, he swam toward her. Rowena's skirts billowed around her like an umbrella, her hair like seaweed in the water. He positioned an arm beneath her head, turning her body upward, so that her eyes stared at him unseeingly. He drew her back against him and began stroking toward the shore, drawing her steadfastly in the direction of the rocks in what seemed an endless journey.

An endless journey—one that was to finish soon, he reminded himself, despite the currents that kept changing and threatening to pull him under. He looked at the raindrops trickling down the windowpane. Alcestor Court had actually made the choices clearer. Smashing the smug, patrician features of the Baron into a pulpy mess would have been highly satisfying, but he realized the benefits of self-restraint. Eliminating the Baron would have accomplished little when Faron was the prize. They believed he would do anything to protect Rowena Woolcott, and so he would feed the delusion with pleasure, including continuing the masquerade of keeping her as his mistress. It was expected, by Sebastian and his watchers. And so public appearances were necessary, at the theater, at Crockford's, even at damned Galveston's on the morrow, he thought acidly.

His bitterness ran deep, the thirst for revenge deeper still. Fleetingly, he saw Kate's face, the passionate brown eyes, the crooked, charming smile, the small, pointed chin. Then it faded away to be replaced by the dark blue eyes and full, mutinous mouth of Rowena Woolcott. He remembered the feel of his hands on her body, the assured touch of a lover who thought he knew the deepest recesses of his beloved's soul.

Cursing, he slammed down the glass and left his study. He needed air.

Thirty minutes later, the sweat and liniment laden air of the West London Boxing Club filled Rushford's lungs. He greeted curtly the odd acquaintance on his way in, nodded to the awaiting valet, and in short order had stripped down to his breeches and was laced into boxing gloves. It was not his regular day for a bout, but no matter, he would be sparring with Nat Langham, the son of poor framework knitters. Langham's trainer, the valet informed him, was looking to put Langham in a serious bout with George Gutteridge the following fortnight. Langham would welcome the practice, and he was already in the ring, shadowboxing with an imaginary opponent. The pugilist stood just under six feet and weighed eleven stone, and his left-handed punch, with his legs wide apart, could render his opponent blind. Langham's punch, Rushford knew, would be a downward left hook, the so-called pickax blow. It was exactly what he needed today, he thought philosophically, climbing into and facing his opponent in the ring, eyeing the brutish face, the tense muscular body.

The circling began slowly, both men narrow eyed, crouching, advancing in progressively smaller circles. No enmity existed between the two, just the tension of the sport. They mirrored each other, tracked each other's moves until, like a snake striking, Langham lunged and caught him with a strike to the abdomen, the air whistling between them.

Rushford was fresh and angry, and before all the breath left his lungs, he launched a blow upward with all his strength, the impact of his fist cracking his opponent's chin. A smaller man would have been felled, but the tree trunk of muscle merely grunted and stumbled, dancing drunkenly away from Rushford. Then he lunged back and his right hand slammed into Rushford's shoulder.

They both fell to the ground, but Rushford's legs were free. Drawing in a breath, he heaved his weight up, forcing all his strength through his legs. Images of Sebastian flickered before his eyes. Then images of Johnston delivering his steady, targeted blows while Rushford sat shackled to a chair. And Rowena, her face pale and steadfast, preparing herself to betray him.

A few men watched the fight from the wooden seats surrounding the ring, murmuring their approval, a series of incomprehensible words floating over the enclosure. But Rushford wasn't listening, hearing other phrases instead rebounding in his head. They would never stop, until he finally stopped Faron. And put his guilt to rest.

He bounced to his feet, and in utter silence, he and his opponent faced each other again. For a full minute, they shambled around one another, advancing, retreating, the one trying a short circular punch delivered with elbows bent, the other a mindless jab. A blissful rhythm to the dance continued until suddenly, the larger man came at Rushford with shuddering speed. Rushford jerked his head aside to protect himself and at the same time delivered a sharp jab to his opponent's solar plexus. Langham landed on his knees, his outstretched hands catching his own face. Rushford was breathing hard and fast, the pressure in his head mounting breath by breath, sweat dripping down his face, the salt stinging his eyes. The well-bred crowd stifled their excitement. The round was to be of three-minutes' duration, as by the rules, with one minute's time between rounds. The well-versed group also knew that if either man fell through weakness, he must get up unassisted within ten seconds. The count began in the stifled silence.

Rushford hung back, watching, as Langham wrenched his body into a sitting position with his last ounce of strength and then with a grunt, rose to his feet and hurled himself forward. Rushford threw himself into a sharp volley of jabs. Then Langham was hanging on the ropes in a helpless state, his toes off the ground. He was unable to acknowledge the rules or his defeat, but considered down after only one round.

Blood thundered in Rushford's ears as he claimed his victory and a measure of catharsis. He pulled the gloves from his hands and swept the sweat from his face. Extending a hand to help his opponent from the ropes, he then stepped outside the ring, oblivious to the hands clapping his shoulders or the towel thrust at him by Sir Richard Archer.

"I hear you didn't even warm up. Just went into the ring bloody cold as ice. Feel better now?" Archer asked, pulling him aside to one of the benches. He drew a small silver flask from his jacket, which Rushford accepted gratefully, taking several deep draughts of water.

"Not really," Rushford said, breathing deeply, mopping the sweat from his torso and returning the flask to Archer.

Unchastized, Archer smiled. "Personally, I didn't think you were doing all that well. Otherwise you might have finished more quickly. The poor sod—Langham acquitted himself bravely."

"Your pledge of confidence is always appreciated." He took in Archer's formal attire, the black breeches, and polished boots, with a jaundiced eye.

Archer's smile broadened. "So what are you feeling so hellish about that you need to take it out on someone in the ring? At least your pretty face didn't get battered, although that bruise I see on your jaw is surely not a souvenir from Langham. Looks too ugly for that." Archer paused. "The visit to Dorset with the Baron did not go well, I presume?"

"Yes and no."

"That answer doesn't help much, Rush," Archer said. "And by the way, I ran into Galveston the other day at White's, and he scurried away from me like the rodent he is."

Rushford grunted in appreciation. "We shall get to him in time, never fear. Justice will have its day."

"All this talk of justice—you are beginning to take on a reputation."

Grimacing, Rushford grabbed the flask and took another drink. "I'm as compromised as the devil himself," he said abruptly. He saw Archer's smile disappear, noted the instant sobering.

"And what of Miss Warren?"

"I'll get to her in a moment," Rushford said.

"I'm certain you will," Archer said after an infinitesimal pause while he took a closer look at his friend. "Never let them see your agony," he said enigmatically. "And by that I mean metaphorically and literally, both in the ring and outside."

"My mistake the first time around," Rushford said, thinking of Kate.

The brooding silence did nothing to help matters along. "And what of the Stone? You have decided upon a plan?" Archer asked in an attempt to turn the course of the conversation. "Of course there is one—I can see it in the steeliness of your eyes," he added with a dose of sarcasm. "I should say that I have your back at Whitehall, for which you owe me by the way. They know nothing of your involvement in this matter and have not questioned me as to my interest in the recent dispatches from France. Which, as you will recall, I shared with you last time we met."

"Much appreciated," Rushford said.

"You could at least show some gratitude," Archer grumbled.

"I thought I had."

"I was thinking more in the way of an all-night card game, copious amounts of brandy, or a visit to our old friend, Mrs. Cruikshank."

"Not in the mood, but you go ahead."

"It was a jest, Rush. Have you not regained a semblance of your old humor?"

"I have lost my train of thought."

"Doubtful. So what's the plan?"

"The situation is actually ideal," Rushford said abruptly, a score of possibilities racing through his mind.

"I'm relieved to hear it."

"Sebastian wants me to secure the Rosetta Stone on Faron's behalf."

They're mad, was Archer's first startled thought. "There's got to be more to it than that."

"They would use Miss Warren against me."

"Kate all over again," Archer said, wiping a hand down his face.

"You would think I'd have learned the first time."

*Forgive yourself, once and for all, damn it. The Duchess of Taunton is not worth it,* Archer wanted to say, but didn't. He saw the pain and guilt etched on his friend's face, the corrosiveness of regret that still worked through him, the stain as vivid and fresh as in the early days of his loss. "And what of Miss Warren?" Archer asked carefully, putting one booted foot up on the bench.

"It's a little more complicated than it looks," Rushford said, explaining in the briefest way possible Miss Warren's true identity and his involvement with her one year earlier.

Listening intently, Archer lifted his mouth in a small smile. "Explains why you were in such a dark mood this past spring. You went to great lengths to ensure Miss Woolcott's survival. Are you certain you don't care for this girl?"

"Don't be ridiculous, Archer. I can't afford to care. And worse still, I don't know how to care. I've proven that, haven't I? Although Miss Woolcott doesn't know what she's doing, they are using her as bait, in the same way they used Kate and Felicity Clarence, to capture my interest and ensure my collaboration. Well, this time it won't work."

"How so?"

"I intend to follow their directives to the letter—and deliver the Rosetta Stone into their hands. Right to Faron's door."

Archer knew his best friend better than that. His eyes

gleamed. "What do you have in mind?" he asked, his eyes alight with sharp intelligence.

"I'll tell you in a moment," Rushford said, tossing the linen towel aside. He looked around for his shirt, the sweat drying on his skin. "But I require your help."

Just as in the old days. Archer had questioned a fortnight ago whether his friend was ready to battle his demons, but tonight he believed that Rushford was coming back to life, and perhaps it had something to do with the young and beautiful Miss Woolcott. Time would tell. In the interim, Archer slapped his hand on his knee. "And have I ever refused?" he asked, "despite the fact that you're a taciturn, surly bastard? Of course I'll help."

The small bell on the door of Mrs. Heppelwhite's establishment chimed cheerily. She looked up from the bolt of sateen that an elderly tenant had recently offered in lieu of rent. It was of good quality, possibly Italian, the landlady speculated, squinting over her spectacles at the beautiful young woman entering her establishment on Holburn Street.

In terms of custom, she was hardly typical of what Mrs. Heppelwhite expected to see walking through the narrow door. Her hair was a thick burnished auburn, swept up under a small cloche hat, and her cloak was of the finest cream cashmere with ivory toggles, suitable for a glorious summer's day. The pure profile, the tilted dark blue eyes—

"Why, Miss Warren," she crowed, moving from behind her counter. "What an unexpected pleasure," she said, managing even a small curtsy.

Miss Warren held out a gloved hand, squeezing her former landlady's arm warmly. "So good of you to remember me, Mrs. Heppelwhite," she said, appearing every inch the lady, her beauty shimmering in the dusty modesty of the small shop. But there was a sadness in the dark blue of her eyes and in the softness of her generous mouth. Where she had once appeared as all but a girl, Miss Warren had been transformed into a woman. They exchanged brief pleasantries, about the weather, their health, and whether certain tenants were still in residence.

"Whatever can I do for you, Miss Warren?" Mrs. Heppelwhite asked at long last, her shrewdness never far from the surface. Her former tenant had done well for herself, clearly, in just several weeks, and it had everything to do with her protector, the landlady speculated. She recalled the day the carriage with its heavy crest had come to collect Miss Warren's valise and small chest, the coachman leaving behind a handsome draft that more than covered six months' rent. Miss Warren had not appeared since.

The young lady appeared nonplussed for the moment, casting about the shop to ensure they were alone before delving into her tasseled reticule to extract a small tissue-wrapped package. A sparkling ruby hair pin emerged from the nest of paper, which Miss Warren placed carefully on the counter between them. "I did not quite know to whom to turn, Mrs. Heppelwhite, and then I thought of you. Of your honesty and kindness toward me when I needed it most."

The landlady demurred, making the appropriate noises, pushing her spectacles up her nose to take a closer look at the pin. Those were rubies, she decided quickly, and sapphires, as dark a blue as Miss Warren's eyes. "It is lovely, my dear, but how can I help?" she asked, feigning ignorance. It was not the first time a young and beautiful woman had brought a piece of jewelry for barter to her establishment. But Miss Warren was different, somewhat more genteel, her protector an obvious disappointment to her and responsible for the sadness in her eyes and the resolute set of her mouth. A series of images popped through Mrs. Heppelwhite's mind, one more heartbreaking than the next.

"I should like to exchange the pin for something of value, Mrs. Heppelwhite, and I thought you might be able to help me."

"Of course, my dear, I should be more than pleased to assist you in any way I can," she said, realizing even with her inexpert eye that the piece was worth far more than Miss Warren would ever get for it. But such was life that others would often exploit tragedy for their own good. "And what would you be needing, my dear, if I might ask?"

Miss Warren paused, looking about the shop again, playing with the tassels on her reticule before replying. "I should like to buy a revolver with the proceeds."

Mrs. Heppelwhite placed a hand to her mouth in shock. "A revolver? Oh, my dear Miss Warren. I do so hope that nothing is amiss." It had taken little more than a fortnight for the blush to leave the rose. Scrutinizing the elegant young woman poised on the other side of her counter, the landlady conjured a myriad of scenarios.

"If your gentleman," she began delicately, "is in any way reluctant to protect you or, heaven forbid, presenting himself as a threat . . . well, my dear, you are always welcome to return to Holburn Street."

Miss Warren shook her head, her eyes casting about the counter. "All is well, Mrs. Heppelwhite, but I should not wish to burden you with my situation. I believe that you do, however, come into possession of such things from time to time." She stared pointedly at a canister of walking sticks in the far corner.

The landlady fidgeted for a moment, hesitating. "You are quite right in your assumption, my dear. A former resident did have in her possession a small pistol, if I could only remember where it is and if, indeed, it is in working condition. It appeared to be more of a keepsake than anything else. Although if truth be told, I do not know much about these things."

"If it is not too much bother, I can take a quick look, Mrs. Heppelwhite, and ascertain whether the device is in good working order." When the older woman raised her brows in astonishment, Rowena added, "I grew up in the countryside, and our overseer, Mr. Mclean, was keen to teach me the fun-

damentals of such things. I do have a small talent in that regard."

"I hesitate to interfere, my dear, and if you feel as though
you need the personal protection . . ."

"I do," Rowena said firmly, her gaze unwavering. Mrs.
Heppelwhite required no further prodding and disappeared
to the small storeroom in the back of the shop. The groan of
drawers opening and closing was followed by scraping
sounds and then the shuffle of feet as she returned to the
counter. Gingerly, as though holding a rodent, she placed a
small box on the counter.

Rowena confidently picked up the pistol, opened its chamber deftly, and nodded. "It even has shells. Perfect," she murmured. "A good oiling should set things to rights."

Mrs. Heppelwhite was struck mute for a moment. Rowena
continued. "However, you understand, I shall soon be in the
position to buy the pin back from you, as it isn't mine but
only borrowed from my gentleman friend," she explained.
Instead of placing the pistol back in its box, she put it into
her reticule.

Mrs. Heppelwhite shook her head, removing her spectacles to look directly at Miss Warren. "Nonsense, dear child.
You earned this pin. Do not tell me differently, so it is yours
to do with as you wish."

"I shall buy it back in good time," she insisted, "if you
would be so kind as to keep it here for me."

"If you wish," she said reluctantly. "Although I do hope
all is well." The landlady wrapped the pin back in its cocoon.

"It is, indeed," Rowena lied, patting the worn hands
folded on the counter between them. She looked around the
shop one more time with something akin to nostalgia, her
eyes on the bolts of fabric piled in a corner and on the clutch
of umbrellas by the entranceway. "I shall return in a few
weeks' time at the most, Mrs. Heppelwhite," she said. "No
need to escort me out. I know how busy you always are."

"Do take care, Miss Warren," Mrs. Heppelwhite called after her, worry in her voice.

The chime rang rustily as Rowena pulled open the door, her skirt sweeping up a swirl of dust from the floor as she smiled over her shoulder at Mrs. Heppelwhite. The older woman raised a hand in salute, her apple-cheeked face wreathed in concern.

Once out on Holburn Street, Rowena quickly secured a hansom cab and asked to be taken to the northwest corner of St. James's Square and to the London Library, occupying the first floor of the Tavellers Club in Pall Mall. Meredith would surely have taken them to the great lending institution, founded by Thomas Carlyle only one year earlier. Thanks to his vision, subscribers enjoyed the wealth of a great national library. Hurrying through the heavy front doors of the building, Rowena refused to think about the collection of books at Montfort or the last time she, Meredith, and Julia had spent an afternoon in the stillness of the library there.

Paying her subscription at the front desk, she sped through to the second floor, murmuring her request to the librarian who, in short order, appeared with several books. Rowena needed something with which to entice Sebastian in her role of Sheherezade, spinning her tales to keep the Frenchman not so much amused but convinced that she had Rushford securely in the palm of her hand.

Which was as far from the truth as could be, but nothing she could think about at present without bursting into tears. And she never cried. Sitting down at a desk piled high with tomes, she closed her eyes, seeing Rushford's face in the red glow behind her eyelids. She could hear his voice, low and accusing, ruthlessly sweeping aside the powerful emotions that had burgeoned between them. He had saved her life. He had promised to help her. He had made love to her over and over again. All of which did not matter, in the end. She still knew that her loyalties lay first and foremost with the family she had vowed to protect.

Forbidding, impatient, unforgiving, of others and most of all himself, Lord Rushford remained a cipher to her. She had always detected a distance in him, even during the most intimate moments of their physical union, as though he had the capability of absenting himself, looking down upon her with cool objectivity. The realization chilled her. Even more frightening, she still felt more bereft than angry, as if she'd been abandoned in the middle of making love.

She straightened, rolled her shoulders, and sorted through the books on the table before her. There were only two other seats occupied in the reading room, and the paneled walls and high ceilings echoed every breath, every turn of the page. She absorbed what she could, aware that Sebastian would already know the basics about the Stone, its import, its history, and its current state. She had been honest with Rushford on that wretched evening at Alcestor Court when she'd said she had no intention of divulging his true plans for the Stone, only fabrications that would have the Frenchman believe her to be of use in some capacity. *Anything that would result in her finding her way to Faron, and keeping Meredith outside his reach.* She thought of the revolver sitting in the recesses of her reticule. Bartering the pin—Rushford's pin—had sickened her. Yet, once she was back at Montfort, she would buy the jewel back from Mrs. Heppelwhite and return it in good order to Rushford.

She returned to the books in front of her. Her fingers traced a map of France, the Loire region, the town of Blois marked in spidery red ink. The fastest route would be from Calais, she calculated. She closed the atlas and replaced it with a heavy tome, the vellum pages rich with drawings and detail regarding Egyptian artifacts. Her eyes skimmed the paragraphs, until a name jumped out at her. Jean-Francois Champollion, she read, a French classical scholar and orientalist who also had deciphered the Egyptian hieroglyphs in 1822, demonstrating that the Egyptian writing system was a combination of phonetic and ideographc signs. Now deceased, he had spent most of his life as Professor of Egyptology at the

College de France. Rowena rummaged through her memory, recalling that Rushford had told her that Montagu Faron was a scientist of sorts, a collector of ancient artifacts and scientific knowledge. She closed the books in front of her.

In her bedchamber later that evening, Rowena's mind continued working feverishly while she prepared for an entertainment that Rushford had insisted they attend. His brief note had been waiting for her on a pewter salver upon her return from St. James's. The Baron would be present, she suspected, and worse still, she would have to pretend that all was well with Rushford despite the grimness of their present relations. She never believed a heart could hurt, but hers did, leaden with disillusionment and anger at herself.

Her thoughts remained incomplete, interrupted by a brief knock. She was startled to see Rushford entering the bedchamber, his dusty boots and wrinkled jacket testament to the fact that he had just returned from riding. The faint purpling of his jaw and granite expression were reminders of the stony ground upon which their relations had fallen since Alcestor Court.

"Leave us, please," he ordered the maid, who instantly dropped a curtsy and departed. Rushford closed the door and regarded Rowena with the flat, unemotional expression she was beginning to hate. "What I am going to tell you now will further our ends regarding Faron," he began with preamble. "You need not know the context—"

"I trust a simple greeting is not in the offing. Have we dispensed with all civility?"

He said tightly, "I don't believe in hypocrisy. And I'd hoped you felt the same."

"Of course," she said bitterly.

He continued. "Sebastian should hear of this without delay. He will understand the importance of the information immediately and will know how to convey it to the right ears with all due speed."

Rowena had turned on her dressing stool at his entrance and now stared at him, her fingers stilled in the act of securing a comb in her upswept hair. "I don't even know where we are going this evening," she protested, "although I assumed it had something to do with the Baron."

"To a small entertainment hosted by Sir Galveston," he answered shortly. In stunned silence, Rowena listened. "You will find the appropriate opportunity to tell Galveston that the Stone will be moved this Friday evening from the British Museum to a more secure setting after the museum's close."

"Is this true?"

"The less you know the better."

Her hands dropped to her sides, the rich silk of her evening dress rustling in the stillness. "If my aunt is in any way jeopardized by this ploy, I need to know. If you refuse to explain matters fully and I don't understand what you want of me, then I don't know if I can possibly help," she said. But she did understand—her purpose was to mislead the Baron—and Faron. She shook her head. "Of course Galveston is keen to do your bidding because he wishes to avoid persecution for the murder of Felicity Clarence." Her voice was sharper than she intended. "Do you like playing God, Rushford?"

Rushford ignored the barb. "I am asking you to do a simple thing, Rowena, one that will work in your favor. It's what the Baron is expecting of us. I will do what's necessary to protect you, and you will do what's necessary to protect your family."

"And I'm to know no more about it than that."

"Why so curious? It causes one to wonder."

Rowena closed her eyes against a sudden surge of anger as she saw the inexorable logic of his thought process. He trusted her so little . . . "Why not simply tell him yourself, then?"

"Because you've already agreed to serve as a conduit of information to the Baron in exchange for learning the whereabouts of Faron and protection for your aunt. I'm surprised that I have to remind you." His mouth curled cynically. "This evening you must reprise your role as my mistress and appear as though you have won my total confidence with your beauty and your wiles."

"As though the Baron would believe it of someone like you," she said wretchedly, watching a faint glimmer of anger in the flatness of his eyes. He had not weakened in the threat of losing the Duchess and he would certainly not weaken in the threat of harm to her family. Nothing worried Rowena more. "Once again, you underestimate not only me but also him, Rushford." She stared at the remaining comb in her hand without seeing it. She felt as if she were teetering on the edge of an abyss.

"We are the most cynical of men, Rowena, never forget. The Baron will believe what he wants to believe of me. He is working both of us. He expects me to relinquish the Rosetta Stone to him for several reasons, among them my disillusionment with Whitehall and my desire to rectify the past. From you, he merely expects confirmation that I am not deviating from the script." Rushford's countenance was impassive, and Rowena reached out blindly for the edge of the stool, holding on to it for balance.

"He would believe that you will do anything to protect me, after what happened . . ." *With the Duchess,* she wanted to add. "In other words, he believes that he has found your weakness. Guilt concerning your actions regarding—"

"Something like that," he interrupted.

Her throat closed against rising panic. "You may use me in your scheme, but please do not jeopardize the well-being of my aunt or my sister. I am warning you, Rushford."

He looked across at her and nodded. "I am forewarned then," he said.

"Do I mean nothing to you?" she asked with a surge of anger.

He replied with equal cruelty, "Nor I to you?"

\*   \*   \*

"Miss Warren is a beautiful woman," observed Sir Ambrose Galveston, leaning over a tray filled with fresh oysters proffered by a footman. In the background, a small orchestra played an aria by Bizet, the cheerful melody an ironic counterpart to his foul mood. Rushford, through Sir Richard Archer, had made his expectations clear, and if Galveston wished to curry the favor of London's court chief justice, he would readily comply.

"Indeed," the Baron agreed somewhat indifferently. "Although I confess I find a certain sophistication and finesse more to my taste."

"Such as our Miss Barry," Ambrose suggested with a heartiness he didn't feel. He popped an oyster in his mouth and made a show of enjoying it with relish. The small ballroom in the town house off Mayfair was a blur of candlelight, winking jewels, and sparkling laughter.

"I thought you would understand," Sebastian conceded, "given your relationship with the late Miss Clarence." He punctuated his sentence with a knowing laugh that grated on Galveston's already exposed nerves.

"But one must admit," Galveston commented, changing the subject hurriedly, "that the Miss Warrens of the world do serve a purpose." As did some actresses, he realized with great regret.

"All too true," the Baron said dryly, and Galveston dutifully laughed. They both kept Rushford and Miss Warren, behind a phalanx of potted palms, in their sights. The latter was resplendent in a shimmering emerald choker and cream silk, looking every inch the indulged mistress. "I'm sure that you are far from impervious to Miss Warren's flirtations," the Baron continued. "Why, I espied you earlier by the French doors in a little tête-à-tête."

"You have sharp eyes and even sharper ears, sir," Galveston said in an attempt at flattery, his own eyes darting around the ballroom to see whether they were being observed with any unusual interest. He had kept the guest list deliberately small, including only those in the demimondaine who would not be known to his wife or anyone else that mattered.

"And what did our Miss Warren have to say?" asked the Baron, smiling at an acquaintance who was trying to catch his attention.

Galveston gave a small bow in the direction of the mutual acquaintance before continuing, lowering his voice. "The object in question will be moved Friday evening."

Sebastian gave a small smile of satisfaction. "Anything more?"

Galveston's brow furrowed. "Yes, some palaver about a man named Champollion. Unfortunately, I did not know what to make of it."

"I'm not surprised," the Baron said, watching Rushford take a glass of champagne from a passing footman and offer it to Rowena Woolcott, who gave him a glittering smile in return. "That will be all this evening, Ambrose, and thank you so much for hosting this wonderful little soiree." He then bowed and excused himself, sauntering into the card room, confident that all was going according to plan.

Rushford sat back against the leather squabs of his coach, his arms folded across his chest, his mood forbidding. Something about the evening at Galveston's town house rankled, his ill humor exacerbated by the woman sitting across from him.

He had not touched Rowena Woolcott for over five days and yet his body still hummed with the memory of her, her scent lingering on his skin, her taste on his tongue. And he damned her for it. Her profile was turned away from him as she watched the London streets pass from the coach's small window, gaslight illuminating the interior of the carriage. She was reckless and had always been, he knew, following impulse and little else. She climbed walls, rode like the devil, and would take on Faron herself if he allowed it.

He rubbed his eyes wearily, suddenly tired of the whole mess. It was over. He was done with his responsibility toward her. He watched as she hunched deeper into her cloak against the early-morning chill. "Well," she asked. Her voice broke the silence with mockery. "Did I fulfill the role of mistress to your liking this evening, Rushford?"

"I saw Galveston and Sebastian with their heads together. So I suppose the answer is yes." He tried to regard her with studied detachment, despite the fact that her eyes were dark with anger.

She threw back the hood of her cloak and ran her hands through her hair, loosening the sparkling combs before leaning back against the squabs. "As long as you are satisfied," she continued in the same sardonic tone. "I await your further instructions."

"There will be none," he said.

She regarded him with a quizzical lift of her eyebrows. "Then I shall be shut up in the town house and await your return with bated breath. Is that it?" As if to taunt him, she leaned forward, touching his knee. "And then what?" She was continuing the charade she had portrayed so winningly earlier in the evening. Throughout the night, she had made certain to stroke his arm, or caress his hand lingeringly, whenever the Baron or Galveston cast a glance their way. It was as though she knew exactly what she was doing, the sexual current of a simple touch jolting him like a bolt of lightning.

"I shall send you home."

"Are you certain of that?" She leaned against the squabs again.

His eyes narrowed. "Isn't that what you've always wanted? Faron will be taken care of."

"I don't trust you."

"The feeling is mutual," he said. "And you may drop the coquettish tone. We're offstage for the moment."

"Coquettish—hardly." As though she had no idea what

she did when she leaned in to him to catch something he was saying, or turned those lush lips up to him in a patently false smile. "Unless," she added, "you are unable to separate fact from fiction, my lord. This evening I was merely fulfilling the role you requested of me."

She looked at him with challenge in her eyes. He moved swiftly to the seat next to her, the rational part of his mind questioning his motives. Perhaps it was her sheer proximity, all evening and now in the coach, that was his undoing. Without waiting for a reply, wishing to silence that rebellious, wilfull mouth, he hooked a finger into the clasp of her cloak, pulling her toward him. His lips met hers in a hard kiss. Quickly, he unclasped the cloak and pushed it off her shoulders, his hands cupping the swell of her breasts under the thin silk of her gown. Her nipples sprang upright in instant response.

"I'm not in the mood for games, damn you," she said hotly against his mouth. "I know what you are trying to do. To subdue me."

"With what? An embrace?" His lips murmured against hers. "You're flushed. I can feel the heat coming off your skin." He lifted his head, and his gaze slowly came up and met hers. A moment passed, and he felt an overwhelming need to assert his control over a situation that was becoming ungovernable. "I can do it again, Rowena, anytime I wish. Bring you to the brink and then leave you there."

"As though our sexual congress has ever solved anything," she said.

"Once you believed it did."

"I was wrong," she said flatly.

"Words have not been of much assistance, either," he said. "However, don't discount the fact that we do have this between us." She gasped and flinched back in shock as his hands deftly arranged her skirt, going to the divide in her pantalets. "Don't forget. Don't ever forget, what I can do to you," he said while his hand smoothed over her already heated sex. She stared, even as her hips jerked and her body reponded to him. Then he lowered his head, parting her legs on the seat between them. She couldn't get away. She did not want to get away; lassitude instantly flooded her mind and her body. His tongue touched her core, and she gasped, her hips lifting from the bench. He focused on her silky wetness and the rhythm of her hips moving up and down, her body tightening against his mouth. And still he laved her, soothed her, kissed her until her body was as tightly wound as a clock. She panted and she gasped, the silk of her thighs tightening.

Somewhere in the recesses of his mind, beyond the deafening drumroll of his pulse, he realized he was lost, adrift in a maze from which there was no escape. He told himself it was what he wanted, what she needed, his lips slanting over her core, the sweet taste of her in his mouth. Her hand curled into the hair at the back of his head, and she clung to him as her other hand roamed restlessly over his back. She was warming now, her dizzying scent taking him over. Somehow he forced himself to slow, to pull away despite her moans of protest. Then he stopped, straightened, and turned away.

Rushford should have known her better. Only a moment passed before Rowena disengaged her hands from her skirts, sat up, and reached for his trousers, pulling them so the buttons snapped free, seemingly by magic. Her dark blue eyes refused to relinquish his gaze as she urged the fine wool down over his hips before shifting from the seat to the floor of the carriage. Taking him between her hands, she kissed him with her lips, then slid him into her mouth in a slow, tight motion that consumed every inch of him. As she drew back, she fed greedily, feeling him grow beneath her tongue. He caught his breath, and she paused to look up at him, satisfaction in her eyes, before he lost his fist in her hair. Again, she took all of him, cupping her hand beneath him as she withdrew, using her other hand to stroke and pump him with a gentle rhythm. His hand tightened in her hair as his breaths became shallower.

When he spoke, his voice was a low groan. "I think we're even now."

She withdrew her mouth but maintained the rhythm of her hand, looking up at him, challenging him to his core. "Are you certain?" Their eyes met, easing the earlier desperation and replacing it with something else. Her lips were full and parted, and he ran a finger along the bottom lip. In return, she ran the flat of her tongue up the length of his shaft moments before he lifted her up to the bench, shoved aside her skirts and entered her with a single thrust. He brought her legs to his shoulders and watched desire cloud her eyes as he thrust into her until he heard her cry out loud over the sounds of the carriage wheels biting into the cobblestones.

When it was over, she lay perfectly still, a hand over her eyes, not looking at him while he adjusted his garments. The wheels of the carriage turned steadily beneath them. Several miles passed in hushed silence. "And what does that prove?" she asked finally, softly into the night. "That I am manageable? That you can bend me to your will? If that makes you feel better, so be it, although for me it changes nothing." Her voice had the ring of finality. She sat up seconds before the carriage slowed and rearranged her skirts as the carriage stopped at the mews behind her apartments. Neither was ready to talk, and Rowena ignored Rushford's hand in assisting her down from the carriage. She stalked past him and into the house.

Her hands shook as she stripped off her cloak. "This situation is out of control, and I don't care for it," she said with her usual forthrightness.

"I didn't hear you protest."

She threw her cloak over the occasional table in the hall. "You are vile."

"And you are dishonest."

"I am going to bed. Good night, Lord Rushford."

His shoulders rested against the door at his back. "We've come to the end, Rowena," he said.

She stopped in midstep, looking over her shoulder at him. "There was never a beginning, was there? Because you would not allow it."

He crossed his arms over his chest, her scent still in his nostrils. "What are you saying?"

"You are still punishing yourself—and punishing me at the same time for something in which I had no part."

"Do not bring up Kate."

"And why not—when her ghost stands between us? It's true. You are always looking for the ghost over your shoulder. Always looking for the Duchess." He did not disagree, but the flat gray of his eyes told her the truth. "It's the reason you can't allow yourself to trust me. The reason that the Baron can do with us as he wishes. Don't you see? I almost wish I'd known her," she continued fearlessly, feeling that she had nothing to lose. "Maybe then I would understand what it takes to inspire that intensity . . ." she paused, "that type of love."

"You don't know what you're saying."

"I believe that I do. And if you could be honest with yourself and with me for once, you would see it also."

"You can't begin to understand what transpired, and what's worse, your ruminations are entirely unproductive," he said harshly. "I meant what I said earlier, Rowena. We have come to an end. This evening was the last time you will be required to pose as my mistress. And if you wish to help me and yourself, you will stay in these apartments until my return."

"Please, Rushford," she said suddenly, her eyes alight. "Why do you not allow me to help you? I don't believe that you cannot find it in yourself to trust me."

Rushford pushed himself away from the door, and his face was neutral, his eyes as hard as stone. "Now please listen to me," he said with soft but deadly intent. "Trust has nothing to do with these circumstances. Your continued involvement will only compound the difficulties for your aunt and sister. As a result, if you so much as think of doing anything impetuous, and unpredictable, as is your wont, I shan't be responsible."

Rowena took an involuntary step back. "I don't know what to do anymore, to convince you."

"There is nothing you can do. You are young and naïve and out of weakness, I allowed myself to believe that becoming further involved with you was wise when it was good for neither of us." He ran a hand through his hair. "I should never have made love to you that first time. And when you returned to me, one year later, I should have done everything to send you on your way again. Not for me—but for you. We are at an end."

"That's not true," she burst out. "I told you I regret none of it. Not one moment. Even when I find myself wondering whether you would sacrifice those close to me for your own ends."

Rushford cut her off with a look before she could continue. There was nothing left to say. "Very well," she said, holding up her palms in a gesture of acceptance. His eyes bored into hers during a brief, tense silence, as if he were reading her mind. Then he exhaled, leaning back against the door. In a rustle of gray silk, she disappeared down the hall, leaving him in the atrium. He swore a savage oath, feeling winded, as if he'd just taken a blow to his stomach.

Rowena did not sleep that night. Instead, she paced the apartments, her mind whirling from one plan to the next, her heart hardening against Rushford. The day began with heavy clouds, and the sun made only a short appearance before setting again, suffusing the satin curtains of her bedchamber with what seemed an ominous glow. It felt as though a lifetime had passed since she had climbed the trellis behind Rushford's town house on Belgravia Square to enlist his aid. Yet, she told herself, despite her conflicting emotions, she was just one step away from Montagu Faron, and closer still to a possession he prized so highly. Gazing into the vermilion glow of the remnants of a fire, she heard the clock strike eight. Only an hour before complete darkness fell. She could hear her own rush of blood pounding in her ears.

It took her no time at all to fling off her day gown and

change into a pair of trousers that she had asked Madame Curzon to make for her, smiling slightly at the memory of the older woman's shocked face when she'd learned of Rowena's preference for a riding costume. Rowena thrust the small, freshly oiled revolver into her pocket, wrapped a cloak around her, and tucked her hair beneath the hood. She had dismissed the maid and cook earlier in the day so there would be no witnesses to her leaving the apartments. Even so, she slipped out from the mews' entrance of the apartments, avoiding the main stairwell, and walked briskly for several minutes before catching a hansom. "Bloomsbury," she said to the driver, not giving a specific address, and pleased he could not discern her trousers beneath the length of her cloak. She sat on the edge of the seat as the vehicle swung around corners, the team of horses making short work of the distance. Rowena wouldn't allow herself to think of anything but her immediate plan. She was determined to arrive at the British Museum ahead of the Baron's men.

The carriage came to a halt in the eerily deserted Russell Square, about half a mile from the museum. Rowena disembarked, wrapped her cloak more closely around her, and skirted the buildings flanking the square. During the day she knew the area to be filled with flower stalls, pigeon coops, and pie vendors, but as darkness settled she could hear only her own feet echoing on the cobblestones. It had been raining earlier, and the puddles glistened in the gaslight, the ground slippery underfoot. She ran through the narrow streets, past pitched roofs and narrow brownstones, cutting her way through Russell Square, heedless of the moisture that soaked the hem of her cloak, her eyes fixed on the corner of Charlotte Street ahead. Upon coming closer, she shifted into a doorway of a narrow series of buildings, pressing back into the shadows before looking up the street. It was dark now, the area curiously deserted save for a group of torches advancing. She fingered the pistol in her pocket, its coldness familiar to her hand.

When the men had passed, she emerged from the shadows, her heart thundering in her chest as she ran toward the monumental south entrance of the museum. Strangely sinister with its colonnades and pediments, it loomed like a Greek architectural colossus in the gathering dark. She skirted a huddled figure in a doorway and ignored a dog frantically barking from a stoop. Picking up her pace, she ran along Charlotte Street to the west façade of the museum, which was more modest in proportion. It was easy to make herself disappear into a niche in the stone wall.

Her breathing became more regular, and she allowed herself to momentarily close her eyes. Suddenly, the hairs on the nape of her neck rose, and her skin crawled. The low murmur of voices came incrementally closer, thinning her blood. Disembodied words catapulted her back to the dark fog of her abduction. The Baron and several other men.

Rowena held her breath, easily identifying Sebastian's voice. The footsteps came closer and then receded before she allowed herself to exhale. She focused instead on Meredith, Julia, and Montfort, her heart easing in acceptance of her fate. Her feelings for Rushford were really of secondary importance; nothing would ever come of them, she knew. He had loved the Duchess, and Rowena Woolcott would always be a postscript, a burden, a responsibility that he had taken on, at best, without thought and, at worst, to staunch his grief for a woman who was lost to him forever.

She paused for another moment, her chemise and shirt sticking to her spine with perspiration from her exertions. Two or three minutes passed, stretching to infinity, while the Baron and his half dozen men moved around to the back of the museum. Rowena could not make out their words but only saw the Baron lift his arm in command before they dispersed, disappearing around the corner, their torchlight lifted high.

Still no sign of Rushford. She began feeling her way along the back wall of the museum, her cloak brushing along the stone until she came to a small set of stairs, clearly an entrance-way, leading to a serviceable-looking door. Rowena did not hesitate. It was slightly ajar, an invitation to go farther, and she quietly slipped inside. Stopping on the threshold, she saw them at once at the far end of a cavernous subterranean vault, stacked high with long wooden boxes holding trea-sures of the museum that did not often see the light of day. Several sconces burned dully, but she identified the two men right away. Rushford and Lord Richard Archer.

To the left, she saw another set of steps leading to a nar-row open walkway above. Wavering only for a moment, she moved silently to creep up the stairs, keeping herself low to the ground until she reached a small platform. She was afraid of what she was about to witness. She knew Lord Rushford was prepared to do what he must to defeat Faron.

"The wagon should be brought around shortly," Rushford said. A chill swept through Rowena at his determined tone. She shifted as far back as she could on the small platform and into the shadows.

"Already done," Archer replied. The two men put their shoulders to a large wooden box, scraping it across the stone floor, their progress slow. "We should be in Calais by early morning, ready to catch the ship out before sunrise."

"The timing couldn't have been better to have your sloop in port."

"I've informed the captain that you're simply on your way to Paris for a fortnight of carousing. Entirely plausible, I thought."

"Always prepared to think the best of me," Rushford replied, his teeth a flash of white in the dimness. "I shouldn't wish to endanger your captain. I think I can manage the *Brig-and* on my own."

"One should hope that ten years in the Royal Navy taught you something."

"I won't lose her, don't worry," he said, glancing at the doorway and the walkway overhead. Rowena sucked in her breath. Then he turned back to Archer. "While I am in France, there is the matter of Miss Woolcott."

Archer, his hand on the crate, said, "She will be well looked after until your return. Never fear. Although I should hope you will have the courage to resolve the issue, Rush."

"Nothing to resolve," he said. "Once I've determined all is well, she can return safely to Montfort."

"Without you?"

"You're as meddlesome as a granny," Rushford said brusquely. "She will not need me to return to Montfort, and in the interim, the less she knows of this the better. Miss Woolcott is difficult enough to manage without her discovering her aunt's life hangs in the balance should this exchange not come off."

Rowena bit her lip, hearing Archer swear softly. "Her aunt is involved? You intend to explain this added complication to me, I trust."

"Not now. There's no time if I'm to meet the ship with the cargo at the appointed hour. Suffice it to say that Miss Woolcott's concerns for her family will be relegated to the past. In exchange for the cargo, Faron will desist with his threats."

"How can you be certain?" Archer's voice in the darkness was somber.

Rushford shrugged and said, "Because I intend to kill him."

*For what he did to Kate.* Rowena's blood ran cold. She pressed herself against the wall at her back, the air suddenly inky dark and thick with dust. She could feel the nightmare terrors nudging at her mind. Once before she'd lain in the dark, the walls pressing down on her, before water had filled her lungs. She imagined Rushford's touch, his strong hands, pulling her back from the currents before she could lose herself in the nightmare again. She forced herself to calm. She watched Rushford closely and realized that he had, always at such moments, a perfect stillness that masked reservoirs of strength. His presence, when she heard the deep murmur of his voice, was like a lifeline unreeling through the darkness.

She clung to the confidence of that voice, allowing herself to wonder why he was so necessary to her life.

A sudden rush of blind panic. I love him, Rowena thought. At that instant, there was nothing else. The power of that fundamental admission shook her to her core, and for the moment, she was unable to absorb it, to envision how it changed everything and nothing at the same time. *I love him.* The words repeated in an endless loop, burning into her consciousness. He would not do anything to harm her family. The relief was like honey on her tongue. But to lose him now . . . She took a deep breath. Baron and his men would come upon them at any moment, their return ensuring that Rushford would deliver on his promise. She squeezed her eyes tight, withdrawing the revolver from the waistband of her trousers.

Opening her eyes, she focused on Rushford, unwilling and unable to look away from the tall figure in the shadows. It was a moment suspended in time, forever written upon her frozen heart. *He is the man I love.* Even though it will all come to nothing, she thought, the silence in the vault stretching like a rope on the verge of snapping.

It was a swinging lantern that first caught her eye. Before she could absorb the implication, a half dozen men catapulted in from the small doorway to effectively surround Archer and Rushford.

The Baron strode into the center, his dark cloak swirling around him, an impresario come to do Faron's work. "Well done, gentlemen," the Baron said, clapping his gloved hands together in a show of applause. "No guards, no constabulary—this is truly marvelous." He gestured to the wooden crate. "I wonder what you told Whitehall, Lord Archer, to have ordered the British Museum to oblige us in such a congenial manner?"

Rushford interrupted. "Your questions are superfluous, Sebastian, when we have more important matters to discuss. We relinquish the prize to Faron himself, as we agreed."

The Baron smiled. "I fear that I have had a change of heart, Lord Rushford. Crompton, Johnston"—he gestured to two men behind him—"remove the crate to the coach waiting outside."

"I don't believe you heard me correctly, Sebastian," Rushford continued calmly. "But then again, I think we had a similar misunderstanding at Alcestor Court." His glance was dark and chill with open contempt.

"You've faced worse in the ring, surely, Lord Rushford. My men are merely amateurs at this sort of thing," the Baron said lightly, shrugging beneath his long, black cloak. "And of course your adventures with the Royal Navy, I have heard said, have prepared you well for challenging encounters of this ilk. Don't stop now," he said to Johnston and Crompton, pushing the crate toward the exit without turning around. "I should like to get on our way."

"I expected as much, Baron," Archer said smoothly, reaching for the inside of his jacket. Almost immediately, four pistols rose in unison in the hands of the men standing behind the Baron. "You obviously didn't anticipate soon enough," the Baron countered. "And how unfortunate it will be for Whitehall to learn that Lord Rushford stole the Rosetta Stone in retaliation for Whitehall not doing enough to protect his duchess. And then another suicide—in a bid to join his departed lover. Always an odd one, that Lord Rushford."

"And what of our agreement regarding the Woolcotts," Rushford asked, remaining calm despite the collection of weapons arrayed against him.

The Baron's sleek brows rose questioningly. "Entirely out of my hands. It would seem that Faron will see to the matter of Rowena Woolcott himself. Quite the turn of events, no?"

"Unlike you, however, I do make good on my promises, Sebastian," Rushford said smoothly. "I recall at Alcestor Court I made mention that once freed from the manacles you so cheerfully provided, I would kill you with my bare hands. And I do believe the time has come."

"The rumors are correct. You do have an unenviable temper, Lord Rushford," the Baron continued, totally unconcerned at the chorus of triggers being pulled back behind him. "If you die in a volley of bullets, so be it. You will be a hero to Whitehall then, rather than a traitor."

Frantically, Rowena searched for a line of sight. The best she could do was create an unexpected melee, giving Rushford and Archer an opportunity to draw their own weapons. She raised her right hand, balancing it on her left, holding the revolver loosely in her fingers. There was no time left to think, only to react. She pulled the trigger.

The sound of three bullets reverberated in the vault as she fired in quick succession. The Baron's men immediately swung away from Rushford and Archer as she'd hoped, toward the platform where she crouched. She pressed closer to the wall as a ricochet of shots sped through the air around her. Huddling back in the shadows, she counted to sixty, knowing it was only a matter of time before she was discovered. There were grunts, the sound of cracking bone and flesh, and suddenly, the vault was plunged into darkness. The sconces had been extinguished. Taking a deep breath, thankful for even a moment's reprieve, she tried to ignore a feeling of wet warmth on her shoulder.

Silence. Her mind conjured one horror more frightening than the next. Rushford. Her mind would not go on . . . Meredith and Julia. She could not just cower in the darkness like a child. A rustle of movement, the acrid smell of a torch being lit. Rowena pulled herself up and held the pistol in both hands, the scene blurring before her swimming eyes.

The Baron, alone. Rushford and Archer and the remaining men were nowhere to be seen. Peering into the space above him, the Baron raised a hand in salute.

"This might be a good time to relinquish the pistol, Miss Woolcott. If you care for the well-being of your dear aunt Meredith." The Baron's tones were silky and measured, as though he had all the time in the world. "No need to fret. We have what we've come for," he said, gesturing with a gloved hand to the wooden crate behind him. "Lord Rushford and Lord Archer have been taken care of by my men, who will return as soon as they dispose of the bodies. Yet more custom for our dear Mrs. Banks. So you see, my dear, your histrionics will do no good."

Rowena's knees went weak. Rushford was dead. The muzzle of her revolver didn't waver, but she didn't trust herself to speak.

"Dare I say that it might have been your poor aim that sent those two to the next world? It only proves that women have no business brandishing pistols. Most unfeminine and unattractive."

Shaking, her shoulder throbbing, Rowena dared herself to speak. "I was not intending to hit a target last time, Baron, but my aim this instance will be true."

The Baron looked downcast. "And what of our agreement, Miss Woolcott?"

"Made under duress and in the poorest of faith."

"Faron will not be pleased when he learns that you have reneged on your promise. I shudder to think of his disappointment and the prospects regarding your dear aunt."

"I shall take that risk once you are dead, Baron." Her right arm and shoulder screaming with pain, she somehow managed to keep hold of the pistol. "I intend to confront Montagu Faron at Claire de Lune myself."

The Baron took a careful step toward her, cocking his head. "And with what will you bargain, my dear? You have precisely nothing, now that we are in possession of the Rosetta Stone. Further, you don't even have the dubious loyalty of Lord Rushford." Rowena's heart refused to contemplate the reality of his words. She could not imagine Rushford lying dead, his body already being carried away by the currents of the Thames. *She would not.*

"You appear positively devastated, my dear Miss Woolcott. I should hope not over the demise of Lord Rushford, when he has only been using you from the start. And not simply in the carnal sense, I might add."

Rowena leveled her pistol, but she felt a sickening desire to hear what the Baron had to say.

"Do you not wonder why he was close by Birdoswald the night he happened to find you in the river? Serendipity, you believe? Hardly, my dear, naïve girl. Lord Rushford, your hero"—he sneered the last word—"was willing to do anything to get closer to Faron in order to avenge the death of the poor Duchess. We made certain to alert him to Faron's impending visit to Eccles House and environs, you see. We knew it would take little to inveigle Rushford in our plans to wreak havoc on your family—if it meant he would find himself closer to Faron. Now do you not feel relieved that the man is dead and gone?"

Rowena could feel the blood trickling from her shoulder through her cloak. Dots danced before her eyes, and a dull nausea settled into the pit of her stomach. "I don't care in the least," she said, her voice strong. "But I do care to resolve this issue once and for all. I shall count to ten before I let go the hammer."

"What are you waiting for, dear girl? You do not have the courage to shoot me, nor do you wish to take the risk that your aunt will pay the price for your impulsiveness." He clucked his tongue against his teeth. "Such a willful girl."

In response, she moved from the shadows toward the center of the small platform. The Baron's face was bloodless in the dim light of the single torch, his eyes dark holes in his pale complexion.

Rowena almost expected him to reach for his silver cigar case. Instead, his right hand extracted a black revolver. "I grow weary, Miss Woolcott," he said, aiming it up at her perch. "And I do believe I shall save Faron the tedium of meeting with you. You are meant to be dead, after all. This time I will take direct responsibility for your demise."

It was true what they said, Rowena thought, about the

moments before death. Montfort rose before her eyes, the figures of her aunt and sister on the distant horizon. And Rushford, she thought, this time with only love in her heart.

She raised her pistol, steeling herself for one last effort before she died, wondering frantically how many shells remained and whether she would have the courage to release the hammer. And then, behind the Baron, *Rushford.* Silhouetted in the torchlight. He was back from the dead to finish what he had started. Taking her last breath, Rowena memorized for eternity all the rage and love she saw in his eyes.

# Chapter 17

He would always think of this summer as one of the most glorious he had ever known. The nighttime scent of lime blossoms lining the estate of Claire de Lune held a dangerous sweetness, recalling a summer many years ago.

Montagu Faron looked away from the opened French doors and the moonlit parterre with its plane trees and disciplined shrubs, and instead paced the length of one of his five laboratories, the aroma of astringent and formaldehyde pinching his nostrils. Two rectangular tables lined the room, topped by rows of microscopes, the instruments adjusted to illuminate a series of prepared specimens. He swept a hand along the table, forcing himself not to look at the blistered flesh on his long fingers, and strong but elegant wrists. The work of Julia Woolcott, he reminded himself. The flames still crackled and licked his flesh, delivering phantom pain from which there was no escape, a memento from their meeting at Eccles House over a year ago.

He stared at a butterfly, its wings pinned back, sacrificed on the altar of his research. The bright yellows and blues mocked him, the colors brilliant against the cold glass upon which they rested. It was all that was left to him now. Knowledge and power.

He knew what he had lost because he thought of Meredith every day, a relentless torture that invaded both his waking and sleeping hours. His life was a palimpsest, layers of bitter-

ness and regret that fueled his appetite for living and now focused on the two wards who were closest to Meredith's
heart. The younger, Rowena, was a rebellious and willful
creature quite different from her more subdued sister. Julia
had brought him to the portals of death from which he'd
only been saved by blind luck and the quick action of his
acolytes nearby. He didn't believe in fate or God but only his
own driving thirst for knowledge and revenge. The first had
made him one of the greatest minds in Europe, but the latter
was increasingly beyond his grasp. His breath whistled behind the finely wrought leather mask as he reluctantly took
stock.

The Rosetta Stone belonged to him. He had not murdered
Champollion all those years earlier to have the Egyptian
tablets remain in England. The professor had been in his employ and yet saw fit to share his knowledge with the greater
world when his work was but the beginning, a mere prelude
to the greater oeuvre Faron could achieve. His was the more
powerful intellect, as focused as a beam of light when he remained free of the facial tremors that overtook him with unexpected viciousness. He had not had an episode since his
return from Eccles House. The irony was cruel. He grimaced
behind the mask and looked out the French doors to the ordered park outside, which had been designed by Le Notre,
esteemed landscaper to Louis the Sun King himself. The roots
of the Faron family in France ran deep, their association with
the Renaissance and the Enlightenment forged in blood and
wealth. The ancient Egyptian artifact was by rights his, a sym-
bol for intellectual breakthrough, not unlike Archimedes's
bath or Newton's apple.

Mysteries surrounding the Stone remained, beckoning him
in a Faustian bargain. Faron felt it in his bones. Each study
was like speaking with the dead, and the dialogue had scarcely
begun. A sensation not unlike a deep thirst overtook him.
The trip to the coast would not require any length of time.
His men were already arrayed along the quay like so many
knights on a chessboard to greet the freight when it arrived.

His library was prepared, a glass niche assembled that would house the tablets in security and safety. Time was of no concern as he had a lifetime to unlock the mysteries the ancient texts would hold. In the shorter term, he would dispatch the Woolcott girl and Rushford like two of his specimens that no longer served any use. That the Englishman had slipped through their grasp not once but twice was unforgivable. As a scientist, he knew the rigors of examining his errors closely. It seemed whenever the Woolcotts were involved, he was doomed to failure.

Without closing his eyes, he saw the past, and his old room in the northeast wing of the chateau. The unforgotten feel of his bed, the elusive scent. Meredith Woolcott's *scent*. He remembered the days after the accident when the act of opening his eyes was torture, the pounding in his head razor sharp. He had forced his lids open and looked around at the light of dawn softening the fleur-de-lis patterns on the silk hangings, the heavy mahogany furniture, the bed curtains pulled back. A tapestry hung on the wall, its unicorn and frolicking maidens all distantly familiar, like a dream. For weeks, he had not been able to think clearly, breaking out in cold sweats, the first of a series of convulsions racking his body. He never learned how long he had drifted in and out of his fevered state of alternating pain and awareness.

But Faron did remember the last time he saw her. *Meredith*. He had been waiting for her on the road to Blois in the gathering light of dawn. He had stiffened his resolve, even as his heart slammed in his chest at the sound of the clattering hooves. She was on a stolen horse, galloping like the wind, her cloak flowing behind her, the masses of titian hair escaping from her hood. He kicked his horse onto the road so she would have to stop, if only for a moment. He drew rein and pivoted his mount to stop her. Her horse, whipped to a frenzy only moments before, tossed its mane and danced impatiently, poised to disappear into the horizon. Meredith cast a quick glance over her shoulder and then met his gaze, her eyes a deep green. Like emeralds. Like the waters of the Loire.

At that moment, she was everything he had ever loved her for in the beginning. Then her expression shuttered. The sounds of pursuit were closer now. He moved his horse nearer and took her chin in his hand, her warmth flowing through him. Twenty years later, he still wondered whether she had seen in the flash of his eyes the intensity of feeling he carried for her in his heart. Then she was gone, leaving behind a shower of mud down the road.

Leaving him a carapace of a man. Leaving him behind a leather mask, with scarred flesh and a scarred mind. His eyes lit briefly on the butterfly, pinned to its crucifix, before walking to the French doors and breathing in the warm scents. It was not the aroma of lime blossoms that held him in thrall. He could scent Calais, not three hundred kilometers away.

Rowena did not have to fire her pistol. Rushford had the Baron in his grip before the man knew that his life was to be snuffed out. Rushford had waited for this moment for over two years, as if the time had come to claim some small share of satisfaction for what had been taken from him. And for what the Baron had been prepared to take from him again— Rowena.

His heart pounded, blasting heat through his veins, despite the fact that he and Archer had just laid waste the Baron's men, Johnston and Crompton included. He was dimly aware of a trickle of blood down his cheek, but then the pain receded. The Baron turned to face him, but he did not have a chance to move away or fire a shot from his revolver. Rushford caught him in the groin with a crashing fist, doubling the Baron over. Although the Frenchman would never know it, the sequence of fists and feet and blows to the back of his neck were merciful, finishing the fight in a series of blindingly fast movements. With a quick glance, Rushford knew the Baron's neck was broken just above the spine.

He took two stairs at a time to the small platform where Rowena stood, the pistol still clutched in her right hand. His glance took in her pale face. "Sit down—don't faint now," he ordered.

"I never faint," she said weakly, an echo of the same words and bravado she had tossed at him just weeks before. Sinking down to the top step, she stared at the scene. By the frozen shock in Rowena's eyes, Rushford discerned that the reality of their situation had yet to penetrate the fog of her brain. The revolver remained in her hand, testament to what she'd been prepared to do. Take a man's life. She looked at the Baron, lying twisted on cold flagstones, his elegant cloak pristinely glistening in the darkness. Then she suddenly became aware of the weapon in her hand. She let it clatter to the ground.

Rushford met her eyes. "I don't know if I could have killed him. To protect Meredith . . ."

"You didn't have to. I did," he said. Her horrified gaze was still fixed on his face. "*I killed him,*" Rushford said simply.

Blood smeared the shoulder of her cloak, but her trembling had ceased. "I can't look at him anymore. I can't because I feel as though I am somehow responsible." She put a hand to her mouth. "I wish to . . . I need to leave."

"A good idea," he said with a glance at her shoulder. He stood abruptly, a hand under her elbow, lifting her to her feet. "I will take you back to the apartments." In the darkness, she looked as though the slightest wind would knock her back to the ground.

"I am going with you," she said, and he saw the flash of pain in her eyes. "I know what's in that wooden crate and where you are intending to take it. I refuse to leave your side."

A thousand emotions clamored for his attention, but he realized crushing anxiety for Rowena Woolcott was uppermost. "I will explain everything once we return to the apartments. I promise you."

"You expected all this, didn't you?" she asked wearily. "And you came back. You did not leave me."

Rushford tore his gaze away from her. As a matter of fact,

he had not expected all of this. "I would not leave you, Rowena. I would never leave you." The words hung in the air between them before he took her head between his hands, his eyes burning with an intensity she had never seen before. "Do you think you are the only one who suffers here?" he asked, his voice soft. "Do you believe that I have not agonized every moment of how to spare you from the ugliness and danger of this situation? I have failed you, I know, since the first day I saw you mere moments away from death," he continued, his voice cracking with emotion. Reflected in her widening eyes was his anguish. It should have moved her, but it didn't. She shook her head mutely, taking his hands away from her face.

"Don't lie to me. To spare my feelings," she said, hiding her face in his chest, the coarse wool of his coat against her cold cheek.

"What if I told you that I'd wanted you from the first moment I saw you," he continued. "Wanted you so badly that I went against logic and reason and good sense. What if I confessed that I was frightened when it became so much more than physical passion between us?"

"Stop it!" She lifted her face. They stared at each other, breathing hard. "You are lying. Lying!" A dry sob was wrenched from her throat.

Pinning her eyes with his, he pressed on relentlessly, his tone a hot whisper. "Would it even matter to you if I said that I can no longer live without you? That when I saw you standing here, so ridiculously courageous with that revolver balanced in your hands, I knew instantly that I loved you, that I had loved you from the first? And that nothing else matters. That losing you would be the darkest moment in my life, worse than anything I have ever known."

Her hands covered her face to escape the intensity of his gaze and words. "How can I believe you, when you refuse to tell me the truth about so much?" Her voice wavered. "About the Duchess." She dropped her hands from her cheeks.

"I don't begin to understand you." She swayed against him, her face bleached white.

"I love you," Rushford repeated quietly. "And as for Kate," he paused. "I was desperately afraid that I would hurt you in some way. In the way I hurt her. The way we hurt each other." In the darkness, under her cloak, she reached for his hands, a mute reply. "I was responsible for her death," he said bleakly. Rowena said nothing, merely let her hands rest in his.

"I love you also, Rushford," she said finally and with a peculiar formality. "But with everything that's happened . . . I don't know if that's enough." He looked into her eyes and saw his own reflection in the deep blue, something he couldn't read, something powerful that had simmered between them from the start. All he wanted to do was catch her head between his hands and bring his mouth to hers, to allow the familiar heady rush of desire to obliterate the past and leave only the present. She sounded so bitter that he wondered if they would ever find their way back again. *It is enough,* he wanted to say fiercely, *that you love me.* He took a deep breath. All they needed was time, he assured himself.

"We will go to Dover together," he said. "I don't dare let you out of my sight. But first, let me take a quick look at that wound in your shoulder."

"It's fine," she said, her lips parched.

He pulled off his cravat. "You're bleeding all over the place. Let me bind it for the moment and I'll look at it closely when we get to Dover." She stood mutely under his ministrations as he loosened the first two toggles of her cloak, exposing a blood-soaked chemise. Stifling a wince, she stood stoically while he examined the red stain seeping through her chemise and shirt. It appeared to be a flesh wound, from what he could discern, the blood already drying. Regardless, he fastened the cravat tightly around her shoulder and under her arm. "I would suggest that you have that attended to here in London and wait for my return—but I know better."

"Don't be absurd." She dismissed his statement, some of the intensity leaving her face, although her eyes still glittered strangely, her emotions running high.

Rushford had estimated a three-hour ride to Dover. It was still a few hours before dawn, so they could vanquish the miles under cloak of darkness. Without asking her permission, he scooped Rowena into his arms, shielding the Baron's body from her gaze, and carried her into the damp London night. Archer had swept the area clean, and there was no sign of the struggle that had taken place that night in the vault and in the shadow of the British Museum. Rushford's mount waited, along with a sleepy lad guarding the leather purse filled with an extra revolver and coins.

They left London through Hyde Park, turning the horse toward the sea, following the Thames to its mouth. Rowena sat quiet in the saddle in front of him, and he sensed that her fatigue enclosed her with a mind-numbing force, protecting her from the pain in her shoulder and the anguish of her spirit. Yet it was enough for him to know that she loved him, even though she shouldn't. She was too young and too inexperienced for him, he told himself, but he wanted her with a single-mindedness that staggered him. He had known it from the first moment he had taken her from the river's grasp, known somehow that this young woman was for him, despite the months he had tried desperately to convince himself otherwise.

The sun was not yet on the horizon when they arrived in Dover, the hour both too late and too early for the usual raucous activity of a port town. Rushford urged his horse onward, cantering easily toward the quay. The *Brigand* was identifiable by her sleek form, moored at the end of the quay, her profile dark. Rushford slipped from his mount, gathering Rowena carefully against him for a moment as she rested her forehead against his chest. She was asleep, her skin flushed but cool. There was no fever developing from the wound to her shoulder, he thought with relief.

The combined odors of fish and sea air swamped him as he

strode down the companionway of the sloop and into the small cabin. Gently depositing Rowena on the cot in the stern, he smoothed the rough ticking of the straw mattress beneath her. He quickly unbuttoned her cloak and loosened her makeshift bandage before dragging a thin blanket over her sleeping form. Taking a last look, he made his way above deck to loosen the moorings and begin their journey to Calais. The moon was almost full, lighting their way.

Rowena awoke to the strong smell of the sea and the swinging of an oil lantern hanging from a low ceiling. The flickering light cast grotesque shadows on the planked bulkhead, and the boat lurched beneath her. Her gaze took in the cabin, the floor covered with gleaming mahogany, the paintings on the bulkhead, the coal-fired stove that provided heat in cooler climes. Two chairs and a settee covered in blue damask filled the port side of the cabin. She heard the groan of a sail running up the masthead. Grabbing the edge of the bed as the boat swung slowly away from deep swells, she listened to the wind fill the mainsail.

It all came crashing over her. Rushford. *He loved her*. Elation swept through her, replaced almost instantly by a jumble of doubts. How could he love her when he didn't trust her and believed that she was but a notch above treachery? And worse still, how could he ever trust her if he could not trust himself, or forgive himself for the demise of the Duchess? The fervency of her unspoken thoughts shocked her.

Rowena's head and shoulder ached as she rose from the narrow bunk, enervated. The world tilted on its axis and she nearly tumbled from where she stood, but she was determined to find Rushford and some blessed fresh air. Ignoring the throbbing in her shoulder, she gathered her cloak around her and made her way up the narrow stairs and onto the deck. She staggered to the rail and threw back her head, looking up into the sky where the moon hung over the boat surrounded by millions of stars. The spray stung her face, but she breathed deeply of the sharp air, her face turning away from the open water to see Rushford emerging from the companionway. He smiled, and her heart leaped at the sight of his face thrown into silver relief by the moonlight. She couldn't prevent her own lips curving in response.

"You have slept deeply. Feeling restored, I trust?" He swept a hand down her cheek, his eyes concerned.

"Much better, thank you." The words were stilted, but she didn't know where to begin. She turned to look out onto the water boiling around a row of jagged rocks. She shivered and drew her cloak tighter around her aching shoulder. Somewhere in the distance a lighthouse glowed weakly in the darkness; the clanging of a warning bell carried faintly across the sound.

"I've never been on open water like this," she said.

Rushford feigned amazement. "Difficult to believe that Rowena Woolcott, along with riding, climbing, and marksmanship, did not learn the fundamentals of sailing."

Her smile widened. "You are always making light of my accomplishments, sir."

"Never, Rowena, do I take your accomplishments for granted. You are a remarkable young woman."

She felt herself flush under his gaze, but silence stretched between them, leaving only the wind that blew stronger now, surging ahead in a rolling expanse of white caps. The *Brigand* rode the waves with ease, but Rowena was not certain how her stomach fared. She intended to stay on deck until they reached Calais. Turning from the rail, she caught sight of a huge wooden crate, its dimensions secured by several heavy chains.

Rushford caught the direction of her gaze.

"Are you prepared to talk about this now?" he asked.

"I've always been prepared," she countered. "But I know you enough to declare that you have no intention of relinquishing the Stone to Faron, Rushford. And please don't tell me otherwise." Her mind grappled with several outstanding details. Such as how the crate had made its journey to Dover without them. "It doesn't matter, does it, given your intention to kill Faron?" She stood at the deck rail, wrapped in her cloak. "And the Rosetta Stone is not even in the crate, is it?" She paused for a moment, taken aback by the troubling intensity of his gaze, which, if she was hard pressed, she might interpret as love.

"Among your many attributes is also keen intelligence," he said.

Unable to bear the force of his gaze, Rowena stared out into the channel, then took a long breath. "How do we know that the threat to Meredith and Julia will end once he is dead?"she asked into the wind. The prospect of murder was too much to contemplate, and she forcibly wiped the recollection of the Baron, his dark cloak spread around him in the vault of the British Museum, from her memory.

Rushford looked at her profile for a moment before answering. "Faron's obsession with the Rosetta Stone stems from the man's insatiable ambitions," he said flatly. "His vendetta against your family is entirely personal. Once he is gone, I don't believe anyone will take up the cause."

She continued to stare moodily over the rail at the dark heavings of the channel. "I need to know what lies behind this madness," she said with grim finality. "Faron's madness."

"You may not wish to know, Rowena."

"Do not try to protect me from the truth," she said urgently, turning to look directly at him. "I acknowledge that you do it out of the best of intentions but—"

He interrupted. "I do it from love, Rowena." He leaned against the rail, and his expression was as open as she had ever seen it.

"So you say," she said with a wan smile. "I don't mean to doubt you. I'm just confused, not only by your feelings but also mine. One moment we're in each other's arms and the next we seem to be plotting against one another, unable to give each other a shred of trust."

He shook his head. "I promised to tell you everything. I need to tell you everything."

Rowena pulled herself up sharply, pain in her gaze. "I only

hope it helps," she said simply. "Because I love you, Rushford, and that fact will never change."

Over the crashing of the waves, his voice was soft. "It will never change, because I won't let it." The statement had the power of a royal decree. "I love you, Rowena. More than I ever thought was possible." In response, because she was almost afraid to hear any more, she rested her head on his shoulder as the *Brigand* cut through the waves. With her cheek on the wet wool of his jacket and his arms around her, she heard the rumble of his voice and breathed in his familiar scent. "I meant what I said to you now and last evening—I love you. And I don't say those words lightly."

The need for honesty between them made her brave. She raised her head to look directly at him. "And I meant what I said. I love you. But I wonder if it is enough," she said softly. "I think I knew it from the first, the reason behind my seeking you out so relentlessly." A faint embarrassment enveloped her. "Do you not need to be at the helm of the ship?" she asked.

He kissed the top of her head. "We're on course for the next several miles. And don't try to squirm out of a difficult conversation. That's hardly like you." But she tucked her head back into the warmth of his chest. "I will have to be the courageous one then," he said softly into her hair.

Rowena closed her eyes, feeling as though she were falling off the edge of the world into nothingness, save for Rushford's arms around her. Words failed her; her emotions were in chaos as she listened to him.

"For the longest time, I felt only the most bitter rage," he said, "and you can guess at the cause. I don't like to lose. As a matter of fact, I had never lost anything I'd cared about in my life. Before Kate."

The ship heaved beneath them, but Rowena felt secure in his arms and with the truth. "So I went after Faron the second time at Birdoswald in an attempt at revenge. Then you came into my life. And everything changed. I mourned for Kate and the love I thought we had, but all the while I wondered how it was possible to feel such a powerful and obsessive emotion for you."

Her silence urged him on. "You must believe me when I say that I had no inkling of Faron's intentions regarding the Woolcotts. I was only at Birdoswald to intercept him before he ventured to Eccles House. And you know the rest."

Rowena breathed in his scent, mingling now with the salt air. "And then you hid," she said simply. "For a year, looking for ways to expiate your guilt. Helping solve the Cruikshank murders—anything to make up for the death of the woman you loved."

"I wish it were that simple, Rowena."

"But I do understand," she insisted. "You were punishing yourself for doing what you did." He had betrayed the Duchess, but Rowena could not say the words. "You sacrificed your love for the Duchess in order to save the Rosetta Stone." She steeled herself for his response.

Rushford took her chin between finger and thumb and brought her face up to his. "I never doubted my love for her. *I doubted her love for me.*" Rowena wanted to close her eyes to hide from the pain she saw in his gaze. "Look at me," he said, softly insistent. "The Duchess of Taunton betrayed me." The words came out evenly, but they must have cost him dearly.

Her eyes widened. "Now I don't understand."

Rushford tightened his arms around her before he continued, gazing into the foam-flecked channel. "Kate was capricious by nature, lively and intelligent and supremely bored as the wife of an elderly diplomat," he said flatly. "It was not surprising that she became too curious about some of the dispatches that arrived on a regular basis for the Earl. As a lark, and perhaps as the ultimate revenge against a husband she increasingly despised, she sought to undermine him by passing highly classified information to the French, the Russians, and to Montagu Faron, as it turned out."

Rowena stiffened. It was as though Rushford had put his finger on an open wound.

"I believe most of the time she had not the slightest idea of the import of the dispatches. It was simply a game to her."

As was their affair, Rowena wanted to say, but dared not.

"In the end, she was using me as well," Rushford continued. Rowena's arms tightened around him.

"Not wittingly at first. She was titillated by what she'd learned about me from the dispatches she'd intercepted, intended for her husband's eyes only. I suppose it was exciting for her to become involved with someone who worked clandestinely on behalf of Whitehall," he said as though telling a story about someone other than himself. "It was only a matter of time before she discovered that I had been asked by Whitehall to prevent the theft of the Rosetta Stone. By that time, she was so inextricably entangled with Faron's people that she had no choice but to divulge every last bit of sensitive information to them or face charges of treason in England." Rushford paused. "I do not blame her. It was not deliberate on her part, I'm convinced."

Rowena strained for breath. "I'm so sorry," she whispered. The rough wool beneath her cheek was damp with her tears.

"As am I," he said with painful honesty. "Because I then betrayed her."

When Rowena was able to speak, she said, "But you had no choice."

"One always has a choice. But I made my decision, and I have to live with it." She felt his muscles stiffen. "And because of it, Faron's men murdered her and then made it look like a suicide by drowning."

"It's why you have had such difficulty trusting me," she said. "You believe I would have betrayed you to Faron for my own purposes, had I known how."

"I was wrong," he said bluntly. "I should have trusted my instincts from the start. And when I saw you ready to defend me with only a pistol, arrayed against Faron's men . . ." He stopped abruptly. "I knew in my head what I'd always known in my heart," he finished.

THE DARKEST SIN   263

She moved out of the circle of his arms to look at him directly. The drizzle of rain enveloped them both. "It's curious, Rushford, but the same thing happened to me. I'd known I loved you for a long time in my heart. It was my head that was causing the difficulties."

"I love you," Rushford said, pulling her back against him. "And I've made my choice. And I damn well won't take no for an answer."

"You're terribly arrogant," she observed, regarding him with her head to one side and a small smile. "But I suppose it's one of the many, many things I love about you."

Rushford dropped his arms and took her head between his hands, his fingers in her hair. "I know I'm terribly flawed, Rowena, but I give you my love, my word, and my life, to do with as you will."

"Is that a proposal, Lord Rushford?" Rainwater dripped into her eyes, mingling with tears of happiness, despite the fact that she never cried.

"More like a demand," he growled. His fingers tightened in her hair, and his eyes burned with an intensity that should have frightened her.

"You know how much I love demands, willful creature that I am," she countered. "But perhaps just this once I shall make an exception." He smiled before bringing his mouth to hers, and Rowena thought, the instant before she was lost in the enveloping heat of the kiss, that love was as irrational as passion and neither she nor Rushford could hope to control either one.

After several moments they pulled back from one another, aware that the coast of France was only several miles away. Rushford took her arm and led her to the front of the sloop, and in moments, her hands were steady on the wheel, her feet braced wide apart, her eyes trained on the mainsail as he'd instructed.

"We are adding to your long list of accomplishments," he said, standing behind her, his eyes searching the horizon. "You are doing an excellent job of keeping the wind in the

mainsail. Simply keep the wind on the left side of your face."
He gently touched her cheek before brushing his lips over the
spot, shocked anew at the surge of passion bolting through
him. Even though they were both drenched by the drizzling
rain and salt spray, his body stirred. Despite the grim circumstances, with a fatal reckoning on the horizon, he was filled
with a heedless and consuming passion for this young
woman whose own courage and determination made his life
suddenly worth living again.

"There's a secluded cove to the west which we can negoti-
ate safely, keeping us well out of sight of Calais," he said,
feeling her warmth against him.

"You've done this before," she noted, her slender hands
now blue with cold, yet sure on the wheel. He covered them
with his own. "I am hoping one day you will regale me with
your stories about your adventures on behalf of Whitehall,"
she said. "I trust they will keep me on the edge of my seat."
He could feel the tension in her shoulders.

"We shall make many stories of our own," he said.

Rowena answered with a half smile. "Beginning with this
one."

And he was determined that it would end well. "Which we
will bring to a conclusion together," he said. He swung the
helm, guiding Rowena's hands beneath his, glancing up at
the sail as it gently pulled on the mainsheet to catch the wind.
The *Brigand* swayed dramatically as the wind filled the sail.

"You have a plan, of course," she stated, matter of factly.

"Which entails that you stay below."

"Stay below?" The wind whipped the dark red of her hair
around her shoulders, her chignon long demolished by nature's force. "And let you confront Faron without me? You
should know me better than that by now, Rushford."

He let go of the helm and stepped in front of her. "How
did you know that we would be meeting Faron on shore and
not at Claire de Lune?"

She shrugged, her eye on the mainsail. "It makes perfect

sense. Firstly, Claire de Lune is most likely an impenetrable fortress. Secondly, you deliberately had me tell Galveston when you would be moving the Rosetta Stone. That gave the Baron more than enough time to let Faron know when you would be coming ashore." She paused. "My assumption is that Faron will meet us at the cove to collect his coveted Stone."

Arms crossed over his chest, Rushford stood with legs apart, clearly comfortable with the sway of the sloop. "Impeccable logic." He smiled. "And your staying below deck will allow us an element of surprise if need be," he said.

Rowena looked at him doubtfully. "Convince me," she said. "And don't dare tell me the less I know, the safer I will be."

"Wouldn't dare." A powerful feeling of protectiveness threatened his equilibrium. The wind whipped back Rowena's dark red hair; her face lifted to his. In the early morning light there were signs of fatigue, but her dark blue eyes were intense and he was again assailed by the desire she effortlessly lit within him. "Faron will not be expecting anyone else but me."

"True." She turned the helm deftly under her hands, a small frown on her smooth forehead. "But he's not expecting the crate to be empty, either."

"He won't be disappointed," Rushford said pointedly. "The crate may not hold the Stone, but it does hold something else."

"You are going to tell me, Rushford."

"Indeed I will. About a quarter ton of ballast, courtesy of London brickworks, and a thoroughly unexpected surprise."

"Surprise?" she repeated.

"Precisely." His eyes tacked the horizon looking for the familiar curve of land behind which the cove lay. Despite the early hour the mist was thickening, and he needed to avoid the rocky shoals leading to the cove. He moved to stand behind Rowena, his hands over hers on the wheel. "The weather is certainly not cooperating," he said. "I've seldom seen fog this thick so close to the coast."

Rowena opened her mouth to continue her questioning but was cut off by a shattering sound that bucked the sloop beneath them. Before she could react, another volley of shots pushed the *Brigand* violently to the side. Rushford suddenly stood in front of her, a pistol in both hands. "Do your best to keep us steady, Rowena," he said tersely.

She knew he wanted her to go below, but his command would have been useless. How long, she wondered, had they been sailing into danger, with Faron watching them from the mist and fog? She clutched the helm beneath her palms, seeing a small boat appear out of the vapor at their bow.

Two men clambered up the side of the *Brigand*, followed by several more. Rushford sprang forward, his pistol firing, as one of the men fell to his knees clutching his abdomen. More men poured onto the deck, until Rowena could no longer discern their number. Smoke mingled now with the heavy mist, and she decided to let go of the helm. The winds had died down and the sloop twirled aimlessly. She wished desperately for the pistol she'd left behind at the British Museum. There was no way that Rushford would survive, she thought desperately, looking around frantically for a weapon.

She had just leaned over to grab an oar beneath the halyard when her arms were gripped from behind. She kicked sideways and drove the oar back into the stomach of one of the men holding her. Her arms were wrenched farther behind her, twisted upward until she swallowed a groan of pain from her injured shoulder. She bit back an overwhelming desire to call Rushford's name, surging forward against her captors' hold and biting her lips against the agony in her limbs. In her mind, she swore at Faron, her rage boundless as she thought of Rushford lying dead, and of Meredith and Julia.

"Let me see Faron," she said. And when no one listened, she said the words again, until she was repeating them like a futile prayer. Someone silenced her with a blow across the mouth, and she tasted her own blood. Dragging her to the middle of the sloop, they bound her wrists behind her and tied her ankles while she frantically sought Rushford in the melee. It was only when she looked up and away from the deck to the ship opposite that she saw him. And her heart stopped. Standing next to Rushford was a tall man wearing a leather mask.

Suddenly all was silent, save for the gentle lapping of the waves against the *Brigand* and the soft murmur of the sails.

When Faron spoke, his voice was low and gravelly. "I did not expect that you would make the journey today with Lord Rushford, Mademoiselle Woolcott," he said. The mist parted momentarily to throw into sharp relief the mask's undulations, sinister and forbidding. Faron's hair was silver and his eyes a fathomless pitch. Rowena stopped struggling against her bonds. From the corner of her eye, she saw Faron's men begin hauling the crate over the side of the *Brigand*.

"I can appreciate that you are experiencing somewhat of a shock, mademoiselle, but as I was just explaining to Lord Rushford," he said with a nod to the man at his side, "once again your continued well-being depends on my discretion."

Rowena's first attempt to speak was only a rasp. She swallowed the metallic taste in her mouth to get the words out. "I have waited a long time for this meeting, monsieur."

"And to what end?" The Frenchman's greatcoat swayed with the gentle rocking of his ship. "I can assure you nothing you can say will change my mind in any way concerning your family. Or more particularly, your dear aunt."

Rowena saw red and wanted to spit and scream at the very thought of Meredith in the hands of the fiend—She swallowed hard, concentrating on the crate that was now being lowered into the cove. Already, Faron's men were scrambling to grab the chains and pull the wooden box alongside the French ship.

Faron smiled behind his mask. "Lord Rushford has been

particularly accommodating, delivering the Rosetta Stone to us, as requested and entirely on schedule." He turned to Rushford. "Many thanks," he said mockingly.

"You have bested me this time, Faron," Rushford said, his eyes a flat, emotionless gray. "I did not expect your ambush nor did I expect that Miss Woolcott would stow away on the *Brigand* and accompany me on this voyage."

"No worries at all," Faron responded sanguinely. "You saved us some trouble. The Baron informed me a week ago that I might be expecting Mademoiselle Woolcott at Claire de Lune."

The Baron was dead, thought Rowena with a savagery that was previously unknown to her.

"And I appreciate your continued cooperation, Lord Rushford, although I don't entirely understand it. You and mademoiselle will both perish once I ascertain that I have the Rosetta Stone in my possession. I'm surprised you haven't leapt at my throat, given your reputation. I hear your rages can be quite deadly."

"I have my reasons, Faron. I should welcome the good fortune if I were you."

"The Baron filled me in on needless details regarding your penchant for the late Duchess and your unwillingness to envision the same fate for Mademoiselle Woolcott here. I should not have believed you to be a sentimental man, still less a moral one."

"That remains to be seen."

Faron's gaze moved from Rushford to Rowena, then back to the crate, which was carefully being lowered onto the deck several feet from where he stood.

Rowena wished again for her pistol. "Since I have a short reprieve," she said across the few feet that separated the two ships, "I should like to know the reason behind this madness. *Your madness,* monsieur."

Rowena thought she saw Rushford tense as Faron admonished her with an upraised finger. "Madness? Did I understand

correctly? Your sister tried to burn me alive, mademoiselle."
With careful deliberation, he stripped a glove from his right
hand to reveal scarred and blistered skin. "Who is the madman—or shall I say madwoman—now?"

Rowena did not flinch. "Julia had her reasons. Without
doubt," she countered, love for her sister welling in her
breast. At least Julia was safe, far away with Strathmore in
Africa. But fear for Meredith robbed Rowena of breath. She
struggled against her bound wrists, trying to read Rushford's
expression. Behind her she counted three men, and there
were at least twice as many on Faron's ship.

Faron laughed appreciatively and then smiled at her with
something like compassion. "If it gives you comfort to believe so in these last moments of your life, then who am I to
deny you?" he said, his breath mingling with the mist. "It
hardly signifies. Once I have the Stone and you are no more,
I shall be free to concentrate my efforts upon your dear aunt."

Rowena's heart all but stopped, a savage desperation making her pull at the ropes digging into her wrists. The pain was
somehow reassuring, telling her that she still had a chance.
"Why do you hate us so?" she burst out.

Faron adjusted his mask. "Hate. Ahh yes, which brings us
to Meredith." He smiled darkly at a memory, his lips a slash
against the leather of his face. "How unfortunate you will
not be available to ask her yourself. It gives me the greatest
pleasure knowing that she has been racked with grief this
past year, believing you to be long dead and her remaining
ward, Julia, virtually in hiding on another continent with her
husband. And all to escape my attentions." He sneered the
last few words.

Rowena stiffened at the cruel twist of his lips. Her shoulder throbbed and was beginning to leak blood again. "You
wish to make us suffer," she said. "Why? I shan't have a chance
to ask again. So at least tell me why," she asked vehemently,
on the verge of begging.

A flash of pride was quickly banked in Faron's eyes. "I ac-cused Lord Rushford here of being a sentimental man." He continued in a distant voice, "Meredith Woolcott was my first love," he said. "And I hers."

It was impossible. Repulsive. Rowena felt nausea overcome her.

"But I do not wear this mask without reason, mademoiselle," Faron continued, his eyes obsidian outlined by leather. "You should well ask what Meredith did to me. Your sister Julia did so. There are wounds that go far beyond the superficialities of the skin and inward to the mind and spirit."

"Faron." Rushford's voice interrupted. "You've waited long enough." He gestured to the crate and the men ready with their metal jacks to pry the lid open. "Talk of the past is useless. If I were you, I'd see that no damage is done to the Stone . . ." He stepped aside.

Faron lifted his gaze from Rowena and turned first to the crate and then to Rushford, something like suspicion in his eyes. "The Baron assured me that you would make good on your promise, Lord Rushford," he said.

"I'm here, aren't I?" Rushford responded. "Disarmed by your men in a totally unexpected and unnecessary ambush. As the Baron no doubt informed you, I wish only to protect Miss Woolcott."

"Since you had no success protecting the Duchess," Faron finished the statement.

Rushford bowed his head slightly. "If you would permit me to at least give some comfort to Miss Woolcott before . . ." He allowed the sentence to drift off.

"And why ever would I do that?"

"Because I believe that I have something that you may covet even more than the Rosetta Stone."

"I doubt that very much."

"Hear me out first," Rushford said.

"I could put a bullet through your head this instant," Faron said coldly.

"You will—but not just yet," Rushford said, equally cool.

"I have a missive. From Meredith Woolcott to you. On the *Brigand*."

For a moment a thick cloud of mist obscured the Frenchman from Rowena's gaze, and then, when the thickness cleared, she saw Faron give a small nod to one of his men, who proceeded to prod Rushford with a pistol at his back. He moved across the deck and then made a short leap over to the *Brigand*. In several strides, Rushford was at her side. Now there were three men and any number of weapons at their backs. Yet, Rowena felt her muscles relax, the throbbing in her wrists, ankles, and shoulder fading away with Rushford's nearness.

"Where is it?" Faron asked softly.

"Below deck," Rushford replied. He made no move to touch her, but Rowena could feel his protectiveness enveloping her like a shield. "In the trunk by the bulkhead."

Faron gave another nod, and two of the men behind Rowena and Rushford disappeared below deck. "In the interim, to prove to you, Lord Rushford, that I am not such a sentimental fool as you appear to be, I shall become reacquainted with the Rosetta Stone. Now that it is mine." Moving toward the crate, he gestured to the men to begin working the lid from it. Several more metal hammers and jacks appeared, grinding into the wood.

Rowena felt Rushford tense beside her for one moment before she heard a crack of what sounded like thunder. The vibration sent her stumbling back before a billowing cloud of smoke from Faron's sloop obscured her vision. Beside her, Rushford slammed into the man behind them, disarming him in a heartbeat and then running across the deck to secure the door that led to the cabin, trapping the remainder of Faron's men below.

"Get down," Rushford hissed, dragging her to the floor while he pushed them both over to the wheel of the *Brigand*. The sails caught the wind, and the sloop began to move away from the Frenchman's now burning ship, wreaths of smoke dancing in the air. Rowena crawled to the edge of the deck, her eyes riveted by the sight of Montagu Faron in the churning waters of the channel.

The mask had yet to come loose, but his eyes were wide with the incomprehension of a child being tortured for reasons he cannot fathom. Rowena's wrists were bound, but for a moment she wondered whether she would have reached out to him if she had been able, remembering her own horror, the flow of the river pulling her down inexorably to her death. The explosion still hammered in her ears, her mind numb with shock. And all she could do was watch as Faron floated farther into the channel, his arms stopping their struggle, the icy water having done its work.

# Epilogue

"I feel decidedly wicked," Rowena declared. It was past noon and she was still abed with her new husband. It was early autumn, and a fire in the grate gave the room a warm glow. "I don't know how ever to explain this to Aunt Meredith. She's expecting us for tea."

"Which is at least four hours away," Rushford growled, sheets pooling around his waist, his torso bared to Rowena's appreciative gaze. A bottle of champagne and a deck of cards lay between them. Rowena had forgotten who had lost the last hand of vingt-et-un. Really they had both won, she thought with a languorous stretch that Rushford did not miss.

"I suppose we have nothing to be embarrassed about," she mused. "We did exert ourselves this morning with an incredibly energetic ride. So we deserve a nap," she concluded with effortless logic. "It is wonderful riding Dragon again, although I beg of you to be honest"—She turned to him with a small frown of concern. "Did you allow me to win the race?"

"And cheat? *Never,*" he avowed with a grin. "Your prowess left me in the dust."

Rowena grinned. "I do ride well, don't I?"

"You do."

She attempted to look modest. "And you did not allow me to win at cards, either."

"I believe it was a draw," he said with a devilish glint in his eyes as they rested on the sheet that had fallen from her breasts. "Besides which, I believe I suddenly have another game in mind, now that we have exhausted cards and riding."

"Chess? Sparring?" she asked provocatively, sliding closer to him. "You promised to show me how to perfect an upper cut, as I recall."

"Not even close." He leaned nearer, his reply a whisper against the warmth of her lips. "I challenge you to guess what I have in mind," he demanded.

She placed a finger on her lips before allowing it to drag over her mouth. "That should not prove too onerous, Rushford," she said, desire suffusing her voice. His hands swept down over her bared breasts, lifting them slightly as they swelled under his touch. The heat of his fingers against her skin sent shivers down her body to her core.

It had been that way between them from the beginning, and nothing seemed to have changed. Insatiable need for each other, both physical and mental, filled their every waking and sleeping hour. As Julia and Strathmore had done before them, they had married quietly in the chapel at Montfort, attended only by Archer and Meredith. Both Meredith and Julia had received the news that Rowena still lived with overwhelming joy, and Julia and Strathmore immediately began making their way back to England. Galveston had been sent into exile, half of Rushford's winnings from his estate returned to Lady Galveston, with the other half going to several charities for indigent women and children in London.

"Rushford," Rowena murmured against his lips. "I just thought of something."

"Have I told you already that you think too much?"

"You love my mind," she reminded him pointedly, gently pushing against him. "I can recall at least several occasions when you made mention of it."

He lifted his head from what he was doing and shifted to

pull her gently onto his lap. "So what is it, my charming bride?" he asked, his expression watchful.

"You lied about the letter, didn't you? To Faron, aboard the *Brigand*. I wish I really knew how Meredith feels—about all of this," she continued carefully. "I do not want to push her, because she's always been so reticent about her past and our beginnings with her here at Montfort."

Rushford stroked the hair back from her face. "Perhaps it is best not to push her, Rowena. She will tell us when she is ready."

Rowena shook her head, the memory of the explosion, and of Faron's drowning, still vivid in her mind. She had listened to Rushford's explanation of the black powder contained in the crate, which was so very easily ignited by the spark of a metal hammer hitting a hard surface. "Am I evil in feeling pleasure that Montagu Faron is gone—out of our lives?"

Rushford shook his head, cradling her in his arms. "You were incredibly courageous, Rowena. You have nothing at all to regret."

"And you?" she asked. "Do you have any regrets?"

"Not one," he answered swiftly. "Unless it is that I wish I had recognized true love sooner."

Rowena looked up at him from beneath her lashes. "I know that I loved you first in my dreams, Lord Rushford," she said softly.

"I asked you to stay with me."

She tilted her head to one side, devouring her beautiful husband with her gaze. "I remember. And I intend to. For the rest of our lives."

And Rushford sealed her vow by lowering his head to hers.

Don't miss BODYGUARDS IN BED,
the anthology from Lucy Monroe, Jamie Denton, and
Elisabeth Naughton, coming next month!

Turn the page for a preview of Lucy's story . . .

Danusia wiggled the key in the lock on her brother's apartment door. Darn thing always stuck, but he wouldn't make her another one. Said she didn't come to stay often enough for it to matter.

Yeah, and he wasn't particularly keen for that to change either, obviously. He'd probably gotten the wonky key on purpose. Just like the rest of her older siblings, Roman Chernichenko kept Danusia at a distance.

She knew why he did it at least, though she was pretty sure the others didn't.

Knowing didn't make her feel any better. Even in her family of brainiacs, she was definitely the odd one out. They loved her, just like she loved them, but they were separated by more than the gap in their ages. She was seven years younger than her next youngest sibling. An unexpected baby, though never unwanted—at least according to her mom.

Still, her sister and brothers might love her, but they didn't get her and didn't particularly want her to get them.

Which was why she was coming to stay in Roman's empty apartment rather than go visit one of the others, or heaven forbid, her parents. She did not need another round of lectures on her single status by her *baba* and mom.

The lock finally gave and Danusia pressed the door open, dragging her rolling suitcase full of books and papers behind her. The fact the alarm wasn't armed registered at the same time as a cold cylinder pressed to her temple.

"Roman, I swear on Opa's grave that if you don't get that gun away from me, I'm going to drop it in a vat of sulfuric acid and then pour the whole mess all over the new sofa Mom insisted you get the last time she visited. If it's loaded, I'm going to do it anyway."

The gun moved away from her temple and she spun around, ready to lecture her brother into an early grave, and help him along the way. "*It is so not okay to pull a gun on your sister. . . .*" Her tirade petered off to a choked breath. "*You!*"

The man standing in front of her was a whole lot sexier than her brother and scarier, which was saying something. Not that she was afraid of him, but *she* wouldn't want him for an enemy.

The rest of the family believed that Roman was a scientist for the military. She knew better. She was a nosy baby sister after all, but this man? Definitely worked with Roman and carried an aura of barely leashed violence. Maxwell Baker was a true warrior.

She shouldn't, absolutely *should not*, find that arousing, but she did.

"You're not my brother," she said stupidly.

Which was not her usual mode, but the six-foot-five black man, who would make Jesse Jackson, Jr. look like the ugly stepbrother if they were related, turned Danusia's brain to serious mush.

His brows rose in mocking acknowledgment of her obvious words.

"Um . . ."

"What are you doing here, Danusia?" Warm as a really good aged whiskey, his voice made her panties wet.

How embarrassing was that? "You know my name?"

Put another mark on the chalkboard for idiocy.

"The wedding wasn't so long ago that I would have forgotten already." He almost cracked a smile.

She almost swooned.

Max and several of Roman's *associates* had done the security at her sister, Elle's, wedding, which might have been overkill. Or not. Danusia suspected stuff had been going on that neither she nor her parents had known about.

It hadn't helped that she'd been focused on her final project for her masters and that Elle's wedding had been planned faster than Danusia could solve a quadratic equation. She'd figured out that something was going on, but that was about it. This time her siblings had managed to keep their baby sister almost completely in the dark.

A place she really hated being.

Not that her irritation had stopped her from noticing the most freaking gorgeous man she'd ever met. Maxwell Baker. A tall, dark dish of absolute yum.

Once she had seen Max with his strong jaw, defined cheekbones, big and muscular body, not much else at the wedding had even registered. Which might help explain why she hadn't figured out why all the security.

"It's nice to see you again." There, that sounded somewhat adult. Full points for polite conversation, right?

"What are you doing here?" he asked again, apparently not caring if he got any points for being polite.

She shrugged, shifting her backpack. "My super is doing some repairs on the apartment."

"What kind of repairs?"

"Man, you're as bad as my brother." They hadn't even made it out of the entry and she was getting the third-degree.

Really as bad as her brother and maybe taking it up a notch. Roman might have let her get her stuff put out of the way before he started asking the probing questions. Then again, maybe not.

"I'll take that as a compliment." Then Max just paused, like he had all the time in the world to wait for her answer.

Like it never even occurred to him she might refuse to respond.

Knowing there was no use in attempted prevarication, she sighed. "They're replacing the front door."

"Why?"

"Does it matter?" Sheesh.

He leaned back against the wall, crossing his arms, muscles bulging everywhere. "I won't know until you tell me."

"Someone broke it." She was proud of herself for getting the words out, considering how difficult she was finding the simple process of breathing right now.

This man? Was lethal.

"Who?" he demanded, frown firmly in place.

Oh, crud, even his not-so-happy face was sexy, yummy, heart-palpitatingly delicious. "I don't know."

Try Dani Harper's sexy debut,
CHANGELING MOON,
out now from Brava!

Freezing rain sliced out of the black sky, turning the wet pavement to glass. Zoey stared out at the freakish weather and groaned aloud. With less than two days left in the month of April, the skies had been clear and bright all afternoon. Trees were budding early and spring had seemed like a sure bet. Now *this*. Local residents said if you didn't like the weather this far north, just wait fifteen minutes. She gave it five, only to watch the rain turn to sleet.

Perhaps she should have asked more questions before taking the job as editor of the *Dunvegan Herald Weekly*. She was getting the peace and quiet she'd wanted, all right, but so far the weather simply sucked. Winter had been in full swing when she'd arrived at the end of October. Wasn't it ever going to end?

Sighing, she buttoned her thin jacket up to her chin and hoisted the camera bag over her shoulder in preparation for the long, cold walk to her truck. All she wanted before bed was a hot shower, her soft flannel pajamas with the little cartoon sheep on them, the TV tuned to *Late Night*, and a cheese and mushroom omelet. Hell, maybe just the omelet. She hadn't eaten since noon, unless the three faded M&Ms she'd found at the bottom of her bag counted as food.

As usual, the council meeting for the Village of Dunvegan had gone on much too long. Who'd have thought that such a small community could have so much business to discuss? It was well past ten when the mayor, the councilors, and the remnants of a long-winded delegation filed out. Zoey had lingered only a few moments to scribble down a couple more notes for her article but it was long enough to make her the last person out of the building.

The heavy glass door automatically locked behind her, the metallic sound echoing ominously. Had she taken longer than she thought? There wasn't a goddamn soul left on the street. Even the hockey arena next door was deserted, although a senior men's play-off game earlier had made parking difficult to find. Now, her truck—a sturdy, old red Bronco that handled the snow much better than her poor little SUV had—was the only vehicle in sight.

The freezing rain made the three-block trek to the truck seem even longer. Not only did the cold wind drive stinging pellets of ice into her face, but her usual business-like stride had to be shortened to tiny careful steps. Her knee-high leather boots were strictly a fashion accessory—her bedroom slippers would have given her more traction on the ice. If she slipped and broke her ankle out here, would anyone even find her before morning?

The truck glittered strangely as she approached and her heart sank. Thick sheets of ice coated every surface, sealing the doors. Nearly frozen herself, she pounded on the lock with the side of her fist until the ice broke away and she could get her key in. "Come on, dammit, come on!"

Of course, the key refused to turn, while the cold both numbed and hurt her gloveless fingers. She tried the passenger door lock without success, then walked gingerly around to the rear cargo door. No luck there either. She'd have to call a tow—

Except that her cell phone was on the front seat of her truck.

Certain that things couldn't get any worse, she tested each door again. Maybe one of the locks would loosen if she kept trying. If not, she'd probably have to walk all the way home, and wasn't that a cheery prospect?

Suddenly a furtive movement teased at her peripheral vision. Zoey straightened slowly and studied her surroundings. There wasn't much to see. The streetlights were very far apart, just glowing pools of pale gold that punctuated the darkness rather than alleviating it. Few downtown businesses bothered to leave lights on overnight. The whispery hiss of the freezing rain was all she could hear.

A normal person would simply chalk it up to imagination, but she'd been forced to toss *normal* out the window at an early age. Her mother, aunts, and grandmother were all powerful psychics—and the gene had been passed down to Zoey. Or at least a watered-down version of it. The talent was reliable enough when it worked, but it seemed to come and go as it pleased. *Like right now.* Zoey tried hard to focus yet sensed absolutely nothing. It was her own fault perhaps for trying to rid herself of the inconvenient ability.

No extrasensory power was needed, however, to see something large and black glide silently from one shadow to another near the building she'd just left. *What the hell was that?* There was nowhere to go for help. The only two bars in town would still be open, but they were several blocks away, as was the detachment headquarters for the Royal Canadian Mounted Police. There was a rundown trailer park a block and a half from the far side of the arena, but Zoey knew there were no streetlights anywhere along that route.

A dog? Maybe it's just a big dog, she thought. A really big dog or a runaway cow. *After all, this was a rural community. And a* northern *rural community at that, so maybe it's just a local moose, ha, ha. . . .* She struggled to keep her fear at bay and redoubled her efforts on the door locks, all the while straining to listen over the sound of her own harsh breathing.

The rear door lock was just beginning to show promise when a low, rumbling growl caused her to drop her keys. She spun to see a monstrous shape emerge from the shadows, stiff-legged and head lowered. *A wolf?* It was bigger than any damn wolf had a right to be. *Jesus.* Some primal instinct warned her not to run and not to scream, that the animal would be on her instantly if she did so.

She backed away slowly, trying not to slip, trying to put the truck between herself and the creature. Its eyes glowed green like something out of a horror flick, but this was no movie. Snarling black lips pulled back to expose gleaming ivory teeth. The grizzled gray fur around its neck was bristling. Zoey was minutely aware that the hair on the back of her own neck was standing on end. Her breath came in short shuddering gasps as she blindly felt for the truck behind her with her hands, sliding her feet carefully without lifting them from the pavement.

She made it around the corner of the Bronco. As soon as she was out of the wolf's line of sight, she turned and half skated, half ran for the front of the truck as fast as the glassy pavement would allow. *Don't fall, don't fall!* It was a litany in her brain as she scrambled up the slippery front bumper onto the icy hood. With no hope of outrunning the creature and no safe place in sight, the roof of the truck seemed like her best bet—if she could make it. *Don't fall, don't fall!* Flailing for a handhold, she seized an ice-crusted windshield wiper, only to have the metal frame snap off in her hand. She screamed as she slid back a few inches.

The wolf sprang at once. It scrabbled and clawed, unable to find a purchase on the ice-coated metal. Foam from its snapping jaws sprayed over her as the beast roared its frustration. Finally it slipped back to the ground and began to pace around the truck.

Zoey managed to shimmy up the hood until she was able to put her back against the windshield, and pull her knees up to her chin. She risked a glance at the roof behind her—she had to get higher. Before she could move, however, the wolf attacked again, scrambling its way up the front bumper. Vicious jaws slashed at her. Without thought, Zoey kicked out at the wolf, knocking one leg out from under it. It slid backward but not before it clamped its teeth on her calf. The enormous weight of the creature dragged at her and she felt herself starting to slide. . . .

One hand still clutched the broken windshield wiper and she used it, whipping the creature's face and muzzle with the frozen blade until she landed a slice across one ungodly glowing eye. The rage-filled snarl became a strangled yelp; the wolf released her leg and slipped from the hood. This time Zoey didn't look, just turned and launched herself upward for the roof rack. She came down hard, adrenaline keeping her from feeling the impact of the bruising metal rails. She was conscious only of the desperate need to claw and grasp and cling and pull until she was safely on the very top of the vehicle.

Except she *wasn't* safe. Not by a long shot. *Crap.* She could plainly see that she wasn't high enough. *Crap, crap, crap.* The enraged wolf leapt upward in spite of the fact that its feet could find little traction on the ice-coated pavement. What it couldn't gain in momentum, the wolf made up for in effort, hurling itself repeatedly against the Bronco. Its snapping jaws came so close that Zoey could see the bleeding welts across its face, see that one of its hellish eyes was now clouded and half-closed. She slashed at it again, catching its tender nose so it howled in frustration and pain as it dropped to the ground. Snarling, it paced back and forth like a caged lion, watching her. Waiting.

The wind picked up and the freezing rain intensified. Huddled on her knees in the exact center of the icy roof, Zoey's adrenaline began to ebb. She was cold and exhausted, and parts of her were numb. But she wasn't helpless; she wouldn't allow herself to think that way. The thin windshield wiper was badly bent with pieces of it missing, but she'd damn well punch the wolf in the nose with her bare fist if she had to. If she still could. . . .

The wolf sprang again.

Good girls should NEVER CRY WOLF.
But who wants to be good?
Be sure to pick up Cynthia Eden's latest novel,
out next month!

Lucas didn't take the woman back to his house on Bryton Road. The place was probably still crawling with cops and reporters, and he didn't feel like dealing with all that crap.

He called his first in command, Piers Stratus, to let him know that he was out of jail and to tell him that there were two unwanted coyotes in town.

The woman—Sarah—didn't speak while he drove. He could feel the waves of tension rolling off her, shaking her body.

She was scared. She'd done a fair job of hiding her fear back at the police station and then at the park, at first anyway. But as the darkness had fallen, he'd seen the fear. Smelled it.

Sarah had known she was being hunted.

He pushed a button on his remote. The wrought-iron gates before him opened and revealed the curving drive that led to his second LA home. In the hills, it gave him a great view of the city below, and that view let him know when company was coming, long before any unexpected guests arrived.

When the gate shut behind him, he saw Sarah sag slightly, settling back into her seat. The scent of her fear finally eased.

Like most of his kind, he usually enjoyed the smell of fear. But he didn't . . . like the scent on her.

He much preferred the softer scent, like vanilla cream, that he could all but taste as it clung to her skin. Perhaps he would get a taste, later.

With a flick of his wrist, he killed the ignition. The house was right in front of them. Two stories. Long, tall windows.

And, hopefully, no more dead bodies.

He eased out of the car, stretching slowly. Then he walked around and opened the door for Sarah. As any man would, Lucas admired the pale flash of thigh when her skirt crept up. And he wondered just what secrets the lovely lady was keeping from him.

"We're going to talk." An order. He wanted to know everything, starting with why the dead human had been at his place.

She gave a quick nod. "Okay, I—"

A wolf bounded out of the house. A flash of black fur. Golden eyes. Teeth.

*Shit.* It wasn't safe for the kid. Not until he found out what was going on—

The wolf ran to him. Tossed back his head and howled.

Sarah laughed softly.

*Laughed.*

His stare shot to her just in time to catch the smile on her lips. His hand lifted, and, almost helplessly, he traced that smile with his fingertips.

Her breath caught.

Lucas ignored the tightening in his gut. "Shouldn't you be afraid?" After the coyotes, he'd expected her to flinch away from any other shifters. And Jordan was one big wolf, with claws and teeth that could easily rip a woman like Sarah apart.

She looked back at the wolf who watched them. "He's so young, little more than a kid. One who's glad you're—"

*No.*

Understanding dawned, fast and brutal in his mind. *I'm more than human.* She'd told him that, he just hadn't understood exactly what she was. Until now.

His hands locked around her arms and Lucas pulled her

up against him. Nose to nose, close enough so that he could see the dark gold glimmering in the depths of her eyes. "Jordan, get the hell out of here." He gave the order to his brother without ever looking away from her.

The wolf growled.

"Go!"

The young wolf pushed against his leg—*letting me know he's pissed, cause Jordan hates when I boss his ass*—and then the wolf backed away.

"Now for you, sweetheart." His fingers tightened. "Why don't we just go back to that part about you not being human?"

Her lips parted. She had nice lips—sexy and plump. He shouldn't be noticing them, not then, but he couldn't help himself. He noticed everything about her. The gold hoops in her dainty ears. The streaks of gold buried deep in her dark hair. The lotion she rubbed on her body—that vanilla scent was driving him wild.

He was turned on, achingly hard, for a woman he barely knew. Not normally a big deal. He had a more than healthy sex drive. Most shifters did. The animal inside liked to play.

But Sarah . . . he didn't trust her, not for a minute, and he didn't usually have sex with women he didn't trust. A man could be vulnerable to attack when he was fucking.

"You know what I am, Lucas," she said and shrugged, the move both careless and fake because he knew that she cared, too much.

"Tell me." Her mouth was so close. He could still taste her. That kiss earlier had just been a tease.

# OFFICIAL RULES
## for *Weekend in London*
## Giveaway Sweepstakes

**SPONSOR**
This promotion is sponsored by author Caroline Richards (a/k/a Anna Sonser) and Kensington Publishing Corp. ("Kensington Publishing Corp."), 119 West 40th Street, New York, New York, 10018. You may write to this address to obtain a list of winners.

**ELIGIBILITY**
NO PURCHASE NECESSARY.

Purchase will not improve the odds of winning. To become eligible to win in the *Weekend in London Giveaway Sweepstakes*, simply fill out the entry form appearing

*(continued on next page)*

at www.readcarolinerichards.com or www.kensingtonbooks.com, or fill out the enclosed entry sheet appearing in this book, and mail it to:

> Kensington Publishing Corp.
> Trip to London Sweepstakes – Dept. AC
> 119 West 40th Street
> New York, NY 10018

Multiple entries are automatically disqualified, and only the first submission will be considered.

The Sweepstakes is open to all legal residents of the United States, excluding Puerto Rico and excluding Rhode Island, 18 years of age and older by May 31, 2011, excluding employees and immediate family members of Caroline Richards a/k/a Anna Sonser and/or of Kensington Publishing Corp. and its parents, subsidiaries, affiliates, assigns, advertising, promotional and fulfillment agents, attorneys, and other representatives and the persons with whom each of the above are domiciled. Offer void outside the United States and wherever prohibited or restricted by law.

**ENTRY PERIOD**
The Sweepstakes will commence on June 1, 2011 (12 a.m. EST). The last entry will be accepted on August 1, 2011 (11:59 p.m. EST).

**PRIZES**
One Grand Prize winner will receive up to a total of $2,000 towards airfare for two adults by coach or equivalent class fare, minimum 4-week advance booking, travel to commence on or after October 1, 2011, and conclude on or before October 1, 2012, plus two nights' accommodations in a standard double room at one of the Romantic Hotel Collection hotels in London (www.roomforromance.com), hotel to be selected by Caroline Richards, no incidentals included. Winner is responsible for all other expenses, including, without limitation, ground transportation to and from local and London airports, any and all hotel incidentals, meals, entertainment, etc.

Only one prize will be awarded. The prize is non-transferable and cannot be sold or redeemed for cash. Any federal, state, or local taxes are the sole responsibility of the winner.

THE ODDS OF WINNING DEPEND UPON THE NUMBER OF ENTRIES.
You have not yet won.

**SELECTION AND NOTIFICATION OF WINNERS**
Winners will be selected by a random drawing from all the entries. Winners will be chosen on or about August 16, 2011, at the offices of Kensington Publishing Corp. The winner will be notified by e-mail by August 19, 2011, at the mail address provided on the winning entry. The winner may be required to sign and return to Kensington Publishing Corp. an affidavit of eligibility and release of liability (the "Affidavit"), and, if the Affidavit is not returned within 7 days of notification, the winner will be deemed to have forfeited the prize, and an alternate winner will be chosen. No fee will be required to sign or return the Affidavit. Winners will receive package by August 31, 2011.

By participating, entrants agree to release, discharge, and hold harmless Caroline Richards a/k/a Anna Sonser and Kensington Publishing Corp., its parent, subsidiaries, affiliates and assigns, and their respective advertising and promotion agencies

from any and all liability or damages associated with acceptance, use or misuse of any prize received in the Sweepstakes.

## CONDITIONS

By participating, entrants agree to be bound by these Official Rules and the decisions of the judge, which shall be final, and waive any right to claim ambiguity in the Sweepstakes and/or these Official Rules.

Acceptance of the prize constitutes permission to use the winner's name, likeness, biography, and prize won for purposes of advertising, promotion and publicity without additional compensation, except where prohibited or re-stricted by law.

The entrants release, discharge, and hold harmless Caroline Richards a/k/a Anna Sonder and Kensington Publishing Corp., its parent, affiliates, subsidiaries, and assigns, and their respective employees, attorneys, representatives and agents, including advertising, promotion and fulfillment agencies, from any and all liability or damages arising from the administration of the Sweepstakes and the use or misuse of any prize received in the Sweepstakes, including, without limitation, the following: (i) late, lost, incomplete, delayed, misdirected or unintelligible entries, (ii) entries that are corrupted or otherwise not received correctly, (iii) any printing, typographical, administrative or technological errors in any materials associated with the Sweepstakes, including, without limitation, entry materials and prize notifications, and (iv) any damage to the entrant's or other person's computer and related equipment and software resulting from entrant's downloading of information regarding the Sweepstakes or participation in the Sweepstakes.

Entry materials and prize notifications that have been tampered with, altered, or do not comply with these Official Rules are void.

Kensington Publishing Corp. may only use the personally identifiable information obtained from the entrants in accordance with these Rules and its privacy policy, available at www.kensingtonbooks.com.

Kensington Publishing Corp. reserves the right, in its sole discretion, to modify, cancel or suspend this Sweepstakes should a virus, bug, computer problem or other causes beyond its control corrupt the administration, security or proper operation of the Sweepstakes. Kensington Publishing Corp. may prohibit you from participating in the Sweepstakes or winning a prize if, in its sole discretion, it determines that you are attempting to undermine the legitimate operation of the Sweepstakes by cheating, hacking or employing other unfair practices or by abusing other entrants or the representatives of Kensington Publishing Corp.

ANY ATTEMPT BY AN ENTRANT TO DELIBERATELY DAMAGE THE WEB SITE OR UNDERMINE THE OPERATION OF THE SWEEPSTAKES MAY BE IN VIOLATION OF CRIMINAL AND CIVIL LAWS, AND, IN SUCH EVENT, KENSINGTON PUBLISHING CORP. RESERVES THE RIGHT TO PURSUE THEIR REMEDIES AND DAMAGES (INCLUDING COSTS AND ATTORNEY'S FEES) TO THE FULLEST EXTENT OF THE LAW.

Any dispute arising from the Sweepstakes will be determined according to the laws of the State of New York, without reference to its conflict of laws principles, and the entrants consent to the personal jurisdiction of the State and Federal Courts located in the State and County of New York over them and agree that such courts have exclusive jurisdiction over all such disputes.